NEW TOEIC

決勝新制多益

聽力6回模擬試題 解析版

作者 ◎ Kim dae Kyun　譯者 ◎ 蔡裴驊／關亭薇

LISTENING

如何下載 **MP3** 音檔

❶ 寂天雲 APP 聆聽： 掃描書上 QR Code 下載「寂天雲 - 英日語學習隨身聽」APP。加入會員後，用 APP 內建掃描器再次掃描書上 QR Code，即可使用 APP 聆聽音檔。

❷ 官網下載音檔： 請上「寂天閱讀網」（www.icosmos.com.tw），註冊會員／登入後，搜尋本書，進入本書頁面，點選「MP3 下載」下載音檔，存於電腦等其他播放器聆聽使用。

決勝新制多益
聽力6回模擬試題 解析版

作者 Kim dae Kyun
譯者 蔡裴驊／關亭薇
編輯 呂敏如
校對 黃詩韻／林蜜琪
主編 丁宥暄
內文排版 謝青秀／林書玉
封面設計 林書玉
製程管理 洪巧玲
發行人 黃朝萍
出版者 寂天文化事業股份有限公司
電話 +886-(0)2-2365-9739
傳真 +886-(0)2-2365-9835
網址 www.icosmos.com.tw
讀者服務 onlineservice@icosmos.com.tw
出版日期 2024 年 5 月 二版一刷 （寂天雲隨身聽APP版）

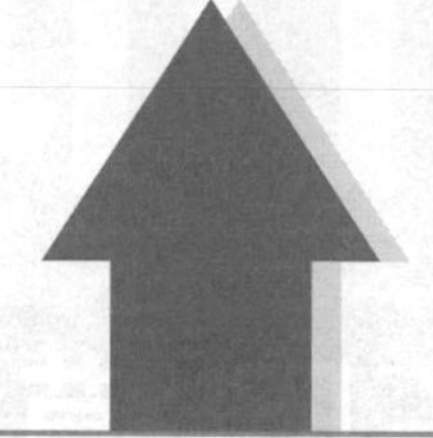

決勝新制多益：聽力6回模擬試題（解析版）（寂天雲隨身聽APP版）/ Kim dae Kyun著；蔡裴驊, 關亭薇譯. -- 初版. --
[臺北市]：寂天文化, 2024.05 面；公分
ISBN 978-626-300-252-4 (16K平裝)
1.CST: 多益測驗
805.1895 113005641

郵撥帳號1998620-0 寂天文化事業股份有限公司
訂書金額未滿1000元，請外加運費100元。

〔若有破損，請寄回更換，謝謝。〕

筆者潛心著筆，將本書出版成冊。為了撰寫出貼近實際測驗的試題，筆者曾多次赴日參加多益測驗，持續致力於新制多益的解題分析。歷經這些過程後，終於完成這套直擊最新命題趨勢的著作。與舊制多益相比，新制多益的整體難度相對提升不少，考生在考前務必要精準掌握出題方向，並勤於練習仿真試題。

根據筆者的透徹分析，新制多益的改制內容與應考對策如下：

PART 1 請務必優先熟記高難度單字。在照片題型中，比起人物，將重點擺在事物上更有利於解題。

PART 2 切勿在聽完題目的當下，立即選填答案。通常需要經過一番思索，才能找出正確答案。

PART 3 為掌握聽力分數的關鍵，請務必充分練習。

PART 4 雖與舊制多益的難易度相當，但聽力的語速加快，這一點請特別留意。

筆者親自監聽錄音檔，精選配音員錄製本書。依照多益聽力測驗語速，完成最貼近實際考試的錄音。

PART 5 與舊制多益的難易度相當。

PART 6 短文填空題的難度提升，請善用本書勤加練習！

PART 7 為掌握閱讀分數的關鍵，充分練習本書的仿真試題，方能取得好成績。

筆者報考過230餘次的多益測驗，自詡是擁有最多滿分經驗的最強權威，至今仍持續參加測驗。這14年來在韓國EBS電台《金大鈞TOEIC KING》擔任內容策劃與主講人，節目不僅獲得大眾的認可，更讓我獲得專業主題類別最佳BJ（註：線上節目主持人）的殊榮。除此之外，就讀金大鈞英語學院的學生，也頻頻獲得滿分的佳績。多益滿分不再遙不可及，相信大家也能做到。我保證在本書的幫助下，大家勢必能快速提升多益成績！

歷史，由你來創造。
身為多益界的不敗傳奇，筆者亦將不負眾望，跨出更大的步伐向前邁進。

向上蒼與讀者致上謝意

金大鈞

目錄

新制多益題型更新重點

PART 1

	新制多益	舊制多益
題型	**照片描述**	照片描述
題數	**總題數6題**	總題數10題

題型不變，照片描述仍為四個選項。

 **題數減少**

PART 2

	新制多益	舊制多益
題型	**應答問題**	應答問題
題數	**總題數25題**	總題數30題

題型不變，應答問題仍為選出適當的選項。

 **題數減少**

PART 3

	新制多益	舊制多益
題型	**簡短對話**	簡短對話
題數	**13組對話（每組3題） 總題數39題**	10組對話（每組3題） 總題數30題

 **新增三人對話題型**  **對話和題數增加**

PART 4

	新制多益	舊制多益
題型	**簡短獨白**	簡短獨白
題數	**10組簡短獨白（每組3題） 總題數30題**	10組簡短獨白（每組3題） 總題數30題

 **新增圖表作答題型**

PART 5

	新制多益	舊制多益
題型	**句子填空**	句子填空
題數	**總題數30題**	總題數40題

題型不變，選出句子中適合填入的單字或片語。

 **題數減少**

PART 6

	新制多益	舊制多益
題型	**段落填空**	段落填空
題數	**總題數16題**	總題數12題

NEW **題型改變**  **題數增加**

PART 7

	新制多益	舊制多益
題型	**單篇閱讀**	單篇閱讀
題數	**10篇單篇閱讀 每篇2–4題 總題數29題**	9篇單篇閱讀 每篇2–5題 總題數28題
題型	**雙篇閱讀**	雙篇閱讀
題數	**兩組雙篇閱讀 每組5題 總題數10題**	四組雙篇閱讀 每組5題 總題數20題
題型	**多篇閱讀**	
題數	**三組多篇閱讀 每組5題 總題數15題**	
題數	**總題數54題**	總題數48題

保留原有的閱讀測驗。

 **新增多篇閱讀題型**  **題數增加**

各大考題最新命題趨勢

新制多益的整體難度相對提升，唯有接受這個事實，認真準備才能取得佳績。本書準確分析出題趨勢，完全比照實際測驗，只要充分練習本書的試題，定能勇奪高分！

PART 1 照片描述 核心攻略

通常只要聽懂**動詞關鍵字**，就能答出大部分的題目，但是仍有不少題目以**高難度單字**和**特殊描寫**命題。在新制多益 PART 1 中，只要聽到 holding、display、casting a shadow（蒙上陰影）、lead to、occupied、unoccupied 這些關鍵字，就是正確選項。然而值得注意的是，你可能會同時聽到**兩個以上**的高難度單字。

1.

(A) A woman is holding an oar. 女子拿著一支槳。
(B) A woman is tying a boat to a pier. 女子把小船繫在碼頭邊。
(C) A woman is getting out of the boat. 女子正從小船上下來。
(D) A woman is swimming across a lake. 女子正泳渡一座湖。

解答 A

第一大題中，只要聽到 holding，就是正確的選項。若同時聽到高難度單字 oar（槳），就能更加肯定它就是正解。雖然 PART 1 中的單字相對容易，但千萬不可小覷，請務必注意單字的發音。vase 通常會唸成 [ves]，但在多益測驗中，若為英國腔，聽起來則像是 [vɑz]。

2.

(A) A knife has been placed on the chair. 刀子放在椅子上。

➜ 照片中並未出現刀和椅子。

(B) Flowers have been put in vases. 花插在花瓶裡。

➜ 這裡的 vases 發音為 [vɑzɪz]（英國腔）。雖然有時會將 vase 唸成 [ves]，但英式唸法 [vɑz] 通常才是正解，請務必熟記！

(C) A woman is watering some flowers. 一名女子正在澆花。

➜ 照片中並未出現人物和動作。

(D) A woman is buying some flowers. 一名女子正在買花。

➜ 照片裡看不到人物。

解答 B

3.

(A) People are gathered at the entryway. 人們聚集在入口處。

(B) A door is beneath a staircase. 樓梯下方有一扇門。

(C) A man is repairing the stairs. 一名男子正在整修樓梯。

(D) Some pictures are propped against a wall. 牆上掛著一些畫。

解答 B

不同於過往題型，題目當中會出現針對事物的特殊描寫。將特殊描寫設為正解，已成為一種出題趨勢。

請特別注意 PART 1 的第五、六題，雖然照片中有出現人物，但答案可能是單純針對事物描寫的選項。

PART 2 應答問題 核心攻略

眾多考生為 PART 2 苦惱不已。值得注意的是，PART 2 可不只是少了五題這麼簡單而已，命題方式反而變得更加巧妙、難度也隨之提升。所謂的「Read between the lines.」，即「**言外之意**」，將大量出現在考題中，考生必須要聽出背後的含意才能找出答案。碰到此類題型時，在聽完題目後，需要經過一番**思考**，才能挑出正確的答案。只要稍不留神，很容易就錯失下一題的解題機會。請務必勤加練習，熟悉此類題型的模式。

7. Sales of the newly published books are higher than we expected.
新出版的書的銷量比我們預期的還要高。

(A) We want to hire her. 我們想僱用她。
➜ hire 僅與 higher 的發音相近，為錯誤選項。

(B) I know they are very popular. 我知道它們很暢銷。
➜ 為最適當的答案，表示「很暢銷」。

(C) What is the bottom line? 主要重點是什麼？

解答 B

8. How will the new members be selected?
新成員會怎麼選出來？

(A) They've already been chosen. 已經選出來了。
➜ selected 可替換成 chosen，為正確答案。

(B) Jane has a monthly membership. 珍持有月會員資格。

(C) Is it on the third floor? 它在三樓嗎？
➜ 不符合單複數一致性（members 為複數，it 為單數），為錯誤選項。

解答 A

9. Why don't you sign up for the TOEIC workshop with us?
你何不和我們一起報名多益工作坊？

(A) I don't have time to go. 我沒空去。
➜ 極為明確的回答，為正確答案。

(B) There is a shop around the corner. 有一間店在轉角處。
➜ shop 僅與 workshop 的發音相近，為錯誤選項。

(C) At the auditorium. 在禮堂。

解答 A

10. Have you made any progress on the merger and acquisition meeting?

併購會議，你們有任何進展嗎？

(A) The company's office. 公司的辦公室。

(B) We're getting together again next Monday. 我們下週一要再聚一次。

➜ 表示「之後將繼續進行」的意思，為需要稍微思考一下的選項。

(C) Acquired immune deficiency syndrome. 後天免疫缺乏症候群。

➜ acquired 僅與 acquisition 的發音相近，為錯誤選項。

解答 B

11. What restaurant did you choose to host the retirement party?

你選擇在哪間餐廳主辦退休歡送會？

(A) He said he will retire next year. 他說他明年退休。

(B) Mark is the host of the show. 馬克是活動的主持人。

(C) I'm still waiting for some price quotes. 我還在等一些報價。

➜ 請熟記 quote 除了有「引用」的意思之外，作為名詞也有「報價」的意思。
quote = estimate

解答 C

12. Didn't Susan already fill an order for this?

蘇珊沒有填這個的訂單嗎？

(A) That was for December. 那是12月的事了。

➜ 需要歷經一番思考才能解出的高難度題目。當出現像(A)這類的選項時，請先標記三角形符號，之後回過頭再聽一次。

(B) Fill her up with unleaded, please. 無鉛加滿，麻煩你。

➜ 當出現和題目相同的單字 fill 時，不是答案的可能性極高。

(C) In chronological order. 照時間順序排列。

➜ order 也是重複出現的單字，不是答案的可能性極高。

解答 A

PART 3 簡短對話 核心攻略

PART 3 不僅對話的**篇幅較長**，特別要注意的是對話**語速也加快了**。從第32題開始，你將聽到語速極快的澳洲口音，而實際測驗中的語速也非常地快，請務必集中精神仔細聆聽。**詢問句意**為何的題目，大多屬於高難度命題，請利用本教材勤加練習！例如：對話中出現「Well, that's a good question.」且題目詢問本句句意為何時，這句話的意思並非是指「這真是個好問題」，而是「He cannot provide the answer.（不太清楚，無法回答）」的意思。

圖表類題型的難度則不如想像中困難。

PART 3 為**掌握聽力分數的關鍵**，同時也是題數最多（39題）、難度較高的大題，請務必好好準備。

PART 4 簡短獨白 核心攻略

PART 4 的難易度與舊制多益相當。在 PART 3 和 PART 4 的命題部分，解題線索不會只放在一個句子裡面，而是要聽懂兩三個句子後，才能找出答案。PART 4 的圖表類題型也是相對容易的部分。

經分析 PART 3 和 PART 4 的答案後，發現**不太會連續出現三次相同的答案**，也就是幾乎不太可能出現像是 AAA、BBB、CCC、DDD 這樣的答案。因此當你沒聽清楚題目時，不要重複選擇和前一題相同的答案，而是改選其他選項，如此一來猜中答案的機率相對較高，請務必牢記這個小訣竅。

PART 5 句子填空 核心攻略

與舊制多益相比，PART 5 的總題數減少了 10 題，難易度不變，因此只要依照過往的準備方式來解題即可。不過偶爾也會出現一些容易誤答的題目。例如：片語 be selective about，正確答案應為 selective（挑剔的、有選擇性的），但選項中會出現 rigorous（嚴格的）作為出題陷阱來誤導你。碰到這類題目時，請務必好好**觀察放入句中的單字是否適當**。

PART 5 會因為每個月考試的難易度而有所差異，讓我們一起挑出難度偏高的題型吧！

101. Tina is one of the most popular musical artists in the world, ------- only Mozart in record sales.

(A) except
(B) into
(C) from
(D) behind

解答 D

本題必須先釐清句意後，才能正確解答。緹娜是位國際級的音樂家，排名第二，僅次於莫札特。這是很多考生都會答錯的題型，請仔細檢視一遍。

中譯 緹娜是位國際知名的音樂家，專輯銷量僅次於莫札特。

102. This year's Kinglish Conference will be held in Seoul, though it has ------- alternated between Tokyo and San Francisco.

(A) traditionally
(B) abruptly
(C) exactly
(D) necessarily

解答 A

本題要從選項中選出最適當的副詞。每次考試都會出現這類題型，難度不亞於上方的範例，請務必多加留意。

中譯 雖然歷來都是在東京和舊金山輪流舉行，但金英大會今年將在首爾舉辦。

103. As they had with the first, organizers of Kinglish Conference ------- managed to find an alternative speaker for the second canceled seminar.

(A) much
(B) excessively
(C) concurrently
(D) likewise

解答 D

本題要從選項中選出最適當的副詞。

中譯 如同上一個場次那般，金英大會主辦方比照辦理，設法為先前取消的第二場研討會找了另一位講師替代。

104. **We should know that the terms are subject to change ------- when oil prices rise or fall.**

(A) heavily
(B) quarterly
(C) still
(D) nearby

解答 B

請先掌握文意，才能找出正確答案。本句的文意為：「條件會隨著季度改變」。

中譯 我們都應該知道，每當油價漲跌時，每季的油價也應隨之調整。

105. **------- the world's tallest building was completed, HaJin and Tina Ltd. had already begun designing a taller one.**

(A) By the time
(B) Whenever
(C) If
(D) Because

解答 A

屬於過去完成式的考題。經常以過去完成式和未來完成式來命題。

By the time＋主詞＋過去式, 主詞＋had p.p.

By the time＋主詞＋現在式, 主詞＋will have p.p.

中譯 當世界最高的建築完工時，哈金與緹娜公司已經在著手設計更高的了。

PART 6 段落填空 核心攻略

PART 6 最難的地方在於要從選項（四個句子）中選出適當的句子填入空格中。這部分為新增加的題型，不僅要花費較多時間解題，平時也應在如何**掌握前後文意**上，下一番功夫。請利用本書徹底釐清觀念，並好好練習本大題的題型！

PART 6 會因每個月考試的難易度而有所差異，難易度較不固定，請務必勤加演練。

PART 7 單/雙/多篇閱讀 核心攻略

最近總是聽到許多人談論 PART 7 的難度很高。PART 7 的總題數增加為 54 題，除了要花費很多時間解題之外，就連題目本身也不太容易理解。如果說 PART 3 是掌握聽力分數的關鍵，那麼 PART 7 就是**掌握閱讀分數的關鍵**。在舊制多益測驗中，原本可以輕鬆解題過關的短文閱讀，難度也大幅提升。而雙篇閱讀和多篇閱讀，也有逐漸變難的趨勢，建議大家可以利用本書精選的試題反覆演練。

另外，考生在寫到第 196–200 題時，常因解題時間不夠，隨便亂猜答案。當各位遇到這種狀況時，請特別留意 ABCD 答案的分配比例都是相同的！從開始實行新制多益測驗，一直到最近本書準備出版之際，我分析了這段期間內 PART 7 中 196–200 題的正確選項後發現：答案為 A 的次數為 18 次；答案為 B 的次數為 18 次；答案為 C 的次數為18次；答案為 D 的次數為 17 次，**ABCD 選項為答案的比例幾乎均等**。因此考生若碰上 PART 7 的作答時間不足，必須猜答案時，請務必分散風險作答。在此提醒，此技巧僅作為解題的輔助手段，希望大家還是以全力以赴解題為優先。

在 PART 7 中，同義詞替換的難度也逐漸提升。例如 retain 這個字最常用的意思為「留存（to keep possession of）」或是「保持」。

例：They insisted on retaining old customs.
他們堅持沿用舊制。

但是你知道其實 retain 也有依合約「聘僱」某人從事有酬工作的意思嗎？
舉例而言：retain a lawyer 意思就是「聘請法律顧問」。

例1：The team failed to retain him, and he became a free agent.
那支球隊無法和他續約，於是他成為自由球員。

例2：They have decided to retain a firm to conduct a survey.
他們決定僱用一間公司來執行調查。

例3：You may need to retain an attorney.
你可能需要聘請律師。

最近在多益閱讀題中，改以 contract 的同義詞 retain 出題，讓眾多考生驚慌失措。這個用法甚至是英英字典裡的最後一個意思。因此當你在複習已經熟悉的單字時，請務必確認這個單字是否還有其他意思，並透過例句來學習，最重要的就是保持學習態度！

做完本書所有試題後，請反覆練習，重點在於**充分理解**所有例句，並維持**做筆記**的習慣。

七大攻略讀熟後，請翻開第一回擬真試題，實際測驗看看吧！

多益權威完美重現實戰考題

32. Where most likely does the man work?
    (A) At a law office
    (B) At a repair company
    (C) At a bookstore
    (D) At a print shop

33. What does the man ask the woman to do?
    (A) Restart some equipment
    (B) Use another machine
    (C) Consult a manual
    (D) Find a reset code

34. What does the man say he can do?
    (A) Locate some equipment
    (B) Copy some documents
    (C) Contact a supplier
    (D) Go to the woman's office

35. Why is the man calling?
    (A) To book tickets for an event
    (B) To inquire about accommodation
    (C) To change a reservation
    (D) To purchase a printer

36. What information does the woman request?
    (A) The number of rooms
    (B) The name of a conference
    (C) A membership card number
    (D) A check-out date

37. What does the woman suggest?
    (A) Upgrading some rooms
    (B) Signing a contract
    (C) Checking a website
    (D) Using a discount code

百分百擬真試題

試題完全比照新制多益出題趨勢；寫完全書共六回題本並讀懂解析，必能輕鬆掌握新制多益答題技巧！

多益權威完美解析

Questions 32–34 refer to the following conversation.

W Hello, this is Suzie Thompson at Pearson Law. [32] I'm calling about a problem with our photocopier. Whenever I try to make copies, the text is so shrunken that it's unreadable.	女 哈囉，我是皮爾森律師事務所的蘇西‧湯普生。[32] 我打電話來，是因為我們的影印機有點問題。我每次影印，字都縮得很小，模糊不清。
M Okay. [32] I think I can help you with that. [33] Have you tried turning it off and then turning it back on?	男 好的。[32] 我想，我可以幫上您的忙。[33] 您試過關機，再重新開機嗎?
W Yes, I did that a few times, but it didn't help. I also tried the reset code you gave me during your last service visit, but that didn't help, either.	女 是的，我試了好幾次都沒用。我也試過你上次來時給的那組重新設定的密碼，但也沒有用。
M I see. Well, I have some time this afternoon. [34] How about I stop by your office and see if I can find out what's wrong?	男 了解。嗯，我今天下午有空。[34] 我順道過去您的辦公室，看看我能不能找出問題，好嗎?

1. 題目原文加詳盡解析，解題重點一網打盡

題目與中譯左右對照，並附詳解，確實理解每題關鍵線索與陷阱！

5

(A) Some workers are moving the chairs.	(A) 一些工人正在搬動椅子。
(B) A waiting room is decorated with pictures.*	(B) 等候室裡裝飾著畫。
(C) A light fixture is being mounted above the doorway.	(C) 門口上方正在裝燈。
(D) Some lampshades have been set on the floor.	(D) 地板上放著一些燈罩。

照片中僅出現事物，因此在聽到 (A) 主詞為人的當下，即可馬上剔除此選項；(C) 為現在進行被動式：be + being + p.p.，表示某個人正在做某件事（Someone is mounting a light fixture above the doorway.），因此也是錯誤的選項；(B) 將焦點放在牆上裝飾的畫，最符合照片情境。

- decorate 裝飾　light fixture 燈具　mount 安裝　above 在……上面　doorway 門口、出入口　lampshade 燈罩　floor 地板

2. 完美解題，瞄準最新出題方向

詳細解說新制多益命題趨勢以及與舊制多益之間的細微差異。

35

Why is the man calling?	男子為何打電話?
(A) To book tickets for an event	(A) 為了預訂某個活動的門票。
(B) To inquire about accommodation*	(B) 為了詢問住房。
(C) To change a reservation	(C) 為了更改預訂資料。
(D) To purchase a printer	(D) 為了購買印表機。

對話第一段，男子提到將會參加會議，並詢問是否有空房（Do you have any rooms available?），因此正確答案為 (B)。

答案改寫 room → accommodation

- inquire 詢問、調查　accommodation 住宿、住房　purchase 購買

36

What information does the woman request?	女子要求什麼資訊?
(A) The number of rooms*	(A) 房間的數量。

3. 單字替換用法一手掌握

提供例題內重點單字「答案改寫」的用法，學會「換句話說」之答題邏輯的同時，還能同步擴充同義字彙量，一舉數得！

M Good morning, my coworkers and I are planning to attend the State Accounting Conference in September. [35] Do you have any rooms available from the 7th to the 10th?	男 早安，我和同事計畫參加九月的國家會計研討會。[35] 你們七日到十日有空房間嗎?
W Let me check our reservation system. Yes, it looks like we have several rooms available. [36] How many would you like to reserve?	女 我查一下訂房系統。有的，看來我們還有好幾間空房。[36] 您要預訂幾間房間?
M There are five of us, so we would prefer to book five single suites. Do your single suites have Internet access?	男 我們有五個人，所以，我們比較想要預訂五間單人套房。你們的單人套房可以上網嗎?
W In that case, [37] I suggest booking five single business suites. For only $10 more per night, each business suite comes with free Internet access and an onsite laser printer.	女 那樣的話，[37] 我建議您預訂五間單人商務套房，升級為商務套房只要每晚再加十元就好。每間商務套房都可以免費上網，房間裡還備有雷射印表機。
M That sounds perfect. Let me discuss it with my coworkers, and I'll call you back within the hour.	男 聽起來非常合適。我和同事討論一下，一

- coworker 同事　attend 參加、出席　accounting 會計　available 可得到的、有空的　check 核對　reservation (n.) 預訂、保留　several 幾個的　reserve (v.) 預訂、保留　prefer 更喜歡、寧可　book 預訂　suite 套房　access 使用　come with 伴隨　onsite 就地、現場

35

Why is the man calling?	男子為何打電話?
(A) To book tickets for an event	(A) 為了預訂某個活動的門票。

4. 高頻單字釋義，加強字彙活用能力

詳列題目重點字彙，幫助確實掌握字詞釋義，快速累積多益高頻字彙量！

ACTUAL
TEST
1

LISTENING TEST 01

In the Listening test, you will be asked to demonstrate how well you understand spoken English. The entire Listening test will last approximately 45 minutes. There are four parts, and directions are given for each part. You must mark your answers on the separate answer sheet. Do not write your answers in your test book.

PART 1

Directions: For each question in this part, you will hear four statements about a picture in your test book. When you hear the statements, you must select the one statement that best describes what you see in the picture. Then find the number of the question on your answer sheet and mark your answer. The statements will not be printed in your test book and will be spoken only one time.

Sample Answer

Statement (C), "A woman is admiring some artwork.," is the best description of the picture, so you should select answer (C) and mark it on your answer sheet.

1.

2.

GO ON TO THE NEXT PAGE

3.

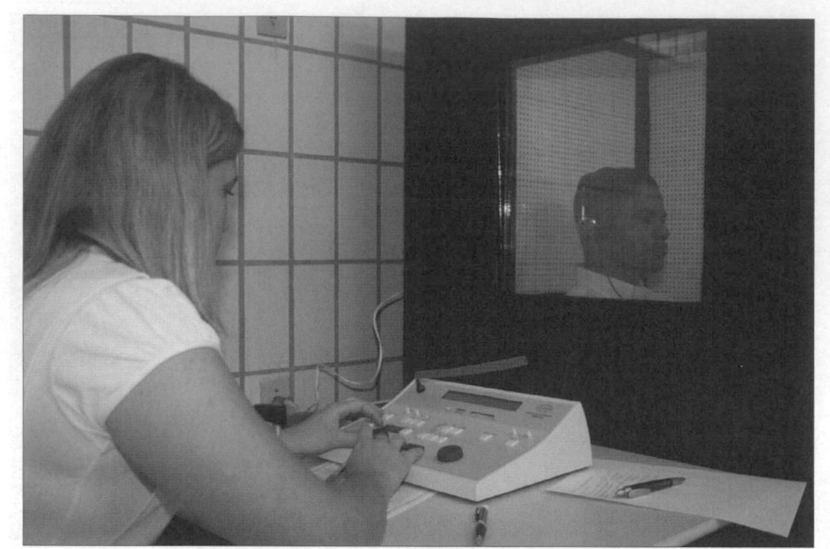

4.

5.

6.

GO ON TO THE NEXT PAGE

PART 2 02

Directions: You will hear a question or statement and three responses spoken in English. They will not be printed in your test book and will be spoken only one time. Select the best response to the question or statement and mark the letter (A), (B) or (C) on your answer sheet.

7. Mark your answer on your answer sheet.
8. Mark your answer on your answer sheet.
9. Mark your answer on your answer sheet.
10. Mark your answer on your answer sheet.
11. Mark your answer on your answer sheet.
12. Mark your answer on your answer sheet.
13. Mark your answer on your answer sheet.
14. Mark your answer on your answer sheet.
15. Mark your answer on your answer sheet.
16. Mark your answer on your answer sheet.
17. Mark your answer on your answer sheet.
18. Mark your answer on your answer sheet.
19. Mark your answer on your answer sheet.
20. Mark your answer on your answer sheet.
21. Mark your answer on your answer sheet.
22. Mark your answer on your answer sheet.
23. Mark your answer on your answer sheet.
24. Mark your answer on your answer sheet.
25. Mark your answer on your answer sheet.
26. Mark your answer on your answer sheet.
27. Mark your answer on your answer sheet.
28. Mark your answer on your answer sheet.
29. Mark your answer on your answer sheet.
30. Mark your answer on your answer sheet.
31. Mark your answer on your answer sheet.

PART 3 ∩ 03

Directions: You will hear some conversations between two or more people. You will be asked to answer three questions about what the speakers say in each conversation. Select the best response to each question and mark the letter (A), (B), (C), or (D) on your answer sheet. The conversations will not be printed in your test book and will be spoken only one time.

32. Where most likely does the man work?
(A) At a law office
(B) At a repair company
(C) At a bookstore
(D) At a print shop

33. What does the man ask the woman to do?
(A) Restart some equipment
(B) Use another machine
(C) Consult a manual
(D) Find a reset code

34. What does the man say he can do?
(A) Locate some equipment
(B) Copy some documents
(C) Contact a supplier
(D) Go to the woman's office

35. Why is the man calling?
(A) To book tickets for an event
(B) To inquire about accommodation
(C) To change a reservation
(D) To purchase a printer

36. What information does the woman request?
(A) The number of rooms
(B) The name of a conference
(C) A membership card number
(D) A check-out date

37. What does the woman suggest?
(A) Upgrading some rooms
(B) Signing a contract
(C) Checking a website
(D) Using a discount code

GO ON TO THE NEXT PAGE

38. What is the conversation mainly about?
(A) An updated menu
(B) A change in a schedule
(C) A writing contest
(D) A volunteer project

39. What is true about the woman?
(A) She will relocate next week.
(B) She is a university professor.
(C) She has a photocopier.
(D) She won an award.

40. What is Mark asked to do?
(A) Take photographs
(B) Develop a design plan
(C) Attend a workshop
(D) Order some supplies

41. What is being discussed?
(A) A business card design
(B) A printing order
(C) A company retreat
(D) New work schedules

42. What was the problem with the sample item?
(A) The paper was damaged.
(B) A logo was outdated.
(C) Some information was incorrect.
(D) The cost was too high.

43. What does the woman ask the man to do?
(A) Contact a company
(B) Return a sample
(C) Hire a new employee
(D) Pay an account

44. Where most likely do the speakers work?
(A) At a subway station
(B) At a dental clinic
(C) At a travel agency
(D) At a marketing firm

45. What project have the women been working on?
(A) Drafting an employee's contract
(B) Creating a television advertisement
(C) Inputting details into a computer
(D) Installing some audio equipment

46. What does the man suggest?
(A) Working some overtime
(B) Moving the deadline
(C) Using different software
(D) Assigning more staff

47. Why is the woman calling?
(A) To request a reservation change
(B) To inquire about a special discount
(C) To ask for a full refund
(D) To upgrade her flight ticket

48. What event does the woman mention?
(A) An animal competition
(B) A veterinary seminar
(C) A tour of a city
(D) An art convention

49. What additional information does the man ask for?
(A) The number of passengers
(B) The dimension of the carriers
(C) The preferred payment method
(D) A membership card number

50. What did the man recently do?
(A) He had an oven repaired.
(B) He printed out a receipt.
(C) He looked at customer feedback.
(D) He corrected an invoice error.

51. Why does the woman say, "I've spent all day training the new cooks"?
(A) To express agreement
(B) To suggest a solution
(C) To request more details
(D) To provide an excuse

52. What will the man mention at the meeting?
(A) Taking orders from people who are waiting
(B) Keeping the business open late on weekends
(C) Removing certain dishes from the menu
(D) Offering more specials during lunchtime

53. What suggestion does the man make?
(A) Organizing workspaces
(B) Being friendly
(C) Working extra hours
(D) Recording information

54. What does the man mean when he says, "It's funny you mention that"?
(A) The woman's suggestion is already true.
(B) He thinks the woman's comment is false.
(C) The woman's idea is strange.
(D) He refuses to answer the question.

55. According to the man, what will happen in October?
(A) A report will be distributed.
(B) A book will become available.
(C) A company will be established.
(D) A project will be started.

56. What is the woman unable to do?
(A) Print some documents
(B) Locate a file
(C) Send some work e-mails
(D) Join the company dinner

57. What did the man do this morning?
(A) Access a server
(B) Visit a department
(C) Fix a computer problem
(D) File a complaint

58. What does the man say he will do?
(A) Demonstrate how to sign in
(B) Submit another form
(C) Update a service request
(D) Reset a company password

59. What did the man do in Chicago?
(A) Sign a new client
(B) Meet with some customers
(C) Attend a workshop
(D) Deliver a sample order

60. What problem does the man mention?
(A) A client canceled a contract.
(B) A CEO was too busy to meet.
(C) A trip was delayed by a week.
(D) A price was not agreed upon.

61. What does the woman suggest doing next?
(A) Flying back to Chicago
(B) Reading an article
(C) Writing a proposal
(D) Reviewing a website

GO ON TO THE NEXT PAGE

Business	Suite
Jane, Baker, and Sons Law	601
Walder Tech Solutions	602
Sedwick International Trade	603
Martin Sound and Recording	604

62. What is the purpose of the woman's visit?

(A) To interview a lawyer
(B) To attend a medical appointment
(C) To purchase a parking pass
(D) To meet with a client

63. What does the man say about parking?

(A) It is free for paying customers.
(B) It is cheaper than most places.
(C) It is only for employees.
(D) It is located on the roof.

64. Look at the graphic. Which office name needs to be updated on the building directory?

(A) Jane, Baker, and Sons Law
(B) Walder Tech Solutions
(C) Sedwick International Trade
(D) Martin Sound and Recording

CONFERENCE ROOM A: WEDNESDAY	
TIME	EVENT
10:00 A.M.	Graphic Design Meeting
11:00 A.M.	Conference Call
2:00 P.M.	Meeting with S&V Fashions
3:00 P.M.	Budget Review

65. Where do the speakers work?

(A) At a fashion house
(B) At an advertising firm
(C) At shipping business
(D) At a medical clinic

66. Look at the graphic. According to the man, what event is Jim in charge of?

(A) Graphic Design Meeting
(B) Conference Call
(C) Meeting with S&V Fashions
(D) Budget Review

67. What does the woman say she will do?

(A) Upgrade a room
(B) Locate some files
(C) Postpone a meeting
(D) Ask for a room change

ITEM or SERVICE	Price
Inkspark 306 Printer	$399.00
2-year extended warranty	$69.00
306 color ink cartridge	$32.00
306 black ink cartridge	$15.00
Total:	$515.00

68. Who most likely is the woman?
(A) A hotel receptionist
(B) A sales clerk
(C) A civil servant
(D) An artist

69. What does the man ask about?
(A) Payment plans
(B) Special discounts
(C) Tax rebates
(D) New products

70. Look at the graphic. Which amount will be removed from the bill?
(A) $399
(B) $69
(C) $32
(D) $15

GO ON TO THE NEXT PAGE

PART 4 04

Directions: You will hear some talks given by a single speaker. You will be asked to answer three questions about what the speaker says in each talk. Select the best response to each question and mark the letter (A), (B), (C), or (D) on your answer sheet. The talks will not be printed in your test book and will be spoken only one time.

71. Where does the speaker work?
(A) At a software company
(B) At an electronics manufacturer
(C) At a computer repair store
(D) At a shipping company

72. What does the speaker say he has done?
(A) Ordered a component
(B) Refunded a fee
(C) Replaced a part
(D) Upgraded some software

73. What does the speaker offer?
(A) To lend a computer
(B) To move some information
(C) To extend a service warranty
(D) To pay for a new computer

74. Why did Ms. Renolds visit Star Insurance's website?
(A) To review a product
(B) To fill out a form
(C) To set up a meeting
(D) To upgrade a service

75. What does the speaker offer Ms. Renolds?
(A) A membership card
(B) A full refund
(C) A discount
(D) A new vehicle

76. According to the speaker, what must Ms. Renolds do by June 23rd?
(A) Sign up for a newsletter
(B) Visit Star Insurance in person
(C) Complete a training course
(D) Make a decision

77. Where is the tour most likely taking place?
(A) At an automotive plant
(B) At a car dealership
(C) At a toy outlet
(D) At a mechanic's shop

78. What does the speaker say has changed about the tour?
(A) The number of guides
(B) The outdoor sites
(C) The cost of tickets
(D) The order of locations

79. What does the speaker offer the listeners?
(A) A limited-time discount
(B) A hands-on workshop
(C) A free membership
(D) A map of the facility

---

80. Why is the mayor visiting the restaurant?
(A) To hold a celebration
(B) To conduct an inspection
(C) To give a speech
(D) To host a birthday party

81. Why does the speaker say, "This shouldn't be any different than usual"?
(A) To stress the importance of a meeting
(B) To reassure employees about an event
(C) To inform of the mayor's special request
(D) To guess the duration of an inspection

82. What must listeners do before the end of the day?
(A) Check an updated schedule
(B) Fill out some information
(C) Purchase some new clothing
(D) Print some new menus

---

83. What does Renton & Sons produce?
(A) Office furniture
(B) Flooring
(C) Appliances
(D) Windows

84. What does the man imply when he says, "ten thousand units is a bit excessive"?
(A) The customer's order may be wrong.
(B) He will have to hire additional workers.
(C) The customer has canceled her order.
(D) He will deliver some materials late.

85. What does the man explain about his products?
(A) They are easy to clean.
(B) They are cheaper in summer.
(C) They are of high quality.
(D) They are large in size.

---

86. Where does the speaker most likely work?
(A) At an employment agency
(B) At a computer store
(C) At a university
(D) At a software company

87. What change to the internship program does the speaker mention?
(A) Employees will submit regular reports.
(B) Interns will be paid for their work.
(C) Fewer students will be selected.
(D) The program length will be extended.

88. What is the purpose of the change?
(A) To ensure interns follow all the rules
(B) To make job candidate selection easier
(C) To provide team leaders with incentives
(D) To allow managers to apply for funding

GO ON TO THE NEXT PAGE

89. According to the speaker, what service will the company begin offering next month?
(A) Discounted products
(B) Free shipping
(C) Cheap memberships
(D) Complimentary samples

90. Why has the company decided to add the new service?
(A) An advertisement failed.
(B) Business has dropped.
(C) Competition has increased.
(D) Some customers complained.

91. What does the speaker say he will do next week?
(A) Conclude an important deal
(B) Test a skincare product
(C) Update an online store
(D) Deliver some products himself

---

92. What type of business is being discussed?
(A) An electronics market
(B) A restaurant chain
(C) A shopping center
(D) A coffee shop

93. Why does the speaker say, "Visitors are already lining up"?
(A) To emphasize interest in an event
(B) To encourage listeners to stay home
(C) To discuss the size of a location
(D) To express concern about crowdedness

94. What will customers receive if they visit the food court?
(A) A free beverage
(B) A 30% refund
(C) A discount coupon
(D) A parking pass

Schedule: *Thursday, March, 2nd*

Time	Event
10:30 A.M.–11:30 A.M.	*Conference Call*
12:00 P.M.–1:20 P.M.	*Lunch Meeting*
1:30 P.M.–3:00 P.M.	*Staff Meeting*
4:00 P.M.–6:00 P.M.	*Meeting at ARF Technology*

95. What is planned for the next week?
(A) A bigger team will be created.
(B) A new product will be launched.
(C) Some managers will retire.
(D) Some meetings will be canceled.

96. Why does the speaker want to meet?
(A) To visit a client's store
(B) To go over some regulations
(C) To introduce some employees
(D) To explain a new contract

97. Look at the graphic. What time does the speaker want to meet?
(A) At 10:30
(B) At 12:00
(C) At 1:30
(D) At 4:00

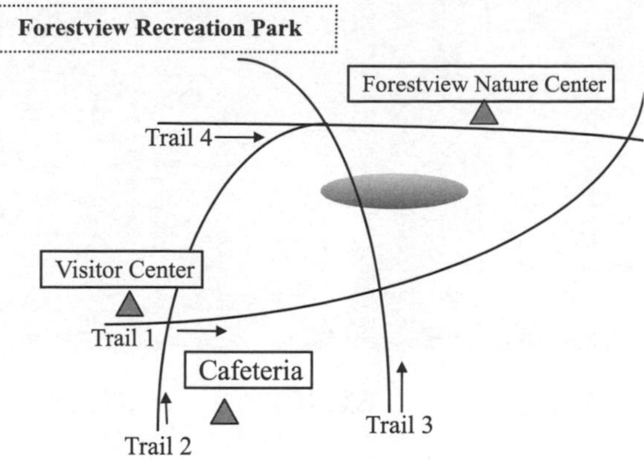

98. Who is the talk intended for?
(A) Park employees
(B) Botany students
(C) Construction workers
(D) Visitors at a park

99. Look at the graphic. Which trail is closed to visitors?
(A) Trail 1
(B) Trail 2
(C) Trail 3
(D) Trail 4

100. What project is the park developing?
(A) A bird-watching club
(B) A research foundation
(C) A study on chipmunks
(D) An educational program

ANSWERS ACTUAL TEST 1

1. (A)	**21.** (B)	**41.** (B)	**61.** (C)	**81.** (B)
2. (A)	**22.** (A)	**42.** (C)	**62.** (B)	**82.** (B)
3. (D)	**23.** (B)	**43.** (A)	**63.** (A)	**83.** (B)
4. (C)	**24.** (A)	**44.** (B)	**64.** (D)	**84.** (A)
5. (B)	**25.** (C)	**45.** (C)	**65.** (B)	**85.** (D)
6. (D)	**26.** (B)	**46.** (D)	**66.** (A)	**86.** (D)
7. (B)	**27.** (C)	**47.** (B)	**67.** (D)	**87.** (A)
8. (A)	**28.** (A)	**48.** (A)	**68.** (B)	**88.** (B)
9. (A)	**29.** (A)	**49.** (B)	**69.** (A)	**89.** (B)
10. (C)	**30.** (A)	**50.** (C)	**70.** (D)	**90.** (D)
11. (B)	**31.** (C)	**51.** (D)	**71.** (C)	**91.** (A)
12. (C)	**32.** (B)	**52.** (A)	**72.** (A)	**92.** (C)
13. (B)	**33.** (A)	**53.** (D)	**73.** (B)	**93.** (A)
14. (B)	**34.** (D)	**54.** (A)	**74.** (B)	**94.** (C)
15. (A)	**35.** (B)	**55.** (B)	**75.** (C)	**95.** (A)
16. (C)	**36.** (A)	**56.** (C)	**76.** (D)	**96.** (C)
17. (B)	**37.** (A)	**57.** (D)	**77.** (A)	**97.** (C)
18. (C)	**38.** (D)	**58.** (A)	**78.** (D)	**98.** (D)
19. (C)	**39.** (D)	**59.** (B)	**79.** (A)	**99.** (D)
20. (A)	**40.** (B)	**60.** (D)	**80.** (A)	**100.** (D)

ACTUAL
TEST
2

LISTENING TEST 05

In the Listening test, you will be asked to demonstrate how well you understand spoken English. The entire Listening test will last approximately 45 minutes. There are four parts, and directions are given for each part. You must mark your answers on the separate answer sheet. Do not write your answers in your test book.

PART 1

Directions: For each question in this part, you will hear four statements about a picture in your test book. When you hear the statements, you must select the one statement that best describes what you see in the picture. Then find the number of the question on your answer sheet and mark your answer. The statements will not be printed in your test book and will be spoken only one time.

Sample Answer

Statement (C), "A woman is admiring some artwork.," is the best description of the picture, so you should select answer (C) and mark it on your answer sheet.

1.

2.

GO ON TO THE NEXT PAGE

3.

4.

5.

6.

GO ON TO THE NEXT PAGE

PART 2 ∩ 06

Directions: You will hear a question or statement and three responses spoken in English. They will not be printed in your test book and will be spoken only one time. Select the best response to the question or statement and mark the letter (A), (B) or (C) on your answer sheet.

7. Mark your answer on your answer sheet.
8. Mark your answer on your answer sheet.
9. Mark your answer on your answer sheet.
10. Mark your answer on your answer sheet.
11. Mark your answer on your answer sheet.
12. Mark your answer on your answer sheet.
13. Mark your answer on your answer sheet.
14. Mark your answer on your answer sheet.
15. Mark your answer on your answer sheet.
16. Mark your answer on your answer sheet.
17. Mark your answer on your answer sheet.
18. Mark your answer on your answer sheet.
19. Mark your answer on your answer sheet.
20. Mark your answer on your answer sheet.
21. Mark your answer on your answer sheet.
22. Mark your answer on your answer sheet.
23. Mark your answer on your answer sheet.
24. Mark your answer on your answer sheet.
25. Mark your answer on your answer sheet.
26. Mark your answer on your answer sheet.
27. Mark your answer on your answer sheet.
28. Mark your answer on your answer sheet.
29. Mark your answer on your answer sheet.
30. Mark your answer on your answer sheet.
31. Mark your answer on your answer sheet.

PART 3 07

Directions: You will hear some conversations between two or more people. You will be asked to answer three questions about what the speakers say in each conversation. Select the best response to each question and mark the letter (A), (B), (C), or (D) on your answer sheet. The conversations will not be printed in your test book and will be spoken only one time.

32. What are the speakers discussing?
(A) A suitcase
(B) A printer
(C) A monitor
(D) A tablet computer

33. What does the man ask about?
(A) The total cost
(B) The available sizes
(C) The warranty options
(D) The free accessories

34. What will the woman most likely do next?
(A) Request payment
(B) Consult a manager
(C) Register an ID
(D) Return an item

35. Why did the man call the woman?
(A) To inform of a change of plans
(B) To offer to call a car service
(C) To explain an event schedule
(D) To reschedule an appointment

36. What does the man suggest?
(A) Canceling an event
(B) Using public transit
(C) Asking a coworker for help
(D) Borrowing a neighbor's car

37. What does the woman say she will do?
(A) Change a reservation
(B) Contact a colleague
(C) Call a tow truck
(D) Pick up a coworker

GO ON TO THE NEXT PAGE

38. What are the speakers discussing?
(A) A new office location
(B) A store's hours
(C) A package delivery
(D) A change of schedule

39. Why is the man's company behind the schedule?
(A) A new store was opened.
(B) Some items were lost.
(C) A few workers were sick.
(D) Some roads were congested.

40. What does the woman say she will do next?
(A) Go to a supermarket
(B) Wait for an item at home
(C) Cancel a purchase
(D) Visit another post office

---

41. What type of services does the man's company offer?
(A) Vehicle upgrades
(B) Home renovations
(C) Window cleaning
(D) Appliance installations

42. Why is the man calling?
(A) To return a phone call
(B) To offer a free service
(C) To discuss a payment plan
(D) To advertise a promotion

43. What does the man offer to do for the woman?
(A) Provide a bigger discount
(B) Mail some carpet samples
(C) Send an employee
(D) Replace some old items

---

44. Where does the woman work?
(A) At a doctor's office
(B) At an insurance company
(C) At a sales office
(D) At a dental clinic

45. What information does the man ask for?
(A) A list of services
(B) A doctor's schedule
(C) The location of a clinic
(D) The price of a service

46. What does the man imply when he says, "I have a business meeting that day"?
(A) He needs another appointment.
(B) He will wear a formal suit.
(C) He will visit another location.
(D) He doesn't mind traveling far.

---

47. What does the woman want to do?
(A) Rent a house overseas
(B) Sign up for a mailing list
(C) Purchase airline tickets
(D) Upgrade a membership

48. What does the man recommend?
(A) Going to a travel agency
(B) Buying a lifetime membership
(C) Using a new travel website
(D) Calling an airline directly

49. What is the woman concerned about?
(A) A delay in payment
(B) The price of a membership
(C) A missing coupon book
(D) The location of an airport

---

50. Who most likely is the woman?
(A) A graphic designer
(B) A store owner
(C) A newspaper reporter
(D) A web developer

51. What is the woman pleased about?
(A) Some seasonal discounts
(B) A new logo design
(C) The price of a service
(D) The annual sales results

52. What does the man offer to do?
(A) Move a company logo
(B) Add a border to a design
(C) Enlarge the size of a picture
(D) Change the color of some words

---

53. What does the woman imply when she says, "I won't be able to leave for a while"?
(A) She had to change her plans.
(B) She is waiting for someone.
(C) She has already eaten dinner.
(D) She doesn't have a car now.

54. What is the woman worried about?
(A) Presenting her findings to her boss
(B) Finishing a report on time
(C) Mending a business relationship
(D) Inspecting some damages

55. What does the man say he will do before he leaves?
(A) Hold a monthly meeting
(B) Pass on some information
(C) Visit a customer's office
(D) Check the status of an order

---

56. Where do the interviewers most likely work?
(A) At a furniture manufacturer
(B) At an interior design company
(C) At an art gallery
(D) At a moving company

57. What job requirement do the speakers discuss?
(A) Meeting deadlines
(B) Cooperating with others
(C) Working long hours
(D) Lifting heavy objects

58. What does the man agree to do next?
(A) Show some documents
(B) Fill out an application
(C) Submit some design samples
(D) Sign an employment contract

---

59. What problem does the woman mention?
(A) A room was damaged.
(B) Some guests complained.
(C) Some workers quit.
(D) A business is slow.

60. What does the man suggest?
(A) Offering free meals to guests
(B) Holding a promotional event
(C) Upgrading room sizes
(D) Merging with another business

61. What does the woman ask the man to do?
(A) Analyze customer feedback
(B) Update a website
(C) Make a mailing list
(D) Prepare some materials

ACTUAL TEST 2 PART 3

GO ON TO THE NEXT PAGE

62. What industry do the speakers most likely work in?

(A) Cosmetics
(B) Engineering
(C) Software
(D) Trade

63. What does the woman say will happen next month?

(A) A convention will take place.
(B) A new product will be manufactured.
(C) A patent will expire.
(D) A new law will be enacted.

64. What does the woman imply when she says, "This diagram is from last year's convention"?

(A) A fee must be paid.
(B) Nothing needs to be done.
(C) This year's figures are not available yet.
(D) Some information is outdated.

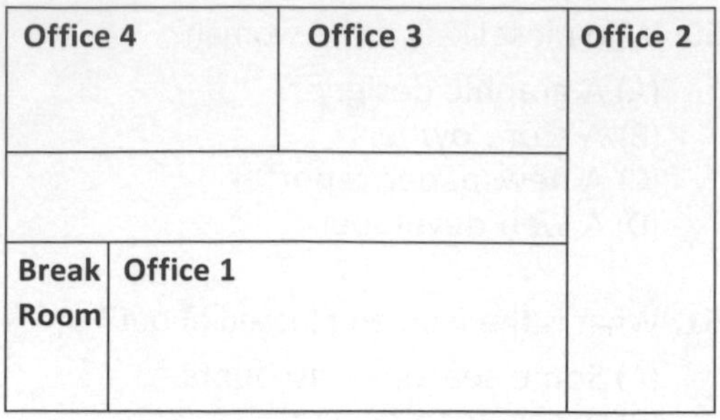

Office 4 **Office 3** **Office 2**

Break Room **Office 1**

65. According to the woman, what will she be doing this afternoon?

(A) Going on vacation
(B) Moving to a new office
(C) Meeting some customers
(D) Drawing up a floor plan

66. Look at the graphic. Which office has been assigned to the woman?

(A) Office 1
(B) Office 2
(C) Office 3
(D) Office 4

67. What does the woman say will take place tomorrow morning?

(A) A visit with clients
(B) An employee meeting
(C) A renovation
(D) A company party

Company	Location
Stanford Design	Chicago
Able Advertising	Miami
Renview Media	New York
Smart Style Design	Atlanta

68. What type of event is the company hosting?

(A) A charity ball
(B) An art gallery opening
(C) A retirement party
(D) A professional conference

69. What is the man concerned about?

(A) The cost of a project
(B) The location of an event
(C) A company's efficiency
(D) A worker's absence

70. Look at the graphic. Which company does the woman suggest?

(A) Stanford Design
(B) Able Advertising
(C) Renview Media
(D) Smart Style Design

GO ON TO THE NEXT PAGE

PART 4 ♫ 08

Directions: You will hear some talks given by a single speaker. You will be asked to answer three questions about what the speaker says in each talk. Select the best response to each question and mark the letter (A), (B), (C), or (D) on your answer sheet. The talks will not be printed in your test book and will be spoken only one time.

71. Where most likely are the listeners?
(A) At an airport
(B) On a ship
(C) At a travel agency
(D) In a shopping mall

72. What is the cause of the delay?
(A) A security issue
(B) Missing passengers
(C) Mechanical problems
(D) Poor weather

73. What does the speaker suggest listeners do?
(A) Request a ticket refund
(B) Obtain a complimentary drink
(C) Book hotel accommodation
(D) Visit an information desk

74. What is the speaker mainly discussing?
(A) A downsizing plan
(B) A company merger
(C) A new office manager
(D) A potential client

75. What does the speaker say will take place at the company once a month?
(A) An employee review
(B) A monthly bonus
(C) A sales meeting
(D) A training course

76. Why will some employees be unavailable in the afternoon?
(A) They are attending a training session.
(B) They are presenting at a trade show.
(C) They are meeting with the head manager.
(D) They are leaving for a company trip.

77. What does the speaker say the business is considering?
(A) Renovating a kitchen
(B) Changing operation hours
(C) Contracting a new chef
(D) Hiring a new supplier

78. Why should listeners visit the head chef's office?
(A) To have an interview
(B) To pick up a coupon
(C) To sample some food
(D) To submit a form

79. What can listeners receive for participation?
(A) Some movie tickets
(B) A vacation package
(C) Some free food
(D) A pay raise

80. Where most likely is the speaker?
(A) At a bus station
(B) At an airport
(C) At her home
(D) In an airplane

81. What does the speaker imply when she says, "It's really too bad"?
(A) She is not well.
(B) She is disappointed.
(C) She lost a lot of money.
(D) She regrets her decision.

82. What does the speaker ask the listener to do?
(A) Drive to an airport
(B) Reschedule a party
(C) Unlock a door
(D) Meet her for dinner

83. Where most likely is this announcement being made?
(A) At pastry shop
(B) At a bookstore
(C) At a supermarket
(D) At a sports center

84. What problem does the speaker mention?
(A) Some employees are sick.
(B) Some items were misplaced.
(C) Some power cables are damaged.
(D) Some areas are flooded.

85. What will employees be informed about this evening?
(A) A store's schedule
(B) A vacation plan
(C) A promotional sale
(D) A city inspection

86. What is the news report about?
(A) Becoming an interior decorator
(B) Selling a home quickly
(C) Taking an online survey
(D) Buying a home abroad

87. What did Channel 6 do on their website recently?
(A) Conduct a survey
(B) Review a service
(C) Advertise a home
(D) Hold a contest

88. According to the speaker, what can listeners do after the break?
(A) View houses on the market
(B) Visit a designer's studio
(C) Hear some advice
(D) Sign up for a newsletter

GO ON TO THE NEXT PAGE

89. According to the speaker, what is the company trying to do?

(A) Increase productivity
(B) Eliminate paper use
(C) Upgrade a computer system
(D) Reduce electricity costs

90. What does the speaker mean when he says, "I know what you must be thinking"?

(A) He wants to stress a key detail.
(B) He wants to caution against disobedience.
(C) He understands the listeners' concerns.
(D) He acknowledges a listener's complaint.

91. What will the listeners be rewarded with?

(A) A free meal
(B) A new computer
(C) A gift card
(D) A promotion

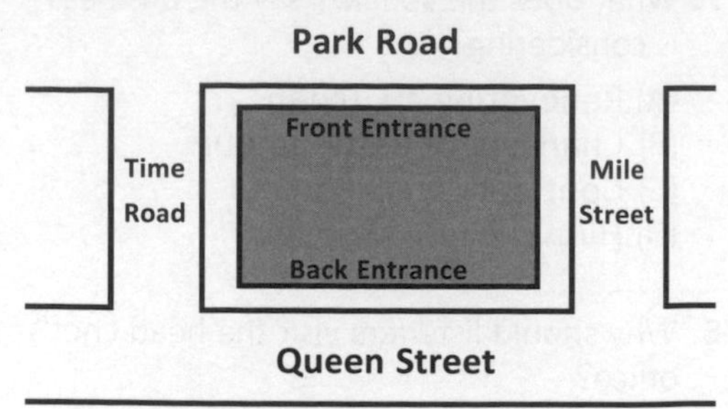

92. What will take place on Friday afternoon?

(A) A contest
(B) A parade
(C) A repair
(D) A sale

93. Look at the graphic. Which street will be closed?

(A) Time Road
(B) Park Road
(C) Mile Street
(D) Queen Street

94. What does the speaker suggest?

(A) Staying home
(B) Attending an event
(C) Parking underground
(D) Taking public transportation

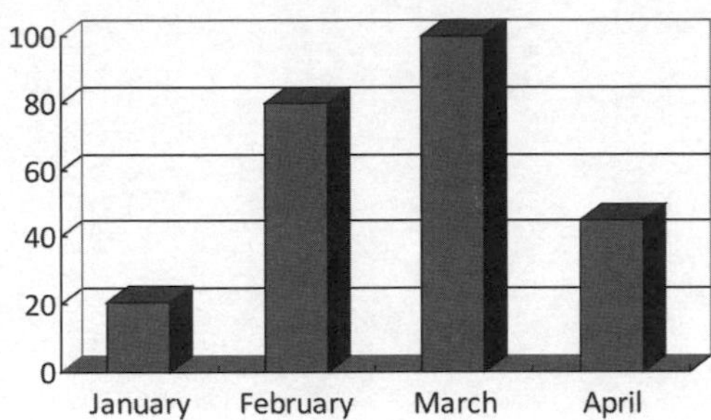

95. Where most likely does the speaker work?
(A) At a home improvement store
(B) At an advertising firm
(C) At a publishing company
(D) At a design company

96. Look at the graphic. When was the discount event held?
(A) In January
(B) In February
(C) In March
(D) In April

97. According to the speaker, what should staff members do by next Friday?
(A) Edit some articles
(B) Prepare a report
(C) Book train tickets
(D) Update a website

	Kimberly Shoe Outlet	**Shoe Source Plus**
Competitive prices	V	X
Free shipping	V	V
Innovative displays	V	X
Online orders	X	V

98. What is the main topic of the meeting?
(A) A new line of products
(B) A manager's promotion
(C) A company's location
(D) A business's success

99. Who most likely is the speaker?
(A) A shoe designer
(B) A store owner
(C) An advertiser
(D) A financial planner

100. Look at the graphic. What will the speaker most likely discuss next?
(A) Competitive prices
(B) Free shipping
(C) Innovative displays
(D) Online orders

ANSWERS ACTUAL TEST 2

1. (B)	**21.** (B)	**41.** (B)	**61.** (D)	**81.** (B)
2. (C)	**22.** (A)	**42.** (D)	**62.** (A)	**82.** (D)
3. (B)	**23.** (A)	**43.** (C)	**63.** (B)	**83.** (C)
4. (C)	**24.** (A)	**44.** (B)	**64.** (D)	**84.** (D)
5. (D)	**25.** (B)	**45.** (D)	**65.** (C)	**85.** (A)
6. (D)	**26.** (B)	**46.** (A)	**66.** (A)	**86.** (B)
7. (C)	**27.** (A)	**47.** (C)	**67.** (B)	**87.** (A)
8. (A)	**28.** (B)	**48.** (C)	**68.** (A)	**88.** (C)
9. (A)	**29.** (B)	**49.** (B)	**69.** (C)	**89.** (B)
10. (A)	**30.** (A)	**50.** (B)	**70.** (D)	**90.** (C)
11. (B)	**31.** (B)	**51.** (B)	**71.** (A)	**91.** (A)
12. (A)	**32.** (D)	**52.** (D)	**72.** (D)	**92.** (B)
13. (C)	**33.** (B)	**53.** (A)	**73.** (B)	**93.** (B)
14. (B)	**34.** (A)	**54.** (C)	**74.** (B)	**94.** (D)
15. (C)	**35.** (A)	**55.** (B)	**75.** (C)	**95.** (C)
16. (A)	**36.** (C)	**56.** (B)	**76.** (A)	**96.** (B)
17. (B)	**37.** (B)	**57.** (D)	**77.** (D)	**97.** (B)
18. (A)	**38.** (C)	**58.** (A)	**78.** (D)	**98.** (D)
19. (B)	**39.** (D)	**59.** (D)	**79.** (A)	**99.** (B)
20. (B)	**40.** (A)	**60.** (B)	**80.** (B)	**100.** (D)

ACTUAL TEST 3

LISTENING TEST 09

In the Listening test, you will be asked to demonstrate how well you understand spoken English. The entire Listening test will last approximately 45 minutes. There are four parts, and directions are given for each part. You must mark your answers on the separate answer sheet. Do not write your answers in your test book.

PART 1

Directions: For each question in this part, you will hear four statements about a picture in your test book. When you hear the statements, you must select the one statement that best describes what you see in the picture. Then find the number of the question on your answer sheet and mark your answer. The statements will not be printed in your test book and will be spoken only one time.

Sample Answer

Statement (C), "A woman is admiring some artwork.," is the best description of the picture, so you should select answer (C) and mark it on your answer sheet.

1.

2.

GO ON TO THE NEXT PAGE

3.

4.

5.

6. 

GO ON TO THE NEXT PAGE

PART 2 ♫ 10

Directions: You will hear a question or statement and three responses spoken in English. They will not be printed in your test book and will be spoken only one time. Select the best response to the question or statement and mark the letter (A), (B) or (C) on your answer sheet.

7. Mark your answer on your answer sheet.
8. Mark your answer on your answer sheet.
9. Mark your answer on your answer sheet.
10. Mark your answer on your answer sheet.
11. Mark your answer on your answer sheet.
12. Mark your answer on your answer sheet.
13. Mark your answer on your answer sheet.
14. Mark your answer on your answer sheet.
15. Mark your answer on your answer sheet.
16. Mark your answer on your answer sheet.
17. Mark your answer on your answer sheet.
18. Mark your answer on your answer sheet.
19. Mark your answer on your answer sheet.
20. Mark your answer on your answer sheet.
21. Mark your answer on your answer sheet.
22. Mark your answer on your answer sheet.
23. Mark your answer on your answer sheet.
24. Mark your answer on your answer sheet.
25. Mark your answer on your answer sheet.
26. Mark your answer on your answer sheet.
27. Mark your answer on your answer sheet.
28. Mark your answer on your answer sheet.
29. Mark your answer on your answer sheet.
30. Mark your answer on your answer sheet.
31. Mark your answer on your answer sheet.

PART 3 11

Directions: You will hear some conversations between two or more people. You will be asked to answer three questions about what the speakers say in each conversation. Select the best response to each question and mark the letter (A), (B), (C), or (D) on your answer sheet. The conversations will not be printed in your test book and will be spoken only one time.

32. Where is the conversation most likely taking place?
(A) At a clothing store
(B) At an outdoor market
(C) At a second-hand shop
(D) At a fabric store

33. What is the problem?
(A) The price was not correct.
(B) A receipt is missing.
(C) An item is defective.
(D) A product is sold out.

34. What does the woman ask the man for?
(A) A membership upgrade
(B) His current address
(C) A credit card number
(D) Proof of payment

35. What is the woman trying to do?
(A) Get a refund
(B) Print some tickets
(C) Reserve a flight
(D) Schedule an event

36. What has caused a problem?
(A) Some tickets are sold out.
(B) An account has expired.
(C) The printer is not working.
(D) Some payment errors occurred.

37. What information does the man ask the woman for?
(A) An address
(B) A credit card number
(C) An account password
(D) A payment total

GO ON TO THE NEXT PAGE

38. What does the woman ask the man to do?
(A) Cancel an appointment
(B) Call a manager
(C) Repair a vehicle
(D) Pick up a coworker

39. What does the man say he needs to do?
(A) Borrow a car
(B) Delay a trip
(C) Hire a driver
(D) Meet a client

40. What does the woman remind the man to do?
(A) Arrive an hour early
(B) Park in the free area
(C) Call a car company
(D) Carry some luggage

---

41. Where do the speakers most likely work?
(A) At a law firm
(B) At a department store
(C) At an art gallery
(D) At a fashion company

42. What does the woman mean when she says, "I can't make any promises"?
(A) She is unable to confirm her participation.
(B) She is busy with other projects.
(C) She will leave her contract early.
(D) She has to hire additional employees.

43. What does the man propose?
(A) Attending a meeting
(B) Calling a supervisor
(C) Delivering a report
(D) Preparing a proposal

---

44. What type of business is the man calling?
(A) A dental clinic
(B) A post office
(C) A moving company
(D) A bookstore

45. What problem does the woman mention?
(A) A payment was not made.
(B) A package was sent back.
(C) An address is wrong.
(D) A form is missing.

46. What will the man most likely do next?
(A) Make a phone call to a client
(B) Check the reverse side of an item
(C) E-mail a document to a colleague
(D) Provide payment information

---

47. Who is the woman?
(A) A veterinarian
(B) A reporter
(C) A shelter owner
(D) An artist

48. What has the man recently done?
(A) Hired new summer employees
(B) Appeared on a television program
(C) Purchased a local animal shelter
(D) Introduced animals to a workplace

49. What does the man say about the cost of the program?
(A) Employees cover most of the costs.
(B) The benefits outweigh the costs.
(C) Donations help offset the costs.
(D) The program does not cost anything.

50. What type of event are the speakers attending?

(A) A job orientation
(B) A staff party
(C) A law conference
(D) An orchestra performance

51. Why does the woman say, "Are you sure that's okay?"?

(A) She wants to leave a meeting early.
(B) She thinks the speakers are too quiet.
(C) She prefers to be in a larger room.
(D) She does not like an option very much.

52. What does the man say about the comment cards?

(A) They include personal information.
(B) They are too small to write on.
(C) They can be handed in after the presentation.
(D) They are reserved for managers only.

---

53. Where most likely does the woman work?

(A) A travel agency
(B) A taxi and limo service
(C) A car rental company
(D) A conference center

54. What does the man say about his trip?

(A) He needs to pick up many people.
(B) He will be traveling for two months.
(C) His company pays for his expenses.
(D) His colleagues are giving presentations.

55. What information does the woman request?

(A) A hotel's location
(B) The cost of flight
(C) The dates of a trip
(D) Some contact information

---

56. What problem does the restaurant have?

(A) It lost some applications.
(B) Its appliances are too old.
(C) Its costs have increased.
(D) It got some negative reviews.

57. What does the woman suggest?

(A) Hiring some new employees
(B) Offering more menu options
(C) Advertising online
(D) Providing refunds

58. What does the woman ask Max to do?

(A) Contact a store manager
(B) Prepare for the next meeting
(C) Host a student job fair
(D) Respond to online reviews

---

59. What are the speakers discussing?

(A) Hiring a training agency
(B) Advertising on the web
(C) Launching a new product
(D) Hosting a conference

60. What type of business does the woman own?

(A) A trade corporation
(B) A web development firm
(C) A landscaping business
(D) A home improvement company

61. What does the man suggest?

(A) Developing a program
(B) Interviewing some clients
(C) Finding a company online
(D) Attending a meeting

GO ON TO THE NEXT PAGE

Admission Price per Person

Students $10
Groups of 6 or more $13
Members $17
Non-members $20
----

62. What type of event are the speakers discussing?
(A) A film release
(B) A restaurant opening
(C) An academic seminar
(D) A musical performance

63. Look at the graphic. What ticket price will the speakers probably pay?
(A) $10
(B) $13
(C) $17
(D) $20

64. What does the woman offer to do?
(A) Pick up some tickets
(B) Make a purchase online
(C) Contact a coworker
(D) Delay an event

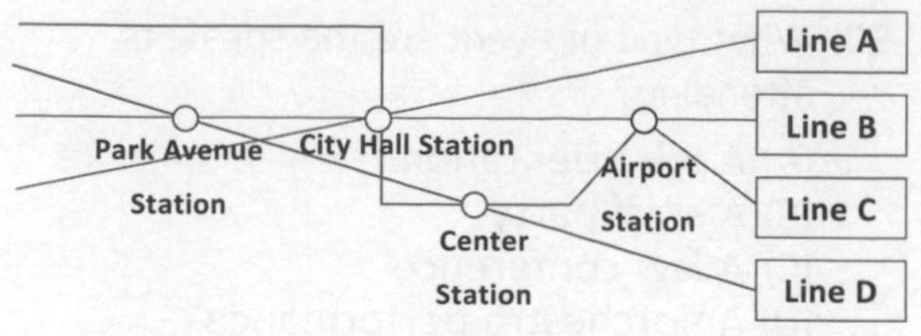

65. Where does the conversation take place?
(A) At a bus stop
(B) In a subway station
(C) At an airport
(D) In an office

66. Look at the graphic. Which line does the man suggest the woman take first?
(A) Line A
(B) Line B
(C) Line C
(D) Line D

67. Why is the woman going to Florida?
(A) To visit with family
(B) To attend a seminar
(C) To go to an office
(D) To meet some clients

FROM	SUBJECT:
Andrew Webber	ATTACHED: August Sales Figures
Anna Stevens	Budget Projection for September
David Skinner	Advertising Meeting Summary
Janine Rogers	CANCELED: Dinner with Mr. Sampson

68. Why is the man unable to access his e-mail?
(A) The company servers are down.
(B) His office connection is not working.
(C) He needs to upgrade his software.
(D) His computer has no battery power.

69. Look at the graphic. Who sent the e-mail the speakers are referring to?
(A) Andrew Webber
(B) Anna Stevens
(C) David Skinner
(D) Janine Rogers

70. What does the man ask the woman to do?
(A) Pass on an e-mail
(B) Attend a meeting
(C) Scan a budget report
(D) Cancel a client dinner

PART 4 12

Directions: You will hear some talks given by a single speaker. You will be asked to answer three questions about what the speaker says in each talk. Select the best response to each question and mark the letter (A), (B), (C), or (D) on your answer sheet. The talks will not be printed in your test book and will be spoken only one time.

71. Where does the speaker work?

(A) At a radio station
(B) At a hospital
(C) At a university
(D) At a newspaper

72. What will Dr. McKay be discussing?

(A) Business finances
(B) Healthy living
(C) Beauty products
(D) Political candidates

73. What does the speaker encourage listeners to do?

(A) Write down tips and information
(B) Call a receptionist with questions
(C) Purchase a new best-selling book
(D) Leave a comment on a website

74. Who most likely are the listeners?

(A) Hotel guests
(B) Supermarket employees
(C) Business managers
(D) Restaurant workers

75. What is the topic of the meeting?

(A) Introducing new menus
(B) Being friendly with customers
(C) Wearing company uniforms
(D) Policies for cleaning workspaces

76. What will the listeners do next?

(A) Watch a film
(B) Complete a survey
(C) Practice a dialogue
(D) Study a pamphlet

77. What event is being introduced?

(A) A store opening
(B) A charity marathon
(C) A product demonstration
(D) A technology sale

78. What did Steven Jones do over the last three years?

(A) Lead several development projects
(B) Review new products in the market
(C) Acquire a few small companies
(D) Coordinate marketing campaigns

79. What should listeners do if they want to attend the question and answer session?

(A) Install a new app
(B) Visit a press room
(C) Log into a website
(D) Hand in a question card

---

80. What did the speaker find out?

(A) His conference was canceled.
(B) His luggage was misplaced.
(C) His reservation was lost.
(D) His speech is too long.

81. What is the speaker scheduled to do on Friday?

(A) Take a vacation
(B) Meet some clients
(C) Review a proposal
(D) Attend a conference

82. Why does the man say, "I know you're busy preparing your presentation"?

(A) To reschedule a trip date
(B) To acknowledge an inconvenience
(C) To offer help with a project
(D) To provide feedback on some work

---

83. According to the news report, what will happen over the next five years?

(A) A city will be planned and developed.
(B) A new highway route will be completed.
(C) A new location for the city hall will be sought.
(D) A tourism sector will be revamped.

84. What benefit to travelers does the speaker mention?

(A) Safer ways to travel
(B) Discounts for families
(C) Beautiful natural landscapes
(D) Shorter travel times

85. What does the speaker say about express passes?

(A) They can be used repeatedly.
(B) They can be ordered online.
(C) They will be distributed free of charge.
(D) They will expire every six months.

---

86. Who most likely are the listeners?

(A) Librarians
(B) Educators
(C) Nurses
(D) Professors

87. What does the woman mean when she says, "we have another group scheduled after lunch"?

(A) A meeting will take place later.
(B) Some refunds will be given.
(C) An event will be canceled.
(D) She cannot wait any longer.

88. What will the speaker distribute to the listeners?

(A) A sign-up form
(B) Music CDs
(C) Training materials
(D) Payment requests

GO ON TO THE NEXT PAGE

89. What does the speaker say about the law firm?

(A) It hired some full-time employees.
(B) It has donated to a local charity.
(C) It will merge with another firm.
(D) It acquired some new cases.

90. According to the speaker, what decision was recently made?

(A) To hire temporary staff
(B) To cancel summer vacations
(C) To increase some rates
(D) To renovate a conference room

91. What does the speaker ask the listeners to do?

(A) Host a training session
(B) Interview candidates
(C) Submit resumes
(D) Fill out a questionnaire

---

92. What is the talk mostly about?

(A) An awards ceremony
(B) A film festival
(C) A local competition
(D) A political speech

93. What does the speaker imply when he says, "You won't want to miss it"?

(A) A local event will be sold out soon.
(B) Some performances will start early.
(C) The show was very popular last year.
(D) A schedule of events is very exciting.

94. Why does the speaker suggest that listeners visit a website?

(A) To get a free parking pass
(B) To see a full list of contestants
(C) To find a map of the event
(D) To sign up to be a performer

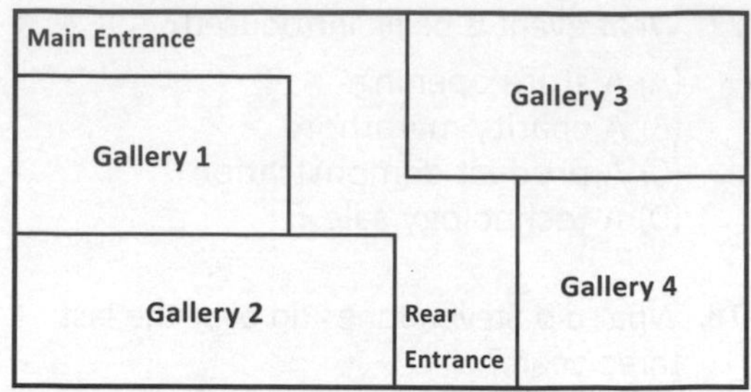

95. What is the gallery featuring this month?

(A) Landscape photography
(B) Watercolor paintings
(C) Abstract installations
(D) Pencil sketches

96. Look at the graphic. In which room is the Cubist art exhibit?

(A) Gallery 1
(B) Gallery 2
(C) Gallery 3
(D) Gallery 4

97. How can listeners attend a guided tour?

(A) By paying a fee
(B) By calling a tour guide
(C) By registering on a website
(D) By signing up on a sheet

September 1	Taxi to Airport: $45	Client Dinner: $98
September 2	Car Rental: $55	Convention Ticket: $35

98. Why is the speaker calling?
(A) An application has been lost.
(B) A submission is incomplete.
(C) A trip has been delayed.
(D) A file is damaged.

99. Look at the graphic. Which expense is the man referring to?
(A) Taxi to Airport
(B) Car Rental
(C) Client Dinner
(D) Convention Ticket

100. What does the speaker say he can do?
(A) Send a form
(B) Pay a fee
(C) Reject a request
(D) Submit a proposal

ANSWERS ACTUAL TEST 3

1. (D)	**21.** (B)	**41.** (D)	**61.** (C)	**81.** (D)
2. (C)	**22.** (B)	**42.** (A)	**62.** (D)	**82.** (B)
3. (A)	**23.** (A)	**43.** (B)	**63.** (B)	**83.** (B)
4. (D)	**24.** (C)	**44.** (B)	**64.** (C)	**84.** (D)
5. (B)	**25.** (B)	**45.** (A)	**65.** (B)	**85.** (A)
6. (D)	**26.** (C)	**46.** (D)	**66.** (D)	**86.** (B)
7. (B)	**27.** (B)	**47.** (B)	**67.** (A)	**87.** (D)
8. (C)	**28.** (A)	**48.** (D)	**68.** (B)	**88.** (C)
9. (C)	**29.** (C)	**49.** (B)	**69.** (A)	**89.** (D)
10. (A)	**30.** (B)	**50.** (A)	**70.** (A)	**90.** (A)
11. (B)	**31.** (A)	**51.** (D)	**71.** (A)	**91.** (C)
12. (B)	**32.** (A)	**52.** (C)	**72.** (B)	**92.** (C)
13. (B)	**33.** (C)	**53.** (C)	**73.** (D)	**93.** (D)
14. (A)	**34.** (D)	**54.** (A)	**74.** (D)	**94.** (B)
15. (A)	**35.** (B)	**55.** (D)	**75.** (B)	**95.** (B)
16. (C)	**36.** (D)	**56.** (D)	**76.** (A)	**96.** (B)
17. (B)	**37.** (B)	**57.** (A)	**77.** (C)	**97.** (D)
18. (A)	**38.** (D)	**58.** (B)	**78.** (A)	**98.** (B)
19. (C)	**39.** (A)	**59.** (A)	**79.** (D)	**99.** (D)
20. (B)	**40.** (B)	**60.** (D)	**80.** (C)	**100.** (A)

ACTUAL TEST

LISTENING TEST 13

In the Listening test, you will be asked to demonstrate how well you understand spoken English. The entire Listening test will last approximately 45 minutes. There are four parts, and directions are given for each part. You must mark your answers on the separate answer sheet. Do not write your answers in your test book.

PART 1

Directions: For each question in this part, you will hear four statements about a picture in your test book. When you hear the statements, you must select the one statement that best describes what you see in the picture. Then find the number of the question on your answer sheet and mark your answer. The statements will not be printed in your test book and will be spoken only one time.

Sample Answer

Statement (C), "A woman is admiring some artwork.," is the best description of the picture, so you should select answer (C) and mark it on your answer sheet.

1.

2.

GO ON TO THE NEXT PAGE

3.

4.

5.

6.

GO ON TO THE NEXT PAGE

PART 2 14

Directions: You will hear a question or statement and three responses spoken in English. They will not be printed in your test book and will be spoken only one time. Select the best response to the question or statement and mark the letter (A), (B) or (C) on your answer sheet.

7. Mark your answer on your answer sheet.
8. Mark your answer on your answer sheet.
9. Mark your answer on your answer sheet.
10. Mark your answer on your answer sheet.
11. Mark your answer on your answer sheet.
12. Mark your answer on your answer sheet.
13. Mark your answer on your answer sheet.
14. Mark your answer on your answer sheet.
15. Mark your answer on your answer sheet.
16. Mark your answer on your answer sheet.
17. Mark your answer on your answer sheet.
18. Mark your answer on your answer sheet.
19. Mark your answer on your answer sheet.
20. Mark your answer on your answer sheet.
21. Mark your answer on your answer sheet.
22. Mark your answer on your answer sheet.
23. Mark your answer on your answer sheet.
24. Mark your answer on your answer sheet.
25. Mark your answer on your answer sheet.
26. Mark your answer on your answer sheet.
27. Mark your answer on your answer sheet.
28. Mark your answer on your answer sheet.
29. Mark your answer on your answer sheet.
30. Mark your answer on your answer sheet.
31. Mark your answer on your answer sheet.

PART 3 15

Directions: You will hear some conversations between two or more people. You will be asked to answer three questions about what the speakers say in each conversation. Select the best response to each question and mark the letter (A), (B), (C), or (D) on your answer sheet. The conversations will not be printed in your test book and will be spoken only one time.

32. Where most likely are the speakers?
(A) In a bank
(B) In a dental clinic
(C) In a shopping mall
(D) In a bookstore

33. What problem does the woman mention?
(A) An appointment will be delayed.
(B) A patient file was misplaced.
(C) An employee called in sick.
(D) A bill was not paid.

34. What does the woman advise the man to do?
(A) Reschedule an appointment
(B) Stay in the office
(C) Take the stairs
(D) Use a specific door

35. What is the purpose of the man's visit?
(A) To extend a warranty
(B) To request a repair
(C) To do some shopping
(D) To deliver an appliance

36. What is the man's job?
(A) Caterer
(B) Architect
(C) Engineer
(D) Farmer

37. What does the woman suggest the man do?
(A) Look at a catalogue
(B) Inspect some merchandise
(C) Shop on a website
(D) Provide an address

GO ON TO THE NEXT PAGE

38. What does the man ask the woman for?
(A) A later deadline
(B) An updated contract
(C) A credit card number
(D) A coworker's e-mail

39. What problem does the man mention?
(A) He lost some client information.
(B) He forgot his login password.
(C) He did not understand some directions.
(D) He had some technical difficulties.

40. What does the woman say she will do?
(A) Send some forms
(B) Contact a manager
(C) Hire some workers
(D) Locate a file

---

41. Where does the man most likely work?
(A) At a library
(B) At a bakery
(C) At a pharmacy
(D) At a law office

42. Why is the woman unavailable during the day?
(A) She is working for a company.
(B) She is taking a college course.
(C) She is traveling out of town.
(D) She is attending a conference.

43. What does the man ask the woman to do?
(A) Submit an updated application
(B) Learn about company systems
(C) Conduct an online survey
(D) Provide written references

---

44. What does the man want to buy?
(A) A refrigerator
(B) Some shoes
(C) A copy machine
(D) Some office furniture

45. Why does the woman apologize?
(A) A discount cannot be used.
(B) Some products are sold out.
(C) A store is closed for renovations.
(D) Some customers complained.

46. What does the man say he will do?
(A) Discuss an issue with a colleague
(B) Visit an online store
(C) Provide an address
(D) Send some measurements

---

47. What are the speakers mainly talking about?
(A) Moving to a new building
(B) Hiring a designer
(C) Updating a customer profile
(D) Editing a document

48. What problem does the woman notice?
(A) An address is outdated.
(B) A form was misplaced.
(C) An employee was late.
(D) A phone number is wrong.

49. Why does the woman say, "It happens to us all"?
(A) To explain a problem
(B) To provide clarification
(C) To prevent an accident
(D) To show compassion

---

50. What is the purpose of the woman's call?
(A) To inquire about test results
(B) To make a payment
(C) To change an appointment
(D) To update insurance information

51. What is the woman doing on Wednesday morning?
(A) Visiting a clinic
(B) Traveling to another city
(C) Meeting a client
(D) Hosting a local event

52. What will the woman most likely do next?
(A) Contact a coworker
(B) Record some information
(C) Go to a hospital
(D) Meet with a consultant

---

53. According to the man, what will happen next year?
(A) A CEO will visit.
(B) A business will fail.
(C) A renovation will occur.
(D) A contract will expire.

54. What does Betina suggest?
(A) Checking a website
(B) Taking a building tour
(C) Extending a lease
(D) Purchasing a building

55. What does Betina agree to do?
(A) Pass on a phone number
(B) Call a real estate agent
(C) Revise a contract
(D) Create a company sign

---

56. What does the woman say is special about the hairpins?
(A) They are made of gold.
(B) They are inexpensive.
(C) They are made in France.
(D) They are all unique.

57. Why does the woman say she no longer wears her hairpin?
(A) She lost it.
(B) She broke it.
(C) She dislikes it.
(D) She gifted it.

58. What does the man imply when he says, "I don't get paid for ten days"?
(A) He usually gets paid every week.
(B) He forgot to pick up his paycheck.
(C) He doesn't have enough money right now.
(D) He recently got a pay increase.

---

59. Who most likely is the woman?
(A) A sales clerk
(B) A web designer
(C) A company receptionist
(D) A post office manager

60. Why does the man visit the office?
(A) To make a delivery
(B) To have a meeting
(C) To inspect a lab
(D) To collect a payment

61. What does the woman imply when she says, "Well, Dr. Strummer is at our Swanson Road laboratory right now"?
(A) Dr. Strummer is a medical scientist.
(B) A storage room is available.
(C) Dr. Strummer cannot sign a form.
(D) An urgent prescription request must be made.

GO ON TO THE NEXT PAGE

62. What type of event are the speakers discussing?
(A) A store's grand opening
(B) An award ceremony
(C) A company anniversary
(D) A retirement party

63. What is the man considering?
(A) Whether to send invitations
(B) Who to hire as a caterer
(C) When to schedule an event
(D) Where to hold an event

64. What does the man say he will do?
(A) Visit a venue
(B) Update a menu
(C) Cancel a reservation
(D) Consult a supervisor

PREMIUM HOME DÉCOR		
Item	**Quantity**	**Total Price**
Panel Curtains	4	$160.00
Cushions	4	$40.00
Shag Rug	1	$79.00
Lamp Shade	2	$44.00

65. What does the woman say she did recently?
(A) She stained her carpet.
(B) She moved to a new house.
(C) She misplaced some items.
(D) She purchased some new furniture.

66. Why does the woman need assistance?
(A) Her order arrived incomplete.
(B) She was charged too much for an item.
(C) She does not like some items.
(D) Her receipt was not in the box.

67. Look at the graphic. How much money will the woman be refunded?
(A) $160.00
(B) $40.00
(C) $79.00
(D) $44.00

Flight	Destination	Gate
AV13	Los Angeles	A56
CP03	Miami	B45
PS55	Paris	B13
AA01	Beijing	A32

68. What type of event are the speakers traveling to?
(A) A holiday vacation
(B) A sales conference
(C) A training session
(D) A corporate workshop

69. Why is the man staying just a short time?
(A) He was unable to get a flight.
(B) He could not reserve a hotel.
(C) He has a conflicting schedule.
(D) He is not well.

70. Look at the graphic. What city are the speakers flying to?
(A) Los Angeles
(B) Miami
(C) Paris
(D) Beijing

GO ON TO THE NEXT PAGE

PART 4 16

Directions: You will hear some talks given by a single speaker. You will be asked to answer three questions about what the speaker says in each talk. Select the best response to each question and mark the letter (A), (B), (C), or (D) on your answer sheet. The talks will not be printed in your test book and will be spoken only one time.

71. Who is Samuel Berkley?
(A) A radio host
(B) A publisher
(C) A writer
(D) A diplomat

72. What is Samuel Berkley planning on doing?
(A) Launching a travel website
(B) Taking a trip around the world
(C) Releasing a book series
(D) Giving a talk about hotels

73. What are listeners instructed to do?
(A) Go to a website
(B) Book a trip
(C) Purchase a book
(D) Post questions online

74. What product is being discussed?
(A) A stereo system
(B) An audio device
(C) A television set
(D) A software program

75. How does the product differ from competitors' products?
(A) It is cheaper to repair.
(B) It is more durable.
(C) It is less expensive.
(D) It has a unique feature.

76. How can listeners win a free product?
(A) By testing out a model
(B) By completing a survey
(C) By visiting a website
(D) By purchasing an item

77. What did the speaker do yesterday?
(A) He went to a restaurant.
(B) He talked to the listener.
(C) He purchased a storage unit.
(D) He signed a lease.

78. What does the speaker say about storage rooms?
(A) They have shelving units inside.
(B) They are an added bonus.
(C) They have security systems.
(D) They are available for a fee.

79. Why does the speaker say, "Several people are interested in the space"?
(A) To explain why the space is no longer available
(B) To encourage the listener to see the space quickly
(C) To request the listener to give up the space
(D) To describe the size and price of the space

---

80. Where does the speaker work?
(A) At a job agency
(B) At a charity
(C) At a concert hall
(D) At a city park

81. Why does the speaker say, "As of now we have enough volunteers for the event"?
(A) To turn down an offer
(B) To stress the success of an event
(C) To voice a concern about a policy
(D) To request more funding

82. What does the speaker ask the listener to do?
(A) Attend a concert
(B) Send an e-mail
(C) Visit a website
(D) Record some information

---

83. Where is the talk taking place?
(A) At a factory
(B) At a yacht club
(C) At a museum
(D) At a travel agency

84. According to the speaker, what did Samuel Welsh do last year?
(A) He made a donation.
(B) He hired an assistant.
(C) He went on a sailing trip.
(D) He opened a gallery.

85. What does the speaker recommend that the listeners do?
(A) Read a booklet
(B) Book a cruise
(C) Go for a swim
(D) Buy a membership

---

86. Who is the advertisement intended for?
(A) Hotel staff
(B) Security guards
(C) Office managers
(D) Bus drivers

87. What does the speaker say is special about the service?
(A) It is offered every day.
(B) It can be booked online.
(C) It can be cancelled easily.
(D) It is done in the evenings.

88. What are listeners encouraged to do?
(A) Ask for an estimate
(B) Call a telephone number
(C) Read some client reviews
(D) Purchase new equipment

ACTUAL TEST 4 PART 4

GO ON TO THE NEXT PAGE

89. What is the main topic of the announcement?
(A) Booking flights online
(B) Paying for travel costs
(C) Training new employees
(D) Canceling out of town travel

90. According to the speaker, why is the change being made?
(A) To respond to employee complaints
(B) To improve employee work efficiency
(C) To make up for a lack of pay raises
(D) To follow a government regulation

91. What are the listeners reminded to do?
(A) Update employee contracts
(B) Pass out new information booklets
(C) Gather reports from employees
(D) Speak with department managers

Tour Date	Departure Time
Monday, May 2	10:30 A.M. / 2:30 P.M.
Tuesday, May 3	11:30 A.M. / 3:30 P.M.
Wednesday, May 4	10:30 A.M. / 2:30 P.M.
Thursday, May 5	11:30 A.M. / 3:30 P.M.

92. What has caused a cancelation?
(A) An absent ship captain
(B) Missing passengers
(C) Poor weather conditions
(D) A damaged boat

93. Look at the graphic. What time will the next boat tour take place?
(A) 10:30 A.M.
(B) 11:30 A.M.
(C) 2:30 P.M.
(D) 3:30 P.M.

94. What does the speaker ask listeners to do?
(A) Wait for a few hours
(B) Try a new restaurant
(C) Stay away from the dock
(D) Visit the front desk

Question: *What improvement would you most like to see?*	
Answer Option	**Number of Votes**
A. A reduction in fares	105
B. Shorter wait times	87
C. More payment options	55
D. Online reservations	32

95. Where most likely does the speaker work?
(A) At a travel agency
(B) At an airline
(C) At a marketing agency
(D) At a bus company

96. Look at the graphic. What survey result does the speaker want to implement?
(A) A reduction in fares
(B) Shorter wait times
(C) More payment options
(D) Online reservations

97. What does the speaker ask the listeners to do?
(A) Recommend employment websites
(B) Interview potential candidates
(C) Review customer information
(D) Upgrade a company system

Ristorante Catoria
50% Off Group Discount Coupon

** Groups may not exceed 15 patrons.*
** Valid until December 31st.*

98. Why is the event being held?
(A) To launch a product line
(B) To host an award ceremony
(C) To announce a promotion
(D) To celebrate a holiday

99. Look at the graphic. Why is the speaker unable to use the coupon for the event?
(A) Not enough guests will attend the event.
(B) The event will occur after the expiration date.
(C) The event will take place on a weekend.
(D) Too many people will be present at the event.

100. What does the speaker ask the listener to do?
(A) Make a list of other restaurants
(B) Call Ristorante Catoria
(C) Change the date of an event
(D) Ask management for more funds

ANSWERS ACTUAL TEST 4

1. (A)	**21.** (C)	**41.** (D)	**61.** (C)	**81.** (A)
2. (A)	**22.** (A)	**42.** (A)	**62.** (C)	**82.** (B)
3. (D)	**23.** (B)	**43.** (B)	**63.** (D)	**83.** (B)
4. (B)	**24.** (A)	**44.** (D)	**64.** (D)	**84.** (A)
5. (A)	**25.** (A)	**45.** (A)	**65.** (D)	**85.** (A)
6. (C)	**26.** (A)	**46.** (B)	**66.** (A)	**86.** (C)
7. (B)	**27.** (C)	**47.** (D)	**67.** (B)	**87.** (D)
8. (A)	**28.** (B)	**48.** (A)	**68.** (D)	**88.** (C)
9. (A)	**29.** (C)	**49.** (D)	**69.** (C)	**89.** (B)
10. (B)	**30.** (A)	**50.** (C)	**70.** (A)	**90.** (A)
11. (B)	**31.** (C)	**51.** (B)	**71.** (C)	**91.** (B)
12. (C)	**32.** (B)	**52.** (B)	**72.** (C)	**92.** (C)
13. (C)	**33.** (A)	**53.** (D)	**73.** (A)	**93.** (B)
14. (B)	**34.** (D)	**54.** (B)	**74.** (B)	**94.** (D)
15. (C)	**35.** (C)	**55.** (A)	**75.** (D)	**95.** (D)
16. (A)	**36.** (A)	**56.** (D)	**76.** (B)	**96.** (B)
17. (C)	**37.** (B)	**57.** (A)	**77.** (B)	**97.** (A)
18. (C)	**38.** (A)	**58.** (C)	**78.** (D)	**98.** (D)
19. (C)	**39.** (D)	**59.** (C)	**79.** (B)	**99.** (D)
20. (B)	**40.** (B)	**60.** (A)	**80.** (B)	**100.** (A)

ACTUAL TEST 5

LISTENING TEST 17

In the Listening test, you will be asked to demonstrate how well you understand spoken English. The entire Listening test will last approximately 45 minutes. There are four parts, and directions are given for each part. You must mark your answers on the separate answer sheet. Do not write your answers in your test book.

PART 1

Directions: For each question in this part, you will hear four statements about a picture in your test book. When you hear the statements, you must select the one statement that best describes what you see in the picture. Then find the number of the question on your answer sheet and mark your answer. The statements will not be printed in your test book and will be spoken only one time.

Sample Answer

Ⓐ Ⓑ ● Ⓓ

Statement (C), "A woman is admiring some artwork.," is the best description of the picture, so you should select answer (C) and mark it on your answer sheet.

1.

2.

GO ON TO THE NEXT PAGE

3.

4.

5.

6.

ACTUAL TEST 5

PART 1

GO ON TO THE NEXT PAGE

PART 2 18

Directions: You will hear a question or statement and three responses spoken in English. They will not be printed in your test book and will be spoken only one time. Select the best response to the question or statement and mark the letter (A), (B) or (C) on your answer sheet.

7. Mark your answer on your answer sheet.
8. Mark your answer on your answer sheet.
9. Mark your answer on your answer sheet.
10. Mark your answer on your answer sheet.
11. Mark your answer on your answer sheet.
12. Mark your answer on your answer sheet.
13. Mark your answer on your answer sheet.
14. Mark your answer on your answer sheet.
15. Mark your answer on your answer sheet.
16. Mark your answer on your answer sheet.
17. Mark your answer on your answer sheet.
18. Mark your answer on your answer sheet.
19. Mark your answer on your answer sheet.
20. Mark your answer on your answer sheet.
21. Mark your answer on your answer sheet.
22. Mark your answer on your answer sheet.
23. Mark your answer on your answer sheet.
24. Mark your answer on your answer sheet.
25. Mark your answer on your answer sheet.
26. Mark your answer on your answer sheet.
27. Mark your answer on your answer sheet.
28. Mark your answer on your answer sheet.
29. Mark your answer on your answer sheet.
30. Mark your answer on your answer sheet.
31. Mark your answer on your answer sheet.

PART 3 ♫19

Directions: You will hear some conversations between two or more people. You will be asked to answer three questions about what the speakers say in each conversation. Select the best response to each question and mark the letter (A), (B), (C), or (D) on your answer sheet. The conversations will not be printed in your test book and will be spoken only one time.

32. What is the woman trying to do?
(A) Lease a new car
(B) Purchase an appliance
(C) Renew an insurance policy
(D) Apply for a credit card

33. What has caused a problem?
(A) An application was rejected.
(B) Some mail did not arrive.
(C) A payment method failed.
(D) Some information was wrong.

34. What does the man offer to do?
(A) Complete a profile
(B) Send a new contract
(C) Cancel a policy
(D) Provide a web address

35. What did the man do on his holiday?
(A) He threw parties.
(B) He visited a farm.
(C) He camped.
(D) He shopped.

36. What does the man say about the places he visited?
(A) They served free food.
(B) They had many discounts.
(C) They were hard to find.
(D) They were next to a park.

37. According to the woman, what did the company do recently?
(A) They gained a client.
(B) They held a sale.
(C) They took a vacation.
(D) They changed management.

GO ON TO THE NEXT PAGE

38. What are the speakers mainly discussing?
(A) An office inspection
(B) A factory opening
(C) A client visit
(D) An advertising launch

39. What does the woman suggest doing?
(A) Presenting a new campaign
(B) Signing a contract
(C) Organizing an inspection
(D) Having some equipment repaired

40. What does the man say he will do?
(A) Pass on some information
(B) E-mail some samples
(C) Update a website
(D) Prepare an itinerary

---

41. What are the speakers discussing?
(A) Moving a business
(B) Negotiating a contract
(C) Traveling for business
(D) Changing event management

42. What does James advise the woman to do?
(A) Schedule another meeting
(B) Make a list of vendors
(C) Hire an assistant
(D) Send receipts by e-mail

43. What does James say he is excited about?
(A) Moving to a new city
(B) Managing more projects
(C) Earning more money
(D) Learning a new sport

---

44. Why is the woman calling the man?
(A) To provide directions to an office
(B) To request a room change
(C) To report a malfunction in equipment
(D) To inquire about a missing file

45. What does the woman mean when she says, "Right now"?
(A) She feels sorry about bothering the man.
(B) She will cancel a meeting.
(C) She wants to delay a repair.
(D) She is pleased with a plan.

46. What does the man say is unusual?
(A) The weather is unseasonably cold.
(B) The office is experiencing many problems.
(C) The meetings have been cancelled.
(D) The woman's schedule is busy.

---

47. What problem does the man mention?
(A) A telephone number was lost.
(B) A ticket price was wrong.
(C) A trip was postponed.
(D) An event was canceled.

48. What does the woman suggest?
(A) A visit to a museum
(B) An evening on a boat
(C) A vacation to Italy
(D) A night at the opera

49. What does the man ask the woman to do?
(A) Inquire about a price
(B) Contact some clients
(C) Refund some tickets
(D) Make a reservation

---

50. Who most likely are Micha and Jennifer?
(A) City inspectors
(B) Potential tenants
(C) Interior designers
(D) Hotel receptionists

51. What are Micha and Jennifer concerned about?
(A) The location of the windows
(B) The size of the rooms
(C) The cost of heating
(D) The noise of the city

52. What is mentioned about the previous couple?
(A) They are no longer working.
(B) They own the whole building.
(C) They prefer warmer climates.
(D) They have not moved yet.

---

53. What will happen on Monday?
(A) A vehicle will be repaired.
(B) A training session will continue.
(C) A trade show will start.
(D) A new product will launch.

54. What did the woman forget to do?
(A) Find some volunteers
(B) Contact a convention center
(C) Set up some tables
(D) Update an itinerary

55. What does the man say is available?
(A) Extra passes into a show
(B) A company banner
(C) Free refreshments
(D) Product samples

---

56. Why does the woman call the man?
(A) To ask for a payment
(B) To return a phone call
(C) To cancel a meeting
(D) To make a hair appointment

57. What did the man recently do?
(A) Hired a graphic designer
(B) Cancelled a subscription
(C) Started a new business
(D) Purchased a billboard

58. What does the man say he will do tomorrow?
(A) Attend a lunch
(B) Get a haircut
(C) Sell some products
(D) Go to an office

---

59. What department do the speakers work in?
(A) Finance
(B) Editorial
(C) Advertising
(D) Design

60. Why does the woman say, "Wow, isn't that too many"?
(A) To express surprise about a decision
(B) To suggest another option
(C) To correct a management mistake
(D) To request a change of policy

61. According to the man, what does the human resources department plan to do?
(A) Prepare a new manual
(B) Host a job fair at an office
(C) Hold a training workshop
(D) Run an advertisement online

GO ON TO THE NEXT PAGE

Package	Rate per Day
All Star Coverage	$35.00
Premium Coverage	$20.00
Advanced Coverage	$15.00
Basic Coverage	$10.00

62. What is the purpose of the phone call?
(A) To inquire about a discount
(B) To apply for a service
(C) To make a reservation
(D) To schedule a meeting

63. Why does the man ask if the employees will do any sports?
(A) To offer some free gifts
(B) To decide on the most suitable package
(C) To recommend a travel destination
(D) To request some medical information

64. Look at the graphic. How much will each employee likely pay per day?
(A) $35
(B) $20
(C) $15
(D) $10

Flight Number	Departure City	On Time/ Delayed	Est. Arrival Time
BT091	Toronto	Landed	11:00
AC550	Alberta	On Time	11:35
HG330	Vancouver	On Time	12:00
DT302	Montreal	Delayed	13:20

65. Look at the graphic. Which city is Michael Park traveling from?
(A) Toronto
(B) Alberta
(C) Vancouver
(D) Montreal

66. According to the man, why should the speakers leave now?
(A) Traffic may cause delays.
(B) The airport is far away.
(C) They need to take the bus.
(D) A flight was early.

67. What does the woman suggest doing while they wait?
(A) Getting some food
(B) Looking in some stores
(C) Seeing a film
(D) Having coffee

Plan	Contract Length	Monthly Payment
Bronze	6 months	$140.00
Silver	12 months	$100.00
Gold	24 months	$60.00
Platinum	36 months	$30.00

68. According to the woman, when is an extra fee charged?
(A) When a product is delivered
(B) When a device gets broken
(C) When a client doesn't pay a bill
(D) When a service is canceled early

69. What does the man say he might do next year?
(A) Purchase a new phone
(B) Go overseas
(C) Sign a new contract
(D) Lease a device

70. Look at the graphic. How much has the man agreed to pay per month?
(A) $140.00
(B) $100.00
(C) $60.00
(D) $30.00

PART 4 ∩ 20

Directions: You will hear some talks given by a single speaker. You will be asked to answer three questions about what the speaker says in each talk. Select the best response to each question and mark the letter (A), (B), (C), or (D) on your answer sheet. The talks will not be printed in your test book and will be spoken only one time.

71. What is the purpose of the talk?
(A) To explain the rules
(B) To name some key features
(C) To ask for payment
(D) To begin a tour

72. What will the speaker distribute?
(A) Some headphones
(B) A museum program
(C) Tickets to a performance
(D) A map of nearby galleries

73. According to the speaker, what will begin at 3:30?
(A) A question and answer session
(B) A classical music concert
(C) An antiques auction
(D) An educational presentation

74. What is being discussed?
(A) Company expense regulations
(B) Training new sales employees
(C) Hiring an office manager
(D) Filling out insurance forms

75. Why will Veronica contact listeners?
(A) To provide payment
(B) To request receipts
(C) To review a policy
(D) To resolve an error

76. What will the company do next month?
(A) Stop using a form system
(B) Begin using a new policy
(C) Lengthen a project deadline
(D) Deposit payments electronically

77. Where is the announcement taking place?

(A) At an outdoor market
(B) At a shopping center
(C) At a bus station
(D) At an art gallery

78. Why does the speaker say, "We have two stations set up"?

(A) To correct a mistake
(B) To explain some locations
(C) To apologize for a delay
(D) To express disappointment

79. What does the speaker offer?

(A) Entrance into a contest
(B) A book of discount coupons
(C) Free beverages at a café
(D) A discount on a purchase

---

80. What is Ms. Bernstein's area of expertise?

(A) Web development
(B) Entertainment
(C) Career guidance
(D) Finance

81. What are the listeners encouraged to do?

(A) Send in résumés
(B) Call Ms. Bernstein
(C) Purchase an e-book
(D) Leave a comment online

82. What does the speaker say happened last month?

(A) A group interview was conducted.
(B) A radio schedule changed.
(C) A free seminar took place.
(D) A line of books was released.

---

83. Who most likely are the listeners?

(A) Restaurant chefs
(B) Café workers
(C) Software designers
(D) Employee trainers

84. What is the purpose of the talk?

(A) To explain a customer complaint
(B) To announce a new sales procedure
(C) To begin a training session
(D) To demonstrate some new equipment

85. What can be found at each cash register?

(A) Announcement signs
(B) Membership cards
(C) Promotional coupons
(D) Updated menus

---

86. What is the purpose of the telephone message?

(A) To order some electronics
(B) To purchase insurance
(C) To apologize for a problem
(D) To ask for a shipping address

87. What problem does the speaker mention?

(A) Some electronics are broken.
(B) Some packaging is damaged.
(C) A payment has been delayed.
(D) A new item is sold out.

88. What does the speaker say he will do?

(A) Pick up an item
(B) Contact a manager
(C) Provide a refund
(D) Send another package

GO ON TO THE NEXT PAGE

89. What industry does the speaker work in?
(A) Internet sales
(B) Fashion retail
(C) Advertising
(D) Publishing

90. Why does the speaker say, "Actually, the design has a few issues"?
(A) To outline the survey results about a design
(B) To suggest that their budget is limited
(C) To indicate a problem with some finished work
(D) To express some safety concerns

91. What does the speaker suggest the listener do?
(A) Study some prior designs
(B) Work on another project
(C) Contact a client directly
(D) Consult a coworker

92. What does the woman imply when she says, "Who knows how many will cancel their orders"?
(A) She wants someone to report an exact figure.
(B) She is worried about a loss of business.
(C) She would prefer to receive online orders.
(D) She was not expecting any problems to occur.

93. What is the topic of the meeting?
(A) Redesigning a book cover
(B) Reducing production costs
(C) Developing a marketing strategy
(D) Attracting new authors

94. What will the speaker probably do this morning?
(A) Attend a weekly meeting
(B) Conduct a telephone consultation
(C) Visit a broadcasting station
(D) Address employee questions

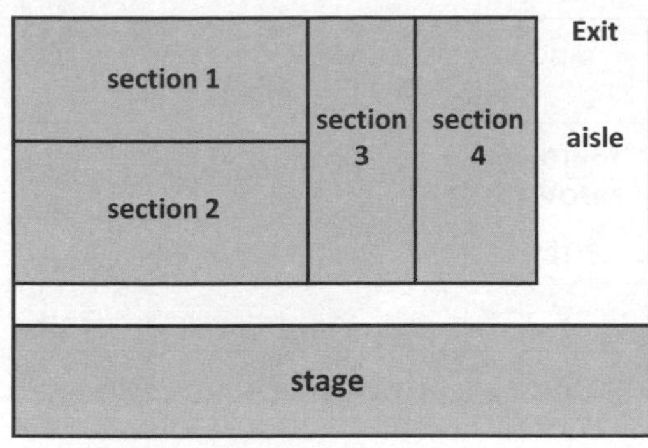

95. Who most likely are the listeners?
(A) Directors
(B) Writers
(C) Performers
(D) Reporters

96. Look at the graphic. What section does the speaker want the listeners to sit in?
(A) Section 1
(B) Section 2
(C) Section 3
(D) Section 4

97. What are listeners asked to do during the audition?
(A) Remain quiet
(B) Take photographs
(C) Avoid cellphone use
(D) Speak to choreographers

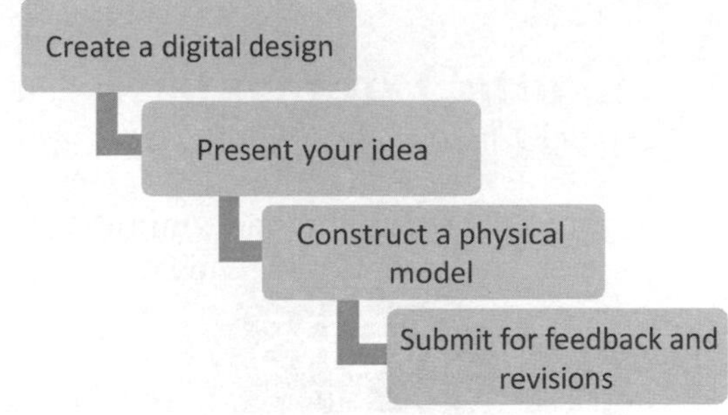

98. What does the speaker say about Frontier Architecture?
(A) They lost several important clients.
(B) They recently merged with another company.
(C) They hired a new design team.
(D) They won an international award.

99. Look at the graphic. According to the speaker, which step was recently added?
(A) Create a digital design
(B) Present your idea
(C) Construct a physical model
(D) Submit for feedback and revisions

100. What problem will the speaker's plan prevent?
(A) Losing digital files
(B) Paying overtime wages
(C) Working in a crowded office
(D) Not finishing work on time

ANSWERS ACTUAL TEST 5

1. (B)	21. (A)	41. (D)	61. (D)	81. (D)
2. (D)	22. (C)	42. (D)	62. (B)	82. (D)
3. (C)	23. (C)	43. (A)	63. (B)	83. (B)
4. (A)	24. (A)	44. (C)	64. (B)	84. (B)
5. (B)	25. (A)	45. (C)	65. (D)	85. (A)
6. (C)	26. (A)	46. (A)	66. (A)	86. (C)
7. (A)	27. (C)	47. (D)	67. (B)	87. (B)
8. (B)	28. (C)	48. (B)	68. (D)	88. (D)
9. (A)	29. (C)	49. (A)	69. (B)	89. (C)
10. (B)	30. (C)	50. (B)	70. (B)	90. (C)
11. (C)	31. (A)	51. (C)	71. (D)	91. (A)
12. (C)	32. (C)	52. (A)	72. (A)	92. (B)
13. (C)	33. (B)	53. (C)	73. (D)	93. (C)
14. (A)	34. (D)	54. (A)	74. (A)	94. (D)
15. (B)	35. (D)	55. (A)	75. (D)	95. (C)
16. (A)	36. (B)	56. (B)	76. (B)	96. (D)
17. (B)	37. (A)	57. (C)	77. (B)	97. (A)
18. (C)	38. (C)	58. (D)	78. (B)	98. (B)
19. (B)	39. (A)	59. (B)	79. (A)	99. (B)
20. (C)	40. (A)	60. (A)	80. (C)	100. (D)

ACTUAL TEST 6

LISTENING TEST 21

In the Listening test, you will be asked to demonstrate how well you understand spoken English. The entire Listening test will last approximately 45 minutes. There are four parts, and directions are given for each part. You must mark your answers on the separate answer sheet. Do not write your answers in your test book.

PART 1

Directions: For each question in this part, you will hear four statements about a picture in your test book. When you hear the statements, you must select the one statement that best describes what you see in the picture. Then find the number of the question on your answer sheet and mark your answer. The statements will not be printed in your test book and will be spoken only one time.

Sample Answer

Ⓐ Ⓑ ● Ⓓ

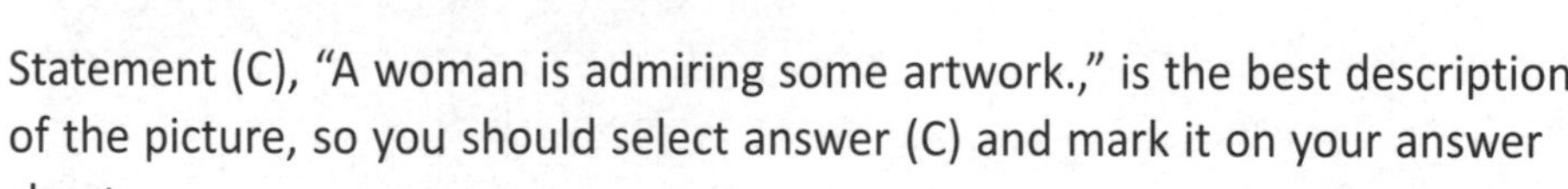

Statement (C), "A woman is admiring some artwork.," is the best description of the picture, so you should select answer (C) and mark it on your answer sheet.

1.

2.

ACTUAL TEST 6

PART 1

GO ON TO THE NEXT PAGE

3.

4.

5.

6.

GO ON TO THE NEXT PAGE

PART 2 ∩ 22

Directions: You will hear a question or statement and three responses spoken in English. They will not be printed in your test book and will be spoken only one time. Select the best response to the question or statement and mark the letter (A), (B) or (C) on your answer sheet.

7. Mark your answer on your answer sheet.
8. Mark your answer on your answer sheet.
9. Mark your answer on your answer sheet.
10. Mark your answer on your answer sheet.
11. Mark your answer on your answer sheet.
12. Mark your answer on your answer sheet.
13. Mark your answer on your answer sheet.
14. Mark your answer on your answer sheet.
15. Mark your answer on your answer sheet.
16. Mark your answer on your answer sheet.
17. Mark your answer on your answer sheet.
18. Mark your answer on your answer sheet.
19. Mark your answer on your answer sheet.
20. Mark your answer on your answer sheet.
21. Mark your answer on your answer sheet.
22. Mark your answer on your answer sheet.
23. Mark your answer on your answer sheet.
24. Mark your answer on your answer sheet.
25. Mark your answer on your answer sheet.
26. Mark your answer on your answer sheet.
27. Mark your answer on your answer sheet.
28. Mark your answer on your answer sheet.
29. Mark your answer on your answer sheet.
30. Mark your answer on your answer sheet.
31. Mark your answer on your answer sheet.

PART 3 23

Directions: You will hear some conversations between two or more people. You will be asked to answer three questions about what the speakers say in each conversation. Select the best response to each question and mark the letter (A), (B), (C), or (D) on your answer sheet. The conversations will not be printed in your test book and will be spoken only one time.

32. Why did the man choose to shop at the store?
(A) The store is next to his home.
(B) He received an e-mail notification.
(C) His friend recommended the store.
(D) The store's selection is very large.

33. What does the woman ask for?
(A) A credit card number
(B) A purchase receipt
(C) A membership card
(D) A discount voucher

34. Why does the man say he will return at a later time?
(A) He left his wallet at the office.
(B) He wants to bring his wife.
(C) He needs to print something.
(D) He has an urgent meeting.

35. Where is this conversation most likely taking place?
(A) At a fabric store
(B) At a supermarket
(C) At a restaurant
(D) At a dry cleaner

36. What is the woman doing on Wednesday?
(A) Traveling out of town
(B) Attending a company event
(C) Making a presentation
(D) Going to a conference

37. What does the man offer to do?
(A) Refund a service
(B) Replace an item
(C) Rush an order
(D) Rent out a garment

GO ON TO THE NEXT PAGE

38. Why will the man visit the woman's office?
(A) To deliver an invoice
(B) To apply for a job
(C) To install some equipment
(D) To pick up a vehicle

39. What does the woman say she will do?
(A) Wait for a worker to arrive
(B) Give a key to an employee
(C) Pay for a service online
(D) Use a discount coupon

40. What does the woman ask the man to put in her mailbox?
(A) Some client paperwork
(B) A tax receipt
(C) A user's manual
(D) Some promotional vouchers

---

41. What is the woman shopping for?
(A) Books
(B) Printer ink
(C) Paper
(D) Folders

42. What does Tim say about some items?
(A) They are still in storage.
(B) They are out of stock.
(C) They are available at another store.
(D) They are currently on sale.

43. What additional service does Tim mention?
(A) Free shipping
(B) In-store printing
(C) Discounted membership
(D) Free book binding

---

44. What are the speakers organizing?
(A) A company trip
(B) A holiday event
(C) An awards dinner
(D) A fundraiser

45. What problem does the woman mention?
(A) A hotel is in need of repair.
(B) A reservation was lost.
(C) Some invitations were misplaced.
(D) Some customers complained.

46. What most likely will the man do next?
(A) Cancel an event
(B) Visit a hotel
(C) Find a contact number
(D) Make a reservation

---

47. Where most likely do the speakers work?
(A) A dance academy
(B) An art school
(C) A paint supply shop
(D) A restaurant

48. What does the woman imply when she says, "Will that be a problem"?
(A) She disagrees with the man's statement.
(B) She does not want to edit a schedule.
(C) She wants to know what she has overlooked.
(D) She is eager to take the man's class.

49. What does the woman offer to do?
(A) Change a classroom
(B) Hire a cleaner
(C) Recruit some students
(D) Pay for art supplies

---

50. What are the speakers discussing?
(A) Preparing for a presentation
(B) Building a new website
(C) Submitting a budget review
(D) Hiring a new advertiser

51. Why was the man unable to complete a task?
(A) A meeting lasted all day.
(B) A website was not working.
(C) Some files went missing.
(D) Some fees were not paid.

52. What does the woman say she will do on Friday?
(A) Meet with a client
(B) Give a presentation
(C) Design a brochure
(D) Print a document

---

53. What is Mr. Holland planning to do?
(A) Purchase a new car
(B) Make an insurance claim
(C) Apply for a license
(D) Rent a vehicle

54. According to the conversation, what did Kevin do yesterday?
(A) He had a car towed.
(B) He ordered some new parts.
(C) He prepared a price quote.
(D) He witnessed a car accident.

55. What does Kevin ask the woman to do?
(A) Process a payment
(B) Call an insurance company
(C) Fill out a form
(D) Print a document

---

56. Why is the man calling?
(A) He received the wrong order.
(B) He wants to return an item.
(C) He would like to visit the store.
(D) He was charged too much for an item.

57. What does the woman explain?
(A) A technical malfunction
(B) A discount policy
(C) A delivery failure
(D) A change in supplier

58. What does the woman ask the man to do?
(A) Send an order back
(B) Locate an invoice
(C) Renew a membership
(D) Describe an item

---

59. Where most likely is the woman?
(A) At a parking entrance
(B) On a bus
(C) In an office
(D) In a stairwell

60. What does the woman ask the man to do?
(A) Call the parking attendant
(B) Deliver a parking pass
(C) Cancel a meeting
(D) Recommend a venue

61. Why does the man say, "I'm just heading into a meeting"?
(A) To acknowledge a problem
(B) To ask for permission
(C) To suggest an option
(D) To decline a request

GO ON TO THE NEXT PAGE

=========== **Front** ===========

Aisle	seat 25C	seat 25D	Window
	seat 26C	seat 26D	

62. What is the purpose of the conversation?
(A) To determine a cost
(B) To request a service
(C) To correct a mistake
(D) To explain a process

63. Look at the graphic. Which seat was the woman originally assigned to?
(A) 25C
(B) 25D
(C) 26C
(D) 26D

64. What will the woman most likely do next?
(A) File a complaint with the airline
(B) Report a change to the flight staff
(C) Get off the plane
(D) Request a vegetarian meal

Stage	Project Type
1	In-ground swimming pool installation
2	Backyard landscaping and gardens
3	Veranda reconstruction (front and back)
4	Final roof repairs

65. What most likely is the man's profession?
(A) Interior decorator
(B) Delivery man
(C) Real estate agent
(D) Contractor

66. Look at the graphic. What stage of the improvements will begin in a couple days?
(A) Stage 1
(B) Stage 2
(C) Stage 3
(D) Stage 4

67. What does the woman ask the man to keep?
(A) Receipts of all costs
(B) A list of available homes
(C) A record of time worked
(D) Photos of his progress

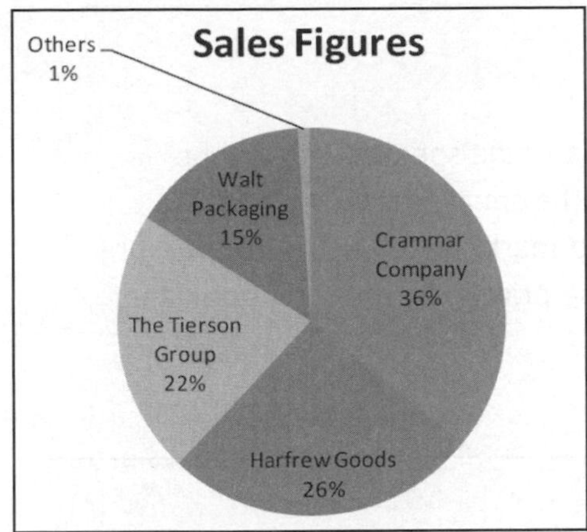

68. What are the speakers mainly discussing?

(A) A company merger
(B) A budget report
(C) Department productivity
(D) Hiring a financial analyst

69. Look at the graphic. Where do the speakers work?

(A) Walt Packaging
(B) Harfrew Goods
(C) The Tierson Group
(D) Crammar Company

70. Why does the woman say she has doubts?

(A) The man did not understand some figures.
(B) A company was excluded from a report.
(C) Her company is located in another state.
(D) A company has not made many sales.

ACTUAL TEST 6
PART 3

GO ON TO THE NEXT PAGE

PART 4 24

Directions: You will hear some talks given by a single speaker. You will be asked to answer three questions about what the speaker says in each talk. Select the best response to each question and mark the letter (A), (B), (C), or (D) on your answer sheet. The talks will not be printed in your test book and will be spoken only one time.

71. What service is being advertised?
(A) Dry cleaning
(B) Furniture delivery
(C) A clothing recycling program
(D) A cooking course

72. How can listeners receive a discount?
(A) By becoming a member
(B) By ordering two items
(C) By registering online
(D) By entering a contest

73. What does the speaker say is available over the phone?
(A) A customer survey
(B) A list of stores
(C) The best discount
(D) An appointment

74. Where is the announcement being made?
(A) At a city hall
(B) At a shopping mall
(C) At a transit station
(D) At a concert venue

75. What does the speaker ask listeners to do?
(A) Proceed to a boarding gate
(B) Keep an original receipt
(C) Use a bank machine
(D) Purchase another ticket

76. According to the speaker, what can customers get at Coffee Madness?
(A) A train ticket
(B) A complimentary drink
(C) A loaned computer
(D) An updated bus schedule

77. What is the purpose of the message?

(A) To locate some materials
(B) To request a meeting
(C) To hire a designer
(D) To ask about a product

78. What does the speaker imply when she says, "The boss is getting impatient"?

(A) Her boss needs to reschedule a project.
(B) She needs to change some paint colors.
(C) The designers will start working soon.
(D) Some selections must be confirmed quickly.

79. What most likely will the speaker do next?

(A) Decide on design samples
(B) Contact a manager
(C) Visit a manufacturing site
(D) Go to a paint supply store

---

80. Where do the listeners work?

(A) At a bank
(B) At a fashion house
(C) At a university
(D) At a real estate agency

81. What will the listeners be doing tomorrow?

(A) Conducting surveys
(B) Interviewing interns
(C) Distributing pamphlets
(D) Cleaning up an office

82. What has the speaker done for the listeners?

(A) Prepared uniforms
(B) Bought some chairs
(C) Shortened a schedule
(D) Paid for a trip

---

83. What is the speaker announcing?

(A) Hiring a new employee
(B) A company fundraiser
(C) An upcoming mentorship program
(D) The winning of an award

84. What did the company sponsor in June?

(A) A sports club
(B) A fundraising event
(C) A financial convention
(D) A university scholarship

85. What does the speaker say about Mona Ruiz's work?

(A) It improved the company image.
(B) It is outlined on the company's website.
(C) It increased the company's charity work.
(D) It doubled the number of clients.

---

86. What is the main topic of the meeting?

(A) Restructuring plans
(B) A new delivery method
(C) A product prototype
(D) Customer feedback

87. What feature of the product does the speaker mention?

(A) Removable grills
(B) Portability
(C) Color options
(D) Energy efficiency

88. What does the speaker imply when he says, "Our website does not display images of each color"?

(A) A website should be edited.
(B) Images have been removed from a website.
(C) A photographer needs to be hired.
(D) Customers mostly chose one color.

GO ON TO THE NEXT PAGE →

89. What is the talk mainly about?

(A) Electing a new town mayor
(B) Planning a city anniversary
(C) Convincing state officials
(D) Forming a charity group

90. What problem does the speaker mention?

(A) Lack of public support
(B) A delay in the release of funds
(C) Damaged facilities
(D) Lost signatures

91. What are listeners asked to do?

(A) E-mail state officials
(B) Volunteer at an event
(C) Sample some food
(D) Contact local media

---

92. What type of business does the speaker work for?

(A) A transit company
(B) A medical facility
(C) An advertising firm
(D) A pharmacy

93. What does the speaker imply when he says, "Not all seats are full right now"?

(A) Some participants have not arrived.
(B) The chairs can be rearranged.
(C) The venue will be changed.
(D) The event is not successful.

94. What does the speaker ask the listeners to do?

(A) Write down their medical history
(B) Go to their assigned departments
(C) Fill out contact information
(D) Review some materials

Quantity	Item Description
10	Ballpoint Pens (10 per package)
20	Black toner cartridge
35	Clear plastic A4 file
60	Glossy copy paper (1000 sheets per box)

95. Look at the graphic. Which quantity on the order form will probably be changed?

(A) 10
(B) 20
(C) 35
(D) 60

96. What will the speaker do before processing the order?

(A) Wait for a confirmation
(B) Give a phone number
(C) Inspect a package
(D) Review a product manual

97. What does the speaker say about Tina?

(A) She will not be in the office.
(B) She will deliver some items herself.
(C) She will take care of shipping problems.
(D) She will refund some purchases.

98. Where does the talk take place?
(A) At a museum
(B) At a restaurant
(C) At a shopping mall
(D) At an office

99. Look at the graphic. Which suggestion will the company begin to work on?
(A) Employee breakrooms
(B) Food court discounts
(C) Better parking spaces
(D) Free transit passes

100. What will employees receive for completing comment cards?
(A) A gift card for the mall
(B) Entrance into a contest
(C) A voucher for a free drink
(D) A new work uniform

ANSWERS ACTUAL TEST 6

1. (D)	**21.** (B)	**41.** (D)	**61.** (D)	**81.** (C)
2. (B)	**22.** (C)	**42.** (A)	**62.** (C)	**82.** (A)
3. (C)	**23.** (B)	**43.** (B)	**63.** (A)	**83.** (D)
4. (B)	**24.** (A)	**44.** (D)	**64.** (B)	**84.** (B)
5. (B)	**25.** (C)	**45.** (A)	**65.** (D)	**85.** (C)
6. (A)	**26.** (B)	**46.** (C)	**66.** (B)	**86.** (D)
7. (B)	**27.** (B)	**47.** (B)	**67.** (C)	**87.** (C)
8. (C)	**28.** (C)	**48.** (C)	**68.** (A)	**88.** (A)
9. (A)	**29.** (B)	**49.** (A)	**69.** (C)	**89.** (C)
10. (B)	**30.** (C)	**50.** (A)	**70.** (D)	**90.** (A)
11. (B)	**31.** (A)	**51.** (B)	**71.** (C)	**91.** (B)
12. (B)	**32.** (B)	**52.** (D)	**72.** (A)	**92.** (B)
13. (A)	**33.** (D)	**53.** (B)	**73.** (D)	**93.** (A)
14. (C)	**34.** (C)	**54.** (C)	**74.** (C)	**94.** (D)
15. (A)	**35.** (D)	**55.** (D)	**75.** (D)	**95.** (D)
16. (B)	**36.** (B)	**56.** (D)	**76.** (B)	**96.** (A)
17. (B)	**37.** (C)	**57.** (A)	**77.** (B)	**97.** (C)
18. (C)	**38.** (D)	**58.** (C)	**78.** (D)	**98.** (C)
19. (B)	**39.** (B)	**59.** (A)	**79.** (A)	**99.** (B)
20. (A)	**40.** (A)	**60.** (B)	**80.** (D)	**100.** (A)

ACTUAL TEST 1
中譯+解析

PART 1 01

1

(A) He is drawing on a screen.*
(B) He is adjusting his watch.
(C) He is signing a document.
(D) He is throwing a pen away.

(A) 他正在螢幕上畫圖。
(B) 他正在調校手錶。
(C) 他正在簽文件。
(D) 他把筆丟開。

本題為單人照片，圖中可見一個人正在畫畫（drawing），而 (A) 針對動作客觀地描述，為正確答案；(B) 和 (D) 雖提及照片中出現的物品（watch, pen），但說明並不符合照片情境；(C) 的說明與照片內容無關。在此提醒，若選項為「正在使用器具」（using a tool）或是「握著器具」（holding a tool），亦可能是正確答案。

• **adjust** 調整、校準　**throw (away)** 投、擲、扔

2

(A) They're setting the table.*
(B) They're arranging some flowers.
(C) They're cooking on a stove.
(D) They're hanging a plant on the wall.

(A) 他們正在擺設餐具。
(B) 他們正在插花。
(C) 他們正在爐子上煮東西。
(D) 他們正把植物掛到牆上。

本題為雙人照片，請先掌握好照片中兩人行為或狀態，是否有共通點或差異之處。(A) 掌握了「擺設餐具」這個重點，符合照片中兩人的動作，為正確答案。

• **arrange** 整理、布置　**stove** 火爐、爐灶　**hang** 把……掛起　**plant** 植物

3

(A) A woman is wiping the windowsill.
(B) A man is playing music.
(C) A man is pulling open a door.
(D) A woman is using some equipment.*

(A) 一名女子正在擦窗台。
(B) 一名男子正在演奏音樂。
(C) 一名男子正拉開門。
(D) 一名女子正在使用某種機器設備。

(A) 和 (C) 提及了照片中出現的窗戶與門，為陷阱選項；照片中的男子正在聽耳機，因此 (B) 加入了 music 這個單字，但 play music 的意思為「演奏音樂」，為錯誤的選項；(D) 的 equipment 代表擺在女子前方的設備，為正確答案。

• **wipe** 擦乾淨　**windowsill** 窗台　**pull open** 拉開　**equipment** 設備、器械

4

(A) A man is waiting to board a bus.	(A) 一名男子正等著上公車。
(B) A man is walking toward a van.	(B) 一名男子正走向一輛小貨車。
(C) A woman is holding a newspaper.*	(C) 一名女子拿著一份報紙。
(D) A woman is getting a book out of her bag.	(D) 一名女子正從袋子中拿出一本書。

正確答案為 (C)，女子雙手拿著報紙（holding a newspaper）符合照片情境。在此補充，正確答案還有可能是「男子戴著帽子（A man is wearing a cap.）」、「男子揹著後背包（A man is carrying a backpack.）」、「女子揹著單肩包（A woman is carrying a shoulder bag.）」、「女子戴著眼鏡（A woman is wearing glasses.）」等。

- **board** 上（船、車、飛機等）　**toward** 朝著　**hold** 握著、抓著

5

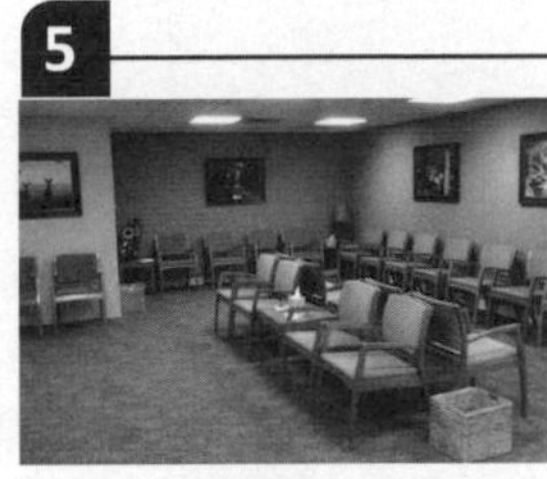

(A) Some workers are moving the chairs.	(A) 一些工人正在搬動椅子。
(B) A waiting room is decorated with pictures.*	(B) 等候室裡裝飾著畫。
(C) A light fixture is being mounted above the doorway.	(C) 門口上方正在裝燈。
(D) Some lampshades have been set on the floor.	(D) 地板上放著一些燈罩。

照片中僅出現事物，因此在聽到 (A) 主詞為人的當下，即可馬上剔除此選項；(C) 為現在進行被動式：be + being + p.p.，表示某個人正在做某件事（Someone is mounting a light fixture above the doorway.），因此也是錯誤的選項；(B) 將焦點放在牆上裝飾的畫，最符合照片情境。

- **decorate** 裝飾　**light fixture** 燈具　**mount** 安裝　**above** 在……上面　**doorway** 門口、出入口　**lampshade** 燈罩　**floor** 地板

6

(A) Pedestrians are crossing a road.	(A) 行人正在過馬路。
(B) A store sign is being replaced.	(B) 正在更換商店的招牌。
(C) A commercial building is under construction.	(C) 正在興建商業大樓。
(D) Some cars are parked on the side of a road.*	(D) 有些車停在馬路邊。

(A) 中的主詞（Pedestrians）正確，但後方說明有誤，若改成「沿著道路行走（walking along the road）」即為正解；(B) 使用了照片中出現的事物（store sign），但說明並不符合照片情境；(C) 的內容從照片中難以判斷；(D) 客觀描述車子停在路邊，為正確答案。

- **pedestrian** 行人　**replace** 更換　**commercial** 商業的　**under construction** 建造中

PART 2 02

7

When did Jeffrey clean out the storage room?
(A) He cleaned the windows.
(B) Sometime this morning.*
(C) A storage container.

傑佛瑞何時打掃了貯藏室？
(A) 他擦了窗戶。
(B) 今天早上某個時候。
(C) 一個置物箱。

When 為詢問「時間」的疑問詞，題目詢問「何時」打掃，(B) 回答了時間資訊，為最適當的答案。回答選項中若重複出現題目中的單字（clean, storage），如 (A) 和 (C)，通常不會是正確答案。

• **storage** 貯藏、保管　**container** 容器、貨櫃

8

What does your store sell?
(A) Secondhand furniture.*
(B) The interns will arrive soon.
(C) A full refund.

你的店賣什麼？
(A) 二手家具。
(B) 實習生很快就來了。
(C) 全額退費。

題目詢問「賣什麼」，(A) 具體回答了產品資訊（furniture 家具），為正確答案。

• **secondhand** 二手的　**arrive** 到達、到來　**refund** 退還、退款

9

Do you know where I can find a newsstand?
(A) I saw one just down the street.*
(B) No, I can't read it.
(C) It's an interesting story.

你知道哪裡有書報攤嗎？
(A) 我看到一家，就在這條街上。
(B) 不，我看不懂。
(C) 這篇故事很有趣。

題目為以「Do you know . . . ?」開頭的間接問句時，請務必聽清楚句子中間的疑問詞。題目為「報攤在哪裡？」，(A) 回答了位置資訊「沿著這條街走」，為最適當的答案。

• **newsstand** 書報攤

10

Can I try those sunglasses on, please?
(A) Sure, I'll work hard.
(B) It has a good location.
(C) Yes, here you are.*

請問我可以試戴那副太陽眼鏡嗎？
(A) 當然，我會努力工作。
(B) 它的位置很好。
(C) 可以，來，給你。

「Can I . . . ?」意思為「請問我可以……嗎？」，本題題目為「請問我可以試戴那副太陽眼鏡嗎？」，回答可以（Yes）並拿出東西最符合語感，因此正確答案為 (C)。請先試想題目問句可能出現在什麼場合或情境，將有助於找出正確答案。

• **try on** 試穿、試戴　**location** 位置、地點

11

Who informed the newcomers of the changes to their assignments?
(A) With the assigned newcomers.
(B) The head of Human Resources.*
(C) One or two minor changes.

誰通知了新同事，他們的工作改變了？
(A) 和指派的新同事。
(B) 人事部的主管。
(C) 一、兩個小改動。

題目以 who 開頭，問「是誰」告知變更事項，(B) 回答了職稱，為正確答案。當題目為 Who 開頭的問句時，答案可能為人名、職稱、部門名稱、公司名稱等。

• **inform** 通知、告知　**newcomer** 新來者、新手　**change** 改變、變動　**assignment** 任務、工作　**assign** 分派、指定　**head** 領導人、主管　**human resources** 人事部門、人力資源　**minor** 較小的、次要的

12

When is the best time to talk to your manager?
(A) You must be in management.
(B) At her downtown office.
(C) Anytime in the afternoon.*

什麼時候最適合和你的經理談話？
(A) 你一定是管理階級。
(B) 在她市區的辦公室。
(C) 下午都可以。

When 為詢問「時間」的疑問詞，重點在詢問「什麼時候最適合說」，(C) 為最自然的回應；(A) 中的 management 與問句中的 manager 字根相同、發音也相似，容易讓人混淆，應特別注意；也請務必記住此類選項極有可能不是答案。

• **management** 管理

13

Would you prefer to take a vacation later this month or after we finish the project?
(A) It's taking up too much space.
(B) I'm okay with either.*
(C) I like project work.

你要在這個月晚一點休假，還是等我們完成專案再說？
(A) 它太佔空間了。
(B) 我都可以。
(C) 我喜歡專案工作。

碰到題目為選擇疑問句時，可以預想到答案應為問句中所包含的兩種選項（①這個月稍晚、②專案結束後）之一，或是排除這兩種選項，以其他內容回覆。本題的重點在於「打算這個月休假？還是專案結束後再休假呢？」，(B)「兩個都可以」屬於以其他方式回覆，為正確答案。在選擇疑問句的題型中，答案通常會出現 both、either 或是 one。

• **prefer** 更喜歡、寧可　**finish** 完成

14

Why did you suggest paying by credit card instead of cash?
(A) A local bank.
(B) Because you can earn points.*
(C) You could write about it.

你為什麼建議用信用卡付款，而非現金？
(A) 一家本地銀行。
(B) 因為你可以得到點數。
(C) 你可以描寫它。

Why 為詢問「原因」的疑問詞，題目句「為何建議我以信用卡結帳呢？」，和 (B) 以連接詞 because 開頭「因為可以累積點數」，兩句構成完整對話。最近經常出現問句 Why 搭配 because 回答的題型。

• pay 支付、付款 instead of 代替 cash 現金 earn 賺到、得到

15

You do know how to make curry, don't you?
(A) I've cooked it over a hundred times.*
(B) At an authentic Indian place.
(C) During lunchtime.

你真的知道怎麼煮咖哩，對嗎？
(A) 我已經煮過不下一百次了。
(B) 在道地的印度餐館。
(C) 在午餐時間。

自己已知的事實，再次向對方確認或是尋求認同時，會使用附加問句。通常會與一般問句「Do you know how to make curry?（你知道怎麼煮咖哩嗎？）」的回答相似，這一點請特別留意。(A) 省略了是（Yes），回答「經常做」為最適當的答覆。

• authentic 正宗的、道地的

16

What task was Ms. Johnson's team given this month?
(A) By the middle of next month.
(B) Sure, I'll speak to her about it.
(C) Reviewing the latest project proposal.*

強生女士的小組這個月的任務是什麼？
(A) 最晚在下個月中之前。
(B) 當然，我會和她說這件事。
(C) 細察最新的提案。

本題詢問的重點為負責了「什麼事」，和 (C) 的回答「檢閱提案書」，兩句構成完整對話，為正確答案。若題目詢問事情的「期限」時，(A) 則為最適當的答案。

• task 任務 middle 中間、中途 review 審查、檢閱 proposal 提案、計畫

17

I would like to go see Jennifer dance in the ballet performance.
(A) No, not here. Over there, please.
(B) It's two hours away by car.*
(C) I must perform well this time.

我想去看珍妮佛的芭蕾舞演出。
(A) 不，不是這裡。請到那邊。
(B) 開車要兩個小時。
(C) 我這次一定要好好表演。

本題的重點為「想去看芭蕾舞演出」，正確答案為 (B) 的回答「車程要兩小時（很累人）」；PART 2 中，選項常會出現與題目中發音相似、或是字根相同的單字，如 (C) 中的 perform，此類選項極有可能不是答案。

• performance (n.) 表演 perform (v.) 表演

18

Is the meeting room big enough to accommodate twenty people?
(A) He is on a conference call.
(B) The company had some financial troubles.
(C) Well, it depends on how we arrange the chairs.*

會議室夠不夠大到足以容納二十個人？
(A) 他正在開電話會議。
(B) 公司有些財務狀況。
(C) 嗯，要看我們椅子怎麼排。

本題詢問的重點為「會議室是否能容納二十個人」，(C) 以婉轉的方式回答「取決於椅子的擺放方式」最為適當。

- **accommodate** 能容納 **conference call** 電話會議 **financial** 財政的、金融的 **depend on** 視某事物而定、取決於某事物 **arrange** 安排

19

When did the company cafeteria open?
(A) It often happens in the morning.
(B) In other departments, too.
(C) After the new CEO was appointed.*

公司的員工餐廳是何時開幕的？
(A) 通常發生在上午。
(B) 其他部門也是。
(C) 在任命新的執行長之後。

本題問句以 When 開頭，詢問「員工餐廳正式營運的時間」，(C) 使用表示時間的介系詞 after，回答「在任命新的執行長之後」，兩句構成完整對話。這題要注意的是，不要一聽到 morning 就馬上選 (A)。

- **department** 部門 **appoint** 任命、指派

20

Do you plan to distribute the sales report at the meeting or before it?
(A) Let's send it now by e-mail.*
(B) No, I will report to him.
(C) She met the sales manager already.

你打算在會議中、還是開會前，分發銷售報告？
(A) 我們現在就用電子郵件寄出吧。
(B) 不，我會向他報告。
(C) 她已經見過業務經理了。

本題屬於選擇疑問句，請務必假設其中一種可能是在兩種選項中擇一：①會議中、或是②會議之前分發報告，抑或可能排除這兩種選項，以其他內容回覆。正確答案為 (A)「現在就以電子郵件寄送」，非常接近②的意思。當選項中出現 Let's 時，極有可能為正確答案。

- **distribute** 分發、散布

21

Let's hire some part-time workers so we can handle all these extra orders.

(A) I'll order them online.

(B) Should we post an advertisement?*

(C) Five hours a day.

我們來僱用一些兼職人員，這樣才能處理這些額外的訂單。

(A) 我會上網訂購。

(B) 我們是否該登個廣告？

(C) 一天五個小時。

本題建議要「僱用員工」，(B) 反問「是否要刊登（徵才）廣告」，兩句構成完整對話，為最適當的選項。(A) 選項中重複出現 order 刻意讓人混淆；若題目詢問工作時間，(C) 則為正確答案。

- **hire** 僱用　**handle** 處理　**extra** 額外的　**order** 訂單　**post** 刊登、張貼　**advertisement** 廣告

22

Do you think the new reception area gives a good impression to visitors?

(A) I would've liked brighter colors.*

(B) I am impressed with him.

(C) Between the first and the seventh floor.

你覺得新的接待區會帶給訪客好印象嗎？

(A) 我原本想要更亮的顏色。

(B) 他令我印象深刻。

(C) 在一樓到七樓之間。

本題詢問「新區域是否合適」，根據對話情境，(A) 的回答「更喜歡明亮些的顏色」最適當，為正確答案。

- **be impressed with** 對……印象深刻

23

How about taking a flight that departs on Friday?

(A) I'm a frequent flier.

(B) It will have to be close to midnight.*

(C) In a department store.

搭星期五出發的航班好嗎？

(A) 我常搭飛機。

(B) 可能會將近半夜。

(C) 在百貨公司。

本題以「How about . . . ?」開頭，提議「搭乘星期五的班機」，(B) 以「可能會接近午夜時分」回覆，最符合對話情境。其他選項故意使用與 flight 和 departs 發音相近的單字，讓人混淆。

- **flight** （飛機的）班次　**depart** 啟程、出發　**frequent** 頻繁的　**department store** 百貨公司

24

Chevon tested the sound equipment, didn't he?

(A) I'll ask him.*

(B) They're equipped for the job.

(C) Our new speakers.

薛峰測試過音響設備了，不是嗎？

(A) 我會問他。

(B) 他們有能力做這個工作。

(C) 我們的新喇叭。

本題為附加問句，基本上與問句「薛峰測試過音響設備了嗎？」類似。 (A) 為最適當的答案，不以 Yes 或 No 答覆，反而回答「我向他確認一下」。PART 2 選項中若出現「I don't know」，極有可能為正確答案。

- **equipment** 設備　**be equipped for** 有能力……、有條件……

25

Have you visited the new community center?
(A) More charity events.
(B) It's written in the manual, I guess.
(C) I haven't had a chance.*

你去過新的活動中心嗎?
(A) 更多慈善活動。
(B) 我想應該是寫在使用手冊裡。
(C) 我還沒有機會去。

本題詢問「是否去過新設立的中心」,(C) 回答「還沒有機會去」,為正確答案。

• **charity** 慈善 **event** 活動 **manual** 使用手冊 **chance** 機會

26

Has the schedule for next week's workshop changed?
(A) Has she worked on it before?
(B) Yes, I'll forward the e-mail to you.*
(C) They will focus on teamwork.

下星期工作坊的日程表更改了嗎?
(A) 她以前做過嗎?
(B) 是的,我會把電子郵件轉發給你。
(C) 他們會專注在團隊合作上。

本題詢問「日程是否有所變動」,(B) 回答「是(Yes),稍後寄給你」,兩句構成完整對話,為正確答案。

• **change** 改變 **focus on** 集中注意力於……

27

Who's in charge of maintaining the photocopiers?
(A) Behind the file cabinet.
(B) Yes, it was fantastic.
(C) You can talk to me.*

誰負責維修影印機?
(A) 在檔案櫃後面。
(B) 是啊,棒透了。
(C) 你可以跟我說。

本題詢問「是誰」負責維護,正確答案為 (C)「請直接跟我説」;(A) 使用易與 photocopier 聯想在一起的單字 file cabinet 誤導答題者;(B) 為錯誤選項,以疑問詞開頭的問句,不得用 Yes 或 No 開頭的答句回覆,聽到的當下即可排除此選項。

• **be in charge of** 負責 **maintain** 維修、保養

28

But I thought you said you would be away next week.
(A) My trip has been canceled.*
(B) A member of the committee.
(C) From the train station.

可是,我以為你說你下星期不在。
(A) 我的行程取消了。
(B) 委員會的成員。
(C) 從火車站來。

最適合回覆本句「我以為你下週不在」的內容為 (A)「行程已被取消」。請注意,當題目為直述句時,務必聽清楚每個選項的內容。

• **cancel** 取消 **committee** 委員會

29

Our electricity cost decreased this year, didn't it?
(A) Yes, by 7%.*
(B) During the election.
(C) It was not our product.

我們今年的電費降低了，不是嗎？
(A) 是的，降了 7%。
(B) 在選舉期間。
(C) 那不是我們的產品。

本題為附加問句，等同於一般問句「電費是否降低」，因此正確答案為 (A)，回答「是的（Yes）」以及電費降低幅度的具體數字。

• **electricity** 電力 **cost** 費用 **decrease** 降低、減少 **election** 選舉 **product** 產品

30

Why aren't they wearing their uniforms?
(A) I forgot to tell them.*
(B) The servers and cooks.
(C) Before Wednesday.

他們為什麼沒穿制服？
(A) 我忘記告訴他們了。
(B) 侍者和廚師。
(C) 在星期三以前。

本題以 Why 開頭詢問「為何不穿制服」，(A) 省略了連接詞「因為（Because）」，答道：「我忘了跟他們說」，兩句構成完整對話，為正確答案。

31

Does Dr. Kwon know he has several appointments today?
(A) A university professor.
(B) It's on the top shelf.
(C) He will arrive in time for them.*

權醫師知道他今天有好幾個約診嗎？
(A) 一位大學教授。
(B) 在架子最上層。
(C) 他會及時抵達看診。

本題以略帶擔憂的口吻詢問「醫師是否知道有預約」，(C) 回覆「他會在預定時間內抵達」使對方安心；(A) 故意使用與問句中提及的 Dr.（博士、醫師）相關的職稱（大學教授）誤導答題者；(B) 與題目文意不符。

• **shelf** 架子、擱板 **in time** 及時

PART 3

03

Questions 32–34 refer to the following conversation.

W Hello, this is Suzie Thompson at Pearson Law. [32] I'm calling about a problem with our photocopier. Whenever I try to make copies, the text is so shrunken that it's unreadable.	女 哈囉，我是皮爾森律師事務所的蘇西・湯普生。[32] 我打電話來，是因為我們的影印機有點問題。我每次影印，字都縮得很小，模糊不清。
M Okay. [32] I think I can help you with that. [33] Have you tried turning it off and then turning it back on?	男 好的。[32] 我想，我可以幫上您的忙。[33] 您試過關機，再重新開機嗎？
W Yes, I did that a few times, but it didn't help. I also tried the reset code you gave me during your last service visit, but that didn't help, either.	女 是的，我試了好幾次都沒用。我也試過你上次來時給的那組重新設定的密碼，但也沒有用。
M I see. Well, I have some time this afternoon. [34] How about I stop by your office and see if I can find out what's wrong?	男 了解。嗯，我今天下午有空。[34] 我順道過去您的辦公室，看看我能不能找出問題，好嗎？

• **shrunken** 縮小的 **unreadable** 字跡模糊的 **turn off** 關掉 **turn on** 打開 **find out** 找出、發現 **wrong** 錯誤的、出毛病的

32

Where most likely does the man work? 男子最可能在哪裡工作？

(A) At a law office (B) At a repair company* (C) At a bookstore (D) At a print shop

(A) 律師事務所。 (B) 維修服務公司。 (C) 書店。 (D) 影印店。

對話第一段，女子提到她因為影印機出問題打了電話（I'm calling about a problem with our photocopier.），男子表示他可以幫忙解決（I think I can help you with that.），因此 (B) 為最適當的答案。

• **repair** 修理、修補

33

What does the man ask the woman to do? 男子要求女子何事？

(A) Restart some equipment * (A) 把某個設備重新開機。
(B) Use another machine (B) 使用另一台機器。
(C) Consult a manual (C) 查閱使用手冊。
(D) Find a reset code (D) 找到重新設定的密碼。

請仔細聆聽對話第一段男子所說的話：「Have you tried turning it off and then turning it back on?（您試過關機，再重新開機嗎？）」，故正確答案為 (A)。

• **equipment** 設備 **consult** 查閱 **manual** 使用手冊

34

What does the man say he can do? 男子說，他可以做什麼？

(A) Locate some equipment (B) Copy some documents (C) Contact a supplier (D) Go to the woman's office*

(A) 安置某個設備。 (B) 影印一些文件。 (C) 聯絡供應商。 (D) 去女子的辦公室。

對話最後一句，男子說要去女子的辦公室一趟（How about I stop by your office），因此正確答案為 (D)。

答案改寫 stop by → go to

• **locate** 把……設置在、確定……的地點 **supplier** 供應商

Questions 35–37 refer to the following conversation.

M	Good morning, my coworkers and I are planning to attend the State Accounting Conference in September. [35] Do you have any rooms available from the 7th to the 10th?	男	早安，我和同事計畫參加九月的國家會計研討會。[35] 你們七日到十日有空房間嗎？
W	Let me check our reservation system. Yes, it looks like we have several rooms available. [36] How many would you like to reserve?	女	我查一下訂房系統。有的，看來我們還有好幾間空房。[36] 您要預訂幾間房間？
M	There are five of us, so we would prefer to book five single suites. Do your single suites have Internet access?	男	我們有五個人，所以，我們比較想要預訂五間單人套房。你們的單人套房可以上網嗎？
W	In that case, [37] I suggest booking five single business suites. For only $10 more per night, each business suite comes with free Internet access and an onsite laser printer.	女	那樣的話，[37] 我建議您預訂五間單人商務套房，升級為商務套房只要每晚再加十元就好。每間商務套房都可以免費上網，房間裡還備有雷射印表機。
M	That sounds perfect. Let me discuss it with my coworkers, and I'll call you back within the hour.	男	聽起來非常合適。我和同事討論一下，一個鐘頭內回電。

- **coworker** 同事 **attend** 參加、出席 **accounting** 會計 **available** 可得到的、有空的 **check** 核對 **reservation (n.)** 預訂、保留 **several** 幾個的 **reserve (v.)** 預訂、保留 **prefer** 更喜歡、寧可 **book** 預訂 **suite** 套房 **access** 使用 **come with** 伴隨 **onsite** 就地、現場

35

Why is the man calling? 男子為何打電話？

(A) To book tickets for an event　(A) 為了預訂某個活動的門票。
(B) To inquire about accommodation*　(B) 為了詢問住房。
(C) To change a reservation　(C) 為了更改預訂資料。
(D) To purchase a printer　(D) 為了購買印表機。

對話第一段，男子提到將會參加會議，並詢問是否有空房（Do you have any rooms available?），因此正確答案為 (B)。

答案改寫 room → accommodation

- **inquire** 詢問、調查 **accommodation** 住宿、住房 **purchase** 購買

36

What information does the woman request? 女子要求什麼資訊？

(A) The number of rooms*　(A) 房間的數量。
(B) The name of a conference　(B) 研討會的名稱。
(C) A membership card number　(C) 會員卡的卡號。
(D) A check-out date　(D) 退房的日期。

本題詢問女子說了什麼話，請務必仔細聆聽女子所說的話。女子回覆尚有幾個空房間，緊接著說「How many would you like to reserve?」即詢問要預約的房間數量，選擇 (A) 最為適當。

37

What does the woman suggest?
(A) Upgrading some rooms*
(B) Signing a contract
(C) Checking a website
(D) Using a discount code

女子有何建議？
(A) 升級一些房間。
(B) 簽署一份合約。
(C) 查看一個網站。
(D) 使用折扣優惠密碼。

請注意聆聽「建議（suggest）」。對話第二段，女子建議對方預訂商務房（I suggest booking five single business suites.），並補充道：「只需加一點費用，就能使用網路與印表機」，因此正確答案為 (A)。

Questions 38–40 refer to the following conversation with three speakers.

M1	Hello. As you are all aware, next month, we will hold the annual charity dinner. I think it is a good idea to create a pamphlet to promote the event to local business owners. [38] Would anyone be interested in leading the project?	男 1	哈囉，你們大家都知道，我們下個月要舉行年度慈善晚宴。我認為，做一份宣傳小冊，向本地商家宣傳這個活動是個好主意。[38] 有人有興趣主持這個專案嗎？
W	I'd love to try it. I have some experience in publishing, and [39] I won the Hartford Essay Contest last year.	女	我很樂意嘗試。我在出版業工作過，而且 [39] 去年還得過哈特福散文獎。
M1	Excellent, Sue. That takes care of the written portion. Is there anyone who would like to work on the pamphlet's overall design?	男 1	太好了，蘇。文章的部分搞定。有人願意做宣傳小冊的整體設計嗎？
W	Mark graduated from Stanford's design program. [40] Maybe he will be able to come up with some fantastic ideas for the design plan.	女	馬克是史丹佛大學的設計學位學程畢業。[40] 也許他能想出一些很棒的設計點子。
M2	Sure. I'd be glad to help out in any way I can.	男 2	當然，我很樂意盡我所能幫忙。
M1	Okay. Let's meet next week to discuss the project more in depth.	男 1	好的。我們下星期碰面，再更深入討論專案內容。

• **aware** 知道的 **hold** 舉行 **annual** 年度的 **charity** 慈善 **promote** 宣傳 **owner** 擁有者、所有人 **take care of** 處理 **portion** 部分 **overall** 全部的、整體的 **come up with** 想出、提供 **discuss** 討論 **in depth** 深入地

38

What is the conversation mainly about?
(A) An updated menu
(B) A change in a schedule
(C) A writing contest
(D) A volunteer project*

這段對話的主題為何？
(A) 一份更新的菜單。
(B) 時程表的一項更動。
(C) 一場寫作比賽。
(D) 一個志工專案。

對話第一段提及年度慈善晚宴宣傳小冊，並徵求有興趣負責此專案的人選（Would anyone be interested in leading the project?），因此選項 (D) 最適當。通常在對話前半部，就可以找到與對話主旨有關的線索。

39

What is true about the woman?
(A) She will relocate next week.
(B) She is a university professor.
(C) She has a photocopier.
(D) She won an award.*

關於女子，何者為真？
(A) 她下星期要搬家。
(B) 她是大學教授。
(C) 她有一台影印機。
(D) 她得過一個獎項。

請仔細聆聽女子所説的話。對話第一段，女子説道：「I won the Hartford Essay Contest last year.」，可以由此得知答案為 (D)。

- **relocate** 搬遷 **award** 獎、獎品

40

What is Mark asked to do?
(A) Take photographs
(B) Develop a design plan*
(C) Attend a workshop
(D) Order some supplies

馬克要做什麼？
(A) 拍照。
(B) 定出設計方案。
(C) 參加一個工作坊。
(D) 訂購一些用品。

請注意聆聽關鍵人名 Mark。對話後半部，女子提到：「馬克畢業於史丹佛大學設計學位學程，他應該會有很棒的設計點子（Maybe he will be able to come up with some fantastic ideas for the design plan.）」，因此 (B) 為最適當的答案。

- **attend** 參加 **order** 訂購 **supply** 補給品、生活用品

Questions 41–43 refer to the following conversation.

W Hello, Tim. [41] I'm wondering if the invitations for the company fundraiser have been delivered yet.
M No, they haven't. [42] I got the sample invitation yesterday, but I noticed that our company name was spelled wrong. I called the design studio about it. They apologized and said they'd send the corrected invitations by next Monday.
W Oh, no. Unfortunately, we can't delay it until Monday. Since the event is Wednesday, we need to make sure the invitations are mailed by Friday. [43] Could you call them back and let them know our deadline is urgent?
M Sure. I'll call them right away.

女 哈囉，提姆。[41] 我想知道公司募款活動的邀請函發出去了沒？
男 沒，還沒有。[42] 我昨天收到邀請函的樣本，但我發現公司名稱拼錯了。我打電話告訴設計工作室。他們道了歉，並說最晚下星期一，會把更正好的邀請函寄過來。
女 喔，糟了。遺憾的是，我們沒辦法等到星期一。因為活動是星期三，我們必須確定邀請函最晚星期五要寄出去。[43] 你可不可以再打一次電話，告訴他們，我們的截稿日期很趕？
男 當然可以。我現在就打給他們。

- **invitation** 邀請、請帖 **fundraiser** 募款活動 **deliver** 投遞、傳送 **apologize** 道歉 **correct** 改正、矯正 **delay** 延緩、耽擱 **make sure** 確定 **deadline** 截止期限 **urgent** 緊急的、急迫的 **right away** 立刻

41

What is being discussed?
(A) A business card design
(B) A printing order*
(C) A company retreat
(D) New work schedules

對話在討論何事？
(A) 名片設計。
(B) 印刷的訂單。
(C) 公司的教育訓練。
(D) 新的工作時程表。

對話第一段，經由女子說的話「I'm wondering if the invitations for the company fundraiser have been delivered yet.」，可以得知對話內容與「邀請函」有關，且接著提及要委託 design studio（設計工作室）趕製，因此 (B) 為最適當的答案。

• **order** 訂單　**retreat** 員工旅遊暨教育訓練

42

What was the problem with the sample item?
(A) The paper was damaged.
(B) A logo was outdated.
(C) Some information was incorrect.*
(D) The cost was too high.

邀請函的樣本有何問題？
(A) 紙張受損。
(B) 商標過時了。
(C) 有訊息錯誤。
(D) 費用太高。

請注意聆聽關鍵字 sample。對話第一段，男子宣稱雖然已收到樣本，但公司名稱有誤（I got the sample invitation yesterday, but I noticed that our company name was spelled wrong.），因此正確答案為 (C)。

答案改寫 company name → some information
wrong → incorrect

• **item** 一件物品　**damage** 損害、毀壞　**outdated** 過時的　**incorrect** 錯誤的　**cost** 費用

43

What does the woman ask the man to do?
(A) Contact a company*
(B) Return a sample
(C) Hire a new employee
(D) Pay an account

女子要求男子何事？
(A) 聯絡一家公司。
(B) 退回一份樣本。
(C) 僱用一名新員工。
(D) 結帳。

請注意聆聽女子所說的話。對話後半部，女子要求對方再打一次電話（Could you call them back），因此 (A) 為最適當的答案。「Could/Can you . . . ?」句型用來表示要求或提議，意思為「可以……嗎？」。

答案改寫 call → contact

• **contact** 聯絡　**hire** 僱用　**pay** 付款　**account** 帳戶

Questions 44–46 refer to the following conversation with three speakers.

M [45] How are you two doing entering all the [44] **patient records** into our clinic's new database program?	男 [45] 把所有 [44] 病歷資料輸入我們診所新資料庫的進度，妳們兩個進行得如何？
W1 We are about half done. Entering the basic information such as names and addresses is easy, but it takes time to include descriptions of all the [44] **dental work** each patient has received.	女 1 我們大概完成一半了。輸入基本資料，像名字和地址很容易，但要包含每個病人做過的所有 [44] 牙科治療說明，就很花時間。
W2 She is absolutely correct. That part slows us down a lot.	女 2 她說得一點也沒錯。那個部分大大拖累我們的進度。
M I see. I was hoping we could finish transferring the records by the end of this week. [46] Do you think you could get it done if I had one of my [44] **dental assistants** look after the descriptions?	男 我知道了。我本來希望可以在這個星期之內，把資料都轉換完畢。[46] 如果我讓一個 [44] 牙醫助理來處理說明的部分，妳們覺得，妳們做得完嗎？
W1 Oh, definitely.	女 1 噢，一定可以。

• **enter** 登錄、將……輸入 **patient** 病人 **include** 包含 **description** 說明、描述 **dental** 牙齒的、牙科的 **receive** 接受 **absolutely** 完全地 **correct** 正確的 **slow . . . down** 減低速度 **transfer** 轉移 **assistant** 助理 **look after** 處理、打理 **definitely** 肯定地、當然

44

Where most likely do the speakers work?
(A) At a subway station
(B) At a dental clinic*
(C) At a travel agency
(D) At a marketing firm

說話者最可能在哪裡工作？
(A) 在地下鐵車站。
(B) 在牙醫診所。
(C) 在旅行社。
(D) 在行銷公司。

本題必須聆聽對話中出現的關鍵字來解題。聽到 patient records、dental work、dental assistants 可以得知正確答案為 (B)。

• **firm** 公司、商行

45

What project have the women been working on?
(A) Drafting an employee's contract
(B) Creating a television advertisement
(C) Inputting details into a computer*
(D) Installing some audio equipment

女子正在進行什麼工作？
(A) 草擬員工的合約。
(B) 創作一支電視廣告。
(C) 把詳細資料輸入電腦。
(D) 安裝某個音響設備。

對話第一段問道：「How are you two doing entering all the patient records into our clinic's new database program?」，詢問所有病歷輸入新資料庫進行得如何，因此正確答案為 (C)。

答案改寫 enter → input
record → detail

• **draft** 草擬 **contract** 合約 **input** 將（資料等）輸入電腦 **install** 安裝、設置 **equipment** 設備

46

What does the man suggest?
(A) Working some overtime
(B) Moving the deadline
(C) Using different software
(D) Assigning more staff*

男子有何建議？
(A) 加一下班。
(B) 更改截止期限。
(C) 使用不同的軟體。
(D) 指派更多人手。

請仔細聆聽男子所說的話。對話後半部，男子詢問若調派一名跟診助理來幫忙，能否按時完成（Do you think you could get it done if I had one of my dental assistants look after the descriptions?），因此正確答案為 (D)。

答案改寫 assistant → staff

• **deadline** 截止期限、最後期限 **assign** 分配、派定

Questions 47–49 refer to the following conversation.

W	Hello, [47] I'm calling about the promotion listed on your website for the month of March. I'm interested in booking flight tickets for myself as well as below-cabin space for five large breed dogs from Boston to New York City.	女	哈囉，[47] 我打來問你們登在網站上的三月促銷活動。我對此有興趣，想要自己訂一張從波士頓到紐約市的機票，同時為五隻大型品種犬訂客艙下的位置。
M	No problem. I can help you with that. Would you like to book return fare, and are there any preferred travel dates?	男	沒問題。我可以幫您處理。您要訂來回機票嗎，有偏好的出發日期嗎？
W	[48] I'm bringing my dogs to compete in the National Dog Show, so I have to arrive on March 13th and stay for at least five days. Can you give me an estimate of the cost?	女	[48] 我要帶我的狗狗去參加全國狗展競賽，因此，我必須在 3 月 13 日到，並且至少待五天。你可以幫我估算一下費用嗎？
M	Well, with the March promotion, you'll receive a 20% discount on an economy seat. [49] Before I can determine the exact cost, can I get the exact size of the carriers for your dogs?	男	嗯，用三月的促銷，您訂經濟艙會打八折。[49] 方便知道您所有狗狗的外出提籠確切尺寸嗎？這樣我才能定下確切的費用。

• **promotion** 促銷、宣傳 **be interested in (+ V-ing)** 對……感興趣 **book** 預訂 **flight** （飛機的）班次 **breed** 品種 **fare** 票價 **preferred** 偏好的、合意的 **compete** 參賽 **arrive** 抵達 **at least** 至少 **estimate** 估價 **cost** 費用 **receive** 得到、收到 **determine** 決定、確定

47

Why is the woman calling?
(A) To request a reservation change
(B) To inquire about a special discount*
(C) To ask for a full refund
(D) To upgrade her flight ticket

女子為何打電話？
(A) 要求更改預訂的資料。
(B) 詢問一個特別的折扣。
(C) 要求全額退費。
(D) 將她的機票升等。

對話前半通常會出現打電話的目的。由對話第一段女子所說的內容「I'm calling about the promotion listed on your website for the month of March.」，可以得知答案為 (B)。答案通常會出現在「I'm calling about . . . ?」或是「I'm calling/phoning to . . . ?」後方。

• **request** 要求　**reservation** 預訂　**change** 改變　**inquire** 詢問

48

What event does the woman mention?
(A) An animal competition*
(B) A veterinary seminar
(C) A tour of a city
(D) An art convention

女子提到什麼活動？
(A) 一場動物競賽。
(B) 一場獸醫研討會。
(C) 一次城市觀光之旅。
(D) 一場藝術大會。

請仔細聆聽女子所說的話，且特別留意「event（活動）」的部分。對話第二段，女子提到：「I'm bringing my dogs to compete in the National Dog Show」，因此答案為 (A)。

• **competition** 比賽　**veterinary** 獸醫的

49

What additional information does the man ask for?
(A) The number of passengers
(B) The dimension of the carriers*
(C) The preferred payment method
(D) A membership card number

男子要求什麼額外資訊？
(A) 乘客的數量。
(B) 外出提籠的尺寸。
(C) 偏好的付款方式。
(D) 會員卡的號碼。

對話最後一句，男子希望對方告知寵物外出提籠的尺寸，以便算出確切的費用（Before I can determine the exact cost, can I get the exact size of the carriers for your dogs?），因此答案為 (B)。

答案改寫 size → dimension

• **dimension** 尺寸

Questions 50–52 refer to the following conversation.

M Hey, Monica. I wanted to sit down with you today to discuss the feedback that customers have submitted through our restaurant's website. [50] I just finished reading all of the comments.	男 嗨，莫妮卡。我今天一直想和妳坐下來討論，顧客在我們餐廳網站上提出的意見回饋。[50] 我剛剛看完所有的意見了。
W [51] I'm sorry. I've spent all day training the new cooks. Did you find any useful tips?	女 [51] 抱歉，我一整天都在訓練新來的廚師。你有找到任何有幫助的點子嗎？
M Yes, one woman suggested [52] giving people the menus while they are waiting for a table. They can also place their orders so that it will be ready by the time a table becomes available.	男 有，有位女士建議，[52] 在人們等候桌位時，提供菜單給他們看，他們也可以先點菜。這樣一來，等有座位時，餐點也準備好了。
W That's a wonderful idea! That would definitely save a lot of time.	女 那點子真棒！那樣肯定能節省很多時間。
M I agree. [52] Let's have a quick meeting with the serving staff right now.	男 我同意。[52] 我們現在和服務人員快速開個會吧。

• **discuss** 討論、商談 **submit** 提出（意見等）、呈遞 **comment** 意見、評論 **cook** 廚師 **useful** 有用的、有幫助的 **place an order** 點餐 **available** 可用的、有空的 **definitely** 肯定的、當然 **save** 節省 **agree** 同意

50

What did the man recently do?
(A) He had an oven repaired.
(B) He printed out a receipt.
(C) He looked at customer feedback.*
(D) He corrected an invoice error.

男子最近做了何事？
(A) 他找人修好了爐子。
(B) 他印出了收據。
(C) 他仔細看了顧客的意見回饋。
(D) 他更正了發票上的錯誤。

對話第一段，男子提及顧客意見，並表示自己已全部看過了（I just finished reading all of the comments.），因此答案為 (C)。

答案改寫 read → look
comment → feedback

• **repair** 修理 **invoice** 發票、發貨單

51

Why does the woman say, "I've spent all day training the new cooks"?
(A) To express agreement
(B) To suggest a solution
(C) To request more details
(D) To provide an excuse*

女子為何說「我一整天都在訓練新來的廚師」？
(A) 為了表示同意。
(B) 為了建議解決方法。
(C) 為了要求更多細節。
(D) 為了提出一個理由。

本題句子的前方出現「I'm sorry.」表示歉意，因此答案 (D) 最為適當。當題目詢問對話中出現的某句子代表什麼意思時，請掌握好該句前後的文意。

• **agreement** 同意、協議 **solution** 解決（辦法） **request** 要求 **provide** 提供 **excuse** 理由、藉口

52

What will the man mention at the meeting?
(A) Taking orders from people who are waiting*
(B) Keeping the business open late on weekends
(C) Removing certain dishes from the menu
(D) Offering more specials during lunchtime

男子將在會議上提及何事？
(A) 接受正在等座位的顧客點菜。
(B) 週末時，讓餐廳開到很晚。
(C) 把某些菜從菜單中刪去。
(D) 午餐時，提供更多特餐。

請注意聆聽本題重點「會議主旨」。對話後半部，男子提到，先提供菜單給候位的顧客（giving people the menus while they are waiting for a table），並和外場人員立刻開會討論一下（Let's have a quick meeting with the serving staff right now.），因此答案為 (A)。

- remove 去掉、消除 dish 菜餚 offer 給予、提供

Questions 53–55 refer to the following conversation.

W You're listening to Radio One with our special guest Tim Schwarz, a renowned consultant and an expert on how to succeed at a new job. Mr. Schwarz, would you be able to share your best tip for those who are starting a new job?	女 您現在收聽的是壹電台，我們的特別來賓是提姆・許瓦茲，他是很有名的諮商師，也是如何做好新工作的專家。許瓦茲先生，您可不可以把你最棒的秘訣，分享給那些正開始從事新工作的聽眾？
M Sure, I'd love to. [53] I think one of the easiest things you can do is to write everything down. Take notes during training and keep a schedule book of all your deadlines and meetings.	男 當然，我很樂意。[53] 我認為，最容易做到的事就是把每件事都寫下來。受訓時記筆記，並把你所有的截止期限和會議都記在記事本裡。
W That's an excellent tip. You should consider publishing your thoughts in a self-help book.	女 真棒的建議。您應該考慮把您的想法出版成一本自助書。
M It's funny you mention that. [54] I'm actually in the process of working with an editor on such a book. [55] It's due to be out next October from Wayward Publishing.	男 妳提到這件事，還真是有趣。[54] 我確實正和一位編輯合作，在寫這樣一本書。[55] 預計明年十月由威沃德出版社發行。

- renowned 著名的 expert 專家 succeed 成功 share 分享 take notes 記筆記 training 訓練 consider 考慮 self-help 自助 mention 提到、說起 actually 實際上 be in the process of 在……的進程中 editor 編輯 due 預計的

53

What suggestion does the man make?
(A) Organizing workspaces (B) Being friendly
(C) Working extra hours (D) Recording information*

男子提出什麼建議？
(A) 整理工作場所。 (B) 待人友善。
(C) 加班。 (D) 記錄資訊。

請注意聆聽男子所說的話。由對話第一段：「I think one of the easiest things you can do is to write everything down.」，可以得知答案為 (D)。

答案改寫 write . . . down → record

- organize 組織、整理 extra 額外的

54

What does the man mean when he says, "It's funny you mention that"?
(A) The woman's suggestion is already true.*
(B) He thinks the woman's comment is false.
(C) The woman's idea is strange.
(D) He refuses to answer the question.

當男子說「你提到這件事，還真是有趣」，意指什麼？
(A) 女子的建議已然成真。
(B) 他認為女子的意見是錯的。
(C) 女子的主意很奇怪。
(D) 他拒絕回答問題。

本題問的是男子對於建議出書的答覆，從最後內容：「I'm actually in the process of working with an editor on such a book.」，可以得知男子已在進行出書前的準備，因此答案為 (A)。

• **suggestion** 建議　**false** 錯誤的、虛假的　**refuse** 拒絕

55

According to the man, what will happen in October?
(A) A report will be distributed.
(B) A book will become available.*
(C) A company will be established.
(D) A project will be started.

根據男子表示，十月會發生何事？
(A) 會發送一份報告。
(B) 一本書會上市。
(C) 一家公司會成立。
(D) 一項計畫會開始。

請仔細聆聽男子對話的內容，並特別留意關鍵時間點 October（十月）。可由對話最後一段：「It's due to be out next October from Wayward Publishing.」，找出答案為 (B)。

• **distribute** 分發、散發　**available** 可獲得的、可買到的　**establish** 建立、創辦

Questions 56–58 refer to the following conversation.

W Hi, Maxwell, [56] I've been trying to send some customer reports through the company e-mail, but it keeps telling me that the servers are down. Have you been able to use your e-mail today?

M No, I've been having the same problem. [57] I already submitted a complaint to the IT department this morning, but you should do the same if we want it to be fixed quickly.

W Okay, how should I go about sending a complaint? Should I contact the department head?

M No, you can just log on to the company message board and submit the complaint there. Here, [58] let me show you how to sign in.

女 嗨，麥斯威爾。[56] 我一直試圖透過公司的電子郵件傳送一些顧客報告，但系統一直告訴我伺服器故障。你今天可以寄送電子郵件嗎？

男 不行，我遇到一樣的問題。[57] 我今天早上已經發了申訴信給 IT 部門，不過，如果我們想要系統快點修好的話，妳也應該發申訴信。

女 好，我該怎麼發這封申訴信？我應該聯絡該部門的主管嗎？

男 不用，妳只需登入公司的布告欄，然後從那裡發出申訴信就可以了。來，[58] 我示範給妳看如何登入。

• **submit** 提出（意見等）、呈遞　**complaint** 抱怨、抗議　**department** 部門　**fix** 修理　**head** 領導人、主管

56

What is the woman unable to do?

(A) Print some documents

(B) Locate a file

(C) Send some work e-mails*

(D) Join the company dinner

女子無法做什麼？

(A) 列印一些文件。

(B) 找出一份檔案。

(C) 傳送一些工作上的電子郵件。

(D) 參加公司的晚餐。

本題重點為「遇到的問題或是困境」，女子在對話第一段說：「I've been trying to send some customer repors through the company e-mail, but it keeps telling me that the servers are down.」，由此得知答案為 (C)。

- **locate** 找出、確定……的地點

57

What did the man do this morning?

(A) Access a server

(B) Visit a department

(C) Fix a computer problem

(D) File a complaint*

男子今天早上做了何事？

(A) 進入伺服器存取。

(B) 造訪一個部門。

(C) 修好一個電腦問題。

(D) 提出申訴。

本題聆聽的重點在 this morning（今天早上），對話第一段，男子說道：「I already submitted a complaint to the IT department this moring」，上午已經傳達了自己的不滿，因此答案為 (D)。

答案改寫 submit → file

- **access** 進入、使用、存取　**file** 提出（申請等）

58

What does the man say he will do?

(A) Demonstrate how to sign in*

(B) Submit another form

(C) Update a service request

(D) Reset a company password

男子說他將會做什麼？

(A) 示範如何登入。

(B) 提出另一份表格。

(C) 更新一項服務要求。

(D) 重新設定電腦密碼。

請仔細聆聽男子所說的話。對話最後一段他說道：「我示範給妳看如何登入（let me show you how to sign in）」，因此答案為 (A)。

- **demonstrate** 示範　**form** 表格

Questions 59–61 refer to the following conversation.

W Welcome back from Chicago, Ted. [59] I know you were visiting our current clients, but I'm wondering if you managed to meet with any new companies that are interested in carrying out their advertising campaigns with us.	女 泰德，歡迎你從芝加哥歸來。[59] 我知道，你去拜訪我們現有的客戶，但我想知道，你有沒有成功和一些新公司會面，使他們有意由我們來執行廣告宣傳活動？
M Yes, I found a potential new client for our firm. The company could be big business for us. [60] However, the CEO mentioned that their current advertising firm charges them 5% less than our standard rates. If we want to sign his company, we'll need to match that cost.	男 有的，我幫公司找到一位潛在的新客戶。這家公司可能會帶給我們一筆大生意。[60] 但是，執行長提到，他們現在的廣告公司收費比我們的標準費率少5%。如果我們想要簽下他的公司，我們的收費必須比得過才行。
W Well, if the company is going to bring in a large amount of business for us, I think the 5% discount may be worthwhile. [61] How about you draw up a proposal and then set up a conference call with the CEO?	女 嗯，如果這家公司會為我們帶進一大筆生意的話，我想，或許值得給5%的折扣。[61] 你來草擬一份提案，然後安排和執行長開個電話會議如何？

• **current** 當前的、現行的 **manage to** 設法做到、成功完成 **carry out** 執行、完成 **potential** 潛在的、可能的 **firm** 公司 **charge** 索價、收費 **rate** 費用、價格 **match** 比得上 **worthwhile** 值得做的 **draw up** 起草 **proposal** 提案、計畫

59

What did the man do in Chicago?
(A) Sign a new client
(B) Meet with some customers*
(C) Attend a workshop
(D) Deliver a sample order

男子在芝加哥時做了何事？
(A) 簽了一個新客戶。
(B) 和一些客戶碰面。
(C) 參加一個工作坊。
(D) 送一份樣品。

請注意聆聽關鍵字 Chicago（芝加哥）。對話第一段，女子向男子說道：「歡迎你從芝加哥歸來」，並提到拜訪客戶一事（I know you were visiting our current clients），因此最適當的答案為 (B)。

答案改寫 visit → meet
client → customer

• **attend** 出席、參加

60

What problem does the man mention?
(A) A client canceled a contract.
(B) A CEO was too busy to meet.
(C) A trip was delayed by a week.
(D) A price was not agreed upon.*

男子提到什麼問題？
(A) 一名客戶中止了合約。
(B) 有位執行長太忙，無法碰面。
(C) 有項行程延後了一星期。
(D) 價格沒有談攏。

從男子的回話「However, the CEO mentioned that their current advertising firm charges them 5% less than our standard rates.」，可以發現答案為 (D)。however 為表示轉折的連接詞，答案通常會出現在其後方。

• **cancel** 取消、中止 **contract** 合約 **delay** 使延期 **agree upon a price** 議定價格、談好價格

61

What does the woman suggest doing next?
(A) Flying back to Chicago
(B) Reading an article
(C) Writing a proposal*
(D) Reviewing a website

女子建議接下來做什麼？
(A) 飛回芝加哥。
(B) 讀一篇文章。
(C) 寫一份提案。
(D) 細查一個網站。

請仔細聆聽女子所說的話，並特別留意她的「提議」。對話最後一段她說道：「先完成提案計劃書後，再進行電話會議（How about you draw up a proposal and then set up a conference call with the CEO?）」，因此答案為 (C)。How about 的意思為「……你看如何？」，答案通常會出現在此。

Questions 62–64 refer to the following conversation and building directory.

Business	Suite
Jane, Baker, and Sons Law	601
Walder Tech Solutions	602
Sedwick International Trade	603
[64] Martin Sound and Recording	604

公司	室
珍與貝克父子法律事務所	601
華德科技公司	602
賽德威國際貿易公司	603
[64] 馬丁音響錄音	604

W Hi, [62] I'm scheduled to see my dentist at 1:30 today. I parked in the underground parking garage, but I'm not sure where I should go to pay for parking.

M No problem, Ma'am. [63] Parking is free for paying visitors. Your dentist's office will stamp your ticket. Just show it to me when you leave and you'll be exempt from paying.

W That's great, thank you. Also, can you point me in the right direction? This is my first visit to Dr. Star, but I can't find his name on the directory.

M Ah, Dr. Star is new to this building, and we haven't been able to change the directory yet. [64] You'll find him in suite 604.

女 嗨，[62] 我今天排好一點半來看牙醫。我的車停在地下停車場，但我不確定要去哪裡付停車費。

男 好的，女士。[63] 付費訪客免停車費。您的牙醫診所會在你的停車卡上蓋章。您離開時，只要把卡給我看，就不用付費。

女 太好了，謝謝你。還有，你可以指給我正確的方向嗎？這是我第一次來看史達醫師的診，但我在公司名錄上找不到他的名字。

男 啊，史達醫師剛搬來這棟大樓，我們還沒有更改名錄。[64] 您可以在 604 室找到他。

- **trade** 貿易 **be scheduled to** 定於…… **dentist** 牙醫 **parking garage** 停車場 **pay for** 支付……的費用 **leave** 離開（某處） **exempt** 免除 **directory** 姓名地址簿、工商名錄

62

What is the purpose of the woman's visit?
(A) To interview a lawyer
(B) To attend a medical appointment*
(C) To purchase a parking pass
(D) To meet with a client

女子造訪的目的為何？
(A) 為了面試一位律師。
(B) 為了赴一場約診。
(C) 為了買停車入場證。
(D) 為了和客戶見面。

對話第一段，由女子說的內容：「I'm scheduled to see my dentist at 1:30 today」，已排定要來看牙醫，可以確認答案即為 (B)。

63

What does the man say about parking?
(A) It is free for paying customers.*
(B) It is cheaper than most places.
(C) It is only for employees
(D) It is located on the roof.

關於停車，男子怎麼說？
(A) 付費的顧客免費停車。
(B) 停車費比大部分地方都便宜。
(C) 只有員工可以停車。
(D) 停車場在頂樓。

請仔細聆聽男子所說的話，並特別留意關鍵字 parking（停車）。由對話第一段，男子說：「Parking is free for paying visitors.」，可以得知答案為 (A)。

答案改寫 visitor → customer

- be located on 使……座落於

64

Look at the graphic. Which office name needs to be updated on the building directory?
(A) Jane, Baker, and Sons Law
(B) Walder Tech Solutions
(C) Sedwick International Trade
(D) Martin Sound and Recording*

請見圖表。公司名錄上的哪一家公司名稱需要更新？
(A) 珍與貝克父子法律事務所。
(B) 華德科技公司。
(C) 賽德威國際貿易公司。
(D) 馬丁音響錄音。

對話最後一句，男子提到尚未更新醫生名字，請她至 604 室（You'll find him in suite 604.），而 604 號相對應的內容即為答案 (D)。

Questions 65–67 refer to the following conversation and schedule.

CONFERENCE ROOM A: WEDNESDAY

TIME	EVENT
10:00 A.M.	Graphic Design Meeting
11:00 A.M.	Conference Call
2:00 P.M.	Meeting with S&V Fashions
3:00 P.M.	Budget Review

會議室 A：星期三

時間	活動
上午十點	平面設計會議
上午十一點	電話會議
下午兩點	與 S&V 服飾開會
下午三點	預算審查

W Rebecca Greenwood of Weston Pharmaceuticals just called. [65] Her company is looking to hire a new advertising firm to sell their new line of vitamins. She'd like to come in Wednesday morning at ten to discuss our services.

M That's great. Weston Pharmaceuticals is a big international company. They could potentially become a large account for us. Can you reserve conference room A that day? It's the most comfortable room.

W Unfortunately, [66] that room is already booked at ten.

M Let me check the schedule. Oh, [66] it's been reserved by Jim. But I'm guessing Jim won't mind using another room instead.

W You're right. [67] I'll call him and ask if he's willing to switch rooms.

女 韋斯頓製藥的蕾貝卡・葛林伍德剛剛打電話來。[65] 她的公司正想要找新的廣告公司來銷售他們的維他命系列新產品。她想要星期三早上十點過來，和我們討論服務內容。

男 太好了。韋斯頓製藥是國際大廠。他們可能會成為我們的大客戶。你可以預訂那天的會議室 A 嗎？那是最適宜的房間。

女 不巧，[66] 那間會議室十點已經有人訂了。

男 我來查一下時間表。噢，[66] 已經被吉姆預訂了。但我想，吉姆不會介意用另一間會議室。

女 你說得對。[67] 我會打給他，問問看他是否願意換場地。

• **budget** 預算　**pharmaceuticals** 製藥　**look to** 想、期待　**potentially** 潛在地、可能地　**account** 客戶　**reserve** 預約、預訂　**comfortable** 舒適的　**book** 預訂　**mind** 介意、反對　**instead** 代替　**switch** 使調換

65

Where do the speakers work?

(A) At a fashion house
(B) At an advertising firm*
(C) At shipping business
(D) At a medical clinic

說話者在哪裡工作？

(A) 在一家時裝公司。
(B) 在一家廣告公司。
(C) 在運輸業。
(D) 在一家診所。

對話第一段提到有客戶正在尋找新的廣告公司（Her company is looking to hire a new advertising firm），因此答案為 (B)。

• **shipping** 航運、運輸　**medical** 醫學的、醫療的

66

Look at the graphic. According to the man, what event is Jim in charge of?
(A) Graphic Design Meeting*
(B) Conference Call
(C) Meeting with S&V Fashions
(D) Budget Review

請見圖表。根據男子所說，吉姆負責什麼活動？
(A) 平面設計會議。
(B) 電話會議。
(C) 與 S&V 服飾開會。
(D) 預算審查。

本題要找出 Jim 當天的日程。女子提到十點已經有人預約了（that room is already booked at ten），經男子確認後發現預約的人為 Jim（It's been reserved by Jim），而十點相對應的日程即為答案 (A)。

- **be in charge of** 負責

67

What does the woman say she will do?
(A) Upgrade a room (B) Locate some files
(C) Postpone a meeting (D) Ask for a room change*

女子說她會做什麼？
(A) 把房間升等。 (B) 找出一些檔案。
(C) 延後會議。 (D) 要求換場地。

請仔細聆聽女子所說的話。在最後一段對話中，女子說道：「I'll call him and ask if he's willing to switch rooms.」，她會詢問對方是否願意更換成其他會議室，因此 (D) 為最適當的答案。

- **locate** 找出、確定……的地點 **postpone** 使延期

Questions 68–70 refer to the following conversation and bill.

ITEM or SERVICE	PRICE
Inkspark 306 Printer	$399.00
2-year extended warranty	$69.00
306 color ink cartridge	$32.00
70 306 black ink cartridge	$15.00
Total:	$515.00

W Is there anything else I can do for you, sir? 68 Or are you set with the new printer, cartridges, and extended warranty?

M Actually, I have a question. 69 I was told that if I paid with my credit card at this store, I could split my payment into three monthly portions. Is that service still available?

W Yes, of course. We accept all major credit cards, and they all have the three-month payment plan option.

M Okay, I think I'd like to try that. Also, 70 I just remembered that this printer comes with its own spare black ink cartridge, so I don't think I'll need this replacement cartridge.

W Okay, I'll remove it from your bill before we proceed with payment.

物品或服務	價格
Inkspark 306 印表機	$399.00
兩年延長保固	$69.00
306 彩色墨水匣	$32.00
70 306 黑色墨水匣	$15.00
總計	$515.00

女 還需要什麼服務嗎，先生？68 還是，您就要新的印表機、墨水匣和延長保固？

男 其實，我有個疑問。69 有人告訴我，如果在這家店用信用卡付款，可以把款項分為三個月分期付款。那項服務還有嗎？

女 當然還有。我們接受所有主要信用卡，它們都享有三個月分期付款方案。

男 好，我想我要用這個方案。還有，70 我剛剛想起來，這台印表機附有備用黑色墨水匣，所以我想，我不需要這個替換墨水匣。

女 好的，我會把它從您的賬單中刪除再結帳。

- **extended** 延伸的 **warranty** 保固、保證書 **split** 切分 **portion** 部分 **accept** 接受 **option** 選擇 **come with** 附有 **spare** 備用的 **replacement** 代替物 **remove** 去掉、消除 **proceed** 繼續進行

68

Who most likely is the woman?
(A) A hotel receptionist
(B) A sales clerk*
(C) A civil servant
(D) An artist

女子最可能是誰?
(A) 飯店的櫃檯接待員。
(B) 售貨員。
(C) 公務員。
(D) 藝術家。

對話第一段,女子詢問對方是否有其他需求,或是只要印表機、墨水匣以及延長保固就好(Or are you set with the new printer, cartridges, and extended warranty),因此 (B) 為最適當的答案。

- receptionist 接待員　civil servant 公務員、文官

69

What does the man ask about?
(A) Payment plans*
(B) Special discounts
(C) Tax rebates
(D) New products

男子詢問何事?
(A) 付款方式。
(B) 特別優惠。
(C) 退稅。
(D) 新產品。

請務必掌握本題的重點「男子詢問的內容」,並仔細聆聽。對話前半部,男子提出問題後說道:「I was told that if I paid with my credit card at this store, I could split my payment into three monthly portions.」,詢問是否有分期付款,因此答案為 (A)。

- rebate 退款

70

Look at the graphic. Which amount will be removed from the bill?
(A) $399
(B) $69
(C) $32
(D) $15*

請見圖表。哪一筆金額會從賬單中刪除?
(A) $399。
(B) $69。
(C) $32。
(D) $15。

本題重點在「要刪除的金額」。對話後半部,男子說道「印表機本身就包含黑色墨水匣,因此不需要替換用的墨水匣(I just remember that this printer comes with its own spare black ink cartridge, so I don't think I'll need this replacement cartridge.)」,從表格中找出黑色墨水匣對應的金額,即為答案 (D)。

- amount 金額

PART 4

04

Questions 71–73 refer to the following telephone message.

M Hello, Jim. [71] This is Ron Fuller calling from Fox Computers. Everything looks fine with your computer except for the hard drive. It must be replaced, so [72] I've ordered a new one. I was able to save some files from your old hard drive. [73] If you'd like, I can transfer those files to your new hard drive when it arrives. Please let me know how you'd like to proceed. You can reach me at 655-098-3334. Thanks.

男 哈囉，吉姆，[71] 我是福斯電腦的羅傳樂。除了硬碟之外，您的電腦看起來都還很好。硬碟必須要換，所以，[72] 我已經訂了一個新的。我把您舊硬碟的一些檔案存出來了。[73] 如果您想要的話，等您的新硬碟來了，我可以把那些檔案轉存進去。請告訴我，接下來您想要怎麼做。您可以撥打 655-098-3334 找我。謝謝。

• **except for** 除了……以外 **replace** 更換、取代 **order** 訂購 **transfer** 搬、轉換 **arrive** (物品等)送來 **proceed** (做完某事後)接著做 **reach** 與……取得聯繫

71

Where does the speaker work?

(A) At a software company
(B) At an electronics manufacturer
(C) At a computer repair store*
(D) At a shipping company

說話者在哪裡工作？

(A) 在一家軟體公司。
(B) 在一家電子零件製造公司。
(C) 在一家電腦維修店。
(D) 在一家船運公司。

獨白開頭說道：「This is Run Fuller calling from Fox Computers.」，介紹自己為 Fox 電腦的 Ron Fuller，隨後提到與電腦維修相關的內容，因此答案為 (C)。

• **electronics** 電子機器、電子零件 **manufacturer** 製造公司、製造商 **repair** 修理 **shipping** 船運、運輸

72

What does the speaker say he has done?

(A) Ordered a component*
(B) Refunded a fee
(C) Replaced a part
(D) Upgraded some software

說話者說他做了何事？

(A) 訂了一個零件。
(B) 退還了一筆費用。
(C) 更換了一個零件。
(D) 把一些軟體升級。

請務必掌握本題重點「已完成的事項」，並仔細聆聽。男子說道：「因為需要更換硬碟，已訂購了新品（I've ordered a new one）」，因此答案為 (A)。

答案改寫 new one (hard drive) → component

• **component** 零件、組成部分 **refund** 退還 **fee** 費用 **part** 部件、零件

73

What does the speaker offer?
(A) To lend a computer
(B) To move some information*
(C) To extend a service warranty
(D) To pay for a new computer

說話者提議做何事？
(A) 出借電腦。
(B) 轉移一些資訊。
(C) 延長服務保固。
(D) 花錢買新電腦。

獨白後半部提到：「If you'd like, I can transfer those files to your new hard drive when it arrives.」，表示收到新的硬碟後，可以協助轉移檔案，因此 (B) 為最適當的答案。

• **lend** 把……借給 **extend** 延長 **warranty** 保證書、保固 **pay for** 支付……的費用

Questions 74–76 refer to the following message.

M Good afternoon, Ms. Renolds. [74] Thank you for visiting Star Insurance's website and filling out an online application form. According to your application, you are interested in getting your tour company's new buses insured. You're in luck, because my company is currently having a two-for-one insurance sale for businesses. For every insurance policy you purchase, you'll receive a second policy absolutely free for the first year. [75] If you'd like to take advantage of this sale, [76] please contact me by June 23rd as the promotion expires the next day.

男 雷諾女士，午安。[74] 謝謝您造訪星辰保險公司網站，並填寫線上申請表。根據您的申請書，您有意為貴遊覽公司的新巴士投保。您真幸運，因為我們公司現正舉辦商務保險買一送一促銷活動。根據您所買的每一張保單，第二張保單首年都完全免費。[75] 若您想要享有這項促銷優惠，[76] 請於 6 月 23 日前和我聯絡，因為促銷在 24 日截止。

• **insurance** 保險 **fill out** 填寫（表格、申請書等） **application** 申請 **according to** 根據、按照 **be interested in (+ V-ing)** 對……感興趣 **insure** （為……）投保 **policy** 保險單 **purchase** 購買 **absolutely** 完全地 **take advantage of** 善用 **contact** 與……聯繫 **promotion** 促銷 **expire** 過期

74

Why did Ms. Renolds visit Star Insurance's website?
(A) To review a product
(B) To fill out a form*
(C) To set up a meeting
(D) To upgrade a service

雷諾女士為何造訪星辰保險公司的網站？
(A) 為了仔細看一項產品。
(B) 為了填寫一份表格。
(C) 為了安排一場會議。
(D) 為了升級一項服務。

從獨白第一句，可以得知聽者為 Renolds 女士。問候完緊接著說道：「感謝您於本網站填寫申請書（Thank you for visiting Star Insurance's website and filling out an online application form.）」，因此 (B) 為最適當的答案。

• **review** 細看、審核 **product** 產品 **set up** 安排

75

What does the speaker offer Ms. Renolds?
(A) A membership card
(B) A full refund
(C) A discount*
(D) A new vehicle

說話者提議什麼服務給雷諾女士？
(A) 一張會員卡。
(B) 全額退費。
(C) 折扣。
(D) 一輛新車。

獨白後半部提到：「If you'd like to take advantage of this sale, please contact me.（如有意參與本次優惠活動，請與我聯繫。）」，因此答案為 (C)。

答案改寫 sale → discount

- **offer** 提議、給予 **vehicle** 車輛、運載工具

76

According to the speaker, what must Ms. Renolds do by June 23rd?
(A) Sign up for a newsletter
(B) Visit Star Insurance in person
(C) Complete a training course
(D) Make a decision*

根據說話者所述，雷諾女士必須在 6 月 23 日前做什麼？
(A) 登記訂閱電子報。
(B) 親自造訪星辰保險公司。
(C) 完成訓練課程。
(D) 作出決定。

聆聽時，請特別留意關鍵時間點 June 23rd（6 月 23 日）。獨白最後一句說道：「請於 6 月 23 日前與我聯繫」，並補充說明優惠活動將於隔天截止（please contact me by June 23rd as the promotion expires the next day）。因此是希望對方儘早決定並告知是否參與優惠活動，(D) 為最適當的答案。

- **sign up for** 登記、報名參加 **in person** 親自 **complete** 完成 **make a decision** 作決定

Questions 77–79 refer to the following tour information.

W Hello, everyone, and [77] welcome to the Spartan Automotive Factory tour. As I'm sure you're aware, Spartan Automotive was the first ever car manufacturer in the country. During this tour, you'll get to see some of the machinery used to make the first cars. [78] Since there is currently another group taking this tour, we'll start in the show room instead of the assembly line. You'll get to see some of the oldest cars ever manufactured. Then, we'll work our way into the assembly line area and conclude at the gift shop. [79] Remember, gift shop purchases are on sale today only.

女 大家好，[77] 歡迎參觀斯巴坦汽車工廠。相信你們都知道，斯巴坦汽車是國內第一家汽車製造廠。在本次導覽中，你們會看到一些用來製造第一批汽車的機器。[78] 由於現在有另一組正在參觀，所以，我們會先從展示廳、而不是裝配線開始參觀。你們會看到一些曾經生產的最古老車款。然後，我們會前往裝配區，最後到禮品部。[79] 記得，禮品部的商品優惠，只有今天。

- **automotive** 汽車的 **aware** 知道的、察覺的 **manufacturer** 廠商、製造公司 **machinery** 機器、機械裝置 **currently** 目前、現在 **instead of** 代替 **assembly** 裝配 **manufacture** 製造、加工 **conclude** 結束 **purchase** 購買、所購之物

77

Where is the tour most likely taking place?
這次導覽最可能在哪裡？

(A) At an automotive plant*
(B) At a car dealership
(C) At a toy outlet
(D) At a mechanic's shop

(A) 一間汽車廠。
(B) 一間汽車經銷商。
(C) 一間玩具暢貨中心。
(D) 一間修車行。

可以由獨白前半部「welcome to the Spartan Automotive Factory tour」確認答案為 (A)。

答案改寫 factory → plant

• **plant** 工廠 **dealership** 專賣店、經銷權 **outlet** 暢貨中心、工廠直銷 **mechanic** 修理工、技工

78

What does the speaker say has changed about the tour?
說話者說參觀行程的什麼部分改變了？

(A) The number of guides
(B) The outdoor sites
(C) The cost of tickets
(D) The order of locations*

(A) 導覽人員的數量。
(B) 戶外的地點。
(C) 票價。
(D) 地點的順序。

從題目和選項內容可以確認本題的重點為「更動事項」。獨白中間內容為「Since there is currently another group taking this tour, we'll start in the show room instead of the assembly line.」，表示「因為其他組的人目前正在參觀裝配線，我們改成先參觀展示廳」，因此答案為 (D)。

• **cost** 費用 **order** 順序 **location** 位置、地點

79

What does the speaker offer the listeners?
說話者提供什麼給聽眾？

(A) A limited-time discount*
(B) A hands-on workshop
(C) A free membership
(D) A map of the facility

(A) 限時折扣。
(B) 動手玩工作坊。
(C) 免費會員資格。
(D) 工廠的地圖。

在獨白後半部，通常會聽到説話者的建議事項。最後提到「紀念品特惠僅限今天（Remember, gift shop purchases are on sale today only.）」，因此答案為 (A)。

• **hands-on** 親自動手的

Questions 80–82 refer to the following excerpt from a meeting.

W Before we conclude our meeting, I'd like to take this time to inform you of an important event. I've just found out that [80] the local mayor will be visiting our restaurant next Wednesday to celebrate his reelection. As you know, the mayor often dines here, and he has requested his usual table for ten at 6:00 P.M. This shouldn't be any different than usual. [81] There's no reason to get nervous. However, I'd like to make sure that the new menus are finalized by the end of this week. I'd also like to distribute our new employee uniforms to ensure we all look our best. [82] Please write down your size on this piece of paper by the end of the day.

女 在我們結束會議之前，我要利用這個時間通知各位一個重要活動。我剛剛發現，[80] 本市的市長下星期三會來我們餐廳慶祝連任。你們都知道，市長常來這裡用餐，他已經要求10日下午六點保留他的老位子。這次應該和平常沒兩樣，[81] 不必緊張不安。不過，我想確認新的菜單可以在這個星期內完成。我也要發放新的員工制服，以確保我們呈現最好的一面。[82] 請在今天下班前，在這張紙上寫下你的衣服尺寸。

- **conclude** 結束 **inform** 通知、告知 **event** 活動 **mayor** 市長 **celebrate (v.)** 慶祝 **reelection** 連任 **dine** 用餐 **request (v.)** 要求、請求 **reason** 理由、原因 **get nervous** 變得緊張不安 **make sure** 確定 **finalize** 完成、定案 **distribute** 分發、分配 **ensure** 保證

80

Why is the mayor visiting the restaurant?

(A) To hold a celebration*
(B) To conduct an inspection
(C) To give a speech
(D) To host a birthday party

市長為何造訪這家餐廳？

(A) 為了舉行慶祝會。
(B) 為了進行檢查。
(C) 為了發表演說。
(D) 為了主持生日派對。

請注意聆聽關鍵字 mayor（市長）。可以從獨白前半部「the local mayor will be visiting our restaurant next Wednesday to celebrate his reelection」，確認答案為 (A)。

答案改寫 celebrate → hold a celebration

- **celebration (n.)** 慶祝 **inspection** 檢查、視察 **give a speech** 發表演說、作報告

81

Why does the speaker say, "This shouldn't be any different than usual"?

(A) To stress the importance of a meeting
(B) To reassure employees about an event*
(C) To inform of the mayor's special request
(D) To guess the duration of an inspection

說話者為何說「這次應該和平常沒兩樣」？

(A) 為了強調會議的重要性。
(B) 為了消除員工對活動的疑慮。
(C) 為了告知市長的特殊要求。
(D) 為了推測檢查持續的時間。

題目句的後方緊接著說道：「毋需感到不安（There's no reason to get nervous.）」，因此 (B) 為最適當的答案。

- **stress** 強調 **importance** 重要、重要性 **reassure** 使放心、使消除疑慮、向……再保證 **request (n.)** 要求、請求的事 **guess** 推測、猜測 **duration** （時間的）持續

82

What must listeners do before the end of the day?
(A) Check an updated schedule
(B) Fill out some information*
(C) Purchase some new clothing
(D) Print some new menus

今天下班前，聽眾必須做何事？
(A) 檢查更新的時程表。
(B) 填寫一些資料。
(C) 購買一些新衣服。
(D) 列印一些新菜單。

聆聽時，請特別留意關鍵時間點 before the end of the day（今天下班前）。在獨白末段說道：「Please write down your size on this piece of paper by the end of the day.」，請對方寫下尺寸，因此答案為 (B)。

答案改寫 write down → fill out
size → information

• **check** 檢查、核對　**fill out** 填寫（表格、申請書等）　**purchase** 購買

Questions 83–85 refer to the following telephone message.

M Hi Jennifer. This is Timothy from Renton & Sons. [83] I'm calling in regards to the online order you submitted for laminate floor panels in white oak for your new office space. I just want to double-check that your order is correct, because . . . well . . . ten thousand units is a bit excessive. [84] Even the biggest office spaces do not require more than five thousand units because [85] our laminate panels are quite wide. Please contact me by Friday to confirm your order. Thank you.	**男** 嗨，珍妮佛，我是連頓父子公司的提摩西。[83] 我打電話來，是關於您為了新辦公室，在線上訂購超耐磨白橡木地板一事。我只是想再次確認您的訂單沒錯，因為，呃，一萬片有點多。[84] 就連最大的辦公空間，最多也就需要五千片，因為 [85] 我們的超耐磨地板還蠻大片的。請在星期五之前與我聯絡，確認您的訂單。謝謝您。

• **in regards to** 關於　**order** 訂單　**submit** 提出　**laminate** 薄片製品、層壓板（補充：**laminate floor** 意指超耐磨木地板）　**correct** 正確的　**excessive** 過多的、過度的　**require** 需要　**confirm** 確定、證實

83

What does Renton & Sons produce?
(A) Office furniture　(B) Flooring*
(C) Appliances　(D) Windows

連頓父子公司生產什麼？
(A) 辦公室家具。　(B) 地板。
(C) 家用電器。　(D) 窗戶。

聆聽時，請特別留意關鍵字 Renton & Sons。從開頭問候語可以得知說話者（第一人稱）的來歷，緊接著說道：「I'm calling in regards to the online order you submitted for laminate floor panels.」，表明打電話來確認超耐磨地板的訂購資訊，因此答案為 (B)。

• **produce** 生產、製造　**appliance** 家用電器、器械

84

What does the man imply when he says, "ten thousand units is a bit excessive"?
(A) The customer's order may be wrong.*
(B) He will have to hire additional workers.
(C) The customer has canceled her order.
(D) He will deliver some materials late.

當男子說「一萬片有點多」時，意指什麼？
(A) 顧客的訂單也許有錯。
(B) 他必須另外僱用工人。
(C) 顧客已經取消她的訂單。
(D) 有些材料，他會晚點送。

題目句後方說道：「就連最大的辦公室也只需不到五千片（Even the biggest office spaces do not require more than five thousand units）」，因此 (A) 為最適當的答案。

- imply 暗示、意味　hire 僱用　additional 額外的　cancel 取消　deliver 運送　material 材料、原料

85

What does the man explain about his products?
(A) They are easy to clean.
(B) They are cheaper in summer.
(C) They are of high quality.
(D) They are large in size.*

男子對他的產品作了什麼說明？
(A) 它們很容易清潔。
(B) 夏季比較便宜。
(C) 它們的品質很好。
(D) 它們的尺寸很大。

請掌握住本題重點「產品特性」，並仔細聆聽。獨白後段提到「our laminate panels are quite wide」，可以得知答案為 (D)。

答案改寫 wide → large

- cheap 便宜的

Questions 86–88 refer to the following announcement.

W I'd like to take this time to say a few words about our fall internship program. Like last year, we've decided to recruit some of the highest achieving students from computer programming schools across the country. Over the next six months, [86] these students will be helping us develop several new software programs for public purchase. Like last year, one intern will be assigned to each team; however, I'd like to try something different this year. [87] Instead of a single end of term intern assessment, I'd like team leaders to provide me with monthly progress reports. [88] This will help my colleagues and I make decisions about who will be offered permanent positions at the company.

女 我想利用這個時間，談一下我們秋天的實習生計畫。就像去年一樣，我們決定從全國各地的電腦程式設計學院，招收一些表現最好的學生。接下來半年，[86] 這些學生會協助我們開發數個要公開販售的新軟體。像去年一樣，每個小組會指派一個實習生。不過，我今年想嘗試不一樣的作法。[87] 我不要實習結束時的單一評估報告，我要的是小組長每個月交進度報告給我。[88] 這可以幫助我和同事決定，誰能得到公司的正職工作。

- decide 決定　high achieving student 高成就學生　develop 開發、發展　purchase 購買　assign 分派　instead of 代替、與其　assessment 評價　provide 提供　colleague 同事　permanent 永久的、固定的　position 職位、工作

86

Where does the speaker most likely work?
(A) At an employment agency
(B) At a computer store
(C) At a university
(D) At a software company*

說話者最可能在哪裡工作？
(A) 在職業介紹所。
(B) 在電腦商店。
(C) 在大學。
(D) 在軟體公司。

獨白前段提到「全國各地的電腦程式設計學院」，並說希望「這些學生協助開發軟體程式（these students will be helping us develop several new software programs）」，因此 (D) 為最適當的答案。

- **employment** 職業、工作

87

What change to the internship program does the speaker mention?
(A) Employees will submit regular reports.*
(B) Interns will be paid for their work.
(C) Fewer students will be selected.
(D) The program length will be extended.

說話者提及實習生計畫有什麼改變？
(A) 員工要定期提出報告。
(B) 實習生的工作有酬勞。
(C) 較少學生會獲選。
(D) 計畫的時間要延長。

請掌握本題重點在於「異動」，並仔細聆聽。獨白中段提到「今年想要嘗試不同的作法，不會等到最後才進行總體評價，而是改成每個月都要提交進程報告書（Instead of a single end of term intern assessment, I'd like ream leaders to provide me with monthly progress reports.）」，因此答案為 (A)。

答案改寫 provide → submit
monthly → regular

- **change** 改變、變化 **submit** 提出 **regular** 定期的 **pay for** 支付……酬勞
length（時間的）長短 **extend** 延長、延伸

88

What is the purpose of the change?
(A) To ensure interns follow all the rules
(B) To make job candidate selection easier*
(C) To provide team leaders with incentives
(D) To allow managers to apply for funding

改變的目的為何？
(A) 為了確保實習生遵守所有規定。
(B) 為了更容易挑選應徵者。
(C) 為了提供小組長獎勵。
(D) 為了讓經理申請資助。

交代完異動部分後，緊接著說道：「This will help my colleagues and I make decisions about who will be offered permanent positions at the company.（這將有助於決定轉正名單）」，因此答案為 (B)。

- **ensure** 保證 **candidate** 候選人、應徵者 **selection** 選擇、選拔 **incentive** 鼓勵、獎勵
allow 允許、使成為可能 **apply for** 申請、請求 **funding** 資助、資金提供

Questions 89–91 refer to the following excerpt from a meeting.

M Before we finish up, I'd like to announce a change in shipping procedures. [89] Starting next month, we will be offering free shipping to customers who purchase products from our premium skincare line. As you know, interest in our premium line has grown significantly over the last year, but [90] many customers have complained about the high prices in addition to the cost of shipping. To help offset product costs and encourage more purchases, we will offer shipping free of charge. [91] I have a meeting set up with Parcel Plus Shipping next week to finalize a deal that will make shipping affordable for us.

男 在我們結束之前，我想宣布一項運送過程的變動。[89] 從下個月開始，凡購買我們精選護膚產品的顧客，我們將提供免運費服務。你們都知道，對我們的精選產品感興趣的人，去年大幅增加，但是，[90] 除了運費之外，很多顧客也抱怨定價太高。為了有助降低產品費用並促進消費，我們將提供免費送貨到府。[91] 我下星期安排了和郵佳貨運公司的會議，確定我們負擔得了的運費，以達成交易。

• **announce** 宣布 **shipping** 運輸、貨運 **procedure** 程序、過程 **interest** 興趣、關注 **significantly** 顯著地 **complain** 抱怨 **in addition to** 除……以外（還有） **cost** 費用、成本 **offset** 補償、抵銷 **encourage** 鼓勵、促進 **free of charge** 免費 **finalize** 敲定、定案 **deal** 交易 **affordable** 負擔得起的

89

According to the speaker, what service will the company begin offering next month?

(A) Discounted products
(B) Free shipping*
(C) Cheap memberships
(D) Complimentary samples

根據說話者所述，公司下個月開始提供什麼服務？

(A) 折扣商品。
(B) 免運費。
(C) 收費低廉的會員資格。
(D) 免費贈送樣品。

聆聽時，請特別留意關鍵時間點 next month（下個月）。獨白前段提到：「Starting next month, we will be offering free shipping to customers」，由此可以確認答案為 (B)。

• **complimentary** 免費贈送的

90

Why has the company decided to add the new service?

(A) An advertisement failed.
(B) Business has dropped.
(C) Competition has increased.
(D) Some customers complained.*

公司為何決定增加新服務？

(A) 廣告無效。
(B) 業績下滑。
(C) 競爭增加。
(D) 有些顧客抱怨。

聆聽時，請掌握住本題的重點為「增加新服務的原因」。獨白中段提到，由於顧客給了很多負面評價（many customers have complained about the high prices in addition to the cost of shipping），因此決定增加新服務來壓低價格並促進銷售，答案即為 (D)。

• **drop** 下降 **competition** 競爭 **increase** 增加

91

What does the speaker say he will do next week?
(A) Conclude an important deal*
(B) Test a skincare product
(C) Update an online store
(D) Deliver some products himself

說話者說，他下星期要做何事？
(A) 議定一筆重要的交易。
(B) 測試一項護膚產品。
(C) 升級線上商店。
(D) 親自運送一些產品。

請注意聆聽本題的關鍵時間點 next week（下週）。獨白最後一句說道：「I have a meeting set up with Parcel Plus Shipping next week to finalize a deal」，由此確認答案為 (A)。

答案改寫 finalize → conclude

• conclude 議定、達成 deliver 運送

Questions 92–94 refer to the following news report.

W Rebecca Strauss here, reporting for Channel 6 news. [92] I'm standing just outside Smithview Mall, which is celebrating its grand opening. Visitors are already lining up. [93] Everybody in town wants to shop in Smithview's two hundred brand new stores. To celebrate its opening, all Smithview stores are having their own special sales. You can expect to receive as much as 30% off in some stores. Additionally, [94] the food court will be giving away free $5 vouchers that can be used at any of the forty restaurants and coffee shops located within the mall. Come on down to Smithview Mall to take advantage of these great discounts.

女 我是第 6 台新聞記者蕾貝卡・史特勞斯，[92] 我現在就在史密斯維購物中心外面，此刻正在慶祝盛大開幕。顧客已經在排隊了。[93] 鎮上的每個人都想逛逛史密斯維裡的兩百間全新商店。為了慶祝開幕，史密斯維的所有商店都推出自己的特賣活動。你可以預期有些商店會打到七折之多。此外，[94] 美食廣場將發送免費五元餐券，購物中心內的 40 家餐廳和咖啡館都可使用。快來史密斯維購物中心，享受這些大優惠。

• celebrate 慶祝 visitor 訪客、遊客 line up 排隊 shop 在（商店）買東西 brand new 全新的 expect 預期 receive 收到、得到 additionally 此外 give away 贈送、分發 voucher 票券 take advantage of 趁機利用

92

What type of business is being discussed?
(A) An electronics market
(B) A restaurant chain
(C) A shopping center*
(D) A coffee shop

文中討論的是什麼型態的企業？
(A) 電器市集。
(B) 連鎖餐廳。
(C) 購物中心。
(D) 咖啡館。

獨白前段中「I'm standing just outside Smithciew Mall, which is celebrating its grand opening.」提到了公司名稱「史密斯維購物中心（Smithview Mall）」，由此可以得知答案為 (C)。選項 (B) 和 (D) 故意提及賣場內的店家，請格外小心別落入陷阱。

93

Why does the speaker say, "Visitors are already lining up"?
(A) To emphasize interest in an event*
(B) To encourage listeners to stay home
(C) To discuss the size of a location
(D) To express concern about crowdedness

說話者為何說「顧客已經在排隊了」？
(A) 為了強調對一項活動的興趣。
(B) 為了鼓勵聽眾留在家裡。
(C) 為了討論某個地區的面積大小。
(D) 為了表達對擁擠人群的關切。

獨白開頭沒幾句就說道：「Everybody in town wants to shop in Smithview's two hundred brand new stores.（鎮上所有的人都想要來此購物）」，表示人聲鼎沸、人氣很旺的意思，因此 (A) 為最適當的答案。當題目詢問獨白內文的意思時，請注意聆聽前後文的文意。

• **emphasize** 強調　**event** 活動　**location** 位置、指定地區　**express** 表達　**concern** 擔心、關切　**crowdedness** 擁擠、擠滿人群

94

What will customers receive if they visit the food court?
(A) A free beverage
(B) A 30% refund
(C) A discount coupon*
(D) A parking pass

如果顧客去美食廣場，他們會得到什麼？
(A) 免費飲料。
(B) 30% 的退款。
(C) 折扣優待券。
(D) 停車通行證。

請注意聆聽本題關鍵字 the food court（美食廣場）。獨白後段說道：「the food court will be giving away free $5 vouchers」，由此確認答案為 (C)。

答案改寫 voucher → coupon

• **beverage** 飲料　**refund** 退款

Questions 95–97 refer to the following telephone message and work schedule.

Schedule: *Thursday, March, 2nd*	
Time	**Event**
10:30 A.M.–11:30 A.M.	*Conference Call*
12:00 P.M.–1:20 P.M.	*Lunch Meeting*
1:30 P.M.–3:00 P.M.	*Staff Meeting*
4:00 P.M.–6:00 P.M.	*Meeting at ARF Technology*

時程表：3 月 2 日，星期四	
時間	活動
上午 10 點 30 分到 11 點 30 分	電話會議
中午 12 點到下午 1 點 20 分	午餐會議
下午 1 點 30 分到 3 點	員工會議
下午 4 點到 6 點	赴 ARF 科技開會

W Hello, Beth. This is Jennifer. I was really excited to hear that our two departments are going to be merging. I think it will really improve our efficiency if we're all on the same team. Since [95] the merger will be taking place next week, [96] I thought it would be good to introduce both teams to each other. [97] I know you have a staff meeting this afternoon. How about I bring my team to your meeting and we can do a short introduction then? I know you have to leave to visit a client right after, so let's keep the introductions short. Call me back and let me know what you think.

女 哈囉，貝絲，我是珍妮佛。聽到我們兩個部門要合併，我真的很興奮。如果我們都在同一個團隊，我想這確實會改善我們的效率。由於 [95] 下星期就要進行合併，[96] 我認為介紹兩個團隊彼此認識會很有幫助。[97] 我知道妳今天下午要開員工會議。我把我的團隊帶去妳的會議，然後，我們可以簡短介紹一下彼此，妳覺得如何？我知道，會議一結束妳就要去拜訪客戶，所以簡短介紹一下就好。再回我電話，讓我知道妳的想法。

• **conference call** 電話會議 **department** 部門 **merge (v.)** 使（公司等）合併 **improve** 改善、增進 **efficiency** 效率 **merger (n.)** 合併 **introduce (v.)** 介紹、引見 **introduction (n.)** 介紹、引見 **leave** 離開

95

What is planned for the next week?
(A) A bigger team will be created.*
(B) A new product will be launched.
(C) Some managers will retire.
(D) Some meetings will be canceled.

下星期規劃了何事？
(A) 將會產生一個較大的團隊。
(B) 將發表一款新產品。
(C) 有幾位經理要退休。
(D) 有幾場會議要取消。

請注意聆聽本題關鍵時間點 next week（下週）。獨白中段提到：「the merger will be taking place next week」，表示「即將於下週進行合併」，因此 (A) 為最適當的答案。

• **launch** 把（商品）上市 **retire** 退休 **cancel** 取消

96

Why does the speaker want to meet?
(A) To visit a client's store
(B) To go over some regulations
(C) To introduce some employees*
(D) To explain a new contract

說話者為何想要碰面？
(A) 為了拜訪客戶的商店。
(B) 為了審查一些規章。
(C) 為了介紹一些員工。
(D) 為了解釋一份新合約。

獨白中段建議「應該要介紹彼此認識（I thought it would be good to introduce both teams to each other.）」，因此答案為 (C)。若不小心漏聽這一小段，後方又再度提到 introduction（介紹認識），仍可由此推測出答案。

• **go over** 審查、察看 **regulation** 規則、條例 **explain** 解釋 **contract** 合約

97

Look at the graphic. What time does the speaker want to meet?
(A) At 10:30
(B) At 12:00
(C) At 1:30*
(D) At 4:00

請見圖表。說話者想要什麼時間碰面？
(A) 10 點 30 分。
(B) 12 點。
(C) 1 點 30 分。
(D) 4 點。

由題目和選項內容可以看出，本題要把握的重點為「會面時間」。獨白中段提到了員工會議的時間（I know you have a staff meeting this afternoon.），並隨即表明「預計在對方開會時，帶組員一同前往參加」。因此可以得知時間應為 1:30 P.M. 至 3 P.M. 之間，答案為 (C)。

Questions 98–100 refer to the following talk and map.

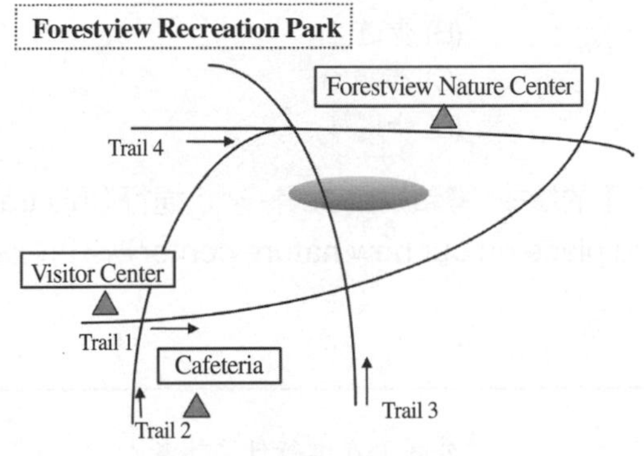

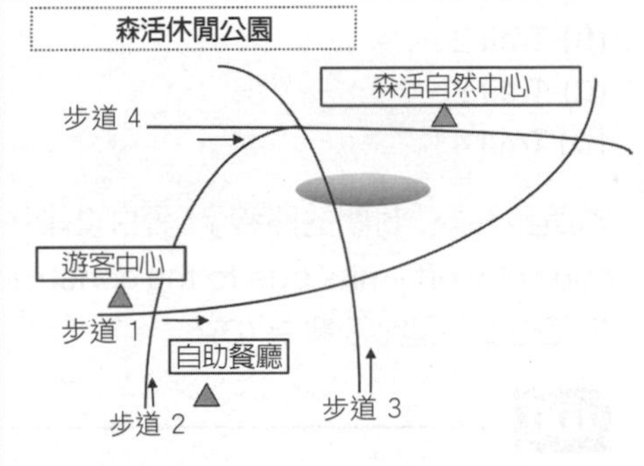

M [98] Welcome to Forestview Recreation Park. We're happy that you chose Forestview for all your outdoor recreation needs. Today, we'll be offering some guided tours of our park. Please take a look at this map. We'll start on Trail 2 where a large chipmunk population lives. You can purchase peanuts to feed the chipmunks for this portion of the tour. From there, we'll travel on the remaining trails along the boardwalks and through the marsh. However, [99] this trail is currently off limits due to the construction taking place on our new nature center. [100] Once the center is complete, you'll be able to partake in our new Nature Education Program. But for now, the construction area is too dangerous to visit.

男 [98] 歡迎來到森活休閒公園。很高興你們選擇森活，來滿足所有的戶外休閒需求。今天，我們會提供園區的導覽。請看一下這份地圖。我們會從步道 2 開始，那裡住著一大群花栗鼠。在這段行程，你們可以買花生餵花栗鼠。從那裡，我們會沿著木棧道，走完其他的步道並穿過沼澤。不過，[99] 由於新的自然中心正在興建中，這條步道目前禁止進入。[100] 一旦中心完工後，你們就可以參加我們新的自然教育計畫。但現在，工程區非常危險，無法參觀。

- **choose** 選擇 **chipmunk** 花栗鼠 **population**（某地區某類）動物（或植物）的總數、人口 **purchase** 購買 **feed** 餵養、飼養 **portion** 部分 **remaining** 剩下的 **boardwalk** 木板路、木板鋪成的步道 **marsh** 沼澤 **currently** 現在、目前 **off limits** 禁止進入 **construction** 建造 **partake** 參加、參與

98

Who is the talk intended for?

(A) Park employees

(B) Botany students

(C) Construction workers

(D) Visitors at a park*

這段話的對象是誰？

(A) 公園的員工。

(B) 植物學的學生。

(C) 營造工人。

(D) 公園的遊客。

由獨白第一句「Welcome to Forestview Recreation Park.（歡迎來到森活休閒公園）」，可以得知答案為 (D)。

• **botany** 植物學

99

Look at the graphic. Which trail is closed to visitors?

(A) Trail 1

(B) Trail 2

(C) Trail 3

(D) Trail 4*

請見圖表。哪一條步道禁止遊客進入？

(A) 步道 1。

(B) 步道 2。

(C) 步道 3。

(D) 步道 4。

本題重點為「封閉的路線」。獨白後段提到「由於施工的緣故，導致道路封閉、禁止通行（this trail is currently off limits due to the construction taking place on our new nature center）」，可由圖中找出施工位置，因此答案為 (D)。

100

What project is the park developing?

(A) A bird-watching club

(B) A research foundation

(C) A study on chipmunks

(D) An educational program*

公園正在進行什麼計畫？

(A) 賞鳥俱樂部。

(B) 研究基金會。

(C) 花栗鼠研究。

(D) 教育計畫。

請注意聆聽「即將施行的專案或計畫」。獨白後段說道：「Once the center is complete, you'll be able to partake in our new Nature Education Education Program.」，表示「待中心完工後，遊客便能參加新設立的教育計畫」，因此答案為 (D)。

• **bird-watching** 賞鳥　**foundation** 基金會　**educational** 有教育意義的

ACTUAL TEST 2
中譯+解析

PART 1 ♫ 05

1

(A) She is trying on a necklace. (A) 她正在試戴項鍊。

(B) She is looking into a store window.* (B) 她正在看商店櫥窗。

(C) She is folding a scarf. (C) 她正在摺一條圍巾。

(D) She is cleaning a glass case. (D) 她正在清理一個玻璃櫃。

請將重點放在照片中出現的人物，並仔細聆聽每一個選項的內容。(B) 客觀描述看向櫥窗內的動作，為正確答案。

- **try on** 試穿（衣服等）、試戴（配件等） **necklace** 項鍊 **fold** 摺疊

2

(A) One of the men is placing his backpack on the floor. (A) 其中一位男子正把背包放到地上。

(B) One of the men is handing out brochures. (B) 其中一位男子正在分發小冊子。

(C) One of the women is holding a flag.* (C) 其中一位女子拿著一面旗子。

(D) One of the women is talking on the phone. (D) 其中一位女子正在講電話。

答案為 (C)，描述最前方女子舉旗的模樣。通常選項中出現 hold 時，即為正確答案。(A) 和 (B) 的內容從照片難以確認；(D) 容易讓人產生混淆，應改為 talk to each other（彼此交談），才會是正解。

- **hand out** 分發 **hold** 握著 **flag** 旗子

3

(A) There's a passenger on a platform. (A) 月台上有位旅客。

(B) The trains are stopped at a station.* (B) 火車停在車站。

(C) Tickets are being purchased from a machine. (C) 透過機器買車票。

(D) Some tracks are being inspected. (D) 一些軌道正在檢查中。

只要看到照片中沒有出現任何人物時，就要先想到錯誤選項中會有現在進行被動式「be being p.p.」，以事物當作主詞。此類句型的後方省略行為者，本意應為「某人正在做某件事」，因此 (C) 和 (D) 分別代表「Someone is purchasing tickets from a machine.」和「Someone is inspecting some tracks.」。由於照片中並未出現人物，因此 (C) 和 (D) 內容皆不符合；(A) 描述月台上「有」乘客，也非答案；正確解釋為 (B)，描述火車靜止的狀態。

- **passenger** 乘客、旅客 **purchase** 購買 **machine** 機器、機械 **inspect** 檢查

4

(A) A woman is strolling on a beach.
(B) A woman is mowing the grass.
(C) A woman is pushing a wheelbarrow near the water.*
(D) A woman is heading toward a bench.

(A) 一名女子正在海灘上散步。
(B) 一名女子正在除草。
(C) 一名女子在近水處推著獨輪手推車。
(D) 一名女子正朝長椅走去。

本題照片的重點在於推著手推車的動作，(C) 的內容符合照片情境，為正確答案。其他的選項僅使用照片中出現的事物（beach、grass、bench）來混淆答題者，並不符合照片情境。

• **stroll** 散步、緩步走　**mow** 割（草坪等的）草　**grass** 草、草地　**wheelbarrow** 獨輪小車、手推車　**head** 朝特定方向前進　**toward** 朝、向　**bench** 長椅、長凳

5

(A) A piece of furniture is on display in a mall.
(B) A vehicle is being parked in a garage.
(C) Some men are stacking some containers.
(D) Some movers are loading a sofa into a truck.*

(A) 購物中心裡展示著一件家具。
(B) 一部車現在停在車庫裡。
(C) 有些人正把一些貨櫃疊起來。
(D) 有些搬家工人正把一張沙發裝上卡車。

(D) 適當描述兩人將沙發搬上卡車的動作，為正確答案；其他選項僅使用照片中出現的事物（a piece of furniture、vehicle、some men），並不符合照片情境，因此在聽到的當下即可排除在外。

• **vehicle** 車輛、運載工具　**garage** 車庫、汽車修理廠　**stack** 堆、疊　**container** 貨櫃　**load** 裝載

6

(A) Some tables are being lined up on a stage.
(B) Plants have been set on top of the tables.
(C) A board has been placed next to the entrance.
(D) Some decorations have been mounted on the walls.*

(A) 正在舞台上把一些桌子排好。
(B) 桌上放了一些植物。
(C) 入口旁擺著一塊板子。
(D) 一些裝飾品固定在牆上。

(A) 省略了行為者，屬於現在進行被動式的句子。因為照片中並未出現人物，所以並不符合照片情境；(B) 包含照片中的植物（plants）和桌子（tables），但位置的說明有誤；(C) 的內容從照片中難以確認；(D) 描述了牆上固定（mounted）畫框等裝飾品（decorations），為正確答案。

• **plant** 植物　**entrance** 入口　**decoration** 裝飾品　**mount** 鑲嵌、固定在……上

PART 2

06

7

How many customers visited the store this morning?
(A) Let's buy them.
(B) The offer ends tomorrow.
(C) Only about 10.*

今天早上有多少客人來過店裡？
(A) 我們把它們買下來吧。
(B) 報價的有效期到明天為止。
(C) 只有大約十個人。

碰到以疑問詞 How 開頭的問句，答題關鍵在於疑問詞後方的單字，請務必仔細聆聽。題目詢問「有多少」顧客來訪，回答 (C) 數字最為適當。

- **offer** 報價、提議 **end** 結束、終止

8

Where is your new cottage located?
(A) It's just past this intersection.*
(B) I haven't seen him today.
(C) It's days from now.

你新買的小屋位在哪裡？
(A) 這個交叉路口過去就是了。
(B) 我今天還沒見到他。
(C) 離現在還有好幾天。

本題為以 Where 開頭的問句，詢問「方位、地點」，(A) 具體回答地點在「過了十字路口之後」，兩句構成完整對話，為正確答案。

- **cottage** 小屋、農舍 **past** 通過、經過 **intersection** 道路交叉口、十字路口

9

Who did you talk to at the restaurant when making the reservation?
(A) His name was Mark.*
(B) Sure, we can book a table for you.
(C) No, I haven't eaten there before.

您訂位時，是和餐廳的哪一位說的？
(A) 他叫馬克。
(B) 當然，我們可以為您預訂一個桌位。
(C) 不，我沒在那裡用餐過。

本題為以 Who 開頭的問句，詢問「和誰説過」，(A) 包含人名「馬克（Mark）」，為正確答案。另外，以疑問詞開頭的問句，不能以 Yes 或 No 回答，因此 (C) 的回應並不適當。

- **reservation (n.)** 預訂 **book** 預訂、預約

10

Would you like to reserve a balcony seat?
(A) Yes, that sounds good.*
(B) No, she didn't.
(C) The local opera house.

您要預訂包廂的位子嗎？
(A) 好啊，聽起來不錯。
(B) 不，她沒有。
(C) 當地的歌劇院。

本句使用的句型為「Would you like to . . . ?」意思為「您要⋯⋯嗎？」。題目詢問「您要預訂包廂席一位嗎？」，(A) 回覆「好（Yes）」，為三個選項中最能和問句構成完整對話的回答。

- **reserve (v.)** 預訂 **local** 當地的、本地的

11

Who submitted these reimbursement forms?
(A) By Tuesday at the latest.
(B) The head of marketing did.*
(C) Sorry, I didn't go.

這些請款單是誰提出的？
(A) 最晚星期二。
(B) 行銷部門的主管。
(C) 抱歉，我沒有去。

本題為以 Who 開頭的問句，詢問「是誰」提交的，(B) 提出人物的相關資訊（行銷部門主管），為正確答案。請記得以 Who 開頭的問句，答句要以人名、職稱、部門名稱或公司名稱回覆。若題目改以 When 開頭，詢問表格的提交期限，則 (A) 便為適當答案。

• **submit** 提出、呈遞　**reimbursement** 退款、償還　**form** 表格　**at the latest** 最晚　**head** 主管

12

Which dates do you need the auditorium for?
(A) From the 3rd to 5th, please.*
(B) It's down the hall.
(C) In the audio-visual room.

你什麼時候需要使用禮堂？
(A) 從 3 日到 5 日，麻煩你。
(B) 在走廊盡頭。
(C) 在視聽室。

題目詢問「哪一天」，(A) 直接回覆具體日期，為正確答案。在此補充，若題目改以「Which room . . . ?」開頭，詢問具體地點，則 (C) 便為適當答案。

• **auditorium** 禮堂、觀眾席　**hall** 走廊、門廳　**audio-visual** 視聽的、視聽教學的

13

This lunch set includes a beverage, doesn't it?
(A) A garage is included.
(B) It was slightly undercooked.
(C) That's correct.*

午餐的套餐包含飲料，不是嗎？
(A) 包含車庫。
(B) 有點不夠熟。
(C) 沒錯。

自己已知的事實（套餐包含飲料），再次向對方確認時，會使用附加問句。這時可用 Yes 或 No 回答，而 (C) 屬於更加積極的回應；(A) 重複使用題目句中的單字 include，並非答案；(B) 僅使用了與「飲料、午餐」相關的單字，不符合文意。

• **beverage** 飲料　**slightly** 稍微地、輕微地　**undercooked** 未煮熟的　**correct** 正確的

14

Aren't we traveling on the same bus?
(A) The bag is over there.
(B) No, I'm on an earlier one.*
(C) He works for a travel agency.

我們不是搭同一班公車嗎？
(A) 袋子在那裡。
(B) 不，我搭較早的一班。
(C) 他在旅行社上班。

碰到否定問句時，只要先將 not 拿掉，視為一般問句，就能更易掌握住題目的重點。本題問句的重點在於「是否搭乘相同的公車」，(B) 的回覆為否定，並說明：「搭乘較早的班車」，與問句構成完整對話，為最適當的答案。題目句中的 bus 可以替換成代名詞 one，這點請特別熟記。

• **early** 早的、早期的　**travel agency** 旅行社

15

Can you tell me who ordered the seafood spaghetti?
(A) I prefer baked salmon.
(B) In the cafeteria.
(C) The man at table 5.*

你能告訴我是誰點了海鮮義大利麵嗎？
(A) 我比較喜歡烤鮭魚。
(B) 在自助餐廳。
(C) 5 號桌的男子。

碰到「Can you tell me . . . ?」或「Do you know . . . ?」等間接問句時，請務必仔細聆聽子句當中的疑問詞。本題問句的重點在於「who ordered . . . ?」，「是誰」點的，因此 (C) 為最適當的答案。

• order 點菜　seafood 海鮮　prefer 更喜歡　baked 烘烤的　salmon 鮭魚

16

Were you able to find the replacement part needed to fix the sink?
(A) I am already working on the next job.*
(B) Sixty words per minute.
(C) Under 30 dollars.

你找到修理水槽所需的替換零件了嗎？
(A) 我已經進行下一個工作了。
(B) 每分鐘 60 字。
(C) 不到 30 元。

本題除了要了解題目為「找到零件了嗎」之外，還要聽懂 (A) 的回覆「（早就找到了），並且已經在做下一件事了」，雖然並未針對問題直接回答，仍和問句構成完整對話。

• replacement 代替、更換　part 零件　fix 修理

17

Please tell me when you're finished with the photocopier.
(A) For our online photos.
(B) Sure, this won't take long.*
(C) No, the page numbering is wrong.

等你用完影印機，請告訴我一聲。
(A) 我們的網路照片要用。
(B) 當然，不會太久。
(C) 不，頁碼編錯了。

本題可以想像成在影印店內的對話內容，題目句為「完成後請通知我」，答案為 (B) 的回覆：「沒問題（Sure），很快就會完成」。

• photocopier 影印機　wrong 錯誤的

18

Should we provide food at the workshop or just something to drink?
(A) Some snacks would be nice.*
(B) At 2:30, every day.
(C) He provided transportation for the participants.

我們的工作坊要提供餐點，還是只有飲料就好？
(A) 一些點心應該不錯。
(B) 每天兩點半。
(C) 他提供與會者交通接送。

碰到題目為選擇疑問句時，可以預想到答案應為問句中所包含的兩種選項之一，或是排除這兩種選項，以其他內容回覆。題目詢問「要準備食物還是飲料」，(A) 婉轉回覆「可以準備一些點心」，為正確答案。

• provide 提供　snack 小吃、點心　transportation 運輸、交通車輛　participant 參與者

19

What's the phone extension for the web designer?
(A) From the 11th of October.
(B) I'm afraid she has the day off.*
(C) By releasing the tension.

網頁設計師的分機是幾號？
(A) 從 10 月 11 日起。
(B) 抱歉，她休假。
(C) 透過釋放壓力。

本題的重點為詢問「分機號碼為何」，(B) 並未具體回答出號碼，而是回覆「對方休假中，可能不方便通話」，亦符合文意，使兩句構成完整對話，為正確答案。PART 2 中常會出現這類需要特別思考，不容易直接找出答案的題型。在此補充，若選項中出現 I'm afraid，通常會是正確答案。

• **extension** 電話分機　**day off** 休息日、休假日　**release** 釋放、放鬆　**tension** 緊張

20

Jennifer Brown only paints in oil, right?
(A) Okay, we'll check if it's in stock.
(B) No, I've seen her watercolor pieces as well.*
(C) Boiled or fried?

珍妮佛・布朗只畫油畫，對嗎？
(A) 好，我們會查查是否有存貨。
(B) 不是，我也看過她的水彩畫作品。
(C) 水煮的還是油炸的？

自己已知的事實（只畫油畫），再次向對方確認時，會使用附加問句。(B) 回覆表示「也曾看過她畫水彩畫」，最符合文意，為正確答案。

• **in stock** 有現貨或存貨　**piece**（藝術）作品　**boiled** 水煮的

21

How will the crew be able to fix the elevator if the building is locked?
(A) It stopped between the 9th and 10th floor.
(B) The security guard was told to let them in.*
(C) The safety inspection will happen on Monday.

如果大樓上鎖，工作人員要如何修理電梯？
(A) 它停在九樓和十樓中間。
(B) 警衛已接獲通知讓他們進來。
(C) 星期一將進行安全檢查。

疑問詞 How 開頭的問句，用來詢問「辦法」。本題問「人員無法進出大樓，該如何修理電梯」，(B) 的回覆為「已經跟警衛說好讓他們進去」，兩句構成完整對話，為最適當的回答。在此補充，因為題目中提到「電梯故障」的情況，(A) 的內容極易讓人誤以為有所關聯，請特別留意。

• **crew** 一組工作人員　**lock** 鎖上　**security** 安全、防衛　**safety** 平安、安全設施　**inspection** 檢查

22

Where should I hang the dentist's professional certification?
(A) Perhaps above his desk.*
(B) For Dr. Batica.
(C) Next Wednesday.

我該把牙醫師的執業證書掛在哪裡？
(A) 也許在他辦公桌的上方。
(B) 給巴緹卡醫師。
(C) 下星期三。

本題為以疑問詞 Where 開頭的問句，詢問證書吊掛的「地點」，(A) 告知具體地點（辦公桌背牆上方），為正確答案。

• **hang** 把……掛起　**dentist** 牙醫　**certification** 證明、證書　**perhaps** 大概、或許　**above** 在……上面

23

Why did the manager cancel the staff meeting?
(A) We don't have a meeting?*
(B) They will receive it soon.
(C) Almost half of the team members.

經理為何取消員工會議？
(A) 我們不開會了？
(B) 他們很快就會收到。
(C) 幾乎一半的團隊成員。

本題詢問「會議為何取消」，(A) 以「不開會了嗎」反問，為最適當的反應。PART 2 中，以反問方式回覆大多是正確答案。最近這類跳脫一般思維邏輯，以反問作為答案的命題方式十分常見。

• **cancel** 取消　**receive** 收到、得到　**almost** 幾乎、差不多　**half** 一半

24

How often do you return to Montreal to visit?
(A) My parents don't live there anymore.*
(B) Yes, it is a huge city.
(C) I usually take the train.

你多久回蒙特婁探訪一次？
(A) 我父母已經不住那裡了。
(B) 是啊，那是個大城市。
(C) 我通常搭火車。

本題詢問的重點為「有多常去」，(A) 並未回答次數或是頻率，而是出乎意料地答覆「父母現在已經不住在那裡了（以此表示自己已經不去了）」，為正確答案。再次提醒，以疑問詞開頭的問句，不能以 Yes 或 No 答覆，聽到的當下即可刪除該選項。

• **return** 返回　**huge** 龐大的

25

Why isn't Mr. Borgald in his office?
(A) I think it started at 2:30.
(B) All division heads are in a meeting.*
(C) Take the stairs at the end of the hall.

博高先生為何不在辦公室？
(A) 我想是兩點半開始的。
(B) 所有部門主管都在開會。
(C) 走通道盡頭的樓梯。

疑問詞 Why 用來詢問「原因」，本題詢問「為什麼」不在辦公室，(B) 省略了 because（因為），回答「全體主管都在開會」，為最適當的答案。本題必須先聯想「博高先生即為主管」，才能順利解答，屬於難度較高的題目。

• **division**（機關、公司等的）部門

26

Which one of us should speak first?
(A) Yes, he did.
(B) Go ahead.*
(C) The first customer.

我們誰要先說？
(A) 是的，是他做的。
(B) 您先請。
(C) 第一個顧客。

本題為「誰要先說」、詢問意見的問句。(B) 向對方表示「您先請」，為正確答案。本題為以疑問詞開頭的問句，不能以 Yes 或 No 答覆，所以可以優先刪除 (A) 選項；(C) 僅重複使用題目中出現的單字 first，回答內容不符合文意。

27

I can't reach the bulb to change it.
(A) Try standing on a chair.*
(B) The light bulbs are in the closet.
(C) This package is quite light.

我手碰不到燈泡，沒辦法更換。
(A) 試試站在椅子上。
(B) 燈泡在櫃子裡。
(C) 這個包裹相當輕。

本題表示「手無法碰到」，(A) 給予建議「站在椅子上（就可以碰到）」，兩句構成完整對話，為正確答案。

• **reach** 伸出手臂（拿或觸摸） **bulb** 電燈泡 **closet** 壁櫥、衣櫥 **quite** 相當、頗

28

Why don't we just postpone the job fair until April?
(A) Yes, we have a booth at the job fair.
(B) The convention center charges cancellation fees.*
(C) His interview is tomorrow morning.

我們何不把就業博覽會延到四月？
(A) 是的，我們在就業博覽會有攤位。
(B) 會議中心要索取取消的費用。
(C) 他的面試是在明天早上。

本題使用了「Why don't we . . . ?」意思為「何不……？」，建議「將就業博覽會延期」，(B) 回答「（那樣做的話）得賠償取消費用」，為正確答案。

• **postpone** 延期、延緩 **charge** 收費、索價 **cancellation** 取消 **fee** 費用

29

How soon can I expect a reply to my loan application?
(A) No, it's a business loan.
(B) We will phone you in a few days.*
(C) Please reply by e-mail.

我的貸款申請預計多快能得到回覆？
(A) 不是，是商業貸款。
(B) 我們幾天內會打電話給您。
(C) 請以電子郵件回覆。

本題詢問「多快（何時）可以得到答覆」，(B) 回答了時間資訊「幾天內」，與題目句構成完整對話。碰到以疑問詞 How 的問句時，請仔細聆聽後方出現的單字。

• **expect** 預期 **reply** 答覆 **loan** 貸款 **application** 申請

30

Are you almost finished packing or do you need more time?

(A) Our train doesn't leave until 4:00.*

(B) The package arrived yesterday.

(C) Is Diana finishing the report?

你差不多打包好了，還是要再多一點時間？

(A) 我們的火車四點才開。

(B) 包裹昨天送來的。

(C) 黛安娜完成報告了嗎？

本題為選擇疑問句，詢問行李已經整理完畢、或是還需要整理的時間，可以預想到答案應為此兩種選項擇一，或是以其他內容回覆。(A) 以其他內容回覆：「火車於四點發車（表示不急、可以慢慢來，時間非常寬裕）」，為正確答案。(B) 提到 package，僅與題目中的單字 packing 發音相似，並非正解；(C) 提及題目中的動詞 finish，意圖誤導答題者，為常見的陷阱選項。

• **pack** 裝（箱）、將（某物）裝入行李　**leave** 離開　**arrive**（郵件、物品等）被送來

31

We don't have any more room in our Dalhousie warehouse.

(A) Yes, we have a room available on the second floor.

(B) That's why I suggested using the one in Hampstead.*

(C) Just two kilometers away from the main road.

我們在戴爾豪斯的倉庫已經沒有空位了。

(A) 是的，我們二樓有一間空房。

(B) 所以，我才建議用漢普斯德那個倉庫。

(C) 離主要道路只有兩公里。

本題表示「倉儲空間不足」，(B) 的回答為「建議使用其他倉庫（warehouse → one）」，兩句構成完整對話，為最適當的選項。

• **room** 場所、空間　**warehouse** 倉庫、貨棧　**available** 可用的　**suggest** 建議

PART 3 07

Questions 32–34 refer to the following conversation.

M [32] I'm interested in buying a new T-pad tablet computer. I've been waiting for it to be released.	男 [32] 我有意購買一台新的 T-pad 平板電腦。我一直在等產品發表。
W Yes, many customers have inquired about the T-pad series recently.	女 好的，最近有許多顧客詢問 T-pad 系列。
M [33] What sizes does it come in?	男 [33] 它有哪些尺寸？
W It comes in three sizes. 6 inch, 8 inch, and 11 inch. However, since we've had a lot of preorders for this tablet series, we don't have all the sizes in stock now.	女 有三種尺寸，6 吋、8 吋和 11 吋。不過，由於我們收到很多這系列平板電腦的預購單，現在不是所有尺寸都有現貨。
M Oh, I see. Well, what sizes do you have?	男 噢，了解。嗯，你們有哪些尺寸？
W We have both the 6 inch and the 11 inch. If you'd like the 8 inch, though, I can order it from the warehouse for you.	女 6 吋和 11 吋都有。不過，如果您想要 8 吋的，我可以幫您從倉庫訂。
M No, that's okay. I'm interested in the 11 inch anyhow. I prefer a bigger screen.	男 不用，沒關係。反正我有興趣的是 11 吋。我比較喜歡大一點的螢幕。
W Okay, great. [34] Let me calculate your total.	女 好的，太好了。[34] 我算一下您的總金額。

• **be interested in (+ V-ing)** 對……感興趣 **release** 發行、發表 **inquire** 詢問 **recently** 最近、近來 **come in** 有（貨） **preorder** 預購 **in stock** 有現貨或存貨 **order** 訂購 **warehouse** 倉庫 **prefer** 更喜歡 **calculate** 計算

32

What are the speakers discussing?
(A) A suitcase
(B) A printer
(C) A monitor
(D) A tablet computer*

說話者在討論什麼？
(A) 行李箱。
(B) 印表機。
(C) 螢幕。
(D) 平板電腦。

對話開頭，男子便說道：「I'm interested in buying a new T-pad tablet computer.」，因此答案為 (D)。

33

What does the man ask about?
(A) The total cost
(B) The available sizes*
(C) The warranty options
(D) The free accessories

男子詢問什麼？
(A) 總金額。
(B) 現有的尺寸。
(C) 保固的選項。
(D) 免費的配件。

請仔細聆聽男子所說的話，可以聽到男子詢問「有哪些尺寸（What sizes does it come in?）」，因此答案為 (B)。

• **cost** 費用 **warranty** 保證書、擔保 **option** 選擇、可選擇的東西 **free** 免費的

34

What will the woman most likely do next?
(A) Request payment*
(B) Consult a manager
(C) Register an ID
(D) Return an item

女子接下來最有可能做什麼？
(A) 要求付款。
(B) 請教經理。
(C) 註冊一個帳號。
(D) 退回一件物品。

當題目詢問「. . . do next?」時，對話後半部會出現解題的關鍵線索。請仔細聆聽女子所說的話，最後一句說道：「Let me calculate your total.」，為男子結帳，因此 (A) 為最適當的答案。

• **request** 要求、請求　**payment** 付款、支付　**consult** 與……商量、請教　**register** 登記、註冊

Questions 35–37 refer to the following conversation.

M Hi, Jen. This is Ronald calling. Sorry, but I'm stuck in traffic now. There's an accident on the highway, so [35] I'm probably not going to be able to pick you up for the company dinner.	**男** 嗨，珍，我是羅納德。抱歉，但我現在遇到塞車，路上有車禍發生，所以，[35] 我很可能沒辦法去接妳參加公司的晚宴。
W Thanks for calling to let me know. I can take a taxi, then.	**女** 謝謝你打電話告訴我。既然這樣，我可以搭計程車。
M Well, [36] why don't you call Maxwell from Marketing to see if he can pick you up? I think he lives near you.	**男** 嗯，[36] 妳何不打給行銷部的麥斯威爾，看看他能不能去接妳？我想他就住在妳家附近。
W Right. I heard he's going to pick up Lila, and I know where she lives. It's not far from here. [37] I'll call him right now and arrange something.	**女** 沒錯。我聽說他要去接萊拉，我知道她住哪裡，離這裡不遠。[37] 我馬上打給他，安排一下。

• **stuck** 被困住　**traffic** 交通　**accident** 意外事故　**probably** 很可能　**arrange** 安排

35

Why did the man call the woman?
(A) To inform of a change of plans*
(B) To offer to call a car service
(C) To explain an event schedule
(D) To reschedule an appointment

男子為何打電話給女子？
(A) 通知計畫有變。
(B) 提議打電話叫車。
(C) 解釋活動的時程表。
(D) 重新安排會面。

對話第一段，男子表示，因公路上發生交通事故，車子卡在車陣中動彈不得，故無法送女方去公司聚餐（I'm probably not going to be able to pick you up for the company dinner.），因此 (A) 為最適當的答案。

• **inform** 通知、告知　**explain** 解釋　**appointment**（會面的）約定、（正式的）約會

36

What does the man suggest?
(A) Canceling an event
(B) Using public transit
(C) Asking a coworker for help*
(D) Borrowing a neighbor's car

男子有何建議？
(A) 取消一個活動。
(B) 利用公共交通運輸系統。
(C) 請求同事的協助。
(D) 借用鄰居的車。

對話第二段，男子說道：「why don't you call Maxwell from Marketing to see if he can pick you up?」，建議女方打電話給麥斯威爾（Maxwell），請他載女子去，因此答案為 (C)。「Why don't you . . . ?」表示「建議」或是「勸告」，通常為解題關鍵。

答案改寫 Maxwell from marketing → coworker

• **transit** 公共交通運輸系統 **coworker** 同事 **borrow** 借入、借用

37

What does the woman say she will do?
(A) Change a reservation
(B) Contact a colleague*
(C) Call a tow truck
(D) Pick up a coworker

女子說她會做什麼？
(A) 更改預約。
(B) 聯絡同事。
(C) 打電話叫拖吊車。
(D) 開車去接同事。

請仔細聆聽女子所說的話。對話最後，她回覆：「I'll call him right now and arrange something.」，由此確認答案為 (B)。

答案改寫 call → contact

• **reservation** 預訂 **colleague** 同事 **tow** 拖、拉、牽引

Questions 38–40 refer to the following conversation.

W [38] I received a text message that a package was being delivered to my home, but when I checked, the package was not there. My name is June Shane.	**女** [38] 我收到簡訊通知，有包裹送到我家，但當我查看時，家裡並沒有包裹。我叫君萱。
M Let me check the computer system. Yes, it looks like the package is on its way back to this location. [39] The traffic was really bad because of the festival downtown, so we're a bit behind schedule, but it should arrive by 3:30 P.M. You can pick it up then or wait for it to be delivered again tomorrow.	**男** 我查一下電腦系統。是的，看來包裹正在運送的途中。[39] 因為市中心的節慶活動，交通實在很擁擠，所以我們比預定時間晚了些，但它應該在下午三點半前會到。你可以到時領取，或等包裹明天再送一次。
W Okay, [40] I have to get some groceries at the store next door, so I'll do that and then come back for the package later.	**女** 好，[40] 我必須去隔壁買些日用品，那我先去買東西，晚點再回來領包裹。

• **package** 包裹 **deliver** 投遞、傳送 **check** 檢查、核對
be on one's way back to 在某人／某物回某地的路上 **location** 位置 **traffic** 交通
behind schedule 比預定時間晚、落後於原計畫 **arrive** （郵件、物品等）被送來 **grocery** 食品雜貨

38

What are the speakers discussing?
(A) A new office location
(B) A store's hours
(C) A package delivery*
(D) A change of schedule

說話者在討論何事？
(A) 新的辦公室地點。
(B) 商店的營業時間。
(C) 包裹的遞送。
(D) 時程表的變動。

從對話第一段「I received a text message that a package was being delivered to my home, but when I checked, the package was not there.」可以聽到 package 和 delivered，得以確認答案為 (C)。在對話前半部，通常可以找到對話的主旨。

• **delivery (n.)** 投遞、傳送

39

Why is the man's company behind the schedule?
(A) A new store was opened.
(B) Some items were lost.
(C) A few workers were sick.
(D) Some roads were congested.*

男子的公司為何比預定時間晚？
(A) 新店面開幕。
(B) 有些物品遺失。
(C) 有些員工生病。
(D) 有些道路擁塞。

聆聽時，請務必掌握本題重點為「延遲送件的原因」。男子在對話中提到「因為交通壅塞，導致送件時間延遲（The traffic was really bad because of the festival downtown, so we're a bit behind schedule.）」，由此確認答案為 (D)。

• **item** 物品　**sick** 生病的　**congest** （使）擁塞

40

What does the woman say she will do next?
(A) Go to a supermarket*
(B) Wait for an item at home
(C) Cancel a purchase
(D) Visit another post office

女子說，她接下來要做什麼？
(A) 去超市。
(B) 在家等一件貨品。
(C) 取消購買。
(D) 去另一家郵局。

本題問句以 do next 結尾，詢問對話結束之後，女子將要做的事情。通常可以從對話後半部聽到相關線索。女子在最後一句說道：「I have to get some groceries at the store next door, so I'll do that and then come back for the package later」，表示打算先去買些日用品，回來後再領取包裹，因此 (A) 為最適當的答案。

答案改寫 store → supermarket

• **cancel** 取消　**purchase** 購買　**post office** 郵局

Questions 41–43 refer to the following conversation.

M Hi, [41] this is Mark Stavros from Stavros Home Improvements. Last year, you hired us to install new flooring in the main floor of your home. [42] I'd like to let you know that we're currently having a special promotion and offering a 25% discount on all floor installations.	男 嗨，[41] 我是史達福居家裝修的馬克史達福。去年，您曾僱我們去您家裡一樓鋪設新地板。[42] 我想通知您，我們目前有特別促銷，所有的地板安裝工程都打七五折。
W Well, my main floor is still in great condition, but I've been thinking about installing carpeting in my upstairs bedrooms. Would that also be discounted?	女 嗯，我一樓的地板狀況還很良好，但我一直想在樓上的臥室鋪地毯。那也有打折嗎？
M Yes, that would still be considered a floor installation. [43] If you'd like, I can send someone by next week to take measurements and discuss carpeting styles.	男 有，那也視為地板安裝。[43] 如果您願意，我可以下星期派個人過去丈量並討論地毯的樣式。

- **improvement** 改進、改善 **hire** 僱用 **install (v.)** 安裝 **flooring** （總稱）室內地板 **currently** 現在 **promotion** （商品等的）促銷 **offer** 給予、提供 **installation (n.)** 安裝 **condition** 情況、狀態 **consider** 認為、把……視為 **measurement** 測量

41

What type of services does the man's company offer? 男子的公司提供何種服務？

(A) Vehicle upgrades (A) 車輛升級。
(B) Home renovations* (B) 住宅翻修。
(C) Window cleaning (C) 窗戶清潔。
(D) Appliance installations (D) 家電安裝。

男子在開頭介紹：「this is Mark Stavros from Stavros Home Improvements」，提及公司名稱「史達福居家裝修（Stavros Home Improvements）」，由此得知答案為 (B)。

- **vehicle** 車輛、運載工具 **renovation** 更新、修理 **appliance** 器具、設備

42

Why is the man calling? 男子為何打電話？

(A) To return a phone call (A) 回一通電話。
(B) To offer a free service (B) 提供免費服務。
(C) To discuss a payment plan (C) 討論付款方案。
(D) To advertise a promotion* (D) 宣傳促銷活動。

男子在對話第一段提到：「I'd like to let you know that we're currently having a special promotion and offering a 25% discount on all floor installations.」，由此確認答案為 (D)。當題目詢問致電原因和目的時，在對話前半部，通常可以聽到關鍵線索。

- **free** 免費的 **payment** 付款、支付

43

What does the man offer to do for the woman?
(A) Provide a bigger discount
(B) Mail some carpet samples
(C) Send an employee*
(D) Replace some old items

男子提議為女子做何事？
(A) 提供更大的折扣。
(B) 郵寄一些地毯的樣品。
(C) 派一個員工來。
(D) 更換一些舊的物品。

請仔細聆聽男子所說的話。最後一句，男子提議：「如果方便的話，他打算派人過去量尺寸（If you'd like, I can send someone by next week to take measurements and discuss carpeting styles.）」，因此答案為 (C)。

答案改寫 someone → employee

• **provide** 提供　**replace** 取代、更換

Questions 44–46 refer to the following conversation.

W	[44] Good afternoon, and thank you for calling Collingwood Insurance. This is Samita speaking. How can I help you?	**女**	[44] 午安，謝謝您致電柯林伍德保險公司。我是莎米塔，請問需要什麼服務？
M	Hi, I'm interested in purchasing life insurance packages for me and my family members. [45] Can you give me a quote of how much it will cost to insure a family of five?	**男**	嗨，我有興趣為我和我的家人購買壽險。[45] 妳可以報價給我，一家五口投保的費用是多少嗎？
W	Well, in order for us to determine your monthly rate, your family members will need to undergo a routine health exam. We have a staff doctor who visits our office every Thursday. Would next Thursday work for you?	**女**	嗯，為了確定你們的月付額，您的家人需要接受例行健康檢查。我們有位專任醫師，每星期四會到辦公室來。您下星期四方便嗎？
M	Actually, I have a business meeting that day. [46] How about the following week?	**男**	其實，我那天有商務會議。[46] 再下一個星期呢？
W	Sure. Does 2:30 work for you?	**女**	當然可以。兩點半您方便嗎？
M	That would be fine. Thank you.	**男**	可以。謝謝妳。

• **insurance** 保險　**be interested in (+ V-ing)** 對⋯⋯感興趣　**purchase** 購買　**quote (n.)** 報價　**cost** 花費　**insure** 為⋯⋯投保　**in order to** 為了⋯⋯　**determine** 確定、決定　**rate** 費用、價格　**undergo** 接受（治療、檢查等）　**routine** 慣例、慣常的程序　**health exam** 健康檢查　**following** 接著的

44

Where does the woman work?
(A) At a doctor's office
(B) At an insurance company*
(C) At a sales office
(D) At a dental clinic

女子在哪裡工作？
(A) 診所。
(B) 保險公司。
(C) 業務部。
(D) 牙醫診所。

對話第一段，女子說道：「Good afternoon, and thank you for calling Collingwood Insurance.」，當中提及公司名稱「柯林伍德保險公司（Collingwood Insurance）」，由此可知答案為 (B)。

• **dental** 牙醫的、牙科的

45

What information does the man ask for?
(A) A list of services
(B) A doctor's schedule
(C) The location of a clinic
(D) The price of a service*

男子詢問何項資訊？
(A) 服務的清單。
(B) 醫師的班表。
(C) 診所的地點。
(D) 服務的費用。

對話第一段，男子要求對方提供家人投保的相關報價（Can you give me a quote of how much it will cost to insure a family of five?），因此答案為 (D)。

答案改寫 quote → price

46

What does the man imply when he says, "I have a business meeting that day"?
(A) He needs another appointment.*
(B) He will wear a formal suit.
(C) He will visit another location.
(D) He doesn't mind traveling far.

當男子說「我那天有商務會議」，意指什麼？
(A) 他需要約別的時間會面。
(B) 他會穿正式的西裝。
(C) 他會造訪另一個地點。
(D) 他不介意長途旅程。

聆聽時，請特別注意題目句後方提及的內容「How about the following week?」，詢問下週時間是否可行，因此 (A) 為最適當的答案。

- formal 正式的

Questions 47–49 refer to the following conversation.

M Hi, Jane. How is everything going?	男 嗨，珍，一切都順利嗎？
W Good. Hey, I wanted to ask you something. [47] I'm thinking of taking a trip to Spain, and I heard you just got cheap tickets to France.	女 很好。嘿，我想問你一件事。[47] 我在考慮要去西班牙旅行，我聽說你剛剛買到前往法國的便宜機票。
M Yes, [48] the tickets were really cheap, because I used the new online ticket website tix4cheap.com. I was able to save several hundred dollars and even got some vouchers for restaurants and hotels, too.	男 是的，[48] 那機票真的很便宜，因為我上了新的線上機票網站 tix4cheap.com。我因此得以省下好幾百元，甚至還得到一些餐廳和旅館的優待券。
W Wow, that sounds great. Can anybody use that website?	女 哇，聽起來真棒。任何人都可以用那個網站嗎？
M Well, you have to sign up for a membership. If you pay to upgrade the membership, you get even more discounts.	男 嗯，妳必須註冊成為會員。如果妳付費升級會員資格，會得到更多折扣。
W [49] Is it expensive? I don't know how often I will use it, so paying for the membership might not be worth it.	女 [49] 會很貴嗎？我不知道我會多常用到，所以，付費會員也許不划算。
M Well, you get the first six months free, so I think it'll be worth it in the end.	男 嗯，前六個月是免費的，所以我想最後是值得的。

- cheap 便宜的、廉價的　save 節省　several 數個的　voucher 票券　sign up for 註冊參加
expensive 高價的、昂貴的　worth 值得（做……）　in the end 最後

47

What does the woman want to do?
(A) Rent a house overseas
(B) Sign up for a mailing list
(C) Purchase airline tickets*
(D) Upgrade a membership

女子想要做什麼？
(A) 在海外租房子。
(B) 註冊加入郵寄名單。
(C) 購買機票。
(D) 升級會員資格。

對話第一段，女子想要詢問對方問題，她打算去西班牙旅遊，聽說男子曾買過便宜的機票（I'm thinking of taking a trip to Spain, and I heard you just got cheap tickets to France.），因此 (C) 為最適當的答案。

- **rent** 租用

48

What does the man recommend?
(A) Going to a travel agency
(B) Buying a lifetime membership
(C) Using a new travel website*
(D) Calling an airline directly

男子推薦什麼？
(A) 去找旅行社。
(B) 買終身會員。
(C) 使用新的旅遊網站。
(D) 直接打電話給航空公司。

請仔細聆聽男子所說的話。男子表示：「the tickets were really cheap, because I used the new online ticket website tix4cheap.com.」，因此答案為 (C)。

答案改寫 online ticket website → travel website

- **recommend** 推薦、介紹

49

What is the woman concerned about?
(A) A delay in payment
(B) The price of a membership*
(C) A missing coupon book
(D) The location of an airport

女子擔心什麼？
(A) 付款延後。
(B) 會員費。
(C) 整本優惠券遺失。
(D) 機場的位置。

聆聽時，請務必掌握本題的重點為「女子擔憂的事情」。對話後半部，女子詢問會費是否很高（Is it expensive?），以消極口吻表示不確定自己是否會經常使用，擔心繳了會費反倒不划算，因此答案為 (B)。

- **delay** 延緩、耽擱

Questions 50–52 refer to the following conversation.

M Hello, Ms. Piper. It's Marcel Shumaker. [50] Did you get a chance to look at the design samples for your advertisement? I e-mailed them yesterday.	男 哈囉，派普太太，我是馬塞爾・許梅克。[50] 您抽空看過廣告的設計樣本了嗎？我昨天用電子郵件寄給您了。
W Hi, Marcel. Yes, I'm looking at them now. I really like sample A. [51] I think the font is very attractive, and I especially love the new store logo you came up with.	女 嗨，馬塞爾。是的，我現在正在看。我真的很喜歡樣本A。[51] 我覺得字型很吸引人，尤其喜歡你們想出的新商標。
M I agree. I think sample A fits [50] your store's style very well. [52] Would you like me to make the words "Summer Sale" a brighter color of red?	男 我也認同。我認為樣本A非常適合 [50] 貴店的風格。[52] 您要我把「夏季特賣」的字樣，用比較亮的紅色嗎？
W Yes, that sounds like a good idea, especially since the advertisement is mainly to let people know about our big upcoming sale.	女 好啊，聽起來是個好主意，尤其是因為，這則廣告主要是讓人們知道我們即將開跑的夏季大特賣。

• **attractive** 有吸引力的、引人注目的 **especially** 特別、尤其 **come up with** （針對問題等）想出
agree 同意、贊同 **fit** 符合、適合於 **mainly** 主要地 **upcoming** 即將來臨的

50

Who most likely is the woman?
(A) A graphic designer
(B) A store owner*
(C) A newspaper reporter
(D) A web developer

女子最有可能是誰？
(A) 平面設計師。
(B) 商店店主。
(C) 報社記者。
(D) 網頁開發工程師。

對話第一段，男子詢問對方是否已經看過廣告設計初稿（Did you get a chance to look at the design samples for your advertisement?），根據文意可得知答案為 (B)。另外，男子在對話中段向女子提到 your store，再次確認答案為 (B)。

• **owner** 所有人 **developer** 開發者

51

What is the woman pleased about?
(A) Some seasonal discounts
(B) A new logo design*
(C) The price of a service
(D) The annual sales results

女子對什麼感到滿意？
(A) 一些季節性的折扣。
(B) 新的商標設計。
(C) 服務的費用。
(D) 年度特賣的結果。

對話第一段，女子説道：「I think the font is very attractive, and I especially love the new store logo you came up with.」，表示自己很滿意字型及新的商標圖案設計，因此答案為 (B)。

• **seasonal** 季節的、季節性的 **result** 結果、效果

52

What does the man offer to do?
(A) Move a company logo
(B) Add a border to a design
(C) Enlarge the size of a picture
(D) Change the color of some words*

男子提議做什麼？
(A) 移除公司的商標。
(B) 為設計加邊線。
(C) 放大照片。
(D) 更改某些字的顏色。

請仔細聆聽男子所說的話，並特別注意「建議」的內容。在對話後半段：「Would you like me to make the words "Summer Sale" a brighter color of red?」，男子詢問是否將紅色字體調亮，因此答案為 (D)。

- **border** 邊緣、邊界　**enlarge** 放大

Questions 53–55 refer to the following conversation.

M Rebecca, why are you still in the office? It's after 6 P.M. [53] I thought you had dinner plans tonight?	男 蕾貝卡，妳怎麼還在辦公室？已經過了六點，[53] 我以為妳今晚有晚餐約會？
W Yes, well, unfortunately I won't be able to leave for a while. I'm still working on some customer feedback reports, and it's not going well.	女 是的，嗯，很遺憾，我暫時還無法離開。我還在忙著做顧客回饋意見報告，而且不太順利。
M Oh no. What happened?	男 噢，不。怎麼回事？
W Well, the Rotary Golf Club has complained that some of our landscapers damaged their fountains last week when they were cutting the grass. [54] I'm so worried because I'm not sure how to convince them to remain our customer.	女 嗯，扶輪高爾夫球社抱怨，我們的園藝設計師上星期除草時，弄壞了他們的噴水池。[54] 我很擔心，因為我不確定要怎麼說服他們繼續作我們的客戶。
M That's too bad. Well, I'm on my way to see the manager now. [55] I'll bring it up with him and let you know what he says before I leave, okay?	男 那真是太糟了。嗯，我現在正要去找經理。[55] 我會和他談這件事，並在我離開前，告訴妳他怎麼說，好嗎？

- **unfortunately** 遺憾地　**leave** 離開　**for a while** 暫時　**complain** 抱怨　**landscaper** 園藝設計師、庭園設計師　**damage** 毀壞　**fountain** 噴泉、噴水池　**convince** 說服　**remain** 保持、仍是　**bring . . . up** 提起⋯⋯、談到⋯⋯

53

What does the woman imply when she says, "I won't be able to leave for a while"?
(A) She had to change her plans.*
(B) She is waiting for someone.
(C) She has already eaten dinner.
(D) She doesn't have a car now.

女子說「我暫時無法離開」，意指什麼？
(A) 她必須改變她的計畫。
(B) 她在等某個人。
(C) 她已經吃過晚餐。
(D) 她現在沒有車。

為了掌握題目句前後的文意，請仔細聆聽對話內容。男子以為女子今晚有約（I thought you had dinner plans tonight?），根據女子的回應，可以得知答案為 (A)。

54

What is the woman worried about?
(A) Presenting her findings to her boss
(B) Finishing a report on time
(C) Mending a business relationship*
(D) Inspecting some damages

女子擔心何事？
(A) 把她的調查結果交給她的上司。
(B) 準時完成報告。
(C) 修補商業關係。
(D) 檢查某些損害。

請注意聆聽女子所擔憂的事情。對話第二段，女子說道：「I'm so worried because I'm not sure how to convince them to remain our customer.」，不曉得該如何挽回顧客的心，重建良好關係，因此 (C) 為最適當的答案。

• **mend** 修補、改善　**inspect** 檢查、審查　**damage** 損害、損失

55

What does the man say he will do before he leaves?
(A) Hold a monthly meeting
(B) Pass on some information*
(C) Visit a customer's office
(D) Check the status of an order

男子說他離開前會做什麼？
(A) 舉行每月會議。
(B) 傳達一些訊息。
(C) 造訪顧客的公司。
(D) 檢查一張訂單的進度。

請特別注意「下班之前」這個時間點，並仔細聆聽男子所說的話。對話最後一句，男子說道：「I'll bring it up with him and let you know what he says before I leave, okay?」，由此得知答案為 (B)。

答案改寫 what he says → information

• **hold** 舉行　**pass** 傳遞　**status** 狀態　**order** 訂單

Questions 56–58 refer to the following conversation with three speakers.

W1 Thank you for coming to our office for an interview, Mr. Bell. [56] I'm Jane Farrah, Human Resources Manager at Country Interior.	女 1 貝爾先生，謝謝你來我們公司參加面試。[56] 我是舉國室內裝修的人事經理珍・法瑞。
W2 And I'm Shannon Rogers. [56] I'm the lead interior designer's assistant.	女 2 我是夏儂・羅傑斯，[56] 首席室內設計師的助理。
M Thanks for inviting me. It's nice to meet both of you.	男 謝謝妳們邀請我，很高興認識兩位。
W1 I've looked over your application package, and it seems that you have a lot of experience installing cabinets, flooring, and windows. I think you would make a great addition to our design crew, but [57] I'm curious about your ability to carry heavy materials.	女 1 我仔細看過你的履歷資料，看來你在安裝櫥櫃、地板和窗戶方面經驗豐富。我想，你對我們的設計團隊會是很大的助力，但 [57] 我想知道你搬運重物的能力。
M That shouldn't be a problem. I've worked several similar jobs and haven't had any problems with the physical demands.	男 應該不成問題。我做過好幾個類似的工作，在體能需求上從來沒遇過任何問題。
W2 Okay, great. [58] Why don't you show us your references? You mentioned in your e-mail that you would bring them.	女 2 好的，好極了。[58] 你何不給我們看看推薦信？你在電子郵件中提過，你會帶來。
M [58] Sure. They're right here.	男 [58] 當然，就在這裡。

• assistant 助理　invite 邀請、徵求　look over 查看、仔細檢查　application 申請、應徵
addition 增加的人　crew 工作人員　ability 能力　carry 搬運、運送　material 材料、原料、建材
physical 身體的、肉體的　demand 需求、請求　reference 推薦函、推薦人

56

Where do the interviewers most likely work?
(A) At a furniture manufacturer
(B) At an interior design company*
(C) At an art gallery
(D) At a moving company

面試官最可能在哪裡工作？
(A) 家具製造廠。
(B) 室內設計公司。
(C) 藝廊。
(D) 搬家公司。

對話前半部，面試官（interviewers）分別說道：「I'm Jane Farrah, Human Resources Manager at Country Interior.」和「I'm the lead interior designer's assistant.」，各自提到公司名稱「舉國室內裝修（Country Interior）」和職稱「首席設計師（lead interior designer）的助理」，由此得知答案為 (B)。

• manufacturer 製造商

57

What job requirement do the speakers discuss?
(A) Meeting deadlines
(B) Cooperating with others
(C) Working long hours
(D) Lifting heavy objects*

說話者在討論什麼工作條件？
(A) 如期完成任務。
(B) 和其他人合作。
(C) 工時很長。
(D) 抬起重物。

聆聽時，請特別注意「職務要求」。對話中段說道：「I'm curious about your ability to carry heavy materials.」，詢問對方是否能提重物，因此答案為 (D)。

答案改寫 carry → lift
material → object

• meet 符合　deadline 最後期限、截止日期　cooperate 合作　lift 舉起、抬起　object 物體

58

What does the man agree to do next?
(A) Show some documents*
(B) Fill out an application
(C) Submit some design samples
(D) Sign an employment contract

男子同意接下來做什麼？
(A) 出示一些文件。
(B) 填寫一份申請書。
(C) 提出一些設計的樣本。
(D) 簽署一份僱傭合約。

當題目問句以「 . . . do next?」結尾時，在對話後半部，會出現解題的關鍵線索。女子向男子詢問能否讓她看一下推薦信（Why don't you show us your references?），男子表示同意（Sure），因此 (A) 為最適當的答案。

答案改寫 reference → document

• fill out 填寫　submit 提出、呈遞　contract 合約

Questions 59–61 refer to the following conversation.

W Hi, Michael. 59 Have you noticed the decrease in reservations lately? We had a lot more reservations booked at this time last year. I think we need to do something to attract more guests. Do you have any suggestions?	女 嗨，麥可。59 你注意到最近訂房的人數減少了嗎？去年這個時候，我們的訂房數多很多。我想，我們必須做點什麼來吸引更多房客。你有什麼建議嗎？
M Well, 60 what if we held a discount event next month? We could send a mass e-mail to our regular visitors and offer them a voucher for 50% off the price of one night's stay. That way, they might book several nights.	男 嗯，60 我們下個月舉行折扣優惠活動怎麼樣？我們可以發送大量電子郵件給常客，提供他們一張住宿一晚的五折優惠券。那樣的話，他們可能會預訂幾個晚上。
W Okay, that sounds like a great idea. 61 How about you design the voucher and draft the e-mail? You can submit them to me by Friday for approval.	女 好，聽起來是很棒的主意。61 你來設計優惠券並草擬電子郵件如何？你可以在星期五之前交給我批准。

• **notice** 注意到　**decrease** 減少　**reservation** 預訂、預訂的房間（或座位）　**lately** 近來、最近　**attract** 吸引、引起（注意、興趣等）　**suggestion** 建議　**event** 活動　**mass** 大量、眾多　**regular** 經常的　**draft** 起草　**submit** 提出、呈遞　**approval** 批准、同意

59

What problem does the woman mention?　女子提及什麼問題？

(A) A room was damaged.　(A) 有個房間損壞。
(B) Some guests complained.　(B) 有些客人抱怨。
(C) Some workers quit.　(C) 有些員工辭職。
(D) A business is slow.*　(D) 生意下滑。

對話第一段，女子提到：「Have you noticed the decrease in reservations lately?」，表示「最近訂房的人數下降」，因此 (D) 為最適當的答案。

• **quit** 辭職

What does the man suggest?　男子有何建議？

(A) Offering free meals to guests　(A) 免費供餐給客人。
(B) Holding a promotional event*　(B) 舉行促銷活動。
(C) Upgrading room sizes　(C) 升等客房大小。
(D) Merging with another business　(D) 與另一家公司合併。

請仔細聆聽男子所說的話。男子提議下個月舉辦促銷活動（what if we held a discount event next month?），由此可以確認答案為 (B)。

答案改寫 discount event → promotional event

• **meal** 一餐　**promotional** 促銷的　**merge** 使（公司等）合併

61

What does the woman ask the man to do?
(A) Analyze customer feedback
(B) Update a website
(C) Make a mailing list
(D) Prepare some materials*

女子要求男子何事？
(A) 分析顧客的回饋意見。
(B) 更新網站。
(C) 列出郵寄名單。
(D) 準備一些資料。

對話最後一句，女子說道：「How about you design the voucher and draft the e-mail?」，要求男子設計優惠券並草擬電子郵件，因此 (D) 為最適當的答案。題目中常會以 How about 和 Why don't you 表示「提議」或「要求」。

答案改寫 design/draft → prepare
voucher/e-mail → materials

• **analyze** 分析 **prepare** 準備、預備

Questions 62–64 refer to the following conversation.

M Hi, Dara. [62] Do you have time to talk about my presentation for the Cosmetics Convention?	男 嗨，黛拉。[62] 妳有空討論我要在化妝品大會發表的簡報嗎？
W Yes. I'm terribly sorry I wasn't able to talk with you yesterday.	女 有的。我很抱歉昨天沒空和你討論。
M That's not a problem. I know you've been busy filing patent applications.	男 沒關係。我知道妳一直在忙專利申請的事情。
W Yes, it's been so complicated, but [63] it looks like our new sunblock line will be ready for manufacturing next month.	女 是的，那很複雜。但是，[63] 看來我們新的防曬系列產品，下個月就可以投入生產。
M Good to hear. Can I show you my PowerPoint presentation?	男 很高興聽到這個消息。我可以把我的 PowerPoint 簡報給妳看嗎？
W Sure. You can use my computer.	女 當然，你可以用我的電腦。
M Okay, here it is. I just wanted to double-check that all of the diagrams are correct.	男 好，就是這個。我只是想要再檢查一次，確認所有圖表都正確。
W It looks good so far. Wait a minute. [64] This diagram is from last year's convention.	女 目前看來都很好。等一下。[64] 這張圖是去年大會的。
M Oh, no. You're right. I'm so glad you caught that.	男 噢，不妙。你說得對。幸好妳發現了。

• **cosmetics** 化妝品 **terribly** 很、非常 **patent** 專利 **application** 申請 **complicated** 複雜的 **manufacture** (大量)製造 **correct** 正確的 **so far** 到目前為止

62

What industry do the speakers most likely work in?
(A) Cosmetics*
(B) Engineering
(C) Software
(D) Trade

說話者最可能在什麼行業工作？
(A) 化妝品。
(B) 工程。
(C) 軟體。
(D) 貿易。

對話開頭，男子說道：「Do you have time to talk about my presentation for the Cosmetics Convention?（有空討論化妝品大會的簡報嗎？）」，由此確認答案為 (A)。

• **trade** 貿易

63

What does the woman say will happen next month?
(A) A convention will take place.
(B) A new product will be manufactured.*
(C) A patent will expire.
(D) A new law will be enacted.

女子說，下個月會發生何事？
(A) 將舉行一場大會。
(B) 將生產一項新產品。
(C) 一項專利權將到期。
(D) 將實施一項新法規。

請特別注意關鍵時間點 next month（下個月），並仔細聆聽女子所說的話。對話中間，提到「下個月將啟動最新研發防曬品的生產線（it looks like our new sunblock line will be ready for manufacturing next month）」，因此答案為 (B)。

答案改寫 sunblock line → product

• take place 舉行、發生　expire （期限）終止　enact 實施

64

What does the woman imply when she says, “This diagram is from last year’s convention”?
(A) A fee must be paid.
(B) Nothing needs to be done.
(C) This year’s figures are not available yet.
(D) Some information is outdated.*

當女子說「這張圖表是去年大會的」時，意指什麼？
(A) 必須支付費用。
(B) 沒有什麼事要做。
(C) 今年的數字還無法得知。
(D) 有些資訊已過期。

女子說這句話的當下，正在準備專利申請要審核的資料，並檢查圖表是否正確無誤，因此根據文意，(D) 為最適當的答案。

• fee 費用

Questions 65–67 refer to the following conversation and floor plan.

Office 4	Office 3	Office 2
Break Room	Office 1	

辦公室 4	辦公室 3	辦公室 2
茶水間	辦公室 1	

M Tracey, do you have time to take a look at the floor plan for our new office space at the Winslow building?

W Sure. [65] I have about ten minutes before I have to leave to meet with some new clients this afternoon.

M Great. Here is the floor plan. Offices 3 and 4 will be for the sales and marketing departments, and [66] you’ll be in the office next to the break room. It’s pretty large, so you’ll have a lot of space to conduct meetings.

男 崔西，你有空看一下我們在溫斯洛大樓新辦公室的平面圖嗎？

女 當然。[65] 我大約有十分鐘，然後我就必須離開，去見今天下午的新客戶。

男 太好了。這是平面圖。3 號和 4 號辦公室會給業務和行銷部門，[66] 妳的辦公室會在茶水間隔壁。那間相當大，所以妳會有充足的空間主持會議。

W That sounds like it'll work out great. Where will you be?	女 聽起來會進行得很順利。那你會在哪裡？
M I'll be in the corner office. That way I can be close to you and the sales department.	男 我會在轉角辦公室。那樣的話，我離妳和業務部都很近。
W Good idea. 67 How about I present this at the staff meeting tomorrow morning?	女 好主意。67 我在明天早上的員工會議上簡報這件事如何？

- **break** 休息、(用茶點的)休息時間 **take a look at** 看一看 **floor plan** 建築的平面圖 **department** 部門 **pretty** 相當、非常 **conduct** 實施、進行 **work out** 發生、進展

65

According to the woman, what will she be doing this afternoon?

根據女子所述，她今天下午會做何事？

(A) Going on vacation
(B) Moving to a new office
(C) Meeting some customers*
(D) Drawing up a floor plan

(A) 去度假。
(B) 搬進一間新辦公室。
(C) 會見一些新客戶。
(D) 草擬一張平面圖。

請特別注意關鍵時間點 this afternoon（今天下午，在文中有「待會兒」的意思），並仔細聆聽女子所說的話。對話第一段，女子說道：「I have about ten minutes before I have to leave to meet with some new clients this afternoon.」，由此可知答案為 (C)。

答案改寫 client → customer

- **draw up** 草擬、起草

66

Look at the graphic. Which office has been assigned to the woman?

請見圖表。哪一間辦公室分配給女子？

(A) Office 1*
(B) Office 2
(C) Office 3
(D) Office 4

(A) 辦公室 1。
(B) 辦公室 2。
(C) 辦公室 3。
(D) 辦公室 4。

聆聽時，請務必掌握解題關鍵在「辦公室的位置」。對話中間，男子說明各辦公室的使用狀況，並告訴女子可以使用茶水間旁的那間辦公室（you'll be in the office next to the break room），因此答案為 (A)。

- **assign** 分配、分派

67

What does the woman say will take place tomorrow morning?

女子說，明天早上會發生何事？

(A) A visit with clients (B) An employee meeting*
(C) A renovation (D) A company party

(A) 拜訪客戶。 (B) 員工會議。
(C) 整修。 (D) 公司派對。

請仔細聆聽女子所說的話，並特別留意 tomorrow morning（明天一早）。對話最後一句提到：「How about I present this at the staff meeting tomorrow morning?」，由此找出答案為 (B)。

答案改寫 staff → employee

- **take place** 舉行、發生 **renovation** 翻修

Questions 68–70 refer to the following conversation and list.

Company	Location
Stanford Design	Chicago
Able Advertising	Miami
Renview Media	New York
70 Smart Style Design	Atlanta

M Hi, Jennifer. 68 I'm so pleased to hear that our company will host a charity gala next month to raise money for the homeless.

W Yes, we can do something for the community and get great publicity. That reminds me. Did you get a chance to look over the list of firms we're considering hiring to advertise the event?

M Yes, I'm looking at it now. 69 I think Renview Media offers great discounts, but we might need somebody who works a bit faster. The last time we hired them, there were many delays.

W Right. I remember that. 70 How about the one that's right here in Atlanta? Their reviews all say they were fast and reasonably priced.

公司	位置
史丹佛設計	芝加哥
艾波廣告	邁阿密
連威媒體	紐約
70 史邁特風格設計	亞特蘭大

男 嗨，珍妮佛。68 真高興聽到我們公司下個月要主辦慈善晚會，為街友募款。

女 是的，我們可以為社區做點事情，並達到很好的公關宣傳。那提醒了我，你有空查看我們考慮要僱用來做活動宣傳的公司名單嗎？

男 有的，我現在正在看。69 我認為「連威媒體」提供很大的優惠，但我們可能需要工作速度快些的公司。我們上一次找他們，有許多事情都拖延了。

女 對，我記得。70 同樣在亞特蘭大的這一家呢？他們的評價都說，他們動作很快而且收費合理。

• **location** 位置、地方 **host** 主辦、主持 **charity** 慈善、善舉 **gala** 盛會 **raise** 募（款）
publicity 宣傳、（公眾的）名聲 **remind** 提醒 **look over** 仔細檢查 **consider** 考慮 **hire** 僱用
offer 提供 **delay** 延遲、耽擱 **reasonably** 合理地

68

What type of event is the company hosting?

(A) A charity ball*
(B) An art gallery opening
(C) A retirement party
(D) A professional conference

公司將主辦哪一種活動？

(A) 慈善晚會。
(B) 藝廊開幕。
(C) 退休派對。
(D) 專業研討會。

聆聽時，請務必掌握本題的關鍵是「活動的類型」。對話第一段，男子說道：「I'm so pleased to hear that our company will host a charity gala」，因此答案為 (A)。

答案改寫 gala → ball

• **ball** 舞會 **retirement** 退休

69

What is the man concerned about?

(A) The cost of a project
(B) The location of an event
(C) A company's efficiency*
(D) A worker's absence

男子擔心何事？

(A) 計畫的費用。
(B) 活動的地點。
(C) 公司的效率。
(D) 某個員工缺席。

請仔細聆聽男子所說的話。對話第二段，男子提及某間公司的優缺點（I think Renview Media offers great discounts, but we might need somebody who works a bit faster.），並補充說道「可能得找其他公司」，因此 (C) 為最適當的答案。

答案改寫 work fast → efficiency

• cost 費用、成本 efficiency 效率、效能 absence 缺席

70

Look at the graphic. Which company does the woman suggest?

(A) Stanford Design
(B) Able Advertising
(C) Renview Media
(D) Smart Style Design*

請見圖表。女子建議的是哪一間公司？

(A) 史丹佛設計。
(B) 艾波廣告。
(C) 連威媒體。
(D) 史邁特風格設計。

對話最後一段，女子說道：「How about the one that's right here in Atlanta?」，提議同樣位在亞特蘭大的公司，因此答案為 (D)。

PART 4 08

Questions 71–73 refer to the following announcement.

W Attention all travelers. [71] This announcement is for passengers of flight FR64 to Paris. [72] Due to unfavorable weather conditions in Paris, your flight has been delayed until further notice. We expect the delay to last no more than two hours. You will be informed as soon as we have a new estimated departure. In the meantime, [73] visit the International Flight Lounge and receive a free beverage by showing your flight FR64 ticket. Thank you for your continued patience.

女 各位旅客請注意。[71] 搭乘 FR64 班機前往巴黎的旅客請注意，[72] 由於巴黎天候不佳，班機已延後起飛，請待進一步通知。我們預計班機延後時間不會超過兩小時。我們一得知新的預估起飛時間，就會通知您。在此期間，[73] 您可以前往國際航班休息室，出示您的 FR64 班機機票就可享有免費飲料一杯。感謝各位耐心等待。

- **announcement** 廣播通知、宣布 **passenger** 旅客、乘客 **flight** 班機 **due to** 因為、由於 **unfavorable** 不利的 **condition** 狀況 **delay** 使延期 **notice** 公告、通知 **expect** 期待、預期 **last** 持續 **inform** 通知、告知 **estimated** 估計的 **departure** 出發、離開 **in the meantime** 在……期間之內、同時 **beverage** 飲料 **continued** 持續的 **patience** 耐心

71

Where most likely are the listeners?
(A) At an airport*
(B) On a ship
(C) At a travel agency
(D) In a shopping mall

聽眾最有可能在何處？
(A) 機場。
(B) 船上。
(C) 旅行社。
(D) 購物中心。

獨白第一句提到「旅客」，即可刪除選項 (D)。後方緊接著說道：「This announcement is for passengers of flight FR64 to Paris.」，表示此廣播的聽眾是搭飛機前往巴黎的乘客，由此得知答案為 (A)。

72

What is the cause of the delay?
(A) A security issue
(B) Missing passengers
(C) Mechanical problems
(D) Poor weather*

延誤的原因為何？
(A) 安全問題。
(B) 旅客行蹤不明。
(C) 機械問題。
(D) 天候不佳。

獨白前半部說道：「Due to unfavorable weather conditions in Paris, your flight has been delayed until further notice.」，表示因為巴黎天候不佳，導致班機誤點，因此答案為 (D)。

答案改寫 unfavorable → poor

- **cause** 原因 **security** 安全、保安 **issue** 問題、爭議 **mechanical** 機械的

73

What does the speaker suggest listeners do?

(A) Request a ticket refund

(B) Obtain a complimentary drink*

(C) Book hotel accommodation

(D) Visit an information desk

說話者建議聽眾做何事？

(A) 要求機票退費。

(B) 取得免費飲料。

(C) 預訂飯店住宿。

(D) 前往服務台。

在獨白後半部，通常會聽到說話者的建議或要求。廣播提到：「乘客可以至休息室享用免費飲品一杯（visit the International Flight Lounge and receive a free beverage）」，因此答案為 (B)。

答案改寫 receive → obtain
free → complimentary
beverage → drink

- **request** 要求、請求 **refund** 退費 **obtain** 取得、得到 **complimentary** 贈送的 **book** 預訂 **accommodation** 住處、住宿

Questions 74–76 refer to the following excerpt from a meeting.

W Today marks our first ever sales meeting since Glasco Merits merged with Summerview Metalworks. [74] I'd like to go over the details of the company merger and what that means for the sales department. As you know, [75] we will be conducting regular meetings for all sales staff on the first Monday of every month. Right now, I'd like to familiarize everybody with our new sales and billing procedures. I'll be distributing updated employee handbooks, which we will go over briefly. [76] I know some of you have a training class this afternoon, so I will try to keep this short.

女 今天是「格拉斯科・美利」與「賽摩威金屬製品」合併後的第一次業務會議。[74] 我想要仔細檢視公司合併的細節，以及對業務部的意義。你們都知道，[75] 我們會在每月的第一個星期一，定期舉行全體業務同仁會議。現在，我想讓各位熟悉新的業務與開立發票的流程。我會分發更新後的員工手冊，我們會從頭到尾簡單帶過。[76] 我知道，你們有些人今天下午有訓練課程，所以，我會努力讓會議簡明扼要。

- **mark** 標示 **merge** 使（公司等）合併（動詞） **go over** 重溫、察看 **merger** （公司等的）合併（名詞） **department** 部門 **conduct** 實施、進行 **familiarize** 使熟悉 **billing** 開立發票 **procedure** 程序、步驟 **distribute** 分發、分配 **briefly** 簡短地

74

What is the speaker mainly discussing?

(A) A downsizing plan

(B) A company merger*

(C) A new office manager

(D) A potential client

說話者主要在討論何事？

(A) 裁減員工計畫。

(B) 公司的合併。

(C) 新的公司經理。

(D) 潛在客戶。

請特別留意，當題目詢問獨白主旨時，在前半部內容中，通常可以聽到關鍵線索。第一句提到，打算在合併後的首次會議上，討論合併後的相關細項與後續影響（I'd like to go over the details of the company merger and what that means for the sales department.），因此答案為 (B)。

- **downsize** 裁減（員工）人數、縮小規模 **potential** 可能的、潛在的

75

What does the speaker say will take place at the company once a month?
說話者說，每個月公司會舉行何事？

(A) An employee review
(B) A monthly bonus
(C) A sales meeting*
(D) A training course

(A) 員工考核。
(B) 每月紅利。
(C) 業務會議。
(D) 訓練課程。

請特別注意聆聽有關「一個月一次」的內容。獨白中間內容為：「we will be conducting regular meetings for all sales staff on the first Monday of every month」，由此得知答案為 (C)。

- **take place** 舉行、發生

76

Why will some employees be unavailable in the afternoon?
為何有些員工下午不在？

(A) They are attending a training session.*
(B) They are presenting at a trade show.
(C) They are meeting with the head manager.
(D) They are leaving for a company trip.

(A) 他們要參加訓練課程。
(B) 他們要出席貿易展。
(C) 他們要和部門經理會面。
(D) 他們要出發去員工旅遊。

請注意聆聽關鍵時間點 afternoon（下午）。獨白最後一句內容為：「I know some of you have a training class this afternoon」，因此答案為 (A)。

答案改寫 class → session

- **unavailable**（忙於他事）抽不開身 **trade** 貿易 **head** 首長、領導人 **leave for** 動身前往

Questions 77–79 refer to the following excerpt from a meeting.

M As I'm sure you've heard, [77] we're thinking of switching to a new company to supply all our restaurant's beverage needs. Next week, a representative will visit the restaurant and bring samples of several different kinds of soda and juice. I'd like some of you to try as many as you can and fill out the feedback questionnaire they will provide. When you're finished, [78] you can drop off your questionnaire in the head chef's office downstairs. To show our appreciation for your participation, management will draw one questionnaire at random and [79] give the winner a pair of movie passes.

男 相信你們都聽說了，[77] 我們正在考慮要換一家新公司供應我們餐廳的飲料。有個業務代表下星期會來拜訪餐廳，並帶好幾種不同的汽水和果汁樣品來。我希望你們一些人盡量試喝，然後填寫他們提供的回饋意見調查問卷。等你們填完，[78] 可以把問卷拿到樓下的總主廚辦公室。為了感謝你們的參與，管理部會隨機抽出一份問卷，[79] 贈送得獎者雙人電影入場券。

- **switch** 使轉換、改變 **supply** 供應、提供 **beverage** 飲料 **representative** 代表、代理人 **several** 數個 **fill out** 填寫（表格、申請書等） **questionnaire** 問卷 **chef** 主廚 **appreciation** 感謝 **participation** 參與 **management** 管理部門 **draw** 抽（籤） **at random** 任意

77

What does the speaker say the business is considering? 說話者說公司正在考慮何事？

(A) Renovating a kitchen (A) 整修廚房。

(B) Changing operation hours (B) 改變營業時間。

(C) Contracting a new chef (C) 與新主廚簽約。

(D) Hiring a new supplier* (D) 僱用新供應商。

本題詢問說話者之後的打算，聆聽時，請務必掌握關鍵點在「變動之處」。獨白前半部說道：「we're thinking of switching to a new company to supply all our restaurant's beverage needs.」，由此可以確認答案為 (D)。

答案改寫 think → consider
company to supply → supplier

- **consider** 考慮 **renovate** 整修、更新 **operation** 經營、營運 **contract** 訂（約） **hire** 僱用 **supplier** 供應商

78

Why should listeners visit the head chef's office? 聽眾為何要去總主廚辦公室？

(A) To have an interview (A) 為了進行面試。

(B) To pick up a coupon (B) 為了領取優惠券。

(C) To sample some food (C) 為了試吃一些食物。

(D) To submit a form* (D) 為了交出一份表格。

聆聽時，請特別留意關鍵字為「the head chef's office（總主廚辦公室）」。獨白後半部要求將調查表繳交至指定地點（you can drop off your questionnaire in the head chef's office downstairs），因此 (D) 為最適當的答案。

答案改寫 questionnaire → form

- **submit** 提出、呈遞 **form** 表格

79

What can listeners receive for participation? 聽眾參與活動可以得到什麼？

(A) Some movie tickets* (A) 一些電影票。

(B) A vacation package (B) 一次套裝旅行。

(C) Some free food (C) 一些免費食物。

(D) A pay raise (D) 加薪。

獨白最後一句提到，將從參與員工當中抽出一位贈送雙人電影入場券（give the winner a pair of movie passes），以表謝意，因此答案為 (A)。

- **free** 免費的 **raise** 加薪、加薪額

Questions 80–82 refer to the following telephone message.

W　Hi, Caroline. This is Trisha calling. [80] My flight was supposed to depart an hour ago, and they've just announced that it's been canceled due to poor weather conditions. It looks like [81] I won't be home in time to attend the dinner to celebrate your promotion. It's really too bad. To make it up to you, [82] I'd love to take you out for dinner next week, maybe on Thursday or Friday evening. Call me and let me know if either of those days works for you.	女　嗨，卡洛琳，我是崔夏。[80] 我的班機應該在一小時前起飛，但他們剛剛廣播，由於天候不佳，班機已取消。看來 [81] 我來不及回家參加妳的升職慶祝晚餐。實在是太遺憾了。為了彌補，[82] 我想下星期請妳出去吃飯，也許星期四或星期五晚上。打電話給我，告訴我哪一天妳可以。

• **flight**（飛機的）班次　**be supposed to** 應該、理應　**depart** 啟程、出發　**cancel** 取消
due to 由於、因為　**condition** 情況、狀態　**attend** 出席、參加　**celebrate** 慶祝　**promotion** 晉升、升職
make up to 補償　**either**（兩者之中）任一個　**work for (someone)** 對（某人）有利

80

Where most likely is the speaker?
(A) At a bus station
(B) At an airport*
(C) At her home
(D) In an airplane

說話者最有可能在何處？
(A) 在巴士車站。
(B) 在機場。
(C) 在她家。
(D) 在飛機上。

獨白前半部說道：「My flight was supposed to depart an hour ago, and they've just announced that it's been canceled due to poor weather conditions.」，表示班機已被取消，最有可能在機場聽到此類的 announcement（廣播公告），因此答案為 (B)。

81

What does the speaker imply when she says, "It's really too bad"?
(A) She is not well.
(B) She is disappointed.*
(C) She lost a lot of money.
(D) She regrets her decision.

當說話者說「實在是太遺憾了」，意指什麼？
(A) 她不舒服。
(B) 她很失望。
(C) 她損失大筆金錢。
(D) 她為她的決定感到懊悔。

題目句後方，說話者表示自己應該無法參加派對（I won't be home in time to attend the dinner to celebrate your promotion），因此答案為 (B)。

• **disappointed** 失望的　**regret** 懊悔、遺憾　**decision** 決定

82

What does the speaker ask the listener to do?
(A) Drive to an airport
(B) Reschedule a party
(C) Unlock a door
(D) Meet her for dinner*

說話者要求聽者做何事？
(A) 開車到機場。
(B) 重新安排派對的時間。
(C) 打開門鎖。
(D) 和她碰面共進晚餐。

在獨白後半部，通常會聽到説話者的要求或建議。説話者詢問聽者是否願意另約時間共進晚餐（I'd love to take you out for dinner next week, maybe on Thursday or Friday evening.），因此 (D) 為最適當的答案。

• **reschedule** 重新安排……的時間 **unlock** 解鎖

Questions 83–85 refer to the following announcement.

W Attention, all staff members. [84] A pipe burst in the stock room overnight and water has rushed into the back offices, [83] **the frozen foods section, and the bakery aisles.** As of now, the managers think it's in our best interest not to open today. Instead, we'd like all available employees to help with the clean-up. If the mess is cleaned up by this evening, we will resume normal operations tomorrow. [85] Your managers will let you know about the schedule before you go home.

女 所有工作人員請注意。[84] 貯藏室裡有根水管昨晚爆裂，水湧進後勤辦公室、[83] **冷凍食品區和烘焙區走道**。現在，經理一致認為，今天最好不要營業。我們希望所有有空的員工轉而協助清理。如果今晚之前可以清理乾淨，我們明天就會恢復正常營運。[85] 你們的經理會在下班時間前，告知日程安排。

• **pipe** 水管 **burst** 爆裂 **stock** 貯存 **aisle** 通道、走廊 **mess** 凌亂的狀態 **resume** 恢復 **normal** 正常的 **operation** 經營、營運

83

Where most likely is this announcement being made?
(A) At pastry shop
(B) At a bookstore
(C) At a supermarket*
(D) At a sports center

這項通知最可能在哪裡發布？
(A) 在糕餅店。
(B) 在書店。
(C) 在超級市場。
(D) 在運動中心。

聆聽時，請仔細找尋與「地點」相關的線索。獨白前半部提到「冷凍食品區以及烘焙區（the frozen foods section, and the bakery aisles）」，因此答案為 (C)。

• **pastry shop** 糕餅店

84

What problem does the speaker mention?
說話者提及什麼問題？

(A) Some employees are sick.　(A) 有些員工生病了。
(B) Some items were misplaced.　(B) 有些物品放錯位置。
(C) Some power cables are damaged.　(C) 有些電纜受損。
(D) Some areas are flooded.*　(D) 有些區域淹水。

獨白前半部說道：「A pipe burst in the stock room overnight and water has rushed into the back offices . . . 」，由於水管破裂導致水湧進後勤部門辦公室等，因此 (D) 為最適當的答案。

• **item** 物品　**damage** 損害、毀壞　**flood** 淹水

85

What will employees be informed about this evening?
員工會在今天晚上收到什麼通知？

(A) A store's schedule*　(A) 商店的時間表。
(B) A vacation plan　(B) 度假的計畫。
(C) A promotional sale　(C) 促銷拍賣。
(D) A city inspection　(D) 市政府的檢查。

聆聽時，請格外留意關鍵時間點 this evening（今天傍晚）。獨白後半部提到，如在今晚前清理完畢，明天將可重新開始營業，緊接著補充：「經理會在下班時間以前，宣布日程安排（Your managers will let you know about the schedule before you go home.）」，因此答案為 (A)。

• **promotional** 促銷的　**inspection** 檢查、檢驗

Questions 86–88 refer to the following news report.

M Welcome to News in Real Estate. I'm Chuck Thompson, and [86] here is the latest news on how to sell your home quickly. [87] A recent survey on Channel 6's website has shown that more and more home owners are using interior decorating services to quickly sell their homes. According to our survey, 75 percent of people who recently sold their home contracted a decorating service. These decorators are experts in giving your home some pleasing upgrades that will attract buyers. If you're on a budget, however, and can't afford a decorator, there are a few ways you can improve the look of your home. [88] Designer Jen Bell will be joining me after the break to give you some tips.

男 歡迎收看不動產新聞，我是查克・湯普森，[86] 這裡有如何快速出售你的房子的最新訊息。[87] 近日，6 號電台網站上有一項調查顯示，有愈來愈多屋主善用室內裝潢來快速售出他們的家。根據我們的調查，近期賣出房子的人，有 75% 與裝潢服務的公司簽約。這些室內裝潢師是專家，帶給你家一些令人滿意的升級項目，以吸引買家。不過，若你的預算有限，請不起室內裝潢設計師，有幾種你可以美化你家外觀的方法。[88] 廣告過後，設計師珍・貝爾會和我一起給大家一些建議。

• **real estate** 不動產、房地產　**recent** 最近的　**survey** 調查、民意調查　**owner** 物主、所有人
according to 根據、按照　**contract** 訂（約）　**decorator** 室內裝潢師　**expert** 專家
pleasing 令人愉快的、使人滿意的　**attract** 吸引、引起（注意、興趣等）　**on a budget** 拮据、節省費用
afford 負擔得起　**improve** 改善、增強　**break** 暫停、休息

86

What is the news report about?
(A) Becoming an interior decorator
(B) Selling a home quickly*
(C) Taking an online survey
(D) Buying a home abroad

這則快訊報導的主題為何？
(A) 成為一位室內裝潢設計師。
(B) 快速售出房子。
(C) 參加線上調查。
(D) 購買國外的房屋。

主旨的關鍵線索，通常會出現在獨白的前半部內容中。介紹過自己的名字後，馬上為大家帶來了最新資訊——快速賣掉房子的好方法（here is the latest news on how to sell your home quickly），因此答案為 (B)。

- **abroad** 在國外

87

What did Channel 6 do on their website recently?
(A) Conduct a survey*
(B) Review a service
(C) Advertise a home
(D) Hold a contest

6 號電台最近在網站上做了何事？
(A) 進行一項調查。
(B) 審核一項服務。
(C) 宣傳一間房子。
(D) 舉行一項競賽。

聆聽時，請特別留意關鍵字 Channel 6（6 號電台）。獨白前半部說道：「A recent survey on Cannel 6's website」，可以由此確認答案為 (A)。

- **conduct** 進行　**advertise** 為……做廣告、為……宣傳　**hold** 舉行

88

According to the speaker, what can listeners do after the break?
(A) View houses on the market
(B) Visit a designer's studio
(C) Hear some advice*
(D) Sign up for a newsletter

根據說話者所述，廣告後聽眾可以做什麼？
(A) 查看市場上的房子。
(B) 造訪設計師的工作室。
(C) 聽到一些建議。
(D) 登記訂閱電子報。

聆聽時，請特別留意關鍵字 after the break（廣告後）。獨白最後一句說道：「Designer Jen Bell will be joining me after the break to give you some tips.」，表示設計師將會告訴大家幾個妙招，因此 (C) 為最適當的答案。

答案改寫 tip → advice

- **sign up for** 註冊、登記報名

Questions 89–91 refer to the following excerpt from a meeting.

M To start today's meeting, 89 I'd like to discuss our new paperless policy. Upper management feels it's important for Parker Refurbishing to be a leader in maintaining a green work environment. So from next week, 89 we're asking that all employees please refrain from using paper. A new database has been set up to handle all our file saving needs. Now, I know what you must be thinking. 90 Last year, we tried and failed to go paperless, but this year, I'm confident that our new database will make it possible. To show their appreciation for your efforts, 91 upper management would like to reward you with a staff lunch at the High Park Hotel Grill.

男 今天的會議一開始，89 我想討論我們新的無紙政策。管理高層認為，「帕克翻新公司」要成為維護綠色工作環境的龍頭，這點很重要。因此，從下星期開始，89 我們要求所有員工節約用紙。我們已經建立了一個新的資料庫，處理所有的檔案保存之需。我知道你們現在一定在想什麼。90 去年，我們嘗試無紙化卻失敗了，但今年，我有信心，我們的新資料庫會讓這政策成功。為了感謝你們的努力，91 管理高層會在「高公園飯店燒烤」舉辦員工午餐作為獎勵。

• **discuss** 討論、商談 **management** 管理、經營 **refurbish** 翻新、再磨光 **maintain** 維持、維護 **environment** 環境 **refrain from** 節制、忍住 **handle** 處理 **confident** 自信的 **appreciation** 感謝 **effort** 努力 **reward** 獎賞、酬謝

89

According to the speaker, what is the company trying to do?

(A) Increase productivity
(B) Eliminate paper use*
(C) Upgrade a computer system
(D) Reduce electricity costs

根據說話者所述，公司正努力做何事？

(A) 增加生產力。
(B) 淘汰紙張的使用。
(C) 升級電腦系統。
(D) 減少電費。

獨白前半部說道：「I'd like to discuss our new paperless policy.」，公司即將頒布一項新政策，希望全體員工節約用紙（we're asking that all employees please refrain from using paper）。其後詳細說明規範內容，因此答案為 (B)。

答案改寫 refrain → eliminate

• **increase** 增加 **productivity** 生產力、生產率 **eliminate** 消除、去除 **reduce** 減少、縮小 **electricity** 電、電力

90

What does the speaker mean when he says, "I know what you must be thinking"?

(A) He wants to stress a key detail.
(B) He wants to caution against disobedience.
(C) He understands the listeners' concerns.*
(D) He acknowledges a listener's complaint.

當說話者說，「我知道你們現在一定在想什麼」，意指什麼？

(A) 他想強調關鍵細節。
(B) 他想告誡大家，別不服從。
(C) 他了解聽者的掛慮。
(D) 他接受一位聽者的抱怨。

請務必掌握題目句的前後文意。說話者提到去年曾經嘗試「無紙化」，最後以失敗告終，但今年勢必會有所不同（Last year, we tried and failed to go paperless, but this year, I'm confident that our new database will make it possible.），因此 (C) 為最適當的答案。

• **stress** 強調 **caution** 告誡、警告 **disobedience** 不服從、違抗 **acknowledge** 承認、接受 **complaint** 抱怨

91

What will the listeners be rewarded with?

(A) A free meal*
(B) A new computer
(C) A gift card
(D) A promotion

聽者會得到什麼獎勵？

(A) 免費的一餐。
(B) 一台新電腦。
(C) 一張禮物卡。
(D) 升職。

聆聽時，請務必掌握住關鍵內容「補償措施」。獨白最後一句說道：「upper management would like to reward you with a staff lunch（高層會提供員工午餐作為獎勵）」，由此可以確認答案為 (A)。

答案改寫 lunch → meal

• **meal** 一餐 **promotion** 晉升

Questions 92–94 refer to the following announcement and map.

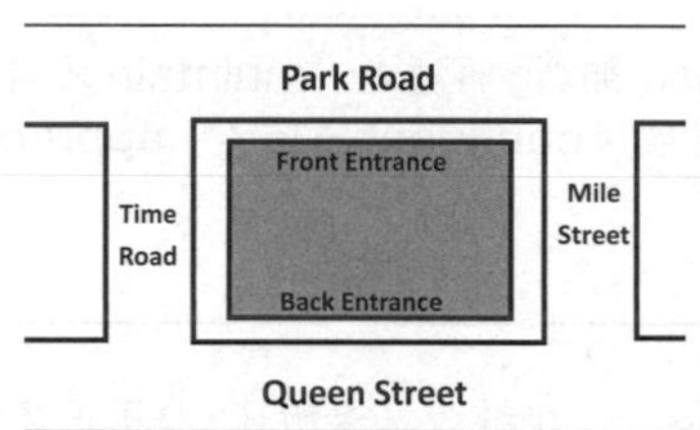

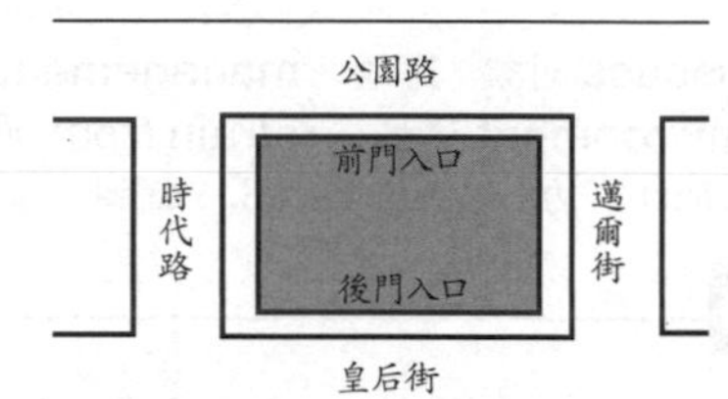

M Attention all businesses located in A&F Building! This is a reminder that [92] the city's winter Christmas Parade will be taking place on Friday afternoon. [93] As the street located in front of our building will be shut down from 11 A.M. to 6 P.M., please make sure to park on the street closest to the back entrance. Also, traffic is expected to be heavy that day, so please ensure you allow yourself enough time during your morning commute. [94] If possible, it might be a good idea to leave your cars at home and take the subway to work.

男 A&F 大樓的所有公司，請注意！提醒大家，[92] 本市的冬季耶誕節遊行將在星期五下午舉行。[93] 由於本大樓前方道路將於上午十一點封閉到下午六點，請務必將車停在最接近後門入口的街上。此外，當天的交通流量預計將會很可觀，因此，請確保自己早晨通勤時間充裕。[94] 如果可以，把車留在家裡搭地下鐵來上班，或許是個好主意。

• **front** 前面、正面 **entrance** 入口 **located in** 座落於 **reminder** 提示、提醒物 **take place** 舉行、發生 **in front of** 在某人／某物前面 **shut down** 關閉 **traffic** 交通、運載量 **expect** 預料、預期 **ensure** 確保 **allow** 容許 **commute** 通勤 **leave** 留下

92

What will take place on Friday afternoon?

(A) A contest
(B) A parade*
(C) A repair
(D) A sale

星期五下午會舉行什麼？

(A) 一場競賽。
(B) 一場遊行。
(C) 維修。
(D) 一場拍賣。

聆聽時，請特別注意關鍵時間點 Friday afternoon（星期五下午）。獨白前半部提到遊行活動（the city's winter Christmas Parade will be taking place on Friday afternoon），因此答案為 (B)。

• **repair** 修理、維修

93

Look at the graphic. Which street will be closed?
(A) Time Road
(B) Park Road*
(C) Mile Street
(D) Queen Street

請見圖表。哪一條街道將封閉?
(A) 時代路。
(B) 公園路。
(C) 邁爾街。
(D) 皇后街。

聆聽時,掌握住關鍵內容為「道路封閉」。獨白中間說道:「As the street located in front of our building will be shut down from 11 A.M. to 6 P.M.」,可由地圖確認「大樓前的道路」為 (B)。

94

What does the speaker suggest?
(A) Staying home
(B) Attending an event
(C) Parking underground
(D) Taking public transportation*

說話者有何建議?
(A) 留在家裡。
(B) 參加一場活動。
(C) 車停在地下樓層。
(D) 搭乘大眾交通運輸工具。

獨白最後一句說道:「If possible, it might be a good idea to leave your cars at home and take the subway to work.」,建議大家不要開車,改搭地鐵上班,因此答案為 (D)。說話者的要求或建議,通常會出現在獨白後半部。

答案改寫 subway → public transportation

• **stay** 停留 **attend** 出席、參加 **public transportation** 公共運輸

Questions 95–97 refer to the following talk and graph.

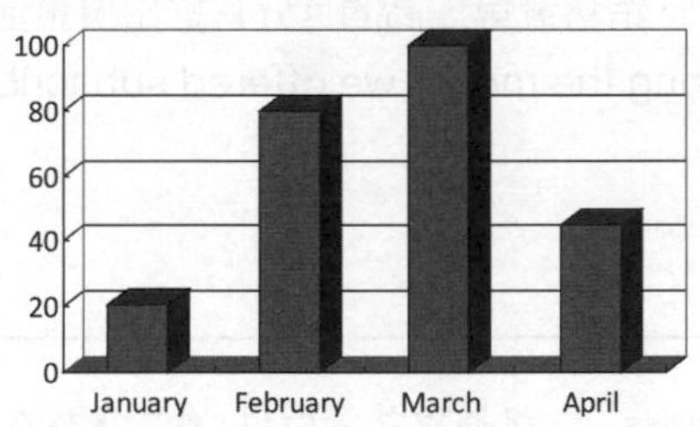

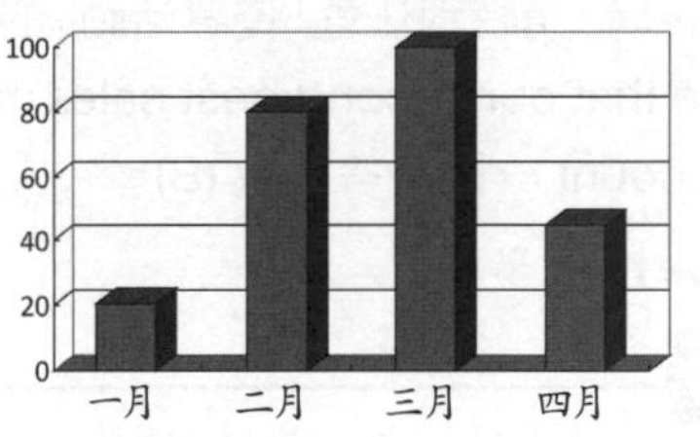

W Good afternoon, staff. [95] I'd like to start our monthly sales meeting by taking a look at our sales progress for our new Garden and Home Monthly Magazine. As you can see, March has been our most successful month in attracting new [95] subscribers. This is probably due to our new advertising campaign that was launched in mid-February. Additionally, [96] you can see that our second best sales month occurred during the month we offered subscribers a 20% discount on [95] **yearly subscriptions**. This month, I'd like to brainstorm ways to increase our subscription rate even more. [97] I'd like each of you to come up with a proposal for either a promotional event or an advertising campaign by next Friday.

女 大家午安。[95] 每月業務會議的一開始,我想先讓各位看一下我們新出版《園藝家居月刊》的銷售進度。你們可以看到,三月是吸引新 [95] 訂戶最為成功的月分。這很可能要歸功於我們在二月中推出的新一波促銷廣告。此外,[96] 你們可以看到,銷量次佳的月分,出現在我們提供訂戶 [95] 訂閱一年八折優惠時。這個月,我要大家腦力激盪,想出讓我們的訂閱率大幅增加的方法。[97] 我希望你們每個人在下星期五前,想出一個促銷活動或廣告宣傳的提案。

• **take a look at** 看一看　**progress** 進步、進展　**successful** 成功的、有成就的　**attract** 吸引　**subscriber** 訂閱者　**probably** 很可能　**due to** 由於、因為　**launch** 發起、使開始從事　**additionally** 此外　**occur** 出現、發生　**yearly** 每年的、一年間的　**subscription** 訂閱　**rate** 率、比率　**come up with**（針對問題等）想出、提供　**promotional** 促銷的、廣告宣傳的

95

Where most likely does the speaker work?
(A) At a home improvement store
(B) At an advertising firm
(C) At a publishing company*
(D) At a design company

說話者最可能在哪裡工作？
(A) 在居家裝修商店。
(B) 在廣告公司。
(C) 在出版公司。
(D) 在設計公司。

獨白前半部說道：「I'd like to start our monthly sales meeting by taking a look at our sales progress for our new Garden and Home Monthly Magazine.」，提到了「Garden and Home Monthly Magazine（園藝家居月刊）」，由此得知答案為 (C)。若不小心漏聽這一小段，後方還提及了「subscribers、yearly subscriptions（訂閱戶、全年訂閱）」，仍可由此推測出答案。切勿因為聽到「廣告（advertising campaign）」兩字，就急著選 (B)。

• **improvement** 改善、改良

96

Look at the graphic. When was the discount event held?
(A) In January
(B) In February*
(C) In March
(D) In April

請見圖表。折扣活動是何時舉行的？
(A) 一月。
(B) 二月。
(C) 三月。
(D) 四月。

聆聽時，請特別注意「優惠活動」的內容。獨白中間提到，銷售量第二高的月分有推出優惠活動（you can see that our second best sales month occurred during the month we offered subscribers a 20% discount），因此答案為 (B)。

• **be held** 舉行

97

According to the speaker, what should staff members do by next Friday?
(A) Edit some articles
(B) Prepare a report*
(C) Book train tickets
(D) Update a website

根據說話者所述，員工應該在下星期五之前做什麼？
(A) 編輯一些文章。
(B) 準備一份報告。
(C) 預訂火車票。
(D) 更新網站。

聆聽時，請特別注意關鍵時間點 next Friday（下週五）。獨白最後一句說道：「I'd like each of you to come up with a proposal for either a promotional event or an advertising campaign by next Friday.」，由此確認答案為 (B)。

答案改寫　come up with → prepare
　　　　　proposal → report

• **edit** 編輯　**article** 文章　**prepare** 準備　**book** 預訂

Questions 98–100 refer to the following excerpt from a meeting and chart.

	Kimberly Shoe Outlet	Shoe Source Plus
Competitive prices	V	X
Free shipping	V	V
Innovative displays	V	X
[100] Online orders	X	V

	金百利鞋子暢貨中心	鞋源加
價格有競爭力	V	X
免運費	V	V
創新的陳列方式	V	X
[100] 線上訂購服務	X	V

W To start the meeting, [98] I'd like to reiterate how impressed I am with our first year of business here at Kimberly Shoe Outlet. [99] When I started planning our opening a year ago, I wasn't sure if we'd do well located near so many other shoe stores. But according to our sales figures, we've managed to beat the competition nearly every month. Now, we need to think of ways to keep that momentum going. Our biggest rival is Shoe Source Plus. As you can see on this chart, we have consistently lower prices than Shoe Source Plus, which has helped to attract customers. [100] Next, I'd like to talk about what Shoe Source Plus launched last month and what we can do to start offering a similar service.

女 會議一開始，[98] 我想重申我對金百利鞋子暢貨中心第一年的業績，印象有多深刻。[99] 當我一年前開始規劃開店時，我不確定在多家鞋店環伺之下，我們是否會成功。但從銷量來看，我們幾乎每個月都成功打敗了對手。現在，我們需要想辦法保持那股衝勁。我們最大的競爭對手是「鞋源加」。你們可以從這張表格看出來，我們的價格始終比「鞋源加」低，這有助吸引顧客。[100] 接下來，我想談談「鞋源加」上個月推出的策略，以及我們可以怎麼做，以便開始提供類似的服務。

- **outlet** 暢貨中心　**competitive** 競爭的、競爭性的　**shipping** 運輸、貨運　**innovative** 創新的、有創意的　**order** 訂購、訂單　**reiterate** 重申　**figure** 數字　**manage** 設法做到　**beat** 打敗、勝過　**competition** 競爭、比賽　**momentum** 動力、衝力　**rival** 對手、競爭者　**consistently** 一貫地、始終如一地　**attract** 吸引　**launch** 發起、開始　**offer** 提供

98

What is the main topic of the meeting?
(A) A new line of products
(B) A manager's promotion
(C) A company's location
(D) A business's success*

會議的主題為何？
(A) 新系列產品。
(B) 經理的升職。
(C) 公司的地點。
(D) 生意的成功。

獨白前半部說道：「I'd like to reiterate how impressed I am with our first year of business here at Kimberly Shoe Outlet.」，想重申對第一年業績的深刻印象，由此可推測出獨白內容為公司首年的營運成果，因此答案為 (D)。

- **promotion** 晉升　**location** 位置、地方

99

Who most likely is the speaker?
(A) A shoe designer
(B) A store owner*
(C) An advertiser
(D) A financial planner

說話者最可能是誰？
(A) 鞋子設計師。
(B) 商店所有人。
(C) 廣告客戶。
(D) 理財專員。

聆聽時，請特別留意是否提及相關「職業」。獨白前半部提到：「When I started planning our opening a year ago」，可以得知說話者一年前開始規劃開店，因此答案為 (B)。

- **owner** 所有人、物主　**advertiser** 廣告客戶　**financial** 財務的

100

Look at the graphic. What will the speaker most likely discuss next?
(A) Competitive prices
(B) Free shipping
(C) Innovative displays
(D) Online orders *

請見圖表。說話者接下來最有可能討論何事？
(A) 有競爭力的價格。
(B) 免運費。
(C) 創新的陳列方式。
(D) 線上訂購服務。

本題詢問獨白結束後，「下個主題」可能為何。答題的關鍵線索通常會出現在獨白後半部。獨白最後一句說道：「Next, I'd like to talk about what Shoe Source Plus launched last month and what we can do to start offering a similar service.」，由此得知之後想討論的是「競爭對手已提供、但我們尚未提供的服務」。對照表格內容後，可得知答案為 (D)。

ACTUAL TEST 3
中譯+解析

PART 1

09

1

(A) He's trimming a tree.
(B) He's wiping a machine.
(C) He's opening a package.
(D) He's holding a container.*

(A) 他在修剪樹木。
(B) 他在擦拭機器。
(C) 他正打開包裹。
(D) 他拿著一個容器。

題目為單人照片時，請特別注意聆聽選項中的動詞。(D) 明確描述圖中人物的動作：握著（holding）某樣東西，為最適當的答案。PART 1 的選項中，不太會明確提到各類瓶罐、箱子、特定容器等名詞字彙，大多以 container 概括。

• **trim** 修剪　**wipe** 擦、抹　**package** 包裹　**hold** 握著、抓住　**container** 容器

2

(A) Some cyclists are racing on a track.
(B) Some cyclists are checking the tires.
(C) Some cyclists are standing next to their bikes.*
(D) Some cyclists are stopping at the traffic light.

(A) 有些自行車騎士正在賽道上比賽。
(B) 有些自行車騎士正在檢查輪胎。
(C) 有些自行車騎士站在他們的單車旁邊。
(D) 有些自行車騎士停在紅綠燈前面。

圖中有一些人站在腳踏車旁，(C) 使用 standing 正確描述動作的狀態，為正確答案。

• **cyclist** 自行車騎士　**race** 競速、參加比賽　**check** 檢查、檢驗　**traffic light** 紅綠燈、交通號誌

3

(A) Some laundry is hanging on the line.*
(B) Towels are being folded.
(C) The grass is being watered.
(D) A man is washing some clothes.

(A) 有些洗好的衣服掛在曬衣繩上。
(B) 正在摺毛巾。
(C) 正在給草坪澆水。
(D) 一名男子正在洗衣服。

看到物品或風景照時，可以推測出主詞應為物品，因此現在進行被動式（be being p.p.）為錯誤選項。當現在進行被動式改成主動語態時，表示某人正在進行某個行為，若照片中未出現人物，則不適合作為照片說明。舉例來說，(B) 代表「Someone is folding towels.」；(C) 為「Someone is watering the grass.」，聽到這兩個選項的當下，即可判斷出與照片情境不符，進而刪除；(D) 的主詞為人，說明亦與照片無關，因此答案為 (A)。

• **laundry** 送洗或洗好的衣服、洗衣店　**hang** 懸掛、吊　**fold** 摺疊　**grass** 草、草坪　**water** 給……澆水

4

(A) Customers are waiting around the cash register.
(B) Some men are examining the vending machine.
(C) One of the men is writing on a clipboard.
(D) A woman is sitting with her knees over the armrest.*

(A) 顧客在收銀機周圍等候。
(B) 有些男子正在檢查自動販賣機。
(C) 其中一名男子正在板夾上寫字。
(D) 一名女子坐著，膝蓋跨在椅子扶手上。

(A) 的內容從照片難以判斷；(B) 僅使用了照片中出現的東西 vending machine，內容並不符合情境；(C) 的說明與照片無關；(D) 女子坐著且把腳抬到椅子扶手上，為適當的描述，因此為正確答案。在此補充，(B) 選項中的單字 examine，有時會搭配有人正在餐廳內看著（examining）菜單的照片。

- **cash register** 收銀機　**examine** 檢查　**vending machine** 自動販賣機　**clipboard** 板夾　**knee** 膝蓋　**armrest**（椅子的）扶手

5

(A) A man is opening the door to the garage.
(B) Some crates are stacked in the back of a vehicle.*
(C) A cart is being pushed up a ramp.
(D) A trailer is being towed by a car.

(A) 一名男子正打開車庫的門。
(B) 一些板條箱堆放在車子的後車廂。
(C) 正把一輛手推車推上斜坡。
(D) 汽車拖著一輛拖車。

照片中僅出現事物，(A) 的主詞為人，因此可以優先刪去。(C) 使用了現在進行被動式，因為句子後方省略了行為者，可以得知 (C) 為錯誤選項；照片中並未看到 trailer（露營拖車），因此 (D) 也是錯誤的選項；(B) 正確描述箱子堆放在後車廂的情景，為最適當的答案。

- **garage** 車庫、修車廠　**crate** 板條箱　**stack** 堆放　**ramp** 斜坡　**vehicle** 車輛　**trailer** 拖車、掛車　**tow** 拖、拉

6

(A) The steps are being repaired.
(B) A tree is growing against the building.
(C) Leaves are being swept out of the path.
(D) A wooden handrail lines a staircase.*

(A) 階梯正在整修。
(B) 一棵樹緊靠著大樓生長。
(C) 正把小徑上的樹葉掃到旁邊。
(D) 木製欄杆沿著樓梯排成一列。

(A) 和 (C) 使用了現在進行被動式，由於照片中並未出現人物，聽到的當下即可刪除這兩個選項；(B) 的內容從照片難以判斷；(D) 敘述扶手與樓梯連接的狀態，為最適當的答案。

- **repair** 修理、修補　**leaf** 葉子　**sweep out of** 從……清除　**path** 小徑、小路　**handrail** 欄杆、扶手　**line** 沿……排列　**staircase** 樓梯、樓梯間

7

When is the training session due to finish? 訓練課程預計何時結束？

(A) I am catching a train. (A) 我在趕火車。

(B) Not until 5.* (B) 直到五點。

(C) From the warehouse. (C) 來自倉庫。

本題為以疑問詞 When 開頭的問句，詢問「預計何時結束」，(B) 回覆至少要到五點，等同於「預計五點結束」，與題目句構成完整對話。(A) 使用了與題目中發音相似的單字（training），此類選項不是答案的可能性高達 99%。

- **training** 訓練 **due** 預期的、應到的 **finish** 結束 **catch** 趕上 **warehouse** 倉庫

8

Where can I use a computer? 哪裡有電腦可用？

(A) Two e-mail messages. (A) 兩封電子郵件訊息。

(B) It's my pleasure. (B) 別客氣。

(C) In the business lounge downstairs.* (C) 樓下的商務貴賓室。

本題為以 Where 開頭的問句，詢問可以使用電腦的「地方」，(C) 回覆「商務休息室」，與題目句構成完整對話。在此補充，(B) 表示「不用客氣」，為常見的慣用句型，請務必熟記。

- **pleasure** 樂事 **downstairs** 樓下的

9

What's the fee for the city bus tour? 市區觀光巴士的車資多少？

(A) I would recommend it to you. (A) 我會推薦給你。

(B) A few famous museums. (B) 一些有名的博物館。

(C) Twelve dollars per person.* (C) 每人 12 元。

本題詢問「車資為多少」，(C) 具體回覆了價格資訊（每人 12 元），為最適當的答案。

- **fee** 費用 **recommend** 推薦 **famous** 有名的 **per** 每一

10

Where is the shareholder meeting taking place? 股東會議在哪裡舉行？

(A) On the 7th floor of the west wing.* (A) 在西側大樓的七樓。

(B) At the end of the month. (B) 在月底。

(C) Yes, we invested in the new factory. (C) 是的，我們投資新工廠。

疑問詞 where 表示詢問「地點」，本題詢問「股東會議在哪裡舉行」，(A) 回覆了確切地點（西側大樓七樓），為正確答案。當題目以 When 開頭，詢問「時間點」時，答案才會是 (B)；(C) 以疑問詞開頭的問句，不可用 Yes 或 No 答句回覆，聽到的當下即可刪除此選項。

- **shareholder** 股東 **take place** 舉行 **invest** 投資 **factory** 工廠

11

How much did sales drop last quarter?
(A) At its headquarters.
(B) By almost 10%.*
(C) Sorry, that's not for sale.

上一季的銷量下跌多少？
(A) 在總公司。
(B) 將近 10%。
(C) 抱歉，那是非賣品。

疑問詞 how 表示詢問「狀態、程度或辦法」，本題為詢問「下降程度為多少」，(B) 以數字回覆「將近 10%」，為正確答案。

• **drop** 下降　**quarter** 季度　**headquarters** 總公司、總部　**almost** 幾乎、差不多

12

Would you like some magazines while you wait?
(A) No, to buy a pair of jeans.
(B) Yes, that would be great.*
(C) The room was too crowded.

在你等候時，想看點雜誌嗎？
(A) 不，去買一條牛仔褲。
(B) 好啊，那太好了。
(C) 房間裡太擁擠了。

本句使用句型「Would you like . . . ?」意思為「你想要……嗎？」。本題詢問「你需要雜誌嗎？」，(B) 回覆好（Yes），和問句構成完整對話，為正確答案。

• **crowded** 擁擠的

13

Who's in charge of cleaning the copy room?
(A) Next to the coffee machine.
(B) It's Daniel's job.*
(C) I didn't expect it.

誰負責打掃影印室？
(A) 在咖啡機旁邊。
(B) 那是丹尼爾的工作。
(C) 我沒料到會這樣。

本題為以 Who 開頭的問句，詢問「由誰」負責清理，(B) 回覆了人名（Daniel），為正確答案。當題目為 Who 開頭的問句時，答案除了人名，還有可能是職稱、部門名稱或公司名稱。另外，PART 2 中，經常會以發音相似的 copy 和 coffee 作為出題陷阱。

• **be in charge of** 掌管、負責　**expect** 預料、期待

14

Isn't the elevator still being repaired?
(A) No, I just came up on it.*
(B) It's made of aluminum.
(C) I need some time to prepare.

電梯不是還在修理嗎？
(A) 沒有，我才剛搭電梯上來的。
(B) 是用鋁做的。
(C) 我需要一些時間準備。

碰到否定問句時，請先將 not 拿掉，視為一般問句，會更容易掌握住題目的重點。本題可以看作是詢問「電梯仍在維修中嗎？」，以 Yes 或 No 答覆即可，因此 (A) 為最適當的答案。

• **repair** 修理　**prepare** 準備

15

The printer in my office is extremely slow.
(A) Make a request for a new one.*
(B) It's not an easy choice.
(C) Yes, the traffic was really bad this morning.

我辦公室的印表機速度非常慢。
(A) 要求換一台新的。
(B) 難以抉擇。
(C) 是的，今天早上的交通狀況確實很糟。

題目表示「印表機出問題」，(A) 回覆「要求再買一台新的印表機（one）」，為正確答案。當選項中出現代名詞 one 時，通常會是答案。

• **extremely** 非常 **request** 要求、請求 **choice** 選擇 **traffic** 交通

16

Which dining table did you buy?
(A) After the holidays.
(B) The restaurants on Green Edge Road.
(C) I chose the smallest one.*

你買了哪一種餐桌？
(A) 假期之後。
(B) 在綠緣路的餐廳。
(C) 我選了最小的那一張。

本題使用疑問詞 which，意思為「哪個、哪些」，詢問「要買哪張餐桌」，(C) 將餐桌換成代名詞 one，回答「最小的那張」，與題目句構成完整對話。在 2016 年 7 月份的官方測驗中，one 曾連續出現在兩道試題中，且皆為正確答案，由此可見代名詞 one 出現機率並不低。

• **dining table** 餐桌 **choose** 選擇

17

Could we postpone the meeting until next week?
(A) Yes, within 24 hours.
(B) I'll be attending a conference in Rochester.*
(C) You can't miss it.

我們可以把會議延到下星期嗎？
(A) 是的，24 小時之內。
(B) 我到時要去羅徹斯特參加研討會。
(C) 你一定找得到。

「Could we . . . ?」的意思為「我們可以……嗎？」。本題以此句型詢問「是否可以將會議延後」，(B) 回覆「下週要出差去其他地方參加會議（所以不行）」，正式回絕，為最適當的答案。最近在 PART 2 中，出現很多這類的高難度題型，必須先推敲出選項中省略的話，才能順利解題。

• **postpone** 使延期、延緩 **attend** 參加 **miss** 錯過

18

The workers are installing the new heating system now, right?
(A) Yes, we will have a warmer office soon.*
(B) An installation art piece.
(C) She's a software developer.

工人現在正在裝設暖氣系統，對嗎？
(A) 是的，我們的辦公室很快就會變暖和了。
(B) 一件裝置藝術作品。
(C) 她是軟體開發人員。

自己已知的事實，再次向對方取得「同意」或「確認」時，會使用附加問句。和一般問句一樣，可以以 Yes 或 No 回答。因此題目詢問「是否正在裝設暖氣」，(A) 回答「是的（Yes）」，為正確答案。

• **install (v.)** 安裝、設置 **installation (n.)** 安裝、設置

19

How do I subscribe to the journal?
(A) On the paper.
(B) They cost six dollars each.
(C) You can simply sign up on this form.*

我該如何訂閱那份期刊？
(A) 在紙上。
(B) 每一份六元。
(C) 你只要在這張表格上登記就可以。

疑問詞 How 開頭的問句，用來詢問「辦法」。本題詢問「如何訂閱」，(C) 回答「請填寫表格申請」，為最適當的答案。在此補充，當題目以「How much . . . ?」詢問「價格或是訂閱費用」時，答案則為 (B)。

• **subscribe** 訂閱　**cost** 價錢為　**sign up** 登記、註冊　**form** 表格

20

I can go to the print shop to collect the brochures.
(A) Yes, many customers like it.
(B) Thanks, that would save me some time.*
(C) When did the designer quit?

我可以去影印店領取廣告小冊子。
(A) 是的，很多顧客喜歡。
(B) 謝謝，那會幫我省下一些時間。
(C) 設計師何時辭職的？

題目為敘述句時，無法推測出固定的回答方式，因此請務必仔細聆聽各選項的內容。題目重點為「去一趟影印店」，(B) 回答「那樣會幫我省下時間」，表示感謝，和題目構成完整對話，為最適當的回應。

• **collect** 領取（信件等）　**save** 節省　**quit** 辭職

21

Could you cover my shift tomorrow?
(A) Some tables.
(B) I have an appointment in the morning.*
(C) They are in a café.

你明天可以幫我代班嗎？
(A) 一些桌子。
(B) 我早上有約。
(C) 他們在咖啡館。

「Could you . . . ?」的意思為「你可以……嗎？」。本題以此開頭請求「可以幫我代班嗎？」，(B) 以「因為已經有約（所以無法幫你代班）」婉轉回絕，與題目句構成完整對話。

• **cover** 代替、頂替（某人的工作或職責）　**shift** 輪班工作時間　**appointment** 約會、約定

22

I think Nadia should deliver the lecture.
(A) In the executive board room.
(B) But Savitri is an expert on the subject.*
(C) A few people were absent.

我認為應該由娜迪亞發表演講。
(A) 在執行董事會會議室。
(B) 但莎薇翠是那個主題的專家。
(C) 有些人缺席。

題目說道：「我認為應該由娜迪亞主講」，(B) 回覆「其他人才是專家」，表示反對意見，最符合對話情境。以 But 開頭的答覆，極可能為正確答案。

• **deliver** 發表　**executive** 執行的、行政上的　**board room** 會議室、董事會會議室　**expert** 專家　**subject** 主題　**absent** 缺席的

23

Your company advertises in several newspapers, doesn't it?
(A) Not this year.*
(B) A weekly report.
(C) She's an editor.

你公司在好幾家報紙上登廣告，不是嗎？
(A) 今年沒有。
(B) 週報表。
(C) 她是編輯。

本題為附加問句，以自己已知的事實（在一些報紙上刊登廣告），再次向對方確認。(A) 回答「今年沒有」，為正確答案。

- **several** 好幾個　**editor** 編輯

24

Can I leave my car here overnight?
(A) The engine sounds strange.
(B) The owner has arrived.
(C) You have to pay a fee.*

我可以把車停在這裡一整晚嗎？
(A) 引擎聽起來有怪聲。
(B) 車主已經到了。
(C) 你必須付費。

本題詢問「是否可以將車停在此過夜」，(C) 省略了 Yes，回覆「（可以）但需要付停車費」，和題目構成完整對話，為正確答案。

- **leave** 留下　**overnight** 整夜　**owner** 物主、所有人　**arrive** 到達、到來　**pay** 付、支付

25

Who took the garbage out?
(A) I can look after the plant.
(B) I did in the morning.*
(C) Several used batteries.

誰把垃圾拿出去倒了？
(A) 我可以照顧植物。
(B) 我今天早上倒的。
(C) 好幾個用過的電池。

本題為以 Who 開頭的問句，詢問「是誰」倒的，(B) 回答「自己」，為正確答案。

- **garbage** 垃圾　**look after** 照顧、照看　**plant** 植物　**used** 舊的、用過的

26

Let's practice our presentation.
(A) The clients were impressed.
(B) An award winner.
(C) Room 305 has a projector.*

我們來練習簡報。
(A) 客戶印象深刻。
(B) 得獎者。
(C) 305 室有投影機。

本題說道「來排練一下吧」，(C) 提供場地資訊，回答在「有投影機的地方」排練，和題目構成完整對話，為最適當的選項。

- **practice** 練習、實習　**impress** 給……極深的印象　**award** 獎、獎品

27

Why did the taxi driver decide to make a detour?
(A) After the trip.
(B) He heard about an accident on the radio.*
(C) Please be there by four.

計程車司機為什麼決定繞道？
(A) 旅行之後。
(B) 他從收音機聽到有車禍。
(C) 請在四點前到那裡。

本題為以 Why 開頭的問句，詢問改道的「原因」，(B) 省略了連接詞 because，回答「聽到廣播中提到發生車禍」，為正確答案。

• **decide** 決定　**make a detour** 繞道而行　**accident** 事故、災禍

28

My plane will depart two hours late.
(A) I hope you don't miss your connecting flight.*
(B) We have a new department.
(C) Gate 7 is on your left.

我的班機會晚兩個小時起飛。
(A) 希望你不會錯過轉接的班機。
(B) 我們有個新的部門。
(C) 七號登機門在你的左邊。

本題說道「班機延遲起飛」，(A) 以「希望你能順利轉機」回覆，和題目句構成完整對話。在此補充，為了刻意使人混淆，(B) 使用了 department，與 depart 的發音相似，內容與題目並無關聯。

• **depart** 起程、出發　**miss** 錯過　**connecting** 連接的　**flight** （飛機的）班次　**department** 部門

29

Do you think we should bring an umbrella, or will the weather get better?
(A) You can bring a friend.
(B) I'd rather do it again.
(C) We will mostly be in the car.*

你覺得我們應該帶傘，還是天氣會好轉？
(A) 你可以帶朋友來。
(B) 我寧願再做一次。
(C) 我們大部分時間會在車上。

碰到題目為選擇疑問句時，可以預想到答案應為問句中所包含的兩種選項（①帶傘、②天氣即將放晴（所以不用帶傘）之一，或是排除這兩種選項，以其他內容回覆。(C) 回覆為「我們幾乎都待著車上（所以可以不用帶傘）」，為最適當的答案。

• **umbrella** 傘　**would rather … (than)** 寧願……（也不要）　**mostly** 大部分

30

I think my new landlord owns several apartments.
(A) I like my neighborhood.
(B) I didn't know you moved.*
(C) We met a real estate agent.

我想，我的新房東擁有好幾間公寓。
(A) 我喜歡我住的那一帶。
(B) 我不知道你搬家了。
(C) 我們遇見一位不動產經紀人。

本題說道「新房東好像有很多間公寓」，(B) 回答「（什麼新房東？）我不知道你搬家了」，與問句構成完整對話。請特別留意，其他選項中亦出現了與「搬家」和「房仲」相關的內容，但皆不符合題目文意。

• **landlord** 房東、地主　**own** 擁有　**neighborhood** 鄰近地區　**real estate** 不動產、房地產

31

Wasn't the swimming pool scheduled to open this week? 游泳池不是預定這個星期開放嗎?

(A) It failed the inspection.* (A) 它沒有通過檢驗。

(B) I'll schedule a pickup. (B) 我會安排接機。

(C) No, only for today. (C) 沒有,只有今天。

本題雖然為否定疑問句,解題時請先將 not 拿掉,視為一般問句,即看作詢問「游泳池這星期會開放嗎?」。(A) 回答「因為未通過檢驗」,為最適當的答案。

- **fail** 沒有通過 **inspection** 檢查、檢驗 **pickup** 用汽車搭載某人或接某人

PART 3 11

Questions 32–34 refer to the following conversation.

M	Hi, I'm wondering if you can help me with a return. [32] I bought this sweater here yesterday, but it seems to be damaged.	男	嗨，不知道你是否可以幫我處理退貨。[32] 我昨天在這裡買了這件毛衣，但它似乎有瑕疵。
W	Oh, that's unfortunate. What seems to be the problem with it? May I have a look?	女	噢，很遺憾，是什麼問題呢？我可以看一下嗎？
M	Sure. I didn't notice it when I tried it on, but there is a white spot on the back of it. I'm hoping I can get a refund.	男	當然。我試穿的時候沒有注意到，但後面有一塊白色汙點。我希望可以退費。
W	I see what you mean. [33] It looks like a flaw that occurred during the dyeing process. I can definitely help you with your return. [34] Just give me your receipt and membership card to start.	女	我了解了。[33] 看起來是染色過程產生的瑕疵。沒問題，我會幫您處理退貨。[34] 首先，請給我您的收據和會員卡。

- **damage** 損害、損傷 **notice** 注意 **spot** 汙點、斑點 **refund** 退款、退還 **flaw** 缺點、瑕疵 **occur** 發生、出現 **dye** 染上顏色 **definitely** 肯定地、當然 **receipt** 收據

32

Where is the conversation most likely taking place?
(A) At a clothing store* (B) At an outdoor market
(C) At a second-hand shop (D) At a fabric store

這段對話最可能在哪裡發生？
(A) 在服飾店。 (B) 在露天市場。
(C) 在二手商店。 (D) 在布料行。

對話第一段，男子說道：「I bought this sweater here yesterday」，表示昨天在此買了毛衣，可由此得知答案為 (A)。

- **market** 市場、市集 **second-hand** 二手的、中古的 **fabric** 織品、布料

33

What is the problem?
(A) The price was not correct. (B) A receipt is missing.
(C) An item is defective.* (D) A product is sold out.

問題是什麼？
(A) 價錢不對。 (B) 收據遺失。
(C) 物品有瑕疵。 (D) 有項產品售完。

女子詢問有什麼問題，男子答道：「衣服上有白色汙點」。之後女子說道：「可能是染色過程中導致的瑕疵（It looks like a flaw that occurred during the dyeing process.）」，答案為 (C)。

答案改寫 flaw → defective

- **correct** 正確的 **missing** 遺失的 **item** 物品 **defective** 有瑕疵的、有缺陷的 **sold out** 售完、賣光

34

What does the woman ask the man for?
(A) A membership upgrade (B) His current address
(C) A credit card number (D) Proof of payment*

女子向男子要求什麼？
(A) 會員升級。 (B) 他目前的地址。
(C) 信用卡卡號。 (D) 付款證明。

請仔細聆聽女子所說的話。對話最後一段，她說道：「Just give me your receipt and membership card to start.」，請男子提供收據和會員卡，由此確認答案為 (D)。

答案改寫 receipt → proof of payment

- **proof** 證據、證明 **payment** 支付、付款

Questions 35–37 refer to the following conversation.

W Hello, I'm calling about my tickets to the National Business Convention. I've just purchased them online. [35] I want to print the tickets, but I can't seem to find them.	女 哈囉，我打電話來是為了我買的全國商業大會入場券。我剛上網訂購，[35] 想要把入場券列印出來，但我似乎找不到票券。
M Yes, [36] we've been having trouble with our payment forms. I'm sorry for the inconvenience. I can check your account for you. What's your full name?	男 是的，[36] 我們的付款表格一直出問題。抱歉造成您的不便。我可以幫您查看帳戶。您的全名是？
W Betty Miller. I'm a premium member of your website.	女 貝蒂・米勒。我是你們網站的尊爵會員。
M Okay, I see your information. It looks like your payment did not go through. [37] If you give me your credit card information, I can complete the transaction and send your tickets to you by e-mail.	男 好的，我看到您的資料了。看來您的付款沒有成功。[37] 如果您給我信用卡資料，我可以完成交易，然後用電子郵件把票寄給您。

• **purchase** 購買 **inconvenience** 不便、麻煩 **check** 檢查 **account** 帳目、帳戶 **go through** 順利完成 **complete** 完成 **transaction** 交易、買賣

35

What is the woman trying to do? 女子想要做什麼？

(A) Get a refund (B) Print some tickets* (C) Reserve a flight (D) Schedule an event

(A) 拿到退款。 (B) 列印一些票券。 (C) 預訂航班。 (D) 安排活動的時間。

對話第一段，女子提到想要印出票券（I want to print the tickets），但找不到列印的地方，因此答案為 (B)。

• **refund** 退還、退款 **reserve** 預約、預訂 **flight**（飛機的）班次 **event** 活動

36

What has caused a problem? 造成問題的原因為何？

(A) Some tickets are sold out. (A) 有些票賣完了。
(B) An account has expired. (B) 有個帳戶到期了。
(C) The printer is not working. (C) 印表機故障。
(D) Some payment errors occurred.* (D) 付款出了問題。

本題的重點在「發生問題的原因」。對話第二段，男子說道：「we've been having trouble with our payment forms」，表示網站上的結帳系統有點問題，因此答案為 (D)。

• **cause** 導致、使發生 **sold out** 售完、賣光 **expire** 到期、終止 **occur** 發生、出現

37

What information does the man ask the woman for? 男子向女子要什麼資料？

(A) An address (B) A credit card number* (C) An account password (D) A payment total

(A) 地址。 (B) 信用卡的卡號。 (C) 帳號密碼。 (D) 付款總金額。

請仔細聆聽男子所說的話。對話最後一句提到：「要請您提供信用卡資訊，將會協助您完成交易（If you give me your credit card information, I can complete the transaction and send your tickets to you by e-mail.）」，因此答案為 (B)。

Questions 38–40 refer to the following conversation.

W	Mike, the district manager is flying back from Chicago today. I just got a call from the car company that was supposed to pick him up. Apparently, they won't be able to get him in time. [38] Can you go to the airport?	女 麥克，區經理今天從芝加哥搭飛機回來。我剛剛接到預定去接機的派車公司電話。看樣子，他們來不及去接他。[38] 你可以去機場嗎？
M	Sure, but my car is out for repairs right now. [39] Could I use your car?	男 當然，但我的車現在送修。[39] 我可以借用妳的車嗎？
W	That would be fine. I suggest leaving around 1:30 because it takes thirty minutes to get there. [40] Make sure to park in the free arrivals section so you don't need to pay for parking.	女 可以。因為到機場要30分鐘，我建議大約一點半出發。[40] 務必把車停在免費入境區，那樣你才不需要付停車費。
M	No problem. I'm sure I can find it.	男 沒問題，我相信我找得到。

• **district** 地區、區域　**be supposed to** 應該、應當　**apparently** 顯然地、似乎　**repair** 修理　**leave** 離開、出發　**make sure** 確定、務必　**arrival** 到達、入境　**pay** 支付、付款

38

What does the woman ask the man to do?　女子要求男子何事？

(A) Cancel an appointment　(A) 取消約會。
(B) Call a manager　(B) 打電話給經理。
(C) Repair a vehicle　(C) 修理汽車。
(D) Pick up a coworker*　(D) 開車去接同事。

對話第一段，女子說道：「因為派車公司出了點問題，無法準時到機場接經理」，向男子詢問能否前往機場一趟（Can you go to the airport?）。因此答案為 (D)。在此補充，(B) 和 (C) 為了混淆視聽，特地使用了對話中出現的單字，請特別留意。

答案改寫 district manager → coworker

• **cancel** 取消　**appointment**（尤指正式的）約會　**repair** 修理　**vehicle** 車輛、運載工具　**coworker** 同事

39

What does the man say he needs to do?　男子說他需要做什麼？

(A) Borrow a car*　(A) 借車。
(B) Delay a trip　(B) 延後行程。
(C) Hire a driver　(C) 僱用一名司機。
(D) Meet a client　(D) 見一位客戶。

請仔細聆聽男子所說的話：「Could I use your car?」，詢問「是否可以使用妳的車」，因此 (A) 為最適當的答案。

• **borrow** 借、借入　**delay** 使延期、延誤

40

What does the woman remind the man to do?
(A) Arrive an hour early
(B) Park in the free area*
(C) Call a car company
(D) Carry some luggage

女子提醒男子何事？
(A) 提早一小時到達。
(B) 停在免費的區域。
(C) 打電話給派車公司。
(D) 搬運一些行李。

本題關鍵在「女子提醒的事項」，請掌握此重點，並仔細聆聽。對話後半部說道：「Make sure to park in the free arrivals section so you don't need to pay for parking.」，提醒對方務必把車停在免費入境區，由此得知答案為 (B)。請特別留意，make sure 常會用來作為「提醒」的開頭語。

答案改寫 section → area

• **carry** （用手、肩等）抱、背、提、搬運 **luggage** 行李

Questions 41–43 refer to the following conversation.

M Hi, Anna. Congratulations on completing our new [41] accessory line. I was really impressed by all the shoes and bags you designed to go with our fall line.	男 嗨，安娜。恭喜妳完成我們的新 [41] 配件系列產品。我真的對你設計來搭配秋裝的所有鞋包印象深刻。
W Thank you. It was a lot of work, but very rewarding.	女 謝謝你。事情雖多，卻很值得。
M Would you consider joining my team for the winter line? I know our designers loved hearing your ideas. I think you could apply your thoughts to outerwear and boots as well.	男 妳要不要考慮加入我的團隊做冬裝？我知道我們的設計師很愛傾聽妳的構想。我認為，妳可以把妳的想法也應用在外套和靴子上。
W That sounds like a great opportunity. I can't make any promises, though. [42] I have a meeting with the director tomorrow to discuss where I'll be assigned.	女 聽起來是很棒的機會。不過我還無法答應。[42] 我明天要和總監開會，討論要指派我到哪個部門。
M [43] How about I call him today to make the suggestion? Then you and he can discuss the idea tomorrow.	男 [43] 我今天打電話給他，提個建議如何？那麼，妳和他明天就可以討論這個想法。
W Great. I'd really appreciate that.	女 太好了。非常感謝。

• **Congratulations** 恭喜、祝賀 **complete** 完成 **be impressed by** 使……留下深刻印象 **rewarding** 值得做的、有意義的 **consider** 考慮 **apply** 應用 **outerwear** （總稱）外套、外衣 **opportunity** 機會 **assign** 指派、分派 **suggestion** 建議 **appreciate** 感謝

41

Where do the speakers most likely work?
(A) At a law firm
(B) At a department store
(C) At an art gallery
(D) At a fashion company*

說話者最可能在哪裡工作？
(A) 在律師事務所。
(B) 在百貨公司。
(C) 在藝廊。
(D) 在時裝公司。

請注意對話中是否使用了特定類別的單字，或是單字間的共同之處。由 accessory、shoes、bags、outerwear、boots 以及 designed、designers 這些相關單字可推測出，說話者最有可能出現在 (D) 行業。

• **law** 法律、律師界 **firm** 商行、公司 **department store** 百貨公司

42

What does the woman mean when she says, "I can't make any promises"?
當女子說「我還無法答應」，意指什麼？

(A) She is unable to confirm her participation.*
(B) She is busy with other projects.
(C) She will leave her contract early.
(D) She has to hire additional employees.

(A) 她無法確定她能參與。
(B) 她忙著做其他的計畫。
(C) 她要提早解約。
(D) 她必須另外僱用員工。

請掌握好題目句前後的文意。後方補充說道：「明天將參加與業務分派有關的會議（I have a meeting with the director tomorrow to discuss where I'll be assigned.）」，因此 (A) 為最適當的答案。

• **confirm** 證實、確定 **participation** 參加、參與 **contract** 合約 **additional** 附加的、額外的

What does the man propose?
男子提議什麼？

(A) Attending a meeting (B) Calling a supervisor*
(C) Delivering a report (D) Preparing a proposal

(A) 參加會議。 (B) 打電話聯絡主管。
(C) 遞交一份報告。 (D) 準備一份提案。

請仔細聆聽男子所說的話。對話後半部說道：「How about I call him today to make the suggestion?」，由此得知答案為 (B)。句型「How about . . . ?」的意思為「……如何？」，常為詢問「提議」的解題線索。

答案改寫 call → contact

• **attend** 出席、參加 **supervisor** 管理者、監督者 **prepare** 準備 **proposal** 提案、建議

Questions 44–46 refer to the following conversation.

M Hello, [44] I am expecting a package from a branch of my company located in Manila. However, it hasn't arrived yet, and I haven't received any notices. My name is James Stone, and I work for Miller Fabric's head office down the street.	男 哈囉，[44] 我在等一件從馬尼拉分公司寄來的包裹。但是，包裹還沒送來，而且我沒有收到任何通知。我是詹姆斯・史東，在這條街的米勒織品總公司上班。
W Yes, Mr. Stone. Your package arrived yesterday. We were planning to notify your company today. [45] As the import fee has not been paid, we cannot deliver it yet.	女 是的，史東先生，您的包裹昨天送達。我們打算今天通知貴公司。[45] 因為進口費用尚未付清，我們便無法遞送。
M Oh, I wasn't aware there were any fees. Do I need to come in to pay it?	男 喔，我不知道有費用。我需要過去付款嗎？
W No, [46] you can pay by credit card over the phone. Just let me pull up your file.	女 不用，[46] 您可以在電話上用信用卡付款。我來找出您的檔案資料。

• **expect** 等待 **branch** 分公司 **located in** 坐落於、位於 **arrive** (郵件、物品等) 被送來
receive 收到、接到 **notice (n.)** 通知 **fabric** 織品、布料 **head office** 總公司
notify (v.) 通知、公告 **import** 進口 **fee** 費用 **deliver** 投遞、運送 **aware** 知道的

44

What type of business is the man calling?
(A) A dental clinic
(B) A post office*
(C) A moving company
(D) A bookstore

男子打電話到什麼類型的行業？
(A) 牙醫診所。
(B) 郵局。
(C) 搬家公司。
(D) 書店。

對話第一段，男子提到預計會收到包裹（I am expecting a package），並補充說明尚未抵達，因此 (B) 為最適當的答案。

• **dental** 牙齒的、牙科的　**post office** 郵局

45

What problem does the woman mention?
(A) A payment was not made.*
(B) A package was sent back.
(C) An address is wrong.
(D) A form is missing.

女子提及什麼問題？
(A) 有款項未付。
(B) 包裹被退回。
(C) 地址有誤。
(D) 表格遺失。

請仔細聆聽女子所說的話，並特別注意「問題」所在。她說：「As the import fee has not been paid, we cannot deliver it yet.」，因為尚未付款，所以仍無法配送，因此答案為 (A)。

答案改寫 pay → make a payment

• **payment** 支付的款項　**wrong** 錯誤的　**form** 表格　**missing** 遺失的

46

What will the man most likely do next?
(A) Make a phone call to a client
(B) Check the reverse side of an item
(C) E-mail a document to a colleague
(D) Provide payment information*

男子接下來最有可能做何事？
(A) 打電話給客戶。
(B) 檢查一個物品的背面。
(C) 以電子郵寄一份文件給同事。
(D) 提供付款資訊。

當題目以「. . . do next?」作結尾時，在對話後半部，會出現解題的關鍵線索。對話最後一段，女子提到可以打電話以信用卡結帳（you can pay by credit card over the phone），(D) 指「信用卡與結帳資訊」，為最適當的答案。

• **make a phone call** 打電話　**check** 檢查、核對　**reverse** 背面的、反面的
item 物品　**colleague** 同事　**provide** 提供

Questions 47–49 refer to the following conversation.

W Hello, Mr. Smith. [47] I'm doing a story for Channel 6's Local News at Five. Can I ask you some questions about your company's new Pets at Work program? I've been hearing great things about it.

M Sure. [48] We implemented the program last year. Basically, [48] we've taken shelter cats and given them a home in our office buildings. The cats are free to roam the office. Employees who interact with the cats have less stress and higher productivity.

W It's also a great way to help out local shelters. But isn't it expensive to feed and maintain the cats?

M Yes, it can get pricey. [49] But we've found the increased productivity more than makes up for it.

女 哈囉，史密斯先生。[47] 我正在為第 6 台的五點鐘地方新聞做專訪。我可以請問您幾個與貴公司的寵物上班計畫有關的問題嗎？我一直聽到關於這個計畫的讚譽。

男 當然。[48] 我們去年開始實行這項計畫。基本上，[48] 我們領養收容所裡的貓，給牠們一個家，就在我們辦公大樓裡。貓咪可以隨意在辦公室裡走動。和貓咪互動的員工壓力較小，生產力較高。

女 這也是一個幫助本地收容所的好方法。但是，飼養這些貓咪不會很貴嗎？

男 是的，可能很花錢。[49] 但是我們發現，增加的產能遠超過這項花費。

• **pet** 寵物 **implement** 實施、執行 **basically** 基本上、根本上 **shelter** 庇護所 **roam** 漫步 **interact** 互動 **productivity** 生產力、產能 **expensive** 昂貴的 **feed** 餵（養）、飼（養） **maintain** 供養 **pricey** 高價的 **increased** 增加的 **make up for** 補償

47

Who is the woman?

(A) A veterinarian
(B) A reporter*
(C) A shelter owner
(D) An artist

女子是誰？

(A) 獸醫。
(B) 記者。
(C) 收容所持有人。
(D) 藝術家。

對話第一段，女子說道：「I'm doing a story for Channel 6's Local News at Five.」，表示正在撰寫報導，因此答案為 (B)。

• **veterinarian** 獸醫

48

What has the man recently done?

(A) Hired new summer employees
(B) Appeared on a television program
(C) Purchased a local animal shelter
(D) Introduced animals to a workplace*

男子最近做了什麼？

(A) 僱用新的夏季員工。
(B) 出現在電視節目中。
(C) 買下一間本地動物收容所。
(D) 將動物帶進工作場所。

女子詢問有關公司的寵物計畫，男子回答：「計畫是從去年開始（We implemented the program last year.）」，接著說道他們把貓咪帶回公司，在公司大樓內為牠們打造了一個家（we've taken shelter cats and given them a home in our office buildings），因此 (D) 為最適當的答案。

答案改寫 implement → introduce
cats → animals
office building → workplace

• **appear** 出現、露面 **introduce** 引進

49

What does the man say about the cost of the program?

(A) Employees cover most of the costs.
(B) The benefits outweigh the costs.*
(C) Donations help offset the costs.
(D) The program does not cost anything.

關於計畫的費用，男子說了什麼？

(A) 員工負擔大部分的費用。
(B) 好處超過開銷。
(C) 捐款有助抵銷開支。
(D) 計畫沒有花任何錢。

請仔細聆聽男子所説的話，並注意關鍵點「費用」。對話最後一句，男子說道：「雖然增加很多開銷，但也相對獲得更多產能（But we've found the increased productivity more than makes up for it.）」，因此答案為 (B)。

答案改寫 size → dimension

- **cover** 足夠支付　**cost** 費用　**benefit** 好處、利益　**outweigh** 比……更重要、比……更有價值　**donation** 捐款　**offset** 抵銷、補償

Questions 50–52 refer to the following conversation.

W I'm so excited to be starting at Wilfred Law. It's one of the best law firms in the country, but [50] I'm a little nervous for the orientation.

M Don't worry. I'm sure everyone is nervous. It looks like the only seats left are in the corner.

W In the corner? Are you sure that's okay? [51] I'd like to be close to the speakers in case I want to ask a question.

M Oh, there won't be any questions this time. But there are some comment cards on the table by the door. [52] You can write your questions and submit them at the end. The questions will be addressed in tomorrow's presentation. Do you want me to get you a card?

女 我對於要開始在魏福德律師事務所上班感到很興奮。這是全國頂尖的律師事務所，但 [50] 我對職前訓練感到有點緊張。

男 別擔心，我相信每個人都很緊張。看來只有角落的位子還空著。

女 角落？你確定這樣沒問題嗎？[51] 我想要靠近講師一些，以防萬一我要問問題。

男 喔，這一次不會有提問時間。但門邊的桌上有意見卡。[52] 你可以把你的問題寫下來，結束時交出去。問題會在明天的演講解決。你要我幫你拿張卡片嗎？

- **nervous** 緊張不安的　**in case** 以防萬一、假如　**submit** 提出、呈遞　**address** 處理、解決

50

What type of event are the speakers attending?

(A) A job orientation*
(B) A staff party
(C) A law conference
(D) An orchestra performance

說話者參加什麼活動？

(A) 職前訓練。
(B) 員工派對。
(C) 法律研討會。
(D) 交響樂團表演。

女子在對話第一段説道：「I'm a little nervous for the orientation」，由此可以聽到解題的關鍵線索，因此答案為 (A)。

- **performance** 表演、演奏

51

Why does the woman say, "Are you sure that's okay"?
(A) She wants to leave a meeting early.
(B) She thinks the speakers are too quiet.
(C) She prefers to be in a larger room.
(D) She does not like an option very much.*

為何女子說「你確定這樣沒問題嗎?」
(A) 她想要提前離開會議。
(B) 她認為講師太安靜了。
(C) 她比較喜歡大一點的空間。
(D) 她不太喜歡某個選項。

請仔細聆聽題目句前後的文意。男子說道:「只剩下角落的位子」,女子向男子再次確認是否只剩下角落空著,並表示自己想要離講師近一點的位置(I'd like to be close to the speakers in case I want to ask a question.)。(D) 將角落的位子改成 an option,為最適當的答案。

52

What does the man say about the comment cards?
(A) They include personal information.
(B) They are too small to write on.
(C) They can be handed in after the presentation.*
(D) They are reserved for managers only.

關於意見卡,男子說了什麼?
(A) 它們包含個人資料。
(B) 它們太小張,無法在上面寫字。
(C) 它們可以在演講結束後交出去。
(D) 它們只保留給經理用。

請仔細聆聽男子所說的話,並注意關鍵字 comment cards(意見卡)。對話最後一段,男子說:「可以先將問題寫在意見卡上,於演講後繳交(You can write your questions and submit them at the end.),問題將在隔天的演講中解答」,因此答案為 (C)。

答案改寫 submit → hand in

• **hand in** 繳交　**reserve** 保留、把……專門留給

Questions 53–55 refer to the following conversation.

M Hi, [53] I'm calling to inquire about your rental cars. [54] I'll be in Chicago for a month on business and I'd prefer to rent a car rather than take public transit.	男 嗨,[53] 我打電話來詢問關於租車的事。[54] 我會到芝加哥出差一個月,我比較喜歡租車,而不是搭乘公共交通運輸工具。
W Okay, great. What kind of car are you looking for, and what is your price range?	女 好的,好極了。您在找什麼樣的車,還有您的價格範圍是?
M Well, [54] I'll be picking up numerous clients and colleagues on our way to and from conferences, so I'd like something roomy with four doors. Since I'll need the car for an entire month, I'd like something in the mid-price range.	男 嗯,[54] 在我們往返研討會的路上,我會去接很多客戶和同事,所以,我想要寬敞的四門汽車。既然我整整一個月都要用到車,我想要中價位的車款。
W Okay, we have several cars that might fit your needs. I can e-mail you a list of cars with photos and prices, and you can get back to me when you've chosen one. [55] What's your e-mail address and phone number?	女 好,我們有幾款車可能符合您的需求。我可以用電子郵件寄一份汽車清單給您,上面有照片和價格,等您選好後,可以回信給我。[55] 您的電子郵件地址和電話號碼是?

• **inquire** 詢問　**rental** 供出租的　**rent (v.)** 租用　**public transit** 公共運輸　**range** 範圍、區域　**numerous** 許多的、為數眾多的　**colleague** 同事　**roomy** 寬敞的、廣闊的　**entire** 整個的、全部的　**several** 數個的　**fit** 適合於

53

Where most likely does the woman work?
(A) A travel agency
(B) A taxi and limo service
(C) A car rental company*
(D) A conference center

女子最有可能在哪裡工作？
(A) 旅行社。
(B) 計程車與豪華禮車服務。
(C) 租車公司。
(D) 會議中心。

男子打電話詢問租車問題（I'm calling to inquire about your rental cars.），因此 (C) 為最適當的答案。請特別留意，有時會出現這類型的題目，必須從另一方的對話內容中尋找答案。

- **travel agency** 旅行社

54

What does the man say about his trip?
(A) He needs to pick up many people.*
(B) He will be traveling for two months.
(C) His company pays for his expenses.
(D) His colleagues are giving presentations.

關於旅程，男子說了什麼？
(A) 他需要開車去接很多人。
(B) 他會旅行兩個月。
(C) 他的公司支付他的開支。
(D) 他的同事要做簡報。

請仔細聆聽男子所說的話，並注意「出差」的內容。對話第一段，男子提到「為期一個月（I'll be in Chicago for a month on business）」；對話第二段則表示接送客戶需要用車（I'll be picking up numerous clients and collegues on our way to and from conferences），因此答案為 (A)。

答案改寫 numerous → many
clients and collegues → people

- **expense** 開支、費用

55

What information does the woman request?
(A) A hotel's location
(B) The cost of flight
(C) The dates of a trip
(D) Some contact information*

女子要求什麼資訊？
(A) 飯店的位置。
(B) 機票的費用。
(C) 旅程的日期。
(D) 一些聯絡資訊。

對話最後一段，女子詢問對方的電子郵件地址和電話號碼（What's your e-mail adderss and phone number?），因此答案為 (D)。

答案改寫 e-mail address and phone number → contact information

Questions 56–58 refer to the following conversation with three speakers.

M1	[56] I'd like to spend today's meeting talking about the bad reviews we've gotten online. Several customers have complained about long wait times at our restaurant. Does anybody have any ideas?	男1	[56] 我想利用今天的會議談談我們最近得到的網路負面評價。好幾個顧客抱怨，在我們餐廳的等候時間很久。有人知道是怎麼回事嗎？
W	Well, we have been short-staffed lately despite being very busy. [57] What about hiring some new part-time workers during peak hours?	女	嗯，儘管很忙，我們最近人手卻一直不足。[57] 在尖峰時段僱用一些新的兼職人員如何？
M1	That's a great idea. Max, you hired the last group of part-time workers, didn't you?	男1	這真是個好主意。麥克斯，上一批兼職人員是你僱用的，不是嗎？
M2	Yes, I did. It wasn't hard. I just advertised on a student job board. We had a lot of applicants.	男2	對，是我。找人不會太難。我只是在學生打工板上打廣告。應徵的人很多。
W	That's great, Max. [58] Would you be willing to collect some résumés that we could review together at the next meeting?	女	那太好了，麥克斯。[58] 你願不願意收集一些履歷表，我們可以在下次會議時一起審核？
M2	Sure. That shouldn't be a problem.	男2	當然，應該不成問題。

• **several** 數個的　**complain** 抱怨、投訴　**short-staffed** 人手短缺　**lately** 近來　**despite** 儘管　**hire** 僱用　**peak** 高峰　**applicant** 應徵者　**collect** 收集　**résumé** 履歷表

56

What problem does the restaurant have?
(A) It lost some applications.
(B) Its appliances are too old.
(C) Its costs have increased.
(D) It got some negative reviews.*

餐廳有什麼問題？
(A) 有些求職信遺失。
(B) 設備太老舊。
(C) 成本增加。
(D) 收到一些負面評價。

對話第一段提到：「I'd like to spend today's meeting talking about the bad reviews we've gotten online.」，想利用今天的會議討論網路負面評價，由此確認答案為 (D)。

答案改寫 bad → negative

• **application** 申請（書）、求職信　**appliance** 器具、（電器）設備　**cost** 費用、成本　**increase** 增加　**negative** 否定的、消極的

57

What does the woman suggest?
(A) Hiring some new employees*
(B) Offering more menu options
(C) Advertising online
(D) Providing refunds

女子有何建議？
(A) 僱用一些新員工。
(B) 提供更多菜單選擇。
(C) 上網打廣告。
(D) 提供退費。

請仔細聆聽女子所說的話。對話前半部，女子建議在用餐尖峰時段增加幾位兼職員工（What about hiring some new part-time workers during peak hours?），因此答案為 (A)。「What about . . . ?」意思為「……如何？」，當題目以 suggest 詢問時，答案通常會出現在這句話中。

答案改寫 worker → employee

• **offer** 提供、給予　**online** 網上的　**provide** 提供　**refund** 退款、退還

58

What does the woman ask Max to do?
(A) Contact a store manager
(B) Prepare for the next meeting*
(C) Host a student job fair
(D) Respond to online reviews

女子要求麥克斯何事？
(A) 聯絡店面經理。
(B) 為下次會議做準備。
(C) 主持學生的就業博覽會。
(D) 回應網路評語

聆聽時，請特別留意關鍵人名 Max。女子叫了 Max 的名字後，說道：「Would you be willing to collect some résumés that we could review together at the next meeting?」，請他收集一些履歷，以便在下次會議中審核，因此 (B) 為最適當的答案。

• **contact** 聯繫、接觸　**prepare** 準備　**host** 主持　**respond to** 回答、回應

Questions 59–61 refer to the following conversation.

W Hi, Mr. Peters. [59] I remember you saying last time that you used Prime Employee Trainers to help train your new staff members. Were you satisfied with their services?	**女** 嗨，畢德斯先生。[59] 我記得你上次說，你採用「一流員工訓練公司」協助訓練新進員工。你對他們的服務滿意嗎？
M Yes. Prime has helped us during several hiring seasons. We're a small company, so we don't have the staff to do our own training.	**男** 是的，「一流」在好幾次招聘季幫上我們的忙。我們是間小公司，所以沒有人手自己訓練。
W That's great. Well, [60] my home renovation company has just hired some new staff members. I'd love to get their training done quickly and affordably.	**女** 太好了。嗯，[60] 我的居家裝修公司才剛僱用一些新員工。我希望他們快點完成訓練，而且收費要公道。
M Actually, I think Prime only does training for IT and accounting departments. I'm not sure they would be able to help you. However, if you're looking to train your administrative workers, I know there are several companies that do that. [61] I'm sure you could find one if you search online.	**男** 事實上，我想「一流」只做 IT 和會計部門的訓練。我不確定他們是否能幫上你的忙。不過，如果妳是要訓練行政人員，我知道有幾家公司是做這方面的訓練。[61] 如果妳上網搜尋，一定可以找到。

• **train** 訓練、培養　**be satisfied with** 感到滿意　**renovation** 翻新　**affordably** 負擔得起地
accounting 會計　**department** 部門　**administrative** 行政的、管理的

59

What are the speakers discussing?
(A) Hiring a training agency*
(B) Advertising on the web
(C) Launching a new product
(D) Hosting a conference

說話者在討論什麼？
(A) 僱用一個訓練機構。
(B) 上網登廣告。
(C) 發表新產品。
(D) 主持研討會。

當題目詢問對話的主旨時，在對話前半部，通常可以聽到關鍵線索。對話第一段，女子提及上次的培訓公司（I remember you saying last time that you used Prime Employee Trainers to help train your new staff members.），並詢問是否滿意，因此 (A) 為最適當的答案。

• **launch** 把（商品）投入市場、推出、發表

60

What type of business does the woman own?
(A) A trade corporation
(B) A web development firm
(C) A landscaping business
(D) A home improvement company*

女子擁有的是何種公司？
(A) 貿易公司。
(B) 網路開發公司。
(C) 景觀美化公司。
(D) 居家裝修公司。

對話第二段，女子說道：「my home renovation company has just hired some new staff members.」，提到公司的說明，由此得知答案為 (D)。

答案改寫 renovation → improvement

• **trade** 貿易 **corporation** 大公司、集團公司 **development** 開發 **firm** 公司 **improvement** 改良、修繕

61

What does the man suggest?
(A) Developing a program
(B) Interviewing some clients
(C) Finding a company online*
(D) Attending a meeting

男子有何建議？
(A) 開發一個程式。
(B) 採訪一些客戶。
(C) 上網找公司。
(D) 參加會議。

請仔細聆聽男子所說的話。對話最後，男子提到他知道有幾家不錯的公司，可以培訓行政人員，並請女子上網搜尋（I'm sure you could find one if you search online.），因此答案為 (C)。

• **develop** 開發、研製 **attend** 參加、出席

Questions 62–64 refer to the following conversation and chart.

Admission Price per Person	單人門票
Students $10	學生 $10
[63] Groups of 6 or more $13	[63] 6人以上團體 $13
Members $17	會員 $17
Non-members $20	非會員 $20

W	[62] Have you heard about the new musical at the theater downtown? Apparently it got rave reviews. Some coworkers and I are planning to go see it. Would you like to come?	女	[62] 你知道鬧區那家劇院新的音樂劇嗎？顯然劇評對它大肆讚揚。我和一些同事打算去看。你要一起去嗎？
M	Sure. I've actually been waiting to see it. How much are the tickets?	男	當然，我其實在等待時機去看。門票多少？
W	There are a few different prices. Here, look at this chart. [63] We already have six people who are interested, so we should be able to get this price.	女	有幾種不同的價位。來，看這張表。[63] 我們已經有六個人有興趣，所以我們應該可以適用這個價格。
M	That sounds good. Are you planning to go this weekend?	男	聽起來很不賴。你們打算這個週末去看嗎？
W	No, probably on Thursday after work. Is that okay for you?	女	不是，也許星期四下班之後。那個時間你可以嗎？
M	That sounds good. Are you going to order the tickets online?	男	聽起來不錯。你們要上網訂票嗎？
W	No. Jenny in the sales department is going to stop by the theater today. [64] I'll call her and tell her to include you.	女	不是。業務部的珍妮今天會順路去劇院。[64] 我會打電話給她，告訴她把你也算進去。

• **admission** 入場費、門票 **apparently** 顯然地 **rave review** 大加讚揚、佳評如潮 **coworker** 同事 **probably** 很可能 **order** 訂購 **stop by** 順路造訪 **include** 算入、包含於……裡面

62

What type of event are the speakers discussing? 說話者在討論什麼活動？

(A) A film release (B) A restaurant opening
(C) An academic seminar (D) A musical performance*

(A) 電影上映。 (B) 餐廳開幕。
(C) 學術研討會。 (D) 音樂劇演出。

對話第一段，女子問道：「Have you heard about the new musical at the theater downtown?」，可由此推測之後的對話內容與「音樂劇」有關，因此答案為 (D)。

• **release** 上映、公映 **academic** 學院的、學術的 **performance** 表演

Look at the graphic. What ticket price will the speakers probably pay? 請見圖表。說話者最可能付哪種票價？

(A) $10 (B) $13*
(C) $17 (D) $20

(A) $10。 (B) $13。
(C) $17。 (D) $20。

聆聽時，請特別留意 ticket price（票價）。對話中間，女子説道：「依照價位表，可以適用六人的價格」。因此由「Groups of 6 or more $13」，可以確認答案為 (B)。

64

What does the woman offer to do?
(A) Pick up some tickets
(B) Make a purchase online
(C) Contact a coworker*
(D) Delay an event

女子提議做什麼？
(A) 去拿票。
(B) 上網購買。
(C) 聯絡同事。
(D) 延後活動。

請仔細聆聽女子所說的話，並特別留意「提議」的內容。對話最後一段提到「將由珍妮去買票，我會打電話告訴她再多追加你一位（I'll call her and tell her to include you.）」，因此 (C) 為最適當的答案。

答案改寫 call → contact

• make a purchase 購買物品　contact 聯繫　coworker 同事　delay 使延期

Questions 65–67 refer to the following conversation and map.

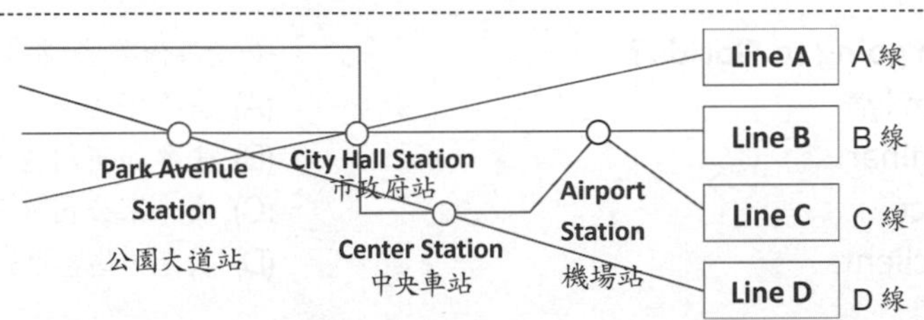

W　Hi, Steve. I'm glad I ran into you. [65] This is my first time at Park Avenue Station, and I'm so confused. I'm trying to get to the airport, but Line B is closed for repairs. Do you know of another way to get to the airport?

M　Here, take a look at my subway map. I usually take this route. However, it's not an express route, so you'll have to transfer. [66] I think you can transfer at Center Station. I don't think it'll take very long, though.

W　Okay. Thank you so much. I hope I don't miss my flight to Florida.

M　Oh, are you traveling for work again?

W　No. Actually, [67] I'm visiting some family members for my vacation.

M　That'll be nice. I guess I won't see you at the office next week, then. Enjoy your trip!

女　嗨，史帝夫，真高興碰巧遇到你。[65] 這是我第一次到公園大道站，我完全搞糊塗了。我想要去機場，但 B 線正封閉整修。你知道其他去機場的路線嗎？

男　來，看一下我的地鐵路線圖。我通常搭這條路線。不過，這不是直達路線，所以妳必須轉車。[66] 我想，妳可以在中央車站轉車。不過我認為不會太久。

女　好的，非常感謝你。希望我不會錯過去佛羅里達的班機。

男　噢，妳又要出差了？

女　不是，其實 [67] 我是休假去看家人。

男　真好。那麼，我猜下星期不會在公司看到妳了。旅途愉快！

• run into 偶然遇見　confused 迷惑的、糊塗的　route 路線　express 直達的　transfer 使換車　miss 未趕上、錯過　flight 班機、航班

65

Where does the conversation take place?
(A) At a bus stop
(B) In a subway station*
(C) At an airport
(D) In an office

這段對話發生在哪裡？
(A) 在公車站。
(B) 在地鐵站。
(C) 在機場。
(D) 在辦公室。

對話第一段，女子說道：「This is my first time at Park Avenue Station」，表示這是她第一次到公園大道站，由此確認答案為 (B)。

66

Look at the graphic. Which line does the man suggest the woman take first?
(A) Line A
(B) Line B
(C) Line C
(D) Line D*

請見圖表。男子建議女子先搭乘哪一條路線？
(A) A 線
(B) B 線
(C) C 線
(D) D 線

請仔細聆聽男子所說的話，並特別留意「轉乘的路線」。男子說道：「現在位於公園大道站，請搭乘至中央車站換車（I think you can transfer at Center Station.）」，因此答案為 (D)。

67

Why is the woman going to Florida?
(A) To visit with family*
(B) To attend a seminar
(C) To go to an office
(D) To meet some clients

女子為何要去佛羅里達？
(A) 去看家人。
(B) 去參加研討會。
(C) 去一家公司。
(D) 去見一些客戶。

聆聽時，請掌握本題的關鍵為「女子出行的目的」。對話後半部，女子說道：「I'm visiting some family members for my vacation」，表示將利用休假時間去看家人，由此得知答案為 (A)。

• **visit with** 看望（某人）、去（某人）家裡作客　**attend** 參加、出席

Questions 68–70 refer to the following conversation and list.

FROM	發信人	SUBJECT:	主旨
69 Andrew Webber	69 安德魯・韋伯	ATTACHED: August Sales Figures	附件：八月銷售數據
Anna Stevens	安娜・史蒂文斯	Budget Projection for September	九月預算
David Skinner	大衛・史基納	Advertising Meeting Summary	廣告會議摘要
Janine Rogers	珍奈・羅傑斯	CANCELED: Dinner with Mr. Sampson	取消：與山普森先生的晚餐

M Hi Trina. 68 Are you having any trouble with your Internet connection?
W No, mine has been fine all morning.
M I see. It must be my office then. I can't seem to access my e-mail or web browsers. 69 Can you tell me if the e-mail with the latest sales figures came in yet?
W Let me check. Yes, it's right here. Do you want to see it on my computer?
M No, that's okay. 70 Can you forward a copy to my assistant? I'll need it for the sales meeting with the CEO this afternoon.

男 嗨，崔娜，68 妳的網路連線有任何問題嗎？
女 沒有，我的網路整個早上都很順。
男 了解。那一定是我辦公室的問題。我似乎無法讀取電子郵件或連上瀏覽器。69 妳可不可以告訴我，最新銷售數據的電子郵件寄來了沒？
女 我查一下。有的，就在這裡。你要在我的電腦上看嗎？
男 不用，沒關係。70 妳可以轉寄一份給我的助理嗎？我今天下午和執行長開的業務會議上需要用到。

• **attach** 把……做為電子郵件的附件　**projection** 預測、推測　**summary** 摘要　**cancel** 取消
connection 連接、銜接　**access** （電腦）讀取、存取　**figure** 數字　**forward** 轉寄　**assistant** 助理

68

Why is the man unable to access his e-mail?
(A) The company servers are down.
(B) His office connection is not working.*
(C) He needs to upgrade his software.
(D) His computer has no battery power.

男子為何無法讀取他的電子郵件？
(A) 公司的伺服器故障。
(B) 他的辦公室無法連上網路。
(C) 他需要升級他的軟體。
(D) 他電腦的電池沒電了。

本題重點在於男子「碰到的問題」。對話第一段，男子說道：「Are you having any trouble with your Internet connection?」，詢問對方能否連上網路，因此 (B) 為最適當的答案。

69

Look at the graphic. Who sent the e-mail the speakers are referring to?
(A) Andrew Webber*
(B) Anna Stevens
(C) David Skinner
(D) Janine Rogers

請見圖表。說話者提及的電子郵件是誰寄出的？
(A) 安德魯・韋伯。
(B) 安娜・史蒂文斯。
(C) 大衛・史基納。
(D) 珍奈・羅傑斯。

聆聽時，請特別留意 e-mail 部分。對話中間，男子想確認是否有銷售數據的郵件（Can you tell me if the e-mail with the latest sales figures came in yet?）。根據相關的郵件主旨，從表格中可以找出寄件人為 Andrew Webber，主旨為「ATTACHED: August Sales Figures」，因此答案為 (A)。

• **refer to** 提到、談論

70

What does the man ask the woman to do?
(A) Pass on an e-mail*
(B) Attend a meeting
(C) Scan a budget report
(D) Cancel a client dinner

男子請求女子何事？
(A) 傳一封電子郵件。
(B) 參加會議。
(C) 掃描一份預算報告。
(D) 取消與客戶的晚餐。

請仔細聆聽男子所說的話。對話最後一段，男子詢問：「Can you forward a copy to my assistant?」，請求對方將郵件轉寄給他的助理，因此答案為 (A)。「Can you . . . ?」的意思為「可以請你⋯⋯嗎？」當題目詢問要求事項時，答案通常會出現在這句話中。

答案改寫 forward → pass on
copy → e-mail

PART 4 12

Questions 71–73 refer to the following introduction.

W [71] We're back with Dr. Ruth McKay on LRT radio. As we heard before the break, Dr. McKay is president of the Natural Life Organization and author of the best-selling book *Eat Natural, Live Natural.* [72] Dr. McKay has joined us to share her best advice on eliminating unnatural products from your life. In just a moment, Dr. McKay will be reading excerpts from her book and then we'll have a question and answer session. [73] To ask a question, visit www.LRTradio.com and comment on Dr. McKay's profile.

女 [71] 回到 LRT 電台，在現場的是茹絲・麥凱博士。我們在廣告之前已經知道，麥凱博士是全國生命組織的主席，並著有暢銷書《吃得天然，活得自然》。[72] 麥凱博士要和我們分享她的最佳建議，告訴我們如何去除生活中的非天然產品。再過一會，麥凱博士會朗讀她書中的節選內容，接著我們會有問答時間。[73] 想問問題的話，請上 www.LRTradio.com 網站，在麥凱博士的人物簡介中留下意見。

• **break** 暫停、休息、廣告時間 **organization** 組織 **author** 作者 **share** 分享 **eliminate** 排除、消除 **unnatural** 非天然的、不自然的 **excerpt** 摘錄、片段

71

Where does the speaker work?

(A) At a radio station*
(B) At a hospital
(C) At a university
(D) At a newspaper

說話者在哪裡工作？

(A) 廣播電台。
(B) 醫院。
(C) 大學。
(D) 報社。

獨白第一句說道：「We're back with Dr. Ruth McKay on LRT radio.」，提到 LRT 電台，由此推測說話者為廣播節目主持人，因此答案為 (A)。

72

What will Dr. McKay be discussing?

(A) Business finances
(B) Healthy living*
(C) Beauty products
(D) Political candidates

麥凱博士將討論什麼？

(A) 商業金融。
(B) 健康生活。
(C) 美容產品。
(D) 政黨候選人。

獨白中段提到將告訴大家如何去除生活當中非自然的產品（Dr. McKay has joined us to share her best advice on eliminating unnatural products from your life.），因此 (B) 為最適當的答案。

• **finance** 金融、財政 **political** 政治的、政黨的 **candidate** 候選人

73

What does the speaker encourage listeners to do?

(A) Write down tips and information
(B) Call a receptionist with questions
(C) Purchase a new best-selling book
(D) Leave a comment on a website*

說話者鼓勵聽眾做什麼？

(A) 寫下建議和資訊。
(B) 打電話給櫃台人員提問。
(C) 購買新的暢銷書。
(D) 在網站上留下意見。

在獨白後半段，通常會出現說話者的建議或是要求事項。最後一句說道：「To ask a question, visit www.LRTradio.com and comment on Dr. McKay's profile.」，提醒聽眾上網留下意見，可由此得知答案為 (D)。

答案改寫 comment → leave a comment

• **encourage** 鼓勵 **purchase** 購買 **leave** 留下

Questions 74–76 refer to the following excerpt from a meeting.

M Good afternoon, everyone. I called this meeting to talk about how we are serving tables during our dinner service. [74] I've noticed that some of the wait staff are very concerned with taking orders and expediting food quickly. However, [75] it's important to interact with our customers. We should make an effort to chat with them and ask how their day has been going. This will make them feel more at home and more likely to dine at our restaurant in the future. [76] Now, I'd like to play a short video that will give you some tips about how to interact with customers.	男 大家午安。我召集這次會議，是為了談談我們在晚餐時段的服務方式。[74] 我注意到，有些服務人員的工作內容高度涉及點餐以及快速送餐。但是，[75] 和顧客互動很重要。我們應該努力和他們聊天，問問他們今天過得如何。這會讓他們感覺比較自在，將來比較可能來我們餐廳用餐。[76] 現在，我想放一段短短的影片，給你們一些如何和顧客互動的訣竅。

• **call a meeting** 召開會議 **notice** 注意 **be concerned with** 涉及、關於 **order** 點菜 **expedite** 加快、加速、迅速完成 **interact** 互動 **make an effort to** 努力 **dine** 用餐 **in the future** 將來、未來 **tip** 訣竅

74

Who most likely are the listeners?

(A) Hotel guests (B) Supermarket employees
(C) Business managers (D) Restaurant workers*

聽眾最有可能是誰？

(A) 飯店的房客。 (B) 超市員工。
(C) 商務經理。 (D) 餐廳員工。

獨白前半部説道：「some of the wait staff are very concerned with taking orders and expediting food quickly」，由此可以推測此為與「點餐」和「送餐服務」有關的企業，因此答案為 (D)。

75

What is the topic of the meeting?

(A) Introducing new menus
(B) Being friendly with customers*
(C) Wearing company uniforms
(D) Policies for cleaning workspaces

會議的主題為何？

(A) 介紹新菜單。
(B) 待客友善。
(C) 穿公司制服。
(D) 清潔工作空間的政策。

説話者指出現在的問題在於服務方式：「it's important to interact with our customers. We should make an effort to chat with them and ask how their day has been going.」，表示需加強與顧客的溝通，並增加日常對話。(B) 以單字 friendly 概括前述的內容，為正確答案。

• **friendly** 友善的 **policy** 政策、方針 **workspace** 工作空間

76

What will the listeners do next?

(A) Watch a film* (B) Complete a survey
(C) Practice a dialogue (D) Study a pamphlet

聽眾接下來會做何事？

(A) 觀看影片。 (B) 完成調查報告。
(C) 練習對話。 (D) 研究一份小冊子。

本題使用「. . . do next?」，詢問獨白結束之後，聽眾將要做的事情，答題線索通常出現在獨白後半部。獨白最後一句説道：「Now, I'd like to play a short video that will give you some tips about how to interact with customers.」，由此得知答案為 (A)。

答案改寫 video → film

• **complete** 完成 **survey** 調查、調查報告 **practice** 練習

Questions 77–79 refer to the following introduction.

W Good afternoon, and [77] welcome to the product launch of ISD Social, a new app designed by software developer Steven Jones. In just a moment, [77] Mr. Jones will introduce his new app and show us some of its features. Mr. Jones is currently lead software designer at Issac Stanford Development. [78] Over the last three years, Mr. Jones has headed several projects at Issac Stanford, the most noteworthy of which is the popular ISD Photo Sharer. Mr. Jones will also be available for a question and answer session later today. [79] Anyone interested in attending can fill out a question card and submit it to me after the presentation. Now, here's Mr. Jones to tell you a bit about his new app.

女 午安，[77] 歡迎參加「ISD 社交」的產品發表會，這是由軟體開發者史蒂芬・瓊斯所設計的新應用程式。再過一會，[77] 瓊斯先生就會介紹他新開發的應用程式，並為我們展示它的一些特色。瓊斯先生目前是艾薩克・史丹佛開發公司的首席軟體設計工程師。[78] 過去三年來，瓊斯先生領導艾薩克・史丹佛的多項專案，最值得注意的是流行的 ISD 照片分享。瓊斯先生今天稍晚也有留時間進行問與答。[79] 有興趣參加的人可以填寫一張提問卡，在簡報之後交給我。現在，就讓瓊斯先生來告訴你，關於他的新應用程式的二三事。

• launch 把（商品）投入市場　introduce 介紹　feature 特色、特徵　head 率領、主管　several 數個的　noteworthy 值得注意的　available 有空的　attend 參加、出席　submit 提出、呈遞

77

What event is being introduced?
(A) A store opening
(B) A charity marathon
(C) A product demonstration*
(D) A technology sale

文中介紹的是什麼活動？
(A) 商店開幕。
(B) 慈善馬拉松。
(C) 產品發表。
(D) 科技產品特賣。

獨白首段說道：「welcome to the product launch of ISD Social」，由此可以推測為「新產品發表會現場」；再加上後面說道：「Mr. Jones will introduce his new app and show us some of its features」，可以更加確定答案為 (C)。

• event 活動　demonstration 示範、演示

78

What did Steven Jones do over the last three years?
(A) Lead several development projects*
(B) Review new products in the market
(C) Acquire a few small companies
(D) Coordinate marketing campaigns

過去三年來，史蒂芬・瓊斯做了什麼？
(A) 領導數個開發計畫。
(B) 細察市場上的新產品。
(C) 收購一些小公司。
(D) 協調行銷活動。

聆聽時，請掌握關鍵在「過去三年的業績」。獨白中段說道：「Over the last three years, Mr. Jones has headed several projects」，由此確認答案為 (A)。

答案改寫 head → lead

• acquire 收購　coordinate 協調

79

What should listeners do if they want to attend the question and answer session?
(A) Install a new app
(B) Visit a press room
(C) Log into a website
(D) Hand in a question card*

聽眾若想參加問答活動，應該做什麼？
(A) 安裝新的應用程式。
(B) 造訪媒體新聞室。
(C) 登入網站。
(D) 遞交提問卡。

本題的關鍵點為「參加條件」。獨白末段提到，想要參與提問時間的朋友，請先將問題寫在提問卡上，並於會後繳交（Anyone interested in attending can fill out a question card and submit it to me after the presentation.），因此答案為 (D)。

答案改寫 submit → hand in

- **install** 安裝、設置 **hand in** 遞交

Questions 80–82 refer to the following telephone message.

M Hello, Anna. This is Max calling. [80] I just found out that the hotel has lost our reservation for [81] our business conference next Friday. I've called a few other hotels, but they're all booked on account of the conference. I remembered your sister is a manager at the Booker Valley Hotel. Is there any way you can call her and see if she can help find us rooms? I know you're busy preparing your presentation. [82] But we really need a place to stay.

男 哈囉，安娜，我是麥克斯。[80] 我剛剛發現，飯店遺失了 [81] 我們下星期五為了參加商務研討會的訂房資料。我已經打給其他幾家飯店，但是因為研討會的關係，它們都客滿了。我記得妳的姊姊是布客谷飯店的經理。妳有沒有辦法打給她，看看她是否能幫我們訂到房間？我知道妳正忙著準備簡報，[82] 但是我們真的需要下榻的地方。

- **lose** 丟失、遺失 **reservation** 預訂 **book** 預訂、預約 **on account of** 由於、因為 **prepare** 準備 **stay** 暫住

80

What did the speaker find out?
(A) His conference was canceled.
(B) His luggage was misplaced.
(C) His reservation was lost.*
(D) His speech is too long.

說話者發現了什麼？
(A) 他的研討會取消了。
(B) 他的行李放錯地方了。
(C) 他的訂房資料不見了。
(D) 他的演講太長了。

獨白前半段說道：「I just found out that the hotel has lost our reservation」，飯店遺失了訂房資料，因此答案為 (C)。雖然 lose 和 misplace 的意思相同，但請特別留意選項中句子的文意，內容完全不同，切勿因為急著答題而選了 (B)。

- **cancel** 取消 **luggage** 行李

81

What is the speaker scheduled to do on Friday?
(A) Take a vacation
(B) Meet some clients
(C) Review a proposal
(D) Attend a conference*

說話者預定星期五要做什麼？
(A) 度假。
(B) 會見一些客戶。
(C) 審核一個提案。
(D) 參加研討會。

聆聽時，請特別留意關鍵時間點 Friday。獨白前半部說道：「our business conference next Friday」，由此得知答案為 (D)。

• **review** 審核、檢閱　**proposal** 提案　**attend** 參加

82

Why does the man say, "I know you're busy preparing your presentation"?
(A) To reschedule a trip date
(B) To acknowledge an inconvenience*
(C) To offer help with a project
(D) To provide feedback on some work

男子為何說「我知道妳在忙著準備妳的簡報？」
(A) 為了重新安排旅程的日期。
(B) 以承認造成不便。
(C) 為了提議幫忙一個專案。
(D) 為了提出工作的回饋意見。

碰到此類題型時，需要先掌握問句前後的文意，才能順利解題。「我知道妳非常忙碌，但我們真的很需要住宿的地方」(But we really need a place to stay.)，根據情境，(B) 為最適當的答案。

• **reschedule** 重新安排……的時間　**acknowledge** 承認　**inconvenience** 不便、麻煩事　**offer** 給予、提議

Questions 83–85 refer to the following news report.

M Yesterday, the State of Mississippi announced that [83] it will build a new express highway over the next five years. The new highway will connect the City of Bradford with Greenwich County. According to the announcement, the new express highway is the first to connect these cities and will [84] lessen driving times by up to six hours. To help sponsor the highway, drivers can purchase [85] express passes that will allow unlimited access to the new highway once it's built. Vicki Brookes, mayor of the City of Bradford, said her community has been waiting a long time for the development of this highway and hopes more routes will be planned.

男 昨天，密西西比州宣布 [83] 將在五年內興建一條新的快速公路。新的公路將連接布拉福市與格林威治郡。根據公告內容，新的快速公路將是第一條連接這兩地的公路，並能 [84] 將開車時間大幅縮短六個小時。為了贊助公路的經費，駕駛人可以購買 [85] 快速通行證，等公路興建完成就可不限次數使用新公路。布拉福市市長薇琪・布魯克斯表示，她的市民等這條公路開發，已經等了很長一段時間，希望日後能規劃更多路線。

• **connect** 使連接　**according to** 根據、按照　**announcement** 宣布、通知　**lessen** 變少、減輕
sponsor 贊助、資助　**purchase** 購買　**allow** 使成為可能　**unlimited** 無限制的　**access** 使用
mayor 市長　**development** 開發、發展　**route** 路線

83

According to the news report, what will happen over the next five years?

(A) A city will be planned and developed.

(B) A new highway route will be completed.*

(C) A new location for the city hall will be sought.

(D) A tourism sector will be revamped.

根據新聞報導，未來五年會發生何事？

(A) 會規劃並開發一座城市。

(B) 會完成一條新的公路。

(C) 會尋找新的市政府位址。

(D) 會改組觀光部門。

聆聽時，請特別留意關鍵時間點 the next five years。獨白第一句後方說道：「it will build a new express highway over the next five years」，由此可以確認答案為 (B)。

• **seek (sought sought)** 尋找 **revamp** 改組

84

What benefit to travelers does the speaker mention?

(A) Safer ways to travel

(B) Discounts for families

(C) Beautiful natural landscapes

(D) Shorter travel times*

說話者提及旅客會得到什麼好處？

(A) 行車更安全。

(B) 家庭有優惠。

(C) 美麗的大自然景色。

(D) 更短的車程。

聆聽時，請掌握住重點為「優點」。獨白中段提到可以減少開車時間（lessen driving times by up to six hours），因此 (D) 為最適當的答案。

• **benefit** 好處、益處

85

What does the speaker say about express passes?

(A) They can be used repeatedly.*

(B) They can be ordered online.

(C) They will be distributed free of charge.

(D) They will expire every six months.

關於快速通行證，說話者說了什麼？

(A) 它們可以重複使用。

(B) 它們可以上網訂購。

(C) 它們將免費發送。

(D) 六個月就會失效。

聆聽時，請特別留意關鍵字為 express passes（快速通行證）。獨白末段說道：「express passes that will allow unlimited access to the new highway once it's built」，表示等到高速公路完工後，通行證將可以無限次使用，因此答案為 (A)。

答案改寫 unlimited → repeatedly

• **repeatedly** 重複地 **expire** 到期、終止、失效

Questions 86–88 refer to the following announcement.

W [86] Welcome to today's seminar for elementary school teachers. Today, we're going to discuss classroom management strategies. I know some people are running late due to traffic, but we have another group scheduled after lunch. [87] While we're waiting for them, let's introduce ourselves. As I'm sure you know, [88] a free workbook is included with your registration fee. [88] I'll hand those out now while you introduce yourselves. You'll notice a complimentary e-book CD in the back of the book. This is in case you want to review the topics we're covering today.	**女** [86] 歡迎來到今天的國小教師研討會，我們今天要討論課堂管理策略。我知道有些人因為交通的關係會晚點到，但午餐時間後已排定另一組上課。[87] 在等他們的同時，我們來自我介紹。相信你們都知道，報名費包含 [88] 免費的練習手冊。[88] 我會趁你們自我介紹時，把這些手冊發下去。你們會發現手冊封底附有免費的電子書 CD。這是考量到你們想要複習今天討論的主題之用。

- **elementary** 初級的、基礎的 **management** 管理 **strategy** 策略 **due to** 由於、因為 **traffic** 交通 **introduce** 介紹 **registration** 登記、註冊、報名 **fee** 費用 **hand out** 分發、免費給予 **notice** 注意 **complimentary** 贈送的 **in case** 假如 **cover** 包含、涉及

86

Who most likely are the listeners?
(A) Librarians
(B) Educators*
(C) Nurses
(D) Professors

聽眾最有可能是誰？
(A) 圖書館員。
(B) 教育工作者。
(C) 護士。
(D) 教授。

獨白第一句說道：「Welcome to today's seminar for elementary school teachers.」，可以得知場合是國小教師研討會，由此確認答案為 (B)。

答案改寫 teacher → educator

- **librarian** 圖書館員 **educator** 教育工作者 **nurse** 護士

87

What does the woman mean when she says, "we have another group scheduled after lunch"?
(A) A meeting will take place later.
(B) Some refunds will be given.
(C) An event will be canceled.
(D) She cannot wait any longer.*

當女子說「午餐時間後已排定另一組上課」，意指什麼？
(A) 稍晚會舉行會議。
(B) 將退還一些款項。
(C) 有個活動會取消。
(D) 她不能再等了。

題目句後方接著說道：「（因為待會還有其他行程）我先利用等待期間，進行自我介紹（While we're waiting for them, let's introduce ourselves.）」，表示要直接開始，因此 (D) 為最適當的答案。

- **take place** 舉行、發生 **refund** 退款、退還 **cancel** 取消

88

What will the speaker distribute to the listeners?
(A) A sign-up form
(B) Music CDs
(C) Training materials*
(D) Payment requests

說話者會發給聽眾什麼？
(A) 報名表。
(B) 音樂 CD。
(C) 訓練教材。
(D) 請款單。

請掌握好本題的重點「發送的東西」，並仔細聆聽。獨白中段中提到了免費練習手冊（a free workbook），接著說道：「要在大家自我介紹時發送給大家（I'll hand those out now while you introduce yourselves.）」，因此答案為 (C)。

答案改寫 hand out → distribute
workbook → training material

• **form** 表格 **material** 資料、素材 **payment** 支付、付款 **request** 要求、請求

Questions 89–91 refer to the following excerpt from a meeting.

W Today, I'd like to discuss our law firm's summer vacation period. As you know, [89] we've just picked up several new cases that will go to trial in the next six months. However, it's important that all full-time staff have a summer vacation. To help deal with the workload during the summer, [90] we've decided to hire some temporary workers. We feel that five part-time workers would help cover some of the administrative work. I posted the job listings online, but um . . . we'd like to fill these positions as soon as possible. If you know anyone who is qualified, [91] please pass their résumé to me.

女 今天我想討論我們律師事務所的夏季休假。你們都知道，[89] 我們剛剛接了幾個會在半年內開庭審理的新案子。然而，重要的是，所有的全職員工夏季都有休假。為了協助處理夏季的工作量，[90] 我們決定僱用一些臨時人員。我們認為，五名兼職人員將有助處理部分行政工作。我把朝聘啟示貼上網，但是，嗯……我們希望這些職缺能盡快補齊。如果你們知道任何適任人選，[91] 請把他們的履歷表傳給我。

• **case** 訴訟案件 **trial** 審判 **deal with** 處理、對待 **workload** 工作量 **decide** 決定 **hire** 僱用 **temporary** 臨時的、暫時的 **cover** 處理 **administrative** 行政的 **position** 職位、職務 **qualified** 具備必要條件的、勝任的 **résumé** 履歷表

89

What does the speaker say about the law firm?
(A) It hired some full-time employees.
(B) It has donated to a local charity.
(C) It will merge with another firm.
(D) It acquired some new cases.*

關於這間律師事務所，說話者說了什麼？
(A) 事務所僱用了一些全職員工。
(B) 事務所捐款給當地的慈善團體。
(C) 事務所會和另一家事務所合併。
(D) 事務所接到一些新案子。

獨白前段說道：「we've just picked up several new cases」，明確提到接了新案子，由此確認答案為 (D)。

答案改寫 pick up → acquire
several → some

• **donate** 捐獻、捐贈 **charity** 慈善團體 **merge** 使合併 **acquire** 取得、獲得

90

According to the speaker, what decision was recently made?

根據說話者所述，最近公司作了什麼決定？

(A) To hire temporary staff*
(B) To cancel summer vacations
(C) To increase some rates
(D) To renovate a conference room

(A) 僱用臨時員工。
(B) 取消夏季休假。
(C) 調升一些費用。
(D) 整修會議室。

聆聽時，請特別留意「決定的事項」。獨白中段提到：「we've decided to hire some temporary workers」，決定要僱用臨時員工，因此答案為 (A)。

答案改寫 workers → staff

• increase 增加　rate 費用、價格、比率　renovate 翻新

91

What does the speaker ask the listeners to do?

說話者要求聽眾做何事？

(A) Host a training session
(B) Interview candidates
(C) Submit résumés*
(D) Fill out a questionnaire

(A) 主持訓練課程。
(B) 面試應徵者。
(C) 呈交履歷表。
(D) 填寫問卷。

說話者的建議或是要求事項，通常會出現在獨白後半部。表示若有適任者，請將他們的履歷提供給我（please pass their résumé to me），因此 (C) 為最適當的答案。

答案改寫 pass → submit

• host 主持　candidate 應徵者、候選人　submit 交出、呈遞　fill out 填寫　questionnaire 問卷

Questions 92–94 refer to the following broadcast.

M　We're back with SSB Radio. [92] I'd just like to remind our listeners in the Smithside area that we're hosting our first summer music competition at the Smithside waterfront next week. [93] The competition will feature numerous local bands and will conclude with a performance by world-famous country music singer Sally Jones. You won't want to miss it! The show starts at 3 P.M. at the northeast pavilion. Make sure to arrive early for free parking. Tickets will be available for a small fee, but children and seniors can enter at no charge. [94] For a complete list of participating bands, please visit www.ssbradio.com/musiccompetition.

男　回到 SSB 電台現場。[92] 我想要提醒史密斯塞德地區的聽眾，下星期我們將在史密斯塞德水岸舉行第一屆夏季音樂大賽。[93] 競賽的亮點將是許多當地樂團，壓軸演出的是世界知名的鄉村歌手莎莉・瓊斯。你絕對不想錯過！表演下午三點在東北館展開。務必提早抵達，才有免費停位。門票費用極低廉，但兒童與年長者還是可以免費入場。[94] 完整的參賽樂團名單，請上 www.ssbradio.com/musiccompetition 查詢。

• remind 提醒　competition 比賽、競賽　numerous 許多的　conclude 結束、終了　performance 表演　miss 錯過　make sure 確定、務必　arrive 到達　at no charge 不收費　complete 完整的、全部的　participating 參加的、參與的

92

What is the talk mostly about?
(A) An awards ceremony
(B) A film festival
(C) A local competition*
(D) A political speech

這段話的主題為何？
(A) 頒獎典禮。
(B) 電影節。
(C) 地方性賽事。
(D) 政治演說。

獨白前段說道：「I'd just like to remind our listeners in the Smithside area that we're hosting our first summer music competition at the Smithside waterfront next week.」，提到當地將主辦夏季音樂大賽，因此答案為 (C)。在獨白的前半段，通常可以聽到獨白的主旨。

• award ceremony 頒獎典禮　political 政治的

93

What does the speaker imply when he says, "You won't want to miss it"?
(A) A local event will be sold out soon.
(B) Some performances will start early.
(C) The show was very popular last year.
(D) A schedule of events is very exciting.*

說話者說「你一定不想錯過」，意指什麼？
(A) 一項當地活動的門票很快就會賣完。
(B) 有些表演會提早開始。
(C) 這場表演去年很受歡迎。
(D) 排定的活動非常令人興奮。

聆聽時，請特別留意題目句前後的文意。題目句前提到將由地方樂團開場，且由舉世聞名的知名歌手壓軸（The competition will feature numerous local bands and will conclude with a performance by world-famous country music singer Sally Jones.），因此 (D) 為最適當的答案。

• sold out （門票等）全部預售完

94

Why does the speaker suggest that listeners visit a website?
(A) To get a free parking pass
(B) To see a full list of contestants*
(C) To find a map of the event
(D) To sign up to be a performer

說話者為何建議聽眾造訪網站？
(A) 以取得免費停車證。
(B) 為了看到完整的參賽者名單。
(C) 為了找到活動的地圖。
(D) 為了登記成為表演者。

聆聽時，請特別留意關鍵字 website（網站）。獨白最後一句說道：「For a complete list of participating bands, please visit www.ssbradio.com/musiccompetition.」，由此確認答案為 (B)。

答案改寫 participating band → contestant

• contestant 參加競賽者　sign up 註冊、報名登記　performer 演出者

Questions 95–97 refer to the following information and floor plan.

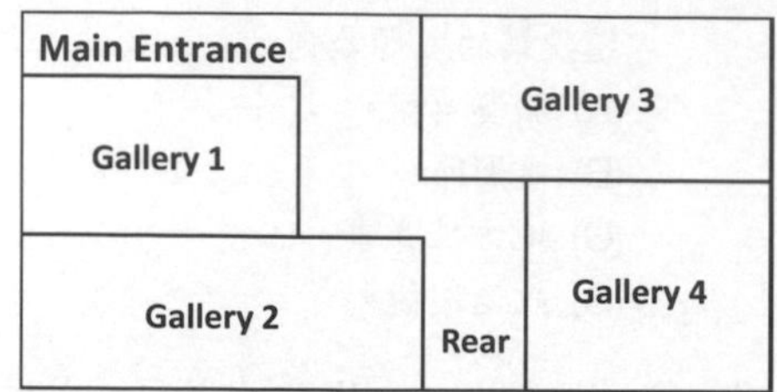

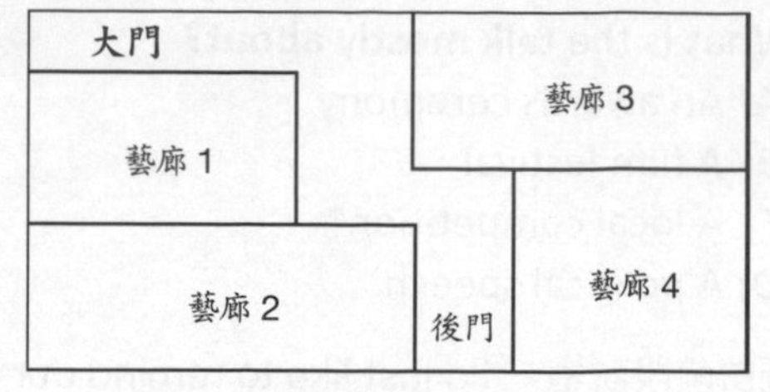

W Thank you for visiting Rutherford's National Art Gallery. [95] This month, we're featuring a wide variety of classic watercolor paintings. I highly recommend visiting the [96] Monet exhibit located in gallery four, as it will only be available for a limited time. Here is a map of the art gallery. [96] We also feature a wide variety of art from the Cubist period, which you can find located near the rear entrance across from the Monet exhibit. Should you like to register for a guided tour of the art gallery, they are held at 11:00 A.M., 2:00 P.M., and 4:00 P.M. every day. [97] Simply sign up on this sheet and return to the front desk at your desired time.

女 謝謝你們來參觀盧瑟福國家美術館。[95] 我們本月特展是各式各樣的經典水彩畫。我大力推薦觀賞 [96] 在四號藝廊展出的莫內展，因為它的展出時間有限。這裡是美術館的地圖。[96] 我們的特展還有立體派時期的許多藝術作品，你們可以在靠近後門的地方看到，就在莫內展的對面。如果你們想要報名參加美術館的導覽，活動時間是每天上午 11 點、下午兩點和四點。[97] 只要在這張表格上簽名登記，然後在你想參加導覽的時間回到櫃台處就可以了。

- **rear** 後面的　**feature** 以……為特色　**a wide variety of** 各式各樣的　**recommend** 推薦　**exhibit** 展覽　**available** 可獲得的　**limited** 有限的　**Cubist** 立體派的、立體派畫家　**period** 時期　**register for** 登記、報名參加　**be held** 舉行　**sign up** 報名登記　**desired** 期望的

What is the gallery featuring this month?
美術館本月特展為何？

(A) Landscape photography
(B) Watercolor paintings*
(C) Abstract installations
(D) Pencil sketches

(A) 風景照。
(B) 水彩畫。
(C) 抽象裝置。
(D) 鉛筆素描。

本題的重點為「本月的展覽」。獨白前段説道：「This month, we're featuring a wide variety of classic watercolor paintings.」，由此聽出答案為 (B)。

- **landscape** 風景、風景畫　**abstract** 抽象的、抽象派的　**installation** 裝置

Look at the graphic. In which room is the Cubist art exhibit?
請見圖表。立體派展覽在哪一間藝廊？

(A) Gallery 1.　(B) Gallery 2*
(C) Gallery 3.　(D) Gallery 4

(A) 藝廊 1。　(B) 藝廊 2。
(C) 藝廊 3。　(D) 藝廊 4。

請掌握重點為「立體派展出藝廊」，並仔細聆聽獨白內容。獨白中段提到位在莫內展的對面、後門旁邊（We also feature a wide variety of Cubist period, which you can find located near the rear entrance across from the Monet exhibit.）。因為莫內展為 4 號藝廊（Monet exhibit located in gallery four），因此答案為 (B)。

97

How can listeners attend a guided tour?
(A) By paying a fee
(B) By calling a tour guide
(C) By registering on a website
(D) By signing up on a sheet*

聽眾如何參加導覽？
(A) 支付費用。
(B) 打電話給導遊。
(C) 上網登記。
(D) 在表格上簽名登記。

聆聽時，請特別留意「申請導覽的方法」。獨白後段，告知導覽時間後提到：「Simply sign up on this sheet and return to the front desk at your desired time.」，表示在紙上登記名字，並在想要的導覽時間交給櫃台即可，因此答案為 (D)。

• **pay** 支付 **fee** 費用

Questions 98–100 refer to the following message and expense report.

September 1 9月1日	**Taxi to Airport:** $45 機場計程車：$45	**Client Dinner:** $98 客戶晚餐：$98
September 2 9月2日	**Car Rental:** $55 租車：$55	**Convention Ticket:** $35 研討會門票：$35

M Hello, Mary. This is Jeff from the accounting department. I've just gotten a chance to review the expense report you submitted after your trip last week. [98] Unfortunately, it seems that one of your receipts is missing from the envelope. [99] Your expense report requests reimbursement for an expense of 35 dollars on September 2, but you did not submit that particular receipt. In order for me to process the payment, I'll need to see the receipt. However, if you've misplaced it and no longer have it, [100] please e-mail me and I'll forward you the Request for Reimbursement Without a Receipt form.

男 哈囉，瑪莉，我是會計部的傑夫。我剛剛才有空檢視妳上星期出差後，送來的費用報告。[98] 不巧的是，似乎有張收據遺失了，不在信封裡。[99] 妳的費用報告中，申請核銷一筆 9 月 2 日的 35 元，但妳並沒有附上那張收據。為了讓我可以處理付款，我需要看到收據。不過，如果妳一時找不到，而且手頭上已經沒有單據，[100] 請寄電子郵件給我，我會轉寄「無收據核銷申請表」給妳。

• **rental** 租賃 **accounting** 會計 **department** 部門 **expense** 費用 **submit** 交出、呈遞 **receipt** 收據、單據 **envelope** 信封 **reimbursement** 報銷、償還 **process** 處理、辦理 **payment** 支付、付款 **misplace** 放錯地方（而一時找不到）

98

Why is the speaker calling?
(A) An application has been lost.
(B) A submission is incomplete.*
(C) A trip has been delayed.
(D) A file is damaged.

說話者為何打電話？
(A) 申請書遺失了。
(B) 提出的文件不完整。
(C) 旅程延後了。
(D) 檔案毀損。

當題目詢問打電話的原因或目的時，在獨白後半部，通常可以聽到答題的關鍵線索。獨白提到，檢查過報告後，發現當中似乎缺了一張收據（Unfortunately, it seems that one of your receipts is missing from the envelope.），因此 (B) 為最適當的答案。當獨白中出現 However 或 Unfortunately 這類表示轉折語氣的單字時，其後方通常就是答案。

答案改寫 missing from → incomplete

- **application** 申請、申請書 **submission** 提出、呈遞 **incomplete** 不完整的 **delay** 使延期 **damage** 損害、損壞

Look at the graphic. Which expense is the man referring to?
(A) Taxi to Airport
(B) Car Rental
(C) Client Dinner
(D) Convention Ticket*

請見圖表。男子提及的是哪一筆費用？
(A) 機場計程車。
(B) 租車。
(C) 客戶晚餐。
(D) 研討會門票。

選項內容即為表格內的項目，因此可以推測出解題關鍵在「日期和費用」。獨白中段說道：「Your expense report requests reimbursement for an expense of 35 dollars on September 2」，由此確認答案為 (D)。

100

What does the speaker say he can do?
(A) Send a form*
(B) Pay a fee
(C) Reject a request
(D) Submit a proposal

說話者說他可以做何事？
(A) 寄送表格。
(B) 支付費用。
(C) 拒絕請求。
(D) 提出計畫。

在獨白後半部，通常會聽到說話者的建議或要求。獨白最後一句說道：「please e-mail me and I'll forward you the Request for Reimbursement Without a Receipt form」，請對方先寄送郵件，然後再將表格回寄給對方，因此答案為 (A)。

答案改寫 forward → send

- **fee** 費用 **reject** 拒絕 **request** 要求、請求 **proposal** 計畫、提案

ACTUAL TEST 4

中譯+解析

1

(A) He's seated in a waiting area.* (A) 他坐在等候區。
(B) He's picking up a book from the table. (B) 他從桌上拿起一本書。
(C) He's arranging the chairs. (C) 他正在排椅子。
(D) He's hanging a picture. (D) 他正在掛一幅畫。

本題為單人照片。(A) 明確描述了坐著（be seated）的狀態，為最適當的答案。雖然其他選項中，也用到了出現在照片中的物品（book, table, chairs, picture），但皆與照片情境無關。在此補充，hang 可以作為及物動詞，或是不及物動詞使用。

- **arrange** 布置、整理　**hang** 把……掛起

2

(A) A woman's working on a flower arrangement.* (A) 女子正在插花。
(B) A woman's choosing a vase from the shelf. (B) 女子從架子上挑選花瓶。
(C) A woman's carrying a bouquet to a party room. (C) 女子拿著一束花進入派對。
(D) A woman's lining up some plants on the table. (D) 女子把一些植物在桌上排好。

(A) 對插花的行為（working on a flower arrangement）進行客觀的描述，為正確答案。雖然其他選項中，也用到了出現在照片中的物品（vase, shelf, bouquet, plants），但內容皆不符合照片情境。

- **flower arrangement** 插花　**choose** 選擇、挑選　**vase** 花瓶　**shelf** 架子　**carry** 攜帶　**bouquet** 花束　**line up** 使排成行　**plant** 植物

3

(A) The counter has been cleared of objects. (A) 櫃台上的物品都清除了。
(B) A man is watering a potted plant. (B) 男子正在給盆栽澆水。
(C) The faucet is being repaired. (C) 正在修理水龍頭。
(D) Some plates are piled on the countertop.* (D) 櫃台檯面上堆著一些盤子。

(D) 以 be piled on 客觀描述流理台上放了許多碗盤，為正確答案。其他選項提及照片中出現的 counter、potted plant、faucet 等相關單字，也請一併熟記。

- **counter** 櫃台　**object** 物品　**water** 澆水　**potted plant** 盆栽　**faucet** 水龍頭　**repair** 修理　**plate** 盤子　**pile** 堆積　**countertop**（廚房的）工作檯面

4

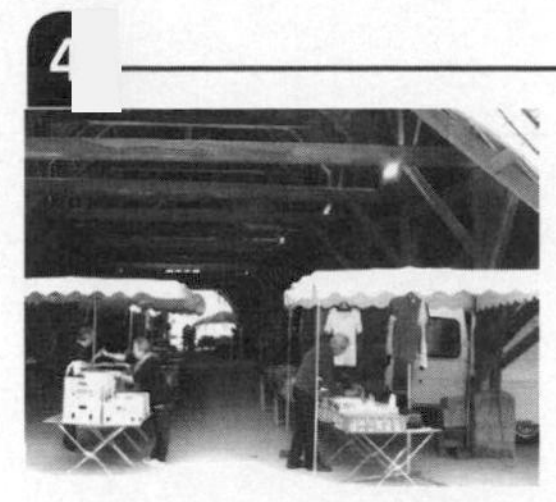

(A) A display case has been set up on the floor.
(B) Tables have been set up under canopies.*
(C) One of the men is trying on a shirt.
(D) Two vendors are shaking hands.

(A) 展示櫃擺放在地板上。
(B) 遮篷下面放置著桌子。
(C) 其中一名男子正在試穿襯衫。
(D) 兩名小販在握手。

(B) 針對照片進行適當的說明：遮篷下方擺了幾張桌子，為正確答案。題目選項中常以 have been set up 作為正確答案。另外，當選項中出現高難度單字時，通常會是答案。像本題答案中的 canopy，意思為（以布或是塑膠作成）類似屋頂的遮蓋物。

• **set up** 安裝、擺放 **canopy** 遮篷、雨篷 **try on** 試穿、試用 **vendor** 小販 **shake hands** 握手

5

(A) Some trees are making shadows.*
(B) A field of grass is being mowed.
(C) Some bushes are being trimmed.
(D) Some benches are being removed.

(A) 有些樹投下陰影。
(B) 正在除一大片草地。
(C) 正在修剪一些灌木叢。
(D) 正在移走一些長椅。

只要照片中沒有出現人物時，就要先想到，極可能會出現現在進行被動式，以照片中的事物當作主詞的錯誤選項。此類句型的後方省略行為者，表示「某人正在做某件事」。舉例來說，(B)、(C) 和 (D) 分別表示「Someone is mowing a field of grass.」、「Someone is trimming some bushes.」、「Someone is removing some benches.」，皆為錯誤選項，因此答案為 (A)。當 PART 1 的題目中出現 shadow 時，多半是答案。

• **field** 原野 **grass** 草、草地 **mow** 割草地上的草 **bush** 灌木、灌木叢 **trim** 修剪 **remove** 移動、搬開

6

(A) Some pedestrians are stepping onto a curb.
(B) A cyclist is examining the wheels.
(C) A bicycle is locked to a pole.*
(D) A road is closed for construction.

(A) 有些行人踩上人行道的路緣。
(B) 自行車騎士正在檢查車輪。
(C) 一輛自行車鎖在柱子旁。
(D) 有條路封閉整建。

圖片中並未出現人物，(A) 和 (B) 以人（pedestrians, cyclist）作為主詞，並不適當，因此聽到的當下即可刪除選項；(D) 的內容無法從照片判斷；所以本題的答案為 (C)。在此補充，若照片中有人在餐廳看著（examine）菜單，選項可能使用 examine the menu，針對照片進行描述。

• **pedestrian** 行人 **curb** （人行道的）路緣 **cyclist** 自行車騎士 **examine** 檢查 **wheel** 輪子、車輪 **lock** 鎖、鎖上 **pole** 柱、竿 **construction** 建造

7

Where is the meeting being held today? 今天的會議在哪裡舉行？
(A) It was boring. (A) 很無聊。
(B) The downtown office.* (B) 市區的辦公室。
(C) No, she hasn't said. (C) 不，她沒說。

本題使用表示「地點」的疑問詞 Where，詢問「在哪裡舉行會議？」。(B) 回覆了具體的地點資訊（downtown office），為正確答案。(C) 以 Yes 或 No 開頭的答句，不適合回覆以疑問詞開頭的問句，為錯誤選項。

• be held 舉行　boring 無聊的

8

Do you need another ticket for the baseball game? 你需要另一張棒球賽的門票嗎？
(A) Yes, I'd like one more.* (A) 是的，我想再要一張。
(B) Please come here. (B) 請過來這裡。
(C) The players are out of town. (C) 球員出城去了。

本題為一般問句，詢問「是否還需要門票？」，可以用 Yes 或 No 開頭的答句回覆，因此答案為 (A)。當選項中出現 one 時，通常即可確定為答案。

• route 路線

9

Who will pick up Mr. Kim from the station? 誰會去車站接金先生？
(A) I live in that area.* (A) 我住在那一區。
(B) He is from Korea. (B) 他是韓國人。
(C) On the express route. (C) 在快速公路上。

當題目為 Who 開頭的問句時，答案可能為人名、職稱、部門名稱或公司名稱。選項 (A) 回覆：「我就住在那一區（所以可以去車站接金先生）」，因此為正確答案。本題的難度較高，需要先理解回覆內容背後所隱藏的含意，才能順利解題。

10

How did the package from England arrive so quickly? 英國寄來的包裹怎麼這麼快就到了？
(A) No, he's a delivery man. (A) 不，他是送貨員。
(B) They used express shipping.* (B) 他們用快捷貨運。
(C) I'm going there on vacation. (C) 我會去那裡度假。

以疑問詞 How 開頭的問句，用來詢問「辦法」。本題詢問「如何快速到達」，(B) 回覆「以快遞配送」，兩句得以構成完整對答，為正確選項。

• package 包裹　arrive（郵件、物品等）被送來　delivery 投遞、送貨　shipping 貨運、運輸

11

Who repaired the projector in this room?
(A) Early this morning.
(B) Our technology specialist.*
(C) The presentation at noon.

這個房間的投影機是誰修好的？
(A) 今天早上稍早。
(B) 我們的技術專員。
(C) 中午的簡報。

本題以疑問詞 Who 開頭，詢問「是誰」修理，(B) 以職稱回覆，最能與問句構成完整對話。當題目改成以 When 詢問修理的時間時，答案則會是 (A)。

• **repair** 修理　**specialist** 專業人員

12

Your parcel should arrive at 4:30 P.M. today.
(A) Yes, I passed the test.
(B) The delivery truck.
(C) I'll be in the office then.*

你的包裹應該在今天下午四點半送到。
(A) 是的，我通過測驗了。
(B) 送貨卡車。
(C) 那個時間，我會在辦公室。

本題表示「包裹預計於下午四點半送達」，(C) 回答「那時我應該會在辦公室（所以可以收包裹）」，為最適當的答案；(A) 故意使用了 pass，與 parcel 的發音相似，為常見陷阱。

• **parcel** 小包、包裹　**pass**（考試等）及格、通過　**delivery** 投遞、交貨

13

When will the employee promotions be announced?
(A) I doubt it is true.
(B) Several other candidates.
(C) Next week at the earliest.*

何時會宣布人事升遷？
(A) 我懷疑是真的。
(B) 其他幾個應徵者。
(C) 最快下星期。

本題為以 When 開頭的問句，詢問「何時」公布，(C) 回答了具體的時間資訊，為正確答案。

• **promotion** 晉升　**announce** 宣布　**doubt** 懷疑　**several** 數個的　**candidate** 應徵者、候選人
at the earliest 最早

14

Are you ready to go get some coffee?
(A) I've been running for twenty minutes.
(B) I have a meeting soon.*
(C) One cup is $5.99.

你要喝點咖啡嗎？
(A) 我跑步跑了 20 分鐘。
(B) 我很快就要去開會。
(C) 一杯 $5.99。

本題為一般問句，詢問「要去喝咖啡嗎」。答句中可以省略 Yes 或 No；(B) 回答「馬上就要開會（不太方便）」，和問句構成完整對話。因為回答中省略了 Yes 或 No，使得答題難度相對提升，這類題型出題機率有逐年增長的趨勢。

15

Why are you waiting outside?
(A) I forgot it at home.
(B) Twenty more minutes.
(C) The café is closed already.*

你為何在外面等？
(A) 我忘在家裡了。
(B) 再 20 分鐘。
(C) 咖啡館已經打烊了。

本題為以疑問詞 Why 開頭的問句，詢問在外面等待的「原因」。(C) 省略了連接詞 because，直接回覆「（因為）咖啡館已經打烊了」，為最適當的答案。

16

How should we arrange the new desks?
(A) Let's make some rows.*
(B) Yes, they were expensive.
(C) No, they are too long.

我們要怎麼排這些新書桌？
(A) 我們排成幾列吧。
(B) 是的，它們很貴。
(C) 不，它們太長了。

以疑問詞 How 開頭的問句，用來詢問「辦法」。本題詢問「如何擺設？」，(A) 建議「排成幾列」，和問句構成完整對話。以疑問詞開頭的問句，不適合以 Yes 或 No 開頭的答句回覆，因此可以直接刪除另外兩個選項。

- **arrange** 布置、安排　**row** 將……列成一排（行）　**expensive** 昂貴的

17

Do you need some help hanging these posters?
(A) They are posted on this site.
(B) Did she design it?
(C) Yes, I'd appreciate it.*

你需要人幫忙掛這些海報嗎？
(A) 它們貼在這個地方。
(B) 是她設計的嗎？
(C) 是的，非常感謝。

本題為一般問句，向對方表示要給予協助。(C) 回覆「好的，謝謝」，和問句構成完整對話。在此補充，(A) 故意使用了 posted，與題目中 posters 的發音相似，為錯誤選項。若選項中使用了發音相似的單字，不是答案的可能性高達 99%。

- **hang** 把……掛起　**post** 貼在……　**appreciate** 感謝、感激

18

Which teams are using this room today?
(A) They are working well.
(B) No, it's the fourteenth.
(C) Just the accounting department.*

哪些單位今天要用這間房間？
(A) 他們進展得很順利。
(B) 不，是第 14 個。
(C) 只有會計部門。

疑問形容詞 Which，意思為「哪個、哪些」。本題詢問「哪個部門要使用這間房間」，(C) 回覆「只有會計部門」，為正確答案；(B) 當中的 (four)teenth，與 teams 的發音相似，為錯誤選項。

- **accounting** 會計、會計學　**department** 部門

19

Are the replacement parts going to get here in time?
(A) In the mail room.
(B) The cost has increased.
(C) I paid for express shipping.*

替換的零件會及時送到這裡嗎？
(A) 在收發室。
(B) 成本增加了。
(C) 我付錢叫了快捷貨運。

本題對於能否準時送達表示擔憂，(C) 回答「已支付了快遞費（表示應該可以很快送達）」，與問句構成完整對話，為正確答案。

- **replacement** 更換、替代 **part** 零件 **cost** 費用、成本 **increase** 增加 **pay for** 為了得到……而付錢 **shipping** 運輸、運送

20

Why is the mall open so late today?
(A) No, I've bought it already.
(B) There's a holiday sale.*
(C) Until 9:00 at night.

購物商場今天為何開到這麼晚？
(A) 不，我已經買了。
(B) 有假期大特賣。
(C) 直到晚上九點。

本題為以 Why 開頭的問句，詢問營業到很晚的「原因」，(B) 回答因為「假期特惠活動」，最能與問句構成完整對話；(A) 以疑問詞開頭的問句，不適合以 Yes 或 No 開頭的答句回覆；題目若改成詢問營業「時間」，(C) 才會是正解。

21

Should I talk to the manager about my vacation plans now or before I leave tonight?
(A) In the conference room.
(B) The sales pitch was very successful.
(C) I heard he is going home before lunch.*

我應該現在和經理談我的休假計畫，還是今晚離開前再說？
(A) 在會議室。
(B) 這套推銷用語非常有效。
(C) 我聽說，他在中午之前就會回家。

碰到題目為選擇疑問句時，可以預想到答案應為問句中所包含的兩種選項之一：①現在說、②今天晚上再說；或是排除這兩種選項，以其他內容回覆。(C) 回答「聽說經理今天會在中午之前下班」，委婉表示應該要現在說，因此為正確答案。

- **pitch** 推銷用語

22

I'm not sure where the conference will be held.
(A) Ask at the front desk.*
(B) It lasts three days.
(C) For all participants.

我不確定會議在哪裡舉行。
(A) 問一下櫃台。
(B) 它持續三天。
(C) 給所有的參加者。

本題的重點在表示自己「不太確定」，(A) 建議「詢問一下」，為最適當的回答。選項若為〈Ask +人或地點〉，極有可能為正確答案。

- **be held** 舉行、發生 **last** 持續 **participant** 參與者

23

I need some more details about the museum opening.
(A) At the main entrance.
(B) No problem. Here is the web address.*
(C) Twelve adult passes.

我需要知道更多關於博物館開幕的詳情。
(A) 在大門口。
(B) 沒問題，這是網址。
(C) 12 張成人票。

本題的重點在要求更多的資訊，(B) 提供了相關資訊的網址，為最適當的回答。其他選項也是與「博物館」相關的內容，答題時請特別留意。

• **entrance** 入口、門口　**pass** 通行證、入場證

24

Where will we go after the plant tour?
(A) Janice has the full itinerary.*
(B) Only the managers, I think.
(C) We plan to hire a few more guides.

參觀完工廠後，我們要去哪裡？
(A) 珍妮絲有完整的行程表。
(B) 我想，只有經理。
(C) 我們打算再多僱一些嚮導。

本題為以 Where 開頭的問句，詢問「要去哪裡」，(A) 沒有回答具體的地點，而是告知擁有地點和行程表的人，為正確答案。請特別留意，當題目為以 Where 開頭的問句時，答案有可能提及「人」。(C) 使用了 plan，與題目中 plant 的發音相似，為誘答選項，並非答案。

• **plant** 工廠　**itinerary** 旅程、路線　**hire** 僱用

25

You can come in for a checkup at 11 o'clock.
(A) What other times are available?*
(B) The dentist was very gentle.
(C) This procedure was cheaper.

你可以十一點來接受檢查。
(A) 還有其他時間可選嗎？
(B) 牙醫很溫和。
(C) 這種療程比較便宜。

本題的重點在建議十一點來，(A) 說道：「（你說的時間我無法配合）方便改成其他時間嗎？」，為最適當的回覆。PART 2 中，若選項以反問的方式回覆，極有可能為正確答案。

• **checkup** 檢查　**dentist** 牙醫　**gentle** 溫和的　**procedure** 手術、療程

26

Should I get another chair for the meeting?
(A) Tom is home sick today.*
(B) I called the meeting.
(C) Yes, it is very comfortable.

我應該再去拿張椅子以供開會時用嗎？
(A) 湯姆今天請病假。
(B) 是我召集會議的。
(C) 是的，椅子非常舒服。

本題詢問「需要再拿一張椅子來嗎？」，(A) 回覆「Tom（參加會議的其中一人）無法參加，（所以椅子數量剛剛好）」，為最適當的答覆。此類題型的難度偏高，需要先理解選項背後代表的含意，才能順利解題。最近經常出現此類題型，使得 PART 2 的整體難度提升。(B) 純粹重複使用了 meeting，並非答案。

• **be home sick** 請病假在家　**call the meeting** 召開會議　**comfortable** 舒服的

27

I forgot my scarf at home.
(A) It is a house with seven rooms.
(B) I am scared, too.
(C) It's pretty warm out today.*

我把圍巾忘在家裡了。
(A) 那棟房子有七間房間。
(B) 我也很害怕。
(C) 今天外面相當溫暖。

本題說道：「忘記帶圍巾」，(C) 回答「今天天氣很溫暖」表示可能用不太到，與問句構成完整對話，為正確答案。(A) 使用了 house，為 home 的同義字；(B) 使用了 scared，僅與 scarf 的發音相似，亦非答案。

- scared 害怕的、吃驚的　pretty 相當、非常

28

The concert tickets for tonight are sold out, aren't they?
(A) The venue is located downtown.
(B) Yes, but you can attend the one tomorrow.*
(C) Two singers have cancelled.

今晚音樂會的票已售完，不是嗎？
(A) 表演場地位於市中心的鬧區。
(B) 是的，但你可以看明天那一場。
(C) 有兩位歌手取消了。

自己已知的事實，再次向對方確認或是尋求同意時，會使用附加問句，與一般問句回答雷同。本題詢問「是否銷售一空」，(B) 回答「是（Yes），但還可以參加明天的場次」，與問句構成完整對話。

- sold out 銷售一空　venue 舉行地點、會場　attend 出席、參加　cancel 取消

29

Do you know where the application packages are?
(A) Not too many.
(B) For external application only.
(C) You can get them from the manager.*

你知道申請文件在哪裡嗎？
(A) 不太多。
(B) 只供外部申請之用。
(C) 你可以跟經理拿。

當題目為以「Do you know . . . ?」開頭的間接問句時，解題關鍵在於句中的疑問詞，因此請務必仔細聆聽。本題詢問的是申請書「在哪裡？」，(C) 將 the application packages 換成 them，回答「可以向經理索取」，為正確答案。

- application 申請、應用　external 外部的、外來的

30

How often do we need to service the copy machine?
(A) I think I threw out the handbook.*
(B) The toner cartridges.
(C) I installed it on Friday.

影印機需要多久維修一次？
(A) 我想我把說明書扔了。
(B) 碳粉匣。
(C) 我星期五安裝好的。

本題使用「How often . . . ?」，詢問需要檢查的頻率。(A) 回答「已經丟掉說明書」，表示自己不太清楚，為最適當的回覆。PART 2 的選項中，只要出現類似 I don't know 的回答，極有可能為正確答案。最近經常出現各式各樣的回答方式，意思其實都是指 I don't know。

- throw out 扔掉　install 安裝、設置

31

Which floor is my hotel room on?
(A) The elevator is over there.
(B) I wish I had a key.
(C) Didn't the clerk tell you?*

我的房間在飯店幾樓？
(A) 電梯在那裡。
(B) 希望我有鑰匙。
(C) 接待員沒告訴你嗎？

本題詢問客房在幾樓，(C) 反問「沒有告訴過你（在幾樓）嗎？」，與問句構成完整對話，為最適當的回應。

PART 3 15

Questions 32–34 refer to the following conversation.

M Hello, I'm Samuel Morgan. [32] I have an appointment with Dr. Baker to have a cavity filled.

W Yes, you're next on the waiting list. [33] However, he's running behind schedule, so it'll be another thirty minutes.

M Oh, I see. Well, I need to stop by the bank across the street, so maybe I'll do that first.

W Sure, [34] just make sure you go out the exit on the left. The elevators on the north side of the building are down for repairs, so you won't be able to use them.

男 哈囉，我是山繆・摩根。[32] 我向貝克醫師預約了要補蛀牙。

女 是的，你是等候名單上的下一位。[33] 不過，他的看診延誤了，所以還要再等 30 分鐘。

男 喔，我知道了。嗯，我得去一下對面的銀行，不然我先去銀行一下。

女 當然好，[34] 只是要確認是從左邊的出口出去。由於大樓北側的電梯待修中，停止運轉，所以你無法搭乘那邊的電梯。

• **appointment** 預約、約會 **cavity** （牙齒的）蛀洞 **fill** 填補（牙齒等） **stop by** 順路造訪 **make sure** 確定 **repair** 修理、修補

32

Where most likely are the speakers?

(A) In a bank
(B) In a dental clinic*
(C) In a shopping mall
(D) In a bookstore

說話者最可能在哪裡？

(A) 在銀行。
(B) 在牙醫診所。
(C) 在購物商場。
(D) 在書店。

當題目詢問對話的地點時，通常可以透過幾個關鍵的單字或是短句進行推測。對話第一段，男子說道：「I have an appointment with Dr. Baker to have a cavity filled.」，由此推測出地點與「預約看牙醫」相關，因此答案為 (B)。

• **dental** 牙齒的、牙科的 **clinic** 診所

33

What problem does the woman mention?

(A) An appointment will be delayed.*
(B) A patient file was misplaced.
(C) An employee called in sick.
(D) A bill was not paid.

女子提及什麼問題？

(A) 有個約診時間會延後。
(B) 有位病人的檔案放錯地方。
(C) 有位員工打電話請病假。
(D) 有張賬單未付。

本題詢問 problem，因此請先標示出各選項的重點單字（delayed, file, sick, bill），再來聆聽對話內容。對話第一段，女子說道：「However, he's running behind schedule, so it'll be another thirty minutes.」，由於前面的人拖延到時間，需要再等三十分鐘，因此 (A) 為最適當的答案。答案通常會出現在 however 的後方。

答案改寫 run behind schedule → delay

• **delay** 拖延、耽擱 **misplace** 誤置、遺忘 **call in sick** 請病假 **bill** 賬單 **pay** 支付

34

What does the woman advise the man to do?
(A) Reschedule an appointment
(B) Stay in the office
(C) Take the stairs
(D) Use a specific door*

女子建議男子何事？
(A) 重新安排預約時間。
(B) 留在辦公室裡。
(C) 走樓梯。
(D) 使用特定的出入口。

對話第二段，女子請對方走左邊的出口（just make sure you go out the exit on the left），並補充說道電梯正待維修，因此答案為 (D)。

答案改寫 exit → door

- **stay** 停留 **specific** 特殊的、特定的

Questions 35–37 refer to the following conversation.

M	Hello, [35] I'm interested in picking up a refrigeration unit for my truck. [36] I run a small catering business and the fridge I currently have is broken.	男	哈囉，[35] 我想要為我的卡車買冷藏設備。[36] 我經營小型的外燴生意，平時在用的冰箱壞了。
W	Great, we have several different models that may suit your needs. And they all come with free installation and a two-year warranty.	女	好的，我們有幾種款式可能符合您的需求，而且含免費安裝以及兩年保固。
M	That sounds good. But my truck is actually quite small, so I'm worried you might not have a unit small enough for it.	男	聽起來很不錯。可是我的卡車其實相當小，所以我擔心，妳也許沒有夠小的款式。
W	Our A4000 series is very compact. I have a few in the back storage room. [37] Why don't you come take a look at them?	女	我們的 A4000 系列非常小巧。我後面的貯藏室裡有幾台。[37] 您何不過來看看？

- **pick up** 獲得、購買、發現 **refrigeration** 冷藏 **catering** 外燴 **fridge** 冰箱 **currently** 目前 **broken** 損壞的 **suit** 適合、與……相配 **come with** 伴隨……發生 **free** 免費的 **installation** 安裝 **warranty** 保證、保證書 **compact** 小巧的、小型的 **storage** 貯藏

35

What is the purpose of the man's visit?
(A) To extend a warranty
(B) To request a repair
(C) To do some shopping*
(D) To deliver an appliance

男子造訪的目的為何？
(A) 延長保固。
(B) 要求修理。
(C) 購物。
(D) 運送一件家電。

對話第一段，男子說道：「I'm interested in picking up a refrigeration unit for my truck.」，由此推測出答案為 (C)。

答案改寫 pick up → shopping

- **extend** 延長 **deliver** 運送、投遞 **appliance** 器械、(尤指) 家用電器

36

What is the man's job?
(A) Caterer*
(B) Architect
(C) Engineer
(D) Farmer

男子的工作為何？
(A) 外燴業者。
(B) 建築師。
(C) 工程師。
(D) 農夫。

與職業或住處相關的線索，通常會出現在對話前半部。對話第一段，男子說道：「I run a small catering business」，表示自己現為外燴業者，因此答案為 (A)。

- **architect** 建築師　**farmer** 農夫

37

What does the woman suggest the man do?
(A) Look at a catalogue
(B) Inspect some merchandise*
(C) Shop on a website
(D) Provide an address

女子建議男子何事？
(A) 看型錄。
(B) 查看一些商品。
(C) 上網購物。
(D) 提供住址。

請仔細聆聽女子所說的話。對話最後一段，女子說道：「Why don't you come take a look at them?」，詢問「何不直接來看一下（A4000 小型冰箱系列）」，因此 (B) 為最適當的答案。當題目提到 suggest 時，答案通常會在「Why don't you . . . ?」句型當中。

答案改寫 take a look → inspect

- **merchandise** 商品、物品

Questions 38–40 refer to the following conversation.

M Hello, this is James calling from the features department. Today is the deadline for the story on the new downtown sports center, but [38] I think I'll need another day or two to finish the piece.	男 哈囉，我是特寫組的詹姆士。今天是那篇市區新運動中心報導的截稿日，但 [38] 我想，我還需要一、二天才能完成這篇報導。
W Oh no. What's the reason? We don't normally allow extensions.	女 喔，不。是什麼原因？我們通常不允許延期。
M Well, unfortunately, [39] my computer crashed and I lost the latest edits on the article. I need to redo a lot of work.	男 嗯，很不幸，[39] 我的電腦當機，我最後修訂的文章不見了。很多工作我必須重來。
W Okay, [40] I'll have to talk with the editorial director about this. In the meantime, please try to get as much done as possible so the proofreaders can get started.	女 好，[40] 我得和總編輯談這件事。在這期間，請努力能做多少是多少，如此一來，校對人員才可以開始作業。

- **feature** 特寫　**deadline** 截止日期　**piece** 作品　**normally** 通常、按慣例　**allow** 允許、准許　**extension** 延長　**crash** （電腦）當機　**lose** 失去　**edit** 編輯、校訂　**article** 文章　**editorial** 編輯的　**proofreader** 校對者

38

What does the man ask the woman for?
(A) A later deadline*
(B) An updated contract
(C) A credit card number
(D) A coworker's e-mail

男子向女子要求何事？
(A) 較晚的截稿日期。
(B) 更新的合約。
(C) 信用卡卡號。
(D) 同事的電子郵地址。

對話第一段，男子表示雖然今天是截止日，但可能還需要一到兩天才能完成（I think I'll need another day or two to finish the piece.），因此 (A) 為最適當的答案。

• **contract** 合約　**coworker** 同事

39

What problem does the man mention?
(A) He lost some client information.
(B) He forgot his login password.
(C) He did not understand some directions.
(D) He had some technical difficulties.*

男子提及什麼問題？
(A) 他弄丟了一些客戶資料。
(B) 他忘記他的登入密碼。
(C) 他不了解某些指令。
(D) 他遇到一些技術問題。

請先標示出各選項中的重點單字，再仔細聆聽男子所說的話。對話第二段提到：「my computer crashed」，可以得知電腦故障。(D) 提到了 technical，與 computer 有關，為正確答案。

• **direction** 指示、指令　**technical** 技術的

40

What does the woman say she will do?
(A) Send some forms
(B) Contact a manager*
(C) Hire some workers
(D) Locate a file

女子說，她會做什麼？
(A) 寄送一些表格。
(B) 聯絡一位管理人員。
(C) 僱用一些人手。
(D) 找出一份檔案。

當題目詢問對話結束後「將發生的事」，在對話後半部，通常可以聽到相關線索。對話最後一段，女子提到之後會跟總編輯說（I'll have to talk with the editorial director about this），因此答案為 (B)。

答案改寫 talk with → contact
editorial director → manager

• **locate** 找出

Questions 41–43 refer to the following conversation.

M Hello, Michelle? This is Andrew Parsons calling. Last week, [41] you interviewed for the legal assistant position at our company. Are you available to come in for a training session this week?	男 哈囉，蜜雪兒？我是安德魯・帕森斯。上星期 [41] 妳來我們公司面試法務助理的工作。這星期妳有空來參加訓練課程嗎？
W Thank you for contacting me, Mr. Parsons. I'd love to come in for training. However, [42] I'm still working for my current employer, so I'm not available during the day.	女 謝謝你打給我，帕森斯先生。我很樂意參加訓練。不過，[42] 我還在目前的公司上班，因此我白天沒有空。
M You could always come in after hours. [43] I'd like to make sure you're familiar with our reporting and communication systems before you start. How does 6:30 P.M. on Wednesday evening sound? I think it will take two to three hours.	男 妳可以下班後隨時過來。[43] 我想確定妳在到任之前，已熟悉我們的通報與通訊系統。星期三下午六點半，這時間聽起來可行嗎？我想會花兩到三個小時。

• **legal** 法律的、有關法律的 **assistant** 助理 **available** 有空的 **current** 現在的 **employer** 僱主 **after hours** 下班後 **be familiar with** 熟悉

41

Where does the man most likely work? 男子最可能在哪裡工作？

(A) At a library (B) At a bakery
(C) At a pharmacy (D) At a law office*

(A) 在圖書館。(B) 在烘焙坊。
(C) 在藥局。(D) 在法律事務所。

對話第一段，男子說道：「you interviewed for the legal assistant position at our company」，提到「我們公司的法務助理」，因此答案為 (D)。

42

Why is the woman unavailable during the day? 女子為何白天沒空？

(A) She is working for a company.* (A) 她在一家公司上班。
(B) She is taking a college course. (B) 她在修習大學課程。
(C) She is traveling out of town. (C) 她去外地旅行。
(D) She is attending a conference. (D) 她去參加研討會。

對話第一段，女子提到 during the day（白天），目前仍在為現任僱主工作，無法抽出時間（I'm still working for my current employer, so I'm not available during the day.），因此答案為 (A)。

• **course** 課程、科目 **attend** 參加、出席

43

What does the man ask the woman to do? 男子要求女子何事？

(A) Submit an updated application (A) 提出更新的應徵資料。
(B) Learn about company systems* (B) 學習公司的系統。
(C) Conduct an online survey (C) 執行線上調查。
(D) Provide written references (D) 提供書面推薦信。

請仔細聆聽男子所說的話，並特別注意「要求」。對話最後一段說道：「I'd like to make sure you're familiar with our reporting and communication systems before you start.」，由此得知答案為 (B)。

答案改寫 be familiar with → learn

• **submit** 提出、呈遞 **application** 申請 **conduct** 實施、進行 **survey** 調查 **reference** 推薦信、推薦人

Questions 44–46 refer to the following conversation.

M Hello, [44] I'm interested in purchasing some new chairs for my office. A colleague mentioned to me that you provide a discount on bulk orders. Does that apply to the Deluxe 500 faux leather model?	男 哈囉，[44] 我想為我的辦公室買一些新椅子。有個同事跟我提到，你們提供大批採購折扣優惠。這適用於 Deluxe 500 人造皮款嗎？
W I'm sorry but, [45] because that is our newest model, our discounts do not apply. However, the Grand 400 faux leather model is available to receive the ten percent discount on bulk orders.	女 很抱歉，[45] 因為那是我們的最新款式，不適用於折扣優惠。不過，Grand 400 人造皮款，大批採購可享有 10% 的折扣。
M Oh, I see. Well, I haven't looked at that specific model. Is it listed on the website?	男 噢，了解。嗯，我還沒看過那一款。它有列在網站上嗎？
W It is, and if you purchase today, I can give you an additional 50 percent off the cost of shipping.	女 有的，而且如果您今天購買，我可以額外替您的運費打五折。
M Oh, that sounds great. [46] Let me check the website and call you back.	男 喔，聽起來很棒。[46] 我看一下網站，再打電話給妳。

• **purchase** 購買 **colleague** 同事 **provide** 提供 **bulk** 大量的、大批的 **apply to** 適用於 **faux** 人造的 **leather** 皮革、皮革製品 **available** 可得到的 **specific** 特定的 **additional** 額外的 **shipping** 運輸、貨運

44

What does the man want to buy? 男子想要買什麼？

(A) A refrigerator (A) 冰箱。
(B) Some shoes (B) 鞋子。
(C) A copy machine (C) 影印機。
(D) Some office furniture* (D) 辦公家具。

對話第一段，男子說道：「I'm interested in purchasing some new chairs for my office.」，由此推測答案為 (D)。

答案改寫 chair for my office → office furniture

• **refrigerator** 冰箱

45

Why does the woman apologize? 女子為何致歉？

(A) A discount cannot be used.* (A) 有項折扣無法使用。
(B) Some products are sold out. (B) 有些產品已售完。
(C) A store is closed for renovations. (C) 有間店關閉整修。
(D) Some customers complained. (D) 有些客戶抱怨。

請特別留意女子所說的話，I'm sorry 後方表示新產品不適用於折扣（because that is our newest model, our discounts do not apply），並提供替代方案，因此 (A) 為最適當的答案。

• **renovation** 更新、修理 **complain** 抱怨

46

What does the man say he will do?
(A) Discuss an issue with a colleague
(B) Visit an online store*
(C) Provide an address
(D) Send some measurements

男子說，他要做什麼？
(A) 和同事討論一個問題。
(B) 造訪線上商店。
(C) 提供地址。
(D) 寄送測量尺寸。

本題詢問的是「對話結束後的狀況」，因此請仔細聆聽對話後半部的內容。對話最後，男子說道：「Let me check the website and call you back.」，表示在網站上確認後會再回電，因此答案為 (B)。

答案改寫 check → visit
website → online store

• **discuss** 討論　**issue** 問題、爭議　**measurement** 尺寸、測量

Questions 47–49 refer to the following conversation.

M Hi, Jan. [47] I've updated the employee handbook that we'll be using this year. Can you check the changes before I send the file to everyone in the office?	男 嗨，珍，[47] 我已經更新了今年要用的員工手冊。妳可以檢查一下修改的地方，我再把檔案寄給大家嗎？
W Okay, this all looks good. Oh, wait a minute. The company address you've used is wrong. [48] This is the old office address before the city changed the street name.	女 好，整體看來很好。噢，等一下。你用的公司地址是錯的。[48] 這是本市更改街道名稱之前的舊辦公地址。
M Oh, wow. I'm so glad you caught that. [49] I can't believe I missed it.	男 噢，哇。幸好妳抓到那個錯誤。[49] 簡直不敢相信我竟然沒發現。
W It happens to us all. Let's send the file to Tina and have her check all the information just to be sure nothing else is wrong.	女 我們難免會遇到這種事。那我們把檔案寄給緹娜，請她檢查所有資料，確認沒有其他錯漏之處。

47

What are the speakers mainly talking about?
(A) Moving to a new building
(B) Hiring a designer
(C) Updating a customer profile
(D) Editing a document*

說話者主要在談何事？
(A) 搬進新大樓。
(B) 僱用一位設計師。
(C) 更新客戶檔案。
(D) 編輯一份文件。

對話一開頭，男子表示已將員工手冊更新（I've updated the employee handbook that we'll be using this year.），要求對方確認，因此 (D) 為最適當的答案。在對話前半部，通常可以聽到對話主旨的相關線索。

答案改寫 the employee handbook → a document

• **edit** 編輯、校訂

48

What problem does the woman notice?
(A) An address is outdated.*
(B) A form was misplaced.
(C) An employee was late.
(D) A phone number is wrong.

女子注意到什麼問題？
(A) 有個地址是舊的。
(B) 有份表格放錯地方。
(C) 有個員工遲到。
(D) 有串電話號碼是錯的。

本題詢問「問題所在」，因此請先標示出各選項中的重點單字（例如：address, form, employee, phone number）。對話第一段，女子提到地址有誤，補充說明「是街道名稱更動以前的舊住址（This is the old office address before the city changed the street name.）」，因此答案為 (A)。

- **outdated** 舊式的、過時的 **misplace** 誤置、遺忘

49

Why does the woman say, "It happens to us all"?
(A) To explain a problem
(B) To provide clarification
(C) To prevent an accident
(D) To show compassion*

女子為何說「我們難免會遇到這種事」？
(A) 以解釋一個問題。
(B) 以澄清意思。
(C) 以防意外事故發生。
(D) 以示同理心。

請留意題目句，並仔細聆聽文中該句前後方的文意。對方對於失誤相當自責（I can't believe I missed it.），女子對其表達想法，因此 (D) 為最適當的答案。

- **clarification** 澄清、說明 **prevent** 防止、預防 **accident** 意外事情 **compassion** 憐憫、同情

Questions 50–52 refer to the following conversation.

W	Hi, this is Becky Hill calling. 50 I need to reschedule my appointment with Dr. Miller. Do you have anything available next week?	女	嗨，我是貝琪・希爾，50 我需要重新安排和米勒醫師的約診時間。下星期什麼時段可以？
M	Let me check our schedule. It looks like Dr. Miller is available next Wednesday morning. Can you come in at 10:00 A.M.?	男	我查一下時間表。看上去，米勒醫師下星期三上午有空。你可以上午十點過來嗎？
W	No, 51 I'll be out of town that day for a business convention. Are there any appointments available on Friday?	女	沒辦法，51 我那一天要出城去參加商務研討會。星期五有任何時段空著嗎？
M	Possibly. Oh, here we go. I see there was a cancellation on Friday, so there's an opening at 3:00 P.M. Does that work?	男	可能有。喔，有了。我看到星期五有個約診取消了，所以，下午三點有個空檔。那個時間可以嗎？
W	That's perfect. 52 I'll write it down in my planner.	女	太好了。52 我會寫在記事本上。

- **reschedule** 重新安排……的時間 **appointment** 約會、預約 **available** 有空的 **be out of town** 出城 **cancellation** 取消 **opening** 空缺、機會

50

What is the purpose of the woman's call?
(A) To inquire about test results
(B) To make a payment
(C) To change an appointment*
(D) To update insurance information

女子打電話的目的為何？
(A) 詢問檢驗的結果。
(B) 付款。
(C) 更改約診。
(D) 更新保險資料。

在對話前半部，通常可以聽到有關目的的關鍵線索。對話第一段，女子介紹完自己的名字後說道：「I need to reschedule my appointment with Dr. Miller.」，表示需要調整一下時間，因此答案為 (C)。

答案改寫 reschedule → change

• inquire 詢問、調查　result 結果　make a payment 付款　insurance 保險

51

What is the woman doing on Wednesday morning?
(A) Visiting a clinic
(B) Traveling to another city*
(C) Meeting a client
(D) Hosting a local event

女子星期三早上要做何事？
(A) 去診所就診。
(B) 到另一個城市出差。
(C) 與客戶碰面。
(D) 主持一個本地活動。

看到題目可以推測出，對話中將會提到關鍵時間點 Wednesday morning（星期三上午）。男子詢問星期三上午十點是否可以來，女子回答：「沒辦法，因為要去別的城市開會（I'll be be out of town that day for a business convention.）」，因此答案為 (B)。

答案改寫 out of town → another city

52

What will the woman most likely do next?
(A) Contact a coworker
(B) Record some information*
(C) Go to a hospital
(D) Meet with a consultant

女子接下來最可能做何事？
(A) 聯絡同事。
(B) 記錄一些資訊。
(C) 前往醫院。
(D) 與諮詢顧問會面。

當題目為「. . . do next?」結尾的問句時，即是詢問對話結束後會做的事情為何，因此答題的關鍵線索會出現在對話後半部。對話最後一句，女子說道：「I'll write it down in my planner.」，由此可以確認答案為 (B)。

答案改寫 write down → record

• record 記錄

Questions 53–55 refer to the following conversation with three speakers.

M	Before we go, let's discuss our office lease. [53] As you know our lease expires next year, which would be a good time to move to a larger office. However, I'd like to get everyone's input before we decide on a location.	男	在開始之前，我們先來討論一下辦公室的租約。[53] 你們都知道，我們的租約到明年，這會是搬到較寬敞辦公室的好時機。不過，在我們決定地點之前，我想聽聽各位的意見。
W1	Betina and I were talking about this yesterday, and she mentioned she saw a sign at the new Roger's building downtown. What did it say, Betina?	女1	貝緹娜和我昨天才在談這件事，她提到，她看到市中心的新羅傑大樓外有個告示牌。上面寫什麼，貝緹娜？
W2	Well, apparently the new building will open next year and they're looking for businesses to rent spaces. [54] We could make an appointment to see the spaces.	女2	嗯，看起來那棟新大樓明年會啟用，而他們現在正在找公司承租。[54] 我們可以約個時間去現場看看。
M	That sounds good. [55] Can you get me the contact number listed on the sign?	男	聽起來還不賴。[55] 妳可以給我告示牌上的聯絡電話嗎？
W2	[55] Sure. I'll stop by there on my way home.	女2	當然可以。我會在回家的路上順道去看。

• **lease** 租約　**expire** 屆期、終止　**input** 投入、貢獻　**decide** 決定　**location** 位置　**sign** 招牌、告示牌　**apparently** 顯然地、表面上、似乎　**rent** 租用　**make an appointment** 與……約定　**stop by** 順路造訪

53

According to the man, what will happen next year?
(A) A CEO will visit.
(B) A business will fail.
(C) A renovation will occur.
(D) A contract will expire.*

根據男子，明年會發生何事？
(A) 有位執行長會來訪。
(B) 有間公司要倒閉。
(C) 要進行整修。
(D) 有份合約要到期。

從對話內容中，通常可以直接聽到題目句的時間副詞。聆聽男子所說的話時，請特別留意 next year。對話第一段說道：「As you know our lease expires next year」，由此可以確定答案為 (D)。

答案改寫 lease → contract

• **renovation** 更新、修理

54

What does Betina suggest?
(A) Checking a website
(B) Taking a building tour*
(C) Extending a lease
(D) Purchasing a building

貝緹娜建議什麼？
(A) 查看一個網站。
(B) 參觀一棟大樓。
(C) 延長租約。
(D) 買下一棟大樓。

聆聽時，請特別留意關鍵人名 Betina。第一位說話的女子向貝緹娜詢問告示牌上寫了什麼，對方回答：「上面寫正在尋找承租業者，或許我們可以約個時間去看一下（We could make an appointment to see the spaces.）」。因此 (B) 為最適當的答案。

• **extend** 延長

55

What does Betina agree to do?
(A) Pass on a phone number*
(B) Call a real estate agent
(C) Revise a contract
(D) Create a company sign

貝緹娜同意做什麼？
(A) 轉達一串電話號碼。
(B) 打電話給不動產經紀人。
(C) 修改一份合約。
(D) 創作公司招牌。

對話後半段，男子詢問了聯絡方式（Can you get me the contact number listed on the sign?），對方回覆「沒問題」，因此答案為 (A)。

- **real estate** 不動產、房地產　**revise** 修改、修訂

Questions 56–58 refer to the following conversation.

M Beth, take a look at these hairpins.	男 貝絲，看看這些髮夾。
W They're really pretty, aren't they? I bought one a while ago. They're made with real pearls from Florida. [56] No two pins are the same. See, they all have different colors.	女 真漂亮，不是嗎？我不久前買了一個。它們是用佛羅里達產的真珠製成的，[56] 每隻髮夾都獨一無二。你看，它們的顏色都不一樣。
M I don't remember you ever wearing a hairpin like this.	男 我不記得妳戴過像這樣的髮夾。
W Actually, [57] I lost it while I was on vacation.	女 事實上，[57] 我去度假時弄丟了。
M That's too bad. I'd love to get one of these for my sister. Her birthday is next week, but, well, I don't get paid for ten days.	男 真慘。我想要買一個這種的給我妹妹。她下星期生日，但是，呃，我已經有十天沒領到薪水了。
W [58] I can lend you the money. You can pay me back when you get paid.	女 [58] 我可以借你錢。等你領到薪水時再還我就好。
M Wow, that's so generous of you.	男 哇，妳真慷慨。

- **pearl** 珍珠　**lend** 借出　**generous** 慷慨的、大方的

56

What does the woman say is special about the hairpins?
(A) They are made of gold.
(B) They are inexpensive.
(C) They are made in France.
(D) They are all unique.*

女子說，這髮夾特別之處為何？
(A) 它們是用黃金做的。
(B) 它們不貴。
(C) 它們是法國製的。
(D) 它們每個都獨一無二。

本題詢問女子說話的內容，因此可以推測答案會出現在女子所說的話當中。對話第一段，女子說道：「No two pins are the same.」，表示沒有一模一樣的髮夾，每個顏色都不一樣，因此 (D) 為最適當的答案。

- **inexpensive** 不貴的、價錢低廉的　**unique** 獨一無二的、獨特的

57

Why does the woman say she no longer wears her hairpin?

(A) She lost it.* (B) She broke it.
(C) She dislikes it. (D) She gifted it.

女子為何說，她不再戴她的髮夾？

(A) 她遺失了。 (B) 她打破了。
(C) 她不喜歡。 (D) 她送人了。

男子表示印象中沒看過女子戴過髮夾，女子回答：「因為度假時不小心弄丟了（I lost it while I was on vacation.）」，因此答案為 (A)。

58

What does the man imply when he says, "I don't get paid for ten days"?

(A) He usually gets paid every week.
(B) He forgot to pick up his paycheck.
(C) He doesn't have enough money right now.*
(D) He recently got a pay increase.

當男子說「我已經有十天沒領到薪水了」，意指什麼？

(A) 他通常每星期領薪水。
(B) 他忘記去領薪水支票。
(C) 他現在沒有足夠的錢。
(D) 他最近加薪。

本題請特別留意題目的句子，並仔細聆聽句子前後的文意。題目句後方，女子接著說道：「I can lend you the money.」，表示願意借錢給男子，可推測出男子現在錢不夠，因此 (C) 為最適當的答案。

- **paycheck** 付薪水的支票 **increase** 增加

Questions 59–61 refer to the following conversation.

W	Welcome to Paxton Pharmaceuticals. [59] How may I help you?	**女**	歡迎光臨帕克斯頓製藥。[59] 需要什麼服務？
M	I'm with Kent Shipping Services. [60] I have a delivery for Dr. Alex Strummer. Can you ask him to come down and sign for it?	**男**	我是肯特貨運。[60] 我有件貨品要給艾力克斯・史楚默博士。你可以請他下來簽收嗎？
W	Is it all right if I sign for him?	**女**	我幫他簽收，可以嗎？
M	Actually, this delivery contains sensitive materials. Only Dr. Strummer is authorized to sign for them.	**男**	事實上，這件貨物內含敏感資料，只有史楚默博士有權利簽收。
W	I see. Well, [61] Dr. Strummer is at our Swanson Road laboratory right now.	**女**	我明白了。嗯，[61] 史楚默博士目前在我們位於史旺生路的實驗室。
M	Okay. [61] I'll come back tomorrow.	**男**	好的，[61] 我明天再來。

- **pharmaceuticals** 藥物 **shipping** 運輸、貨運 **delivery** 一次投遞的郵件或貨物 **contain** 包含 **sensitive** 敏感的 **material** 材料、資料 **authorize** 授權給、允許 **laboratory** 實驗室

59

Who most likely is the woman?

(A) A sales clerk
(B) A web designer
(C) A company receptionist*
(D) A post office manager

女子最可能是誰？

(A) 銷售員。
(B) 網頁設計師。
(C) 公司的櫃檯人員。
(D) 郵局的經理。

本題詢問女子的職業，聆聽時，請特別留意對話第一段內容。女子介紹公司名稱後，緊接著詢問對方有什麼需要（How may I help you?），因此 (C) 為最適當的答案。

- **clerk** 職員、店員 **receptionist** 接待員 **post office** 郵局

60

Why does the man visit the office?
(A) To make a delivery*
(B) To have a meeting
(C) To inspect a lab
(D) To collect a payment

男子為何造訪這家公司？
(A) 為了遞送貨物。
(B) 為了開會。
(C) 為了視察實驗室。
(D) 為了收取款項。

對話第一段，男子表示自己是貨運公司的人員，送來一件貨品（I have a delivery for Dr. Alex Strummer.）。因此答案為 (A)。

答案改寫 have a delivery → make a delivery

- **collect** 收（租、稅、帳等）

61

What does the woman imply when she says, "Well, Dr. Strummer is at our Swanson Road laboratory right now"?
(A) Dr. Strummer is a medical scientist.
(B) A storage room is available.
(C) Dr. Strummer cannot sign a form.*
(D) An urgent prescription request must be made.

當女子說「嗯，史楚默博士目前在我們位於史旺生路的實驗室」，意指什麼？
(A) 史楚默博士是位醫學科學家。
(B) 有一間貯藏室空著可用。
(C) 史楚默博士無法簽文件。
(D) 必須要求緊急處方。

當題目詢問話者的意圖時，請務必掌握說話者的話與前後句之間的關聯，再進行解題。男子表示「必須由史楚默博士簽名」，女子回答題目中的那句話之後，男子便說道：「I'll come back tomorrow.」，表示自己明天再來。因此 (C) 為最適當的答案。

- **medical** 醫學的、醫療的 **available** 可利用的 **urgent** 緊急的 **prescription** 處方 **make a request** 提出請求

Questions 62–64 refer to the following conversation.

W Hi, Marco. [62] Our company's 10th anniversary party is just a month away. Did you get a chance to call the hotel yet?	女 嗨，馬可，[62] 再一個月就是我們公司的十週年派對，你撥出時間打電話給飯店了嗎？
M Yes, and unfortunately, the Hill Park Hotel's banquet rooms are all booked. [63] I was thinking of contacting the Royal Hotel. I believe their banquet rentals are even cheaper and they include a fully catered buffet.	男 有，但遺憾的是，希爾公園飯店的宴會廳全都被訂走了。[63] 我想聯絡皇家飯店。我相信他們的宴會廳租金還更便宜些，而且包含全套自助餐。
W Oh, that sounds good. But wait, isn't the hotel too far for most people to drive to? Aren't there any hotels closer to the office?	女 喔，聽起來很好。但是，等一下，那家飯店對大部分的人來說，要開車去不是太遠了嗎？沒有任何離公司比較近的飯店嗎？
M Yes, but they are quite expensive. I'm not sure we can afford them on our budget. [64] I will e-mail the office manager this afternoon and get his opinion.	男 有，但他們收費相當昂貴。我不確定以我們的預算能否負擔得起。[64] 我今天下午會寫電子郵件給經理，詢問他的意見。

- **anniversary** 週年紀念、週年紀念日 **banquet** 宴會 **book** 預訂 **rental** 租金 **cater** （為宴會等）供應酒筵、承辦酒席 **afford** 支付得起 **budget** 預算 **opinion** 意見

62

What type of event are the speakers discussing?
(A) A store's grand opening
(B) An award ceremony
(C) A company anniversary*
(D) A retirement party

說話者在討論何種活動？
(A) 商店的盛大開幕。
(B) 頒獎典禮。
(C) 公司的週年紀念。
(D) 退休派對。

對話第一段，女子說道：「Our company's 10th anniversary party is just a month away.」，由此可以聽到解題的關鍵線索，因此答案為 (C)。

• **award ceremony** 頒獎典禮　**retirement** 退休

63

What is the man considering?
(A) Whether to send invitations
(B) Who to hire as a caterer
(C) When to schedule an event
(D) Where to hold an event*

男子在考慮何事？
(A) 是否要寄送邀請函。
(B) 僱用誰承辦酒席。
(C) 把活動安排在何時。
(D) 在哪裡舉行活動。

聆聽時，請特別留意「考量與煩惱的事項」。對話第一段，男子提到「因為預約全滿，正在考慮要不要聯絡其他場地（I was thinking of contacting the Royal Hotel.）」，因此 (D) 為最適當的答案。

• **invitation** 邀請、請帖

64

What does the man say he will do?
(A) Visit a venue
(B) Update a menu
(C) Cancel a reservation
(D) Consult a supervisor*

男子說他會做何事？
(A) 去看一個場地。
(B) 更新菜單。
(C) 取消預訂。
(D) 請教主管。

請仔細聆聽男子「之後的計畫」。對話最後一段說道：「I will e-mail the office manager this afternoon and get his opinion.」，表示之後會寄郵件給經理，詢問對方的意見。因此答案為 (D)。

答案改寫 office manager → supervisor

• **venue** 舉行地點、會場　**reservation** 預訂、預約　**consult** 請教、諮詢　**supervisor** 監督者、管理者

Questions 65–67 refer to the following conversation and packing slip.

PREMIUM HOME DÉCOR		
Item	**Quantity**	**Total Price**
Panel Curtains	4	$160.00
[67] Cushions	4	$40.00
Shag Rug	1	$79.00
Lamp Shade	2	$44.00

優質居家裝潢		
項目	**數量**	**總計**
片簾	4	$160.00
[67] 靠墊	4	$40.00
長絨地毯	1	$79.00
燈罩	2	$44.00

M Hello, Ma'am. How can I help you?

W Hi, [65] I bought a new sofa recently and found that most of my décor no longer matches. So, I ordered several furnishings from your online store. [66] They arrived yesterday, but only two of the cushions I ordered were delivered instead of four.

M Oh, I'm sorry to hear that. May I have a look at your packing slip?

W Sure. It's right here.

M Hmm. Unfortunately, the color you ordered is out of stock. You seem to have gotten the last two. I'm not sure when we'll get more, so [67] how about I refund the full cost of the cushions, and you can keep the two you did get for free.

W That would be great. Thank you!

男 哈囉，女士，需要什麼服務？

女 嗨，[65] 我最近買了張新沙發，卻發現大部分的裝潢都不搭了。所以我在你們的線上商店訂了一些家具。[66] 昨天送來了，但我訂的靠墊只送來兩個，而不是四個。

男 喔，發生這種狀況真的很抱歉。我可以看一下您的出貨單嗎？

女 當然，就在這裡。

男 嗯。很不巧，您訂的顏色缺貨。您似乎買到最後兩個。我不確定我們何時會有貨。那麼，[67] 我把靠墊的費用全額退給您，已經收到的那兩個您可以自己留著，等同免費，這樣好嗎？

女 太好了，謝謝你！

• **quantity** 數量 **shag** (地毯)長絨的 **rug** 小地毯 **shade** 燈罩 **match** 和……相配 **furnishing** 家具、室內陳設 **arrive** (郵件、物品等)被送來 **deliver** 投遞、運送 **packing slip** 出貨單、裝箱單 **slip** (通常為條形的)單子 **out of stock** 無庫存、無現貨 **refund** 退款 **cost** 費用

65

What does the woman say she did recently?

(A) She stained her carpet.

(B) She moved to a new house.

(C) She misplaced some items.

(D) She purchased some new furniture.*

女子說她最近做了何事？

(A) 她弄髒了地毯。

(B) 她搬新家。

(C) 有些東西她放錯地方了。

(D) 她買了新家具。

聆聽時，請特別留意女子的「近況」。對話第一段，女子說道：「I bought a new sofa recently」，由此確認答案為 (D)。

答案改寫 sofa → furniture

• **stain** 沾上汙漬 **misplace** 誤置

66

Why does the woman need assistance?
(A) Her order arrived incomplete.*
(B) She was charged too much for an item.
(C) She does not like some items.
(D) Her receipt was not in the box.

女子為何需要協助？
(A) 她訂的貨沒有全部送來。
(B) 某件貨品的收費太高。
(C) 有些物品她不喜歡。
(D) 她的收據不在盒子裡。

請仔細聆聽女子所說的話。對話第一段，女子提到「昨天只有收到兩個靠墊（They arrived yesterday, but only two of the cushions I ordered were delivered instead of four.）」，因此 (A) 為最適當的答案。

• **assistance** 協助　**incomplete** 不完全的、不完整的　**charge** 索價

67

Look at the graphic. How much money will the woman be refunded?
(A) $160.00　(B) $40.00*
(C) $79.00　(D) $44.00

請見圖表。女子可以收到多少退款？
(A) $160.00。(B) $40.00。
(C) $79.00。(D) $44.00。

聆聽時，請務必先掌握解題關鍵為「退費金額」。對話末段，男子說道：「how about I refund the full cost of the cushions」，由此可以得知為「靠墊的總額」，對照表格後，可確認答案為 (B)。

Questions 68–70 refer to the following conversation and sign.

Flight	Destination	Gate
AV13	[70] Los Angeles	A56
CP03	Miami	B45
PS55	Paris	B13
AA01	Beijing	A32

W Where are your bags, Steve? Did you already take them to the baggage drop off?
M No. I'm only bringing this carry-on. I packed light because [68] I won't be staying for the entire workshop.
W Oh? Why not?
M [69] I have an important marketing meeting in the middle of the week. I couldn't reschedule it, so I'll only be attending the first two days of the workshop.
W That's too bad. You're going to miss out on a lot of the presentations by the regional managers. Oh, look at the time! We'd better get to our departure gate.
M Right. [70] The departure board says we're at A56. We still have to go through airport security, so let's hurry.

航班	目的地	登機門
AV13	[70] 洛杉磯	A56
CP03	邁阿密	B45
P555	巴黎	B13
AA01	北京	A32

女 史帝夫，你的行李在哪裡？你已經送去托運了嗎？
男 沒有，我只帶了這個手提行李。我的行李很輕便，因為 [68] 我不會待到整個工作坊結束。
女 哦？為什麼不？
男 [69] 這星期到一半時，我有個很重要的行銷會議。我無法重新安排時間，所以我只會參加前兩天的工作坊。
女 真是太掃興了。你會錯過很多地區經理的報告。噢，你看時間！我們最好過去登機門。
男 是啊。[70] 班機起飛看板上說，我們是 A56。我們還必須通過機場的安檢，所以我們趕快吧。

• **baggage drop off** 行李託運　**carry-on** 隨身行李、手提行李　**pack** 收拾行李　**entire** 全部的、整個的　**attend** 參加、出席　**miss out on** 未得到、錯失　**regional** 地區的、局部的　**departure** 離開、出發　**security** 安全、安全措施　**hurry** 趕緊

68

What type of event are the speakers traveling to?
(A) A holiday vacation (B) A sales conference
(C) A training session (D) A corporate workshop*

說話者要飛去參加的是哪種活動？
(A) 休假。 (B) 銷售研討會。
(C) 訓練課程。 (D) 企業的工作坊。

對話第一段，男子說道：「I won't be staying for the entire workshop.」，由此可以確認答案為 (D)。

69

Why is the man staying just a short time?
(A) He was unable to get a flight.
(B) He could not reserve a hotel.
(C) He has a conflicting schedule.*
(D) He is not well.

男子為何只會停留短暫的時間？
(A) 他無法搭上飛機。
(B) 他訂不到飯店。
(C) 他的行程有衝突。
(D) 他不舒服。

女子向男子詢問為何要提早離開，男子表示有重要的會議，無法更動行程（I have an important marketing meeting in the middle of the week. I couldn't reschedule it, so I'll only be attending the first two days of the workshop.），因此 (C) 為最適當的答案。

- **reserve** 預約、預訂 **conflicting** 衝突的 **well** 健康的

70

Look at the graphic. What city are the speakers flying to?
(A) Los Angeles* (B) Miami
(C) Paris (D) Beijing

請見圖表。說話者要飛往哪座城市？
(A) 洛杉磯。 (B) 邁阿密。
(C) 巴黎。 (D) 北京。

聆聽對話時，請找出解題線索「目的地」。對話最後一段，男子提到了登機口的號碼（The departure board says we're at A56.），對照表格後，可確認答案為 (A)。

PART 4 16

Questions 71–73 refer to the following broadcast.

M Welcome back to KTM radio, and thank you for listening to our new program, Travel Talk. [71, 72] Respected travel writer, Samuel Berkley, has joined us to talk about his new travel book series titled *A Trekker's Guide to the World*, which will be published early next year. Each book focuses on one popular tourist country and includes useful information, such as where to eat, where to stay, and what to see. [73] Those of you who are interested in learning more about Berkley's new series can check it out online at www.trekkersguide.com.	男 歡迎回到 KTM 電台，感謝您收聽我們的新節目「旅遊閒談」。[71, 72] 備受景仰的旅遊作家山繆・柏克利來到節目，和我們談談他將於明年初出版的新系列旅遊叢書《背包客的世界指南》。每一本書各聚焦在一個受歡迎的旅遊國家，並包含實用的資訊，像是去哪裡吃、去哪裡住宿和要看什麼。[73] 若您有興趣瞭解柏克利新系列叢書，詳情請上 www.trekkersguide.com 查詢。

• **respected** 受尊敬的、受敬重的 **trekker** 背包客 **publish** 出版 **focus on** 集中（於焦點）
popular 受歡迎的、流行的 **include** 包含 **useful** 有用的、有助益的

71

Who is Samuel Berkley?

(A) A radio host (B) A publisher
(C) A writer* (D) A diplomat

山繆・柏克利是誰？

(A) 電台主持人。 (B) 出版商。
(C) 作家。 (D) 外交官。

在人名的前後方，通常會提及身分或是職業，聆聽時，請特別留意 Samuel Berkley。獨白前半部說道：「Respected travel writer, Samuel Berkley」，由此確認答案為 (C)。

• **host** （電視或廣播節目的）主持人 **diplomat** 外交官

72

What is Samuel Berkley planning on doing?

(A) Launching a travel website
(B) Taking a trip around the world
(C) Releasing a book series*
(D) Giving a talk about hotels

山繆・柏克利打算做何事？

(A) 推出旅遊網站。
(B) 環遊世界。
(C) 發行系列書籍。
(D) 分享有關飯店的談話。

獨白中段說道：「Samuel Berkley, has joined us to talk about his new travel book series titled *A Trekker's Guide to the World*, which will be published early next year.」，提到預計於明年出版旅遊系列書籍，因此 (C) 為最適當的答案。

• **launch** 啟動、推出 **release** 發行

73

What are listeners instructed to do?

(A) Go to a website* (B) Book a trip
(C) Purchase a book (D) Post questions online

聽眾被告知要做何事？

(A) 造訪網站。 (B) 預訂旅程。
(C) 買書。 (D) 上網提問。

在獨白後半部，通常會聽到說話者的建議或要求。獨白最後一句提到：「更多相關資訊，請至官網查詢（Those of you who are interested in learning more about Berkley's new series can check it out online at www.trekkersquide.com.）」，由此得知答案為 (A)。

答案改寫 online at www.trekkersguide.com → website

• **book** 預訂

Questions 74–76 refer to the following talk.

M Hello everyone. Welcome to the Audio Visual Technology Exhibition here in San Francisco. My name is Jackson, and I'm an employee at Southern Tech. [74] Today, I'd like to introduce you to a new type of headphones my company just released. [75] What sets our design apart from others is its wireless capability. You can actually upload music into the headphones and wear them without using another device. Everyone here today is eligible to win a free set. [76] All you need to do is fill out a survey telling us about the devices you currently own.	男 大家好，歡迎來到舊金山的視聽科技展。我是傑克生，南方科技的員工。[74] 今天要為各位介紹我們公司才剛發表的新型耳機。[75] 我們的設計與眾不同之處在於它的無線功能。你真的可以不必使用別的裝置，就能上傳音樂到耳機並且戴著聽。今天在場的各位都可以免費贏得一副耳機，[76] 只需填寫一份調查，告訴我們你現在擁有的裝置就可以了。

• **audio visual** 視聽的 **exhibition** 展覽 **release** 發行、發表 **set apart from** 使……與眾不同或優於其他 **wireless** 無線的 **capability** 能力、功能 **device** 設備、裝置 **eligible** 有資格的 **fill out** 填寫 **survey** 調查 **own** 擁有

74

What product is being discussed? 文中討論的是什麼產品？

(A) A stereo system 立體音響系統。
(B) An audio device* 音訊裝置。
(C) A television set 電視機。
(D) A software program 軟體程式。

從歡迎問候語中，可以推測在視聽展示會場。獨白中段，可以聽到即將介紹最新型的耳機（Today, I'd like to introduce you a new type of headphones my company just released.），因此答案為 (B)。

答案改寫 headphones → an audio device

75

How does the product differ from competitors' products? 這項產品與競爭對手的產品有何不同？

(A) It is cheaper to repair. 修理費用較便宜。
(B) It is more durable. 比較持久耐用。
(C) It is less expensive. 價格較低廉。
(D) It has a unique feature.* 有一項獨有的特色。

聆聽獨白時，請掌握解題關鍵為「不同之處」。獨白中段說道：「What sets our design apart from others is its wireless capability.」，表示與其他產品的不同之處為無線功能，由此確認 (D) 為最適當的答案。

答案改寫 set apart from → differ from
capability → feature

• **differ from** 與……不同 **competitor** 競爭者、對手 **cheaper** 較便宜 **repair** 修理、修補 **durable** 持久的、耐用的 **expensive** 昂貴的

76

How can listeners win a free product?
(A) By testing out a model
(B) By completing a survey*
(C) By visiting a website
(D) By purchasing an item

聽眾如何贏得一項免費產品?
(A) 充分檢測一個款式。
(B) 完成一份調查。
(C) 造訪一個網站。
(D) 購買一個物品。

獨白後半部提到,只要填寫問卷,就有機會獲得免費的產品(All you need to do is fill out a survey telling us about the devices you currently own.),因此答案為 (B)。

答案改寫 fill out → complete

• **complete** 完成 **purchase** 購買 **item** 物品

Questions 77–79 refer to the following telephone message.

M Hello, Ms. Choi. This is Mike Burton calling from Burton and Sons properties. [77] It was nice speaking with you on the phone yesterday, and I hope you're still interested in seeing the restaurant space on Miller Road. You asked about basement storage space, and I wanted to let you know [78] that storage rooms can be rented for a monthly fee. Anyway, several people are interested in the space, [79] so we should probably go see it as soon as possible. That way, we can sign a lease before someone else does.	男 哈囉,崔女士,我是博頓父子房地產公司的麥克・博頓。[77] 很高興昨天和您通電話,希望您還有興趣看米勒路上的那間餐廳。您詢問了地下室貯藏空間的問題,我想通知您,[78] 貯藏室可以月租。不過,有好幾個人都對這個空間感興趣,[79] 因此我們應該盡快去看看。那樣的話,我們就可以趕在其他人之前簽下租約。

• **property** 房地產、資產 **basement** 地下室 **storage** 貯藏、保管 **rent** 租用 **fee** 費用 **several** 好幾個 **probably** 很可能 **lease** 租約

77

What did the speaker do yesterday?
(A) He went to a restaurant.
(B) He talked to the listener.*
(C) He purchased a storage unit.
(D) He signed a lease.

說話者昨天做了何事?
(A) 他去了一家餐廳。
(B) 他和聽者談話。
(C) 他買下一個貯藏空間。
(D) 他簽了一份租約。

在獨白中,通常可以聽到題目內提及的關鍵時間副詞,因此聆聽時,請特別留意 yesterday(昨天)。獨白前段說道:「It was nice speaking with you on the phone yesterday」,由此確認答案為 (B)。

答案改寫 speak with → talk to

78

What does the speaker say about storage rooms?
(A) They have shelving units inside.
(B) They are an added bonus.
(C) They have security systems.
(D) They are available for a fee.*

關於貯藏室，說話者怎麼說？
(A) 裡面有層架。
(B) 是額外的好處。
(C) 有保全系統。
(D) 可付費使用。

聆聽時，請特別留意關鍵字 storage rooms（貯藏室）。獨白中段提到「地下倉庫也可以提供月租（that storage rooms can be rented for a monthly fee）」，因此答案為 (D)。

• shelving 架子（總稱）　security 安全、防護

79

Why does the speaker say, "Several people are interested in the space"?
(A) To explain why the space is no longer available
(B) To encourage the listener to see the space quickly*
(C) To request the listener to give up the space
(D) To describe the size and price of the space

說話者為何說「有好幾個人都對這個空間感興趣」？
(A) 解釋這個空間為何不再能租。
(B) 鼓勵聽者趕快點去看這個地點。
(C) 要求聽者放棄這個地點。
(D) 形容這個空間的大小與價格。

請先讀過題目並記下句子後，再聆聽獨白內容。題目句後方緊接著說道：「so we should probably go see it as soon as possible」，以催促的口吻表示得盡可能快點去看才行，因此 (B) 為最適當的答案。

• no longer 不再　encourage 鼓勵、激發　request 要求　describe 形容、描寫

Questions 80–82 refer to the following phone message.

W　Hi, this is a message for David Taylor. [80] This is Beatrice calling from Eastside Homeless Shelter. Thank you very much for signing up to help out at our annual concert fundraiser downtown. As of now we have enough volunteers for the event. [81] However, we are looking for volunteers to work one Sunday a month in our soup kitchen. We really need the extra help there, so you'd be doing your community a great service. If you're interested, [82] please e-mail me at beatrice@eastsideshelter.com, so I can send you an application.

女　嗨，這是給大衛・泰勒的訊息。[80] 我是東岸街友庇護所的畢翠絲，非常感謝您報名要當我們於市中心舉行的年度募款音樂會的義工。目前，我們已有足夠的活動義工。[81] 不過，我們正在尋找能一個月抽出一個星期日，在我們的慈善廚房幫忙的義工。我們那裡真的很需要額外的幫手，所以，您會幫上社區很大的忙。如果您有興趣，[82] 請寄電子郵件到 beatrice@eastsideshelter.com 給我，好讓我能寄申請書給您。

• shelter 避難所、掩蔽　sign up 報名登記、註冊　annual 年度的　fundraiser 募款活動
as of now 現在、此刻　volunteer 義工、志願者　soup kitchen 慈善廚房　community 社區、社會
application 申請、申請書

80

Where does the speaker work?
(A) At a job agency
(B) At a charity*
(C) At a concert hall
(D) At a city park

說話者在哪裡工作？
(A) 職業介紹所。
(B) 慈善團體。
(C) 音樂廳。
(D) 市立公園。

從專有名詞，可以得知說話者職業的相關資訊。前段問候內容中說道：「This is Beatrice calling from Eastside Homeless Shelter.」，提到了自己的名字和所屬單位，因此 (B) 為最適當的答案。

• **charity** 慈善團體、慈善事業、博愛

81

Why does the speaker say, "As of now we have enough volunteers for the event"?
(A) To turn down an offer*
(B) To stress the success of an event
(C) To voice a concern about a policy
(D) To request more funding

說話者為何說「目前，我們已有足夠的活動義工」？
(A) 以回絕一個提議。
(B) 以強調一場活動的成功。
(C) 以表達對一項政策的關心。
(D) 以要求更多資金。

題目句之後提出了其他方案（However, we are looking for volunteers to work one Sunday a month in our soup kitchen.），根據前後文意，確認答案為 (A)。

• **turn down** 拒絕 **stress** 強調 **voice** 表達、說出 **funding** 資金

82

What does the speaker ask the listener to do?
(A) Attend a concert (B) Send an e-mail*
(C) Visit a website (D) Record some information

說話者要求聽者做何事？
(A) 參加一場音樂會。(B) 寄送電子郵件。
(C) 造訪一個網站。 (D) 記錄一些資訊。

獨白最後一句說道：「please email me at beatrice@eastsideshelter.com, so I can send you an application.」，請對方以電子郵件寄送，因此答案為 (B)。Please 開頭的命令句型，大多是用來表示說話者的要求事項。

Questions 83–85 refer to the following talk.

W [83] Now that we've had a chance to view the yacht club banquet hall, I'd like to take everyone out onto the docks, where we will see a variety of boats owned by the club. [84] Our entire collection of vessels was donated to us by retired engineer Samuel Welsh last year. Mr. Welsh designed these boats himself and has graciously given them to us to host private events on. If you'd like to learn more about Mr. Welsh's work, [85] I highly recommend picking up a pamphlet near the exit, which details his amazing career.

女 [83] 現在，既然我們已經參觀過遊艇俱樂部的宴會廳，我想帶大家出去到碼頭上，在那裡，我們可以看到俱樂部擁有的各種不同船隻。[84] 我們的所有船隻都是退休工程師山繆・韋爾許去年捐贈的。韋爾許先生親自設計這些船隻，並好心送給了我們，以便遊艇俱樂部在上面舉辦私人活動。如果你們想更了解韋爾許先生的作品，[85] 我極力推薦各位拿一份出口附近的小冊子，上面詳述他令人嘖嘖稱奇的生涯。

• **chance** 機會 **banquet** 宴會 **dock** 碼頭 **a variety of** 各種各樣的 **entire** 整個的、全部的 **collection** 一批、一群 **vessel** 船、艦 **donate** 捐獻、捐贈 **retired** 退休的 **graciously** 親切地、仁慈地 **host** 主辦 **private** 私人的 **recommend** 推薦、建議 **exit** 出口 **detail** 詳述、詳細說明 **amazing** 令人吃驚的、驚奇的

83

Where is the talk taking place?
(A) At a factory
(B) At a yacht club*
(C) At a museum
(D) At a travel agency

這段談話發生在哪裡？
(A) 在一間工廠。
(B) 在一個遊艇俱樂部。
(C) 在一間博物館。
(D) 在一家旅行社。

獨白前半部，通常可以聽到說話者所在地點的關鍵線索。獨白第一句說道：「Now that we've had a chance to view the yacht club banquet hall, I'd like to take everyone out onto the docks, where we will see a variety of boats owned by the club.」，由此確認答案為 (B)。

• **take place** 發生、舉行 **factory** 工廠 **travel agency** 旅行社

84

According to the speaker, what did Samuel Welsh do last year?
(A) He made a donation.*
(B) He hired an assistant.
(C) He went on a sailing trip.
(D) He opened a gallery.

根據說話者所述，山繆・韋爾許去年做了何事？
(A) 他捐贈了東西。
(B) 他請了一個助理。
(C) 他去航海旅行。
(D) 他開了一家藝廊。

聆聽時，請特別留意關鍵字 last year（去年）。獨白前段提到，全部的遊艇皆由山繆・韋爾許捐贈（Our entire collection of vessels was donated to us by retired engineer Samuel Welsh last year.），因此答案為 (A)。

答案改寫 donate → make a donation

• **make a donation** 捐獻 **hire** 僱用 **assistant** 助理

85

What does the speaker recommend that the listeners do?
(A) Read a booklet*
(B) Book a cruise
(C) Go for a swim
(D) Buy a membership

說話者推薦聽者何事？
(A) 閱讀一份小冊子。
(B) 預訂搭船遊覽。
(C) 去游泳。
(D) 購買會員資格。

獨白最後一句說道：「I highly recommend picking up a pamphlet near the exit, which details his amazing career.」，由此確認答案為 (A)。題目的關鍵字 recommend 或 suggest，通常會直接出現在獨白內容當中。

答案改寫 pick up → read
pamphlet → booklet

• **book** 預訂、預約 **cruise** 乘船遊覽

Questions 86–88 refer to the following advertisement.

M [86] Do you have a difficult time keeping your office space and lobby clean? Is it hard to find trustworthy and affordable after-hours cleaners? Corporate Custodian Services is a reliable and cheap way to keep your office clean and tidy. [87] We understand your busy schedule, which is why all our cleaners start work after you've gone home for the day. Imagine arriving at work to a freshly cleaned office every morning. With Corporate Custodian Services, you never have to worry about taking out the trash or sweeping again. Don't believe us? [88] Visit www.corporatecustodianservices.com/feedback to read postings from our satisfied customers.

男 [86] 要保持辦公室與大廳整潔，是否有困難？要找到值得信任而且負擔得起，在下班之後來的清潔人員是不是很難？「企業守衛服務」是維持您辦公室潔淨整齊、既可靠又價廉的方式。[87] 我們了解您的時程表很忙碌，所以，我們所有清潔人員會在你們下班回家後才開始工作。想像一下，每天早上到一個剛打掃乾淨的辦公室來上班。有了「企業守衛服務」，您再也不必煩惱要把垃圾拿出去倒或者打掃了。難以置信嗎？[88] 請至 www.corporatecustodianservices.com/feedback，看看我們的客戶滿意意見回饋。

- **trustworthy** 值得信任的 **affordable** 負擔得起的 **after-hours** 下班後、下課後 **corporate** 公司的、團體的 **custodian** 管理人、監護人、守衛 **reliable** 可靠的、確實的 **tidy** 整潔的、整齊的 **trash** 垃圾 **sweep** 清掃、打掃 **satisfied** 感到滿意的

86

Who is the advertisement intended for?
這則廣告的對象是誰？

(A) Hotel staff　(A) 飯店員工。
(B) Security guards　(B) 保全人員。
(C) Office managers*　(C) 辦公室經理。
(D) Bus drivers　(D) 公車司機。

當題目詢問廣告的對象時，可以從一兩個關鍵字中找出線索。獨白第一句說道：「Do you have a difficult time keeping your office space and lobby clean?」，由此推測為與辦公場所（office）和清掃（clean）相關的服務，因此 (C) 為最適當的答案。

- **security** 安全、保安

87

What does the speaker say is special about the service?
說話者說，這項服務的特別之處為何？

(A) It is offered every day.　(A) 每天提供。
(B) It can be booked online.　(B) 可以上網預約。
(C) It can be cancelled easily.　(C) 可以輕鬆取消。
(D) It is done in the evenings.*　(D) 在傍晚履行。

聆聽獨白時，請掌握重點在於「特點」或是「強項」。獨白中段說道：「We understand your busy schedule, which is why all our cleaners start work after you've gone home for the day.」，表示下班後才會開始作業，因此答案為 (D)

答案改寫 after you've gone home for the day → in the evenings

88

What are listeners encouraged to do?
(A) Ask for an estimate
(B) Call a telephone number
(C) Read some client reviews*
(D) Purchase new equipment

廣告鼓勵聽眾做何事？
(A) 要求估價。
(B) 打某個電話號碼。
(C) 看一些客戶意見。
(D) 購買新設備。

本題詢問說話者的提議或是要求事項，請務必仔細聆聽獨白後半段內容。獨白最後一句說道：「Visit www.corporatecustodianservices.com/feedback to read postings from our satisfied customers.」，表示可上網看客戶滿意意見，由此得知答案為 (C)。

答案改寫 posting → review
customer → client

• **estimate** 估價、估計

Questions 89–91 refer to the following announcement.

W Before we wrap up, [89] I'd like to let you all know about a change in our company's travel expense reimbursement. Currently, employees are only allowed to ask for expense reimbursement when they travel out of town. However, [90] many of our employees who travel within the city for client meetings have expressed displeasure about the lack of reimbursement for their expenses. In the interest of keeping things fair, the company will begin expense reimbursement for all employees regardless of where they are traveling. [91] Please distribute the new expense handbooks by the end of this month and be prepared to explain them to your respective departments.

女 在我們結束之前，[89] 我想要讓你們所有人知道，我們公司交通旅資報銷的改變。目前，只有到外地的費用，員工才准予報銷。不過，[90] 有許多員工在城裡往來，是為了與客戶會面，他們對於費用無法報銷表示不滿。為了公平起見，公司會開始讓所有員工報銷費用，不論目的地是哪裡。[91] 請在本月底前將新的費用手冊發下去，並準備好向你們各自的部門解釋更動內容。

• **wrap up** 完成、結束 **expense** 費用 **reimbursement** 報銷、退還 **currently** 現在 **allow** 准許、允許 **displeasure** 不滿、生氣 **lack** 缺少、沒有 **in the interest of** 為某事物的緣故 **fair** 公平的 **regardless of** 不管、不顧 **distribute** 分發、分配 **prepare** 使……準備好 **respective** 各自的、分別的 **department** 部門

89

What is the main topic of the announcement?
(A) Booking flights online
(B) Paying for travel costs*
(C) Training new employees
(D) Canceling out of town travel

這項聲明的主題為何？
(A) 上網預訂航班。
(B) 支付旅費。
(C) 訓練新員工。
(D) 取消外地旅行。

獨白前半部說道：「I'd like to let you know about a change in our company's travel expense reimbursement.」，可以推測主題與交通旅資報銷有關，由此得知答案為 (B)。

答案改寫 expense → cost

• **book** 預訂、預約 **flight** （飛機的）班次 **cost** 費用 **cancel** 取消

90

According to the speaker, why is the change being made?
(A) To respond to employee complaints*
(B) To improve employee work efficiency
(C) To make up for a lack of pay raises
(D) To follow a government regulation

根據說話者所述，公司為何做出這項改變？
(A) 為了回應員工的抱怨。
(B) 為了改善員工的工作效率。
(C) 為了補償未能加薪。
(D) 為了遵守政府規定。

本題的解題關鍵為「變更的原因」。獨白中段提到「為了緩解出差職員的不滿（many of our employees who travel within the city for client meetings have expressed displeasure about the lack of reimbursement for their expenses）」，因此 (A) 為最適當的答案。

答案改寫 displeasure → complaint

• **respond to** 對……做出反應、對……做出回答　**complaint** 抱怨、抗議　**improve** 改善、增進　**efficiency** 效率、效能　**make up for** 彌補　**pay raise** 加薪　**follow** 聽從、採用　**regulation** 規定、規章

91

What are the listeners reminded to do?
(A) Update employee contracts
(B) Pass out new information booklets*
(C) Gather reports from employees
(D) Speak with department managers

說話者提醒聽眾做何事？
(A) 更新員工合約。
(B) 分發新的資訊小冊子。
(C) 收集員工的報告。
(D) 和部門經理談話。

雖然題目中用到了 listeners 這個字，但本題要問的其實是說話者的建議和要求事項。在獨白後半段，通常可以找到相關線索。獨白最後一句說道：「Please distribute the new expense handbooks by the end of this month and be prepared to explain them to your respective departments.」，由此確認答案為 (B)。答案通常就在 Please 開頭的句子當中。

答案改寫 distribute → pass out
handbook → booklet

• **remind** 提醒　**contract** 合約、契約　**pass ~ out** 分發、分配　**gather** 收集

Questions 92–94 refer to the following announcement and schedule.

Tour Date	Departure Time
Monday, May 2	10:30 A.M. / 2:30 P.M.
Tuesday, May 3	11:30 A.M. / 3:30 P.M.
Wednesday, May 4	10:30 A.M. / 2:30 P.M.
[93] Thursday, May 5	11:30 A.M. / 3:30 P.M.

旅行日期	出發時間
5月2日，星期一	10:30 A.M. / 2:30 P.M.
5月3日，星期二	11:30 A.M. / 3:30 P.M.
5月4日，星期三	10:30 A.M. / 2:30 P.M.
[93] 5月5日，星期四	11:30 A.M. / 3:30 P.M.

M Attention, all passengers of Barbados Boat Tours. [92] Due to an approaching tropical storm, all tours have been canceled for today, Tuesday, and Wednesday. We expect the storm to have passed by the following day, and [93] our business will resume Thursday morning. We would like to offer all ticket holders complete refunds. Simply [94] visit the front desk to have your ticket refunded or changed for another day. Thank you very much for your understanding, and we apologize for the inconvenience.

男 巴巴多輪船旅遊的乘客請注意，[92] 由於熱帶暴風雨即將來襲，今天、星期二和星期三的所有行程皆已取消。暴風雨預計在第二天會經過，而 [93] 我們會在星期四早上恢復營業。我們會提供所有購票的旅客全額退費。您只需要 [94] 到櫃台退票或更改日期。非常感謝您的諒解，造成您的不便，敬請見諒。

• **departure** 出發、離開 **passenger** 乘客、旅客 **due to** 因為、由於 **approaching** 將近、靠近 **tropical** 熱帶的 **storm** 暴風雨 **cancel** 取消 **expect** 預期、預計……可能發生（或來到） **resume** 恢復、重新開始 **offer** 給予、提供 **holder** 持有者 **complete** 全部的、完整的 **refund** 退還、退款 **apologize** 道歉 **inconvenience** 不便、麻煩

92

What has caused a cancelation?

(A) An absent ship captain

(B) Missing passengers

(C) Poor weather conditions*

(D) A damaged boat

什麼原因導致取消？

(A) 輪船船長缺席。

(B) 乘客失蹤。

(C) 天候不佳。

(D) 輪船受損。

聆聽獨白時，請先掌握解題的關鍵在於「取消的原因」。獨白前段說道：「Due to an approaching tropical storm, all tours have been canceled」，可知取消原因與熱帶暴風雨（tropical storm）有關由此確認答案為 (C)。請務必熟記 due to 可用來表示原因。

答案改寫 tropical storm → poor weather

• **cause** 導致、使發生 **cancelation** 取消 **absent** 缺席的 **condition** 情況

93

Look at the graphic. What time will the next boat tour take place?

(A) 10:30 A.M.

(B) 11:30 A.M.*

(C) 2:30 P.M.

(D) 3:30 P.M.

請見圖表。下一班輪船旅程是何時？

(A) 上午10點30分。

(B) 上午11點30分。

(C) 下午2點30分。

(D) 下午3點30分。

聆聽時，請特別留意「下一次導覽」。獨白中段提到，預計於星期四上午再度行駛（our business will resume Thursday morning），因此答案為 (B)。

• **take place** 發生、舉行

94

What does the speaker ask listeners to do?
(A) Wait for a few hours
(B) Try a new restaurant
(C) Stay away from the dock
(D) Visit the front desk*

說話者要求聽眾何事?
(A) 等幾個小時。
(B) 試試新餐廳。
(C) 遠離碼頭。
(D) 前往櫃台。

獨白後段,通常可以聽到說話者的建議事項。當中說道:「可以全額退費,請到櫃台直接退款或是改成其他日期(visit the front desk to have your ticket refunded or changed for another day)」,因此答案為 (D)。

• **stay away** (與某人/某事物)保持距離、不打擾 **dock** 碼頭

Questions 95–97 refer to the following excerpt from a meeting and survey results.

Question: What improvement would you most like to see?

Answer Option	Number of Votes
A. A reduction in fares	105
[96] B. Shorter wait times	87
C. More payment options	55
D. Online reservations	32

W Let's start the meeting by looking at the results of [95] a survey we recently conducted with the passengers onboard our express buses. First, let's look at the answers to the first question, "What improvement would you most like to see?" As you can see, most survey participants said they would prefer fare decreases. However, we are really not in a position to offer discounts at this point. But, [96] we could hire a few more drivers in order to implement the second-most popular answer. [97] If you know of any websites we could post advertisements on, please let me know at the end of the meeting.

問題:您最想看到什麼樣的改進?

答案選項	票數
A. 票價調降	105
[96]B. 候車時間縮短	87
C. 更多付款方式選擇	55
D. 線上訂票	32

女 [95] 最近針對搭乘我們快捷巴士的旅客,我們做了調查,會議一開始,先來看看結果。首先,來看第一題的答案:「您最想看到什麼樣的改進?」正如你們所見,大部分參與調查的人說,他們比較希望票價調降。不過,我們目前真的無法提供折扣。不過,[96] 我們倒是可以僱用更多司機,實現票數第二高的答案。[97] 如果你們知道哪些網站可以張貼廣告,請在會議之後告訴我。

• **improvement** 改進、改善的事物 **option** 選擇、選擇權 **vote** 票、選票 **reduction** 減少、縮小 **fare** (交通工具的)票價 **reservation** 預訂 **result** 結果 **survey** 調查、民意調查 **conduct** 實施、處理 **passenger** 乘客、旅客 **onboard** 搭乘交通工具 **participant** 參與者 **decrease** 減少 **position** 形勢、立場 **implement** 實踐 **post** 貼出

95

Where most likely does the speaker work?
(A) At a travel agency
(B) At an airline
(C) At a marketing agency
(D) At a bus company*

說話者最可能在哪裡工作?
(A) 旅行社。
(B) 航空公司。
(C) 行銷公司。
(D) 巴士公司。

獨白第一句說道:「a survey we recently conducted with the passengers onboard our express buses」,提到了快捷巴士(express buses)。由此得知答案為 (D)。

96

Look at the graphic. What survey result does the speaker want to implement?

(A) A reduction in fares
(B) Shorter wait times*
(C) More payment options
(D) Online reservations

請見圖表。說話者打算執行哪一項調查結果？

(A) 票價調降。
(B) 候車時間縮短。
(C) 更多付款方式選擇。
(D) 線上訂票。

獨白後段提到，為了解決得票數「第二高」的問題，打算僱用更多的司機（we could hire a few more drivers in order to implement the second-most popular answer），繼 105 票之後，第二高的票數為 87 票，因此答案為 (B)。

97

What does the speaker ask the listeners to do?

(A) Recommend employment websites*
(B) Interview potential candidates
(C) Review customer information
(D) Upgrade a company system

說話者要求聽者何事？

(A) 推薦求職網站。
(B) 面試可能的人選。
(C) 檢閱顧客資料。
(D) 升級公司的系統。

獨白最後一句說道：「If you know of any websites we could post advertisements on, please let me know at the end of the meeting.」，請聽眾告知可張貼的廣告的網站，由此確認答案為 (A)。

答案改寫 let me know → recommend

• **recommend** 推薦 **potential** 可能的、潛在的 **candidate** 求職應徵者、人選

Questions 98–100 refer to the following telephone message and coupon.

> **Ristorante Catoria**
> **50% Off Group Discount Coupon**
> [99] ** Groups may not exceed 15 patrons.*
> ** Valid until December 31st.*

> 卡多麗亞餐廳
> 團體 5 折優惠券
> [99]* 團體不得超過 15 人。
> *12 月 31 日前有效。

W Hello, this is Jan. [98] I'm calling about the holiday party we're organizing for our department this year. Now . . . we've already decided the party will be on December 22nd, and it's great to hear that [99] the number of guests has been jumped to twenty. However, it looks like we won't be able to use the coupon for Ristorante Catoria. We might want to make a reservation at a cheaper buffet. Also, it would be nice to find a place that has a party room available that can accommodate all our guests. [100] Can you do some research and prepare a list of potential places?

女 哈囉，我是珍。[98] 我打電話來問關於正在籌備的今年度部門佳期派對。那麼，我們已經決定派對在 12 月 22 日舉行，而且很高興聽到 [99] 賓客人數已激增到 20 人。不過，這樣看來我們無法使用卡多麗亞餐廳的優惠券了。我們可能要預訂較低廉的自助餐。還有，如果能找到一個備有派對室的場地，足以容納我們所有賓客的話就更好了。[100] 你可以調查一下，準備一份可能行得通的場地清單嗎？

• **exceed** 超過 **patron** 顧客、常客 **valid** 有效的 **organize** 組織、籌畫 **jump** 激增
make a reservation 預定 **accommodate** 容納 **potential** 可能的

98

Why is the event being held?
(A) To launch a product line
(B) To host an award ceremony
(C) To announce a promotion
(D) To celebrate a holiday*

為何舉行這個活動？
(A) 為了推出一條產品線。
(B) 為了主辦頒獎典禮。
(C) 為了宣布升遷。
(D) 為了慶祝假期。

獨白前段說道：「the holiday party we're organizing for our department this year」，提到了「佳期派對（holiday party）」，因此 (D) 為最適當的答案。holiday 在此可用來表示聖誕節、感恩節或是復活節。

• **award ceremony** 頒獎典禮　**promotion** 升遷

99

Look at the graphic. Why is the speaker unable to use the coupon for the event?
(A) Not enough guests will attend the event.
(B) The event will occur after the expiration date.
(C) The event will take place on a weekend.
(D) Too many people will be present at the event.*

請見圖表。說話者為何無法將優惠券用於本次活動？
(A) 參加活動的賓客人數不足。
(B) 活動會在有效日期之後舉行。
(C) 活動在週末舉行。
(D) 活動的出席人數太多。

請特別注意聆聽「使用優惠券的資格」。獨白中段提到，當顧客數量超過二十人時（the number of guests has been jumped to twenty），可能無法使用優惠券。優惠券上也寫著：「限十五人以下團體（Groups may not exceed 15 patrons）」，綜合前述所有資訊，答案應為 (D)。

• **expiration** 期滿、終結　**take place** 舉行、發生

100

What does the speaker ask the listener to do?
(A) Make a list of other restaurants*
(B) Call Ristorante Catoria
(C) Change the date of an event
(D) Ask management for more funds

說話者要求聽者做什麼？
(A) 列一張其他餐廳的清單。
(B) 打電話給卡多麗亞餐廳。
(C) 更改活動日期。
(D) 向管理階層要求更多資金。

獨白最後一句說道：「Can you do some research and prepare a list of potential places?」，要求查詢可以容納的場地，並整理成目錄繳交，因此答案為 (A)。在獨白後段，通常可以聽到說話者的要求或提議的內容。

答案改寫 prepare → make
potential → other
place → restaurant

• **fund** 資金、專款

ACTUAL TEST 5

中譯+解析

PART 1 17

1

(A) He's checking in at an airport.
(B) He's pulling a suitcase.*
(C) He's packing for a trip.
(D) He's opening his luggage.

(A) 他正在機場辦理登機手續。
(B) 他拉著行李箱。
(C) 他正在為旅行打包。
(D) 他打開他的行李箱。

本題為單人照片，(B) 針對動作重點描述：「拉著（pulling）行李箱（suitcase）」，為正確答案。(D) 也提到了照片中的東西（luggage），但內容並不符合照片情境，因此為錯誤選項。

- **check in**（在機場）辦理登機手續　**pull** 拖、拉　**pack** 收拾行李　**luggage** 行李箱、行李

2

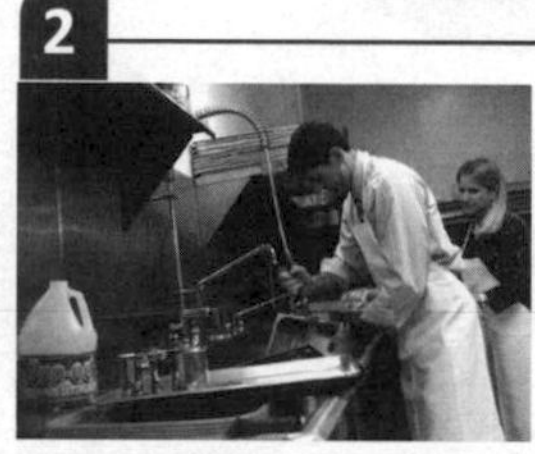

(A) They are making a dish.
(B) They are cleaning the kitchen.
(C) They are spraying water on the floor.
(D) They are wearing aprons.*

(A) 他們正在做菜。
(B) 他們正在清理廚房。
(C) 他們把水灑在地上。
(D) 他們穿著圍裙。

題目為雙人照片時，請注意兩人是否有共通點或差異之處。(D) 描述圍著圍裙的狀態（wearing aprons），為正確答案。在此補充，wear 用來表示穿戴的狀態；put on 則是表示動作，請特別留意。put on 的動作難以藉由照片表現，因此大多為錯誤選項。(A) 中 dish 的意思並非是碗盤，而是指菜餚；(B) 應改成 cleaning the dishes；(C) 應改成 spraying water on the trays，才會是正確答案。

- **dish** 一盤菜、菜餚　**spray** 噴灑　**apron** 圍裙

3

(A) A man is taking an order.
(B) A woman is trying on a pair of sunglasses.
(C) Some merchandise is arranged on the table.*
(D) Some posters are being put up.

(A) 男子正在接受點單。
(B) 女子正在試戴太陽眼鏡。
(C) 桌上排列著一些商品。
(D) 掛起一些海報。

在聆聽各選項的同時，請一邊對照照片，並刪除不適當的選項。 (A) 的內容無法從照片判斷；(B) try on（試用或試穿）與照片中女子的動作無關，並非答案；(D) 沒有看到正在貼 poster 的人，因此也非答案；(C) 在照片中央，可以看到桌子上面擺著太陽眼鏡，以單字 merchandise（商品）描述此狀態，為正確答案。

- **take an order** 接受點菜　**merchandise** 商品、貨物　**be arranged on** 布置、排列

4

(A) People are seated on the stairs.* (A) 人們坐在台階上。
(B) People are stepping down from the platform. (B) 人們走下月台。
(C) People are walking beneath the tree. (C) 人們走在樹下。
(D) People are moving across the showroom. (D) 人們穿越展示廳。

(A) 描述人們坐在（are seated）樓梯上（stairs）的情景，為正確答案。seated、sitting 或 standing 皆有可能為正確答案，但答案為 seated 的頻率最高。

- **stair** 樓梯、梯級　**step down** 走下　**beneath** 在……之下

5

(A) A lecture is being given outdoors. (A) 課程正在戶外進行。
(B) Some people are watching a demonstration.* (B) 有些人正在觀看操作示範。
(C) A man is filling a container with some tools. (C) 男子正利用一些工具把容器裝滿。
(D) Some bottles are being cleared off the table. (D) 正把桌上的一些瓶子清掉。

(A) 選項後半部為 outdoors（在戶外），並不正確；(C) 和 (D) 僅使用了照片中出現的人和物品（a man 和 some bottles）作為主詞，意圖使人混淆，後半部內容皆不正確；因此答案為 (B)。在此補充，clear off the table 意思為「收拾餐桌」，請把它當成慣用語熟記。

- **outdoors** 在戶外　**demonstration** 示範操作、實地示範　**fill** 裝滿、填滿　**tool** 工具　**bottle** 瓶子

6

(A) A man is backing a vehicle into a garage. (A) 男子正倒車進入車庫。
(B) Workers are unloading some supplies. (B) 工人正卸下一些日用品。
(C) A vehicle is being examined.* (C) 正在檢查一輛車。
(D) Equipment is being loaded onto a cart. (D) 正把設備裝上手推車。

(C) 針對「檢查車輛」進行描述，為最適當的答案；其他的選項僅使用了出現在照片中的人和物（vehicle, garage, workers, equipment），說明並不符合照片情境，皆非正解。在此補充，若針對兩個人的動作或狀態進行描寫（The men are wearing uniforms, . . . using some tools, . . . working on a vehicle, . . . examining a vehicle 等），皆有可能為正確答案。

- **vehicle** 車輛、運載工具　**garage** 車庫、修車廠　**unload** 卸貨　**supply** 日用品、生活必需品　**examine** 檢查　**equipment** 設備、用具　**load** 裝、裝載

PART 2

18

7

How long does it take to reach Paris?
(A) Seven hours in the air.*
(B) To go sightseeing.
(C) The plane landed.

到巴黎要多久？
(A) 搭飛機七個小時。
(B) 去觀光遊覽。
(C) 飛機降落了。

以疑問詞 How 開頭的問句，後方的單字即為解題關鍵。本題詢問「要花多久的時間」，(A) 回答出具體的時間，為正確答案。在此補充，當題目改成以 Why 詢問去巴黎的「目的」時，答案才可以選 (B)。

• **sightseeing** 觀光、遊覽　**land** 降落、登陸

8

Where should I hang these pictures in the office?
(A) We need to take a picture.
(B) I prefer them in the break room.*
(C) No, he's not in the office.

我該把這些畫掛在辦公室的哪裡？
(A) 我們需要拍張照片。
(B) 我比較喜歡掛在休息室。
(C) 不，他不在辦公室。

本題為以 Where 開頭的問句，詢問可以掛畫的「地方」，(B) 回覆了具體的地點（break room 休息室），為正確答案。在此補充，(C) 以疑問詞開頭的問句，不可用 Yes 或 No 來回答，因此聽到的當下即可刪除此選項。

• **hang** 懸掛、吊起　**take a picture** 拍照　**prefer** 寧可、更喜歡

9

Who will be in charge of organizing the company picnic?
(A) The office manager.*
(B) In the park.
(C) One day this weekend.

誰要負責籌劃公司的野餐？
(A) 辦公室經理。
(B) 在公園。
(C) 這個週末的其中一天。

本題為以 Who 開頭的問句，詢問「負責人」是誰，(A) 回答了職稱，為適當的答案。題目為 Who 開頭的問句時，除了職稱之外，答案還可能為人名、部門名稱、公司名稱；(B) 適用於以 Where 詢問野餐地點的問句；當題目改以 When 詢問野餐時間時，答案才會是 (C)。

10

Would you like a hamburger or a hotdog?
(A) In the frozen foods section.
(B) I'm not all that hungry now.*
(C) A package of twelve.

你要漢堡還是熱狗？
(A) 在冷凍食品區。
(B) 我現在還不是很餓。
(C) 一袋十二個。

碰到題目為選擇疑問句時，可以預想到答案應為問句中所包含的兩種選項（①漢堡、②熱狗）之一，或是兩者皆非，以其他內容回覆。(B) 回答「我現在不餓（表示兩個都不想吃）」，沒有選擇任一選項，為正確答案。

• **all that** 非常

11

Don't we need a key to get into the building?
(A) Her response is key.
(B) She's already in her room.
(C) Yes, but I forgot mine.*

我們進入大樓不需要用鑰匙嗎？
(A) 她的回應是關鍵。
(B) 她已經在她的房間了。
(C) 要，但我忘記帶我的了。

碰到否定問句時，只要先將 not 拿掉，視為一般問句，就能更加容易掌握住題目的重點。本句重點為詢問「是否需要鑰匙」，(C) 表示同意（Yes），接著說自己忘了帶鑰匙，和問句構成完整對話，為正確答案。(B) 僅使用 He 或 She 作為主詞，並未明確指出對象是誰，這類選項通常不會是答案。

- **key** 鑰匙、關鍵　**response** 回覆、反應

12

Where did you save the insurance files?
(A) I saved you some time.
(B) She called the insurance company.
(C) On your desktop.*

你把保險檔案存在哪裡了？
(A) 我替你省了些時間。
(B) 她打電話給保險公司。
(C) 在你的桌面。

疑問詞 Where 用來詢問「地點」，本題詢問保險資料「儲存在哪裡」，(C) 回覆了確切的地點（your desktop 你的電腦桌面），為正確答案。(A) 重複使用了題目中的單字，這類選項多半不會是答案。

- **save** 儲存、節省　**insurance** 保險　**desktop** （電腦）桌面

13

Why have we ordered the team T-shirts from a different website?
(A) By next Monday.
(B) From the online store.
(C) The colors were better.*

我們為什麼從不同的網站訂購團隊 T 恤？
(A) 下星期一之前。
(B) 從線上商店。
(C) 顏色比較好看。

疑問詞 Why 用來詢問「原因」，本題詢問「為何要在其他地方訂購」，(C) 省略了連接詞 Because，回答「（因為）顏色更好看」，為最適當的回覆。這類題型的答案，選項中通常會省略 Because。

- **order** 訂購

14

How did you get such a good interest rate?
(A) I visited the bank in person.*
(B) It's 2% each month.
(C) No, I'm not buying a house.

你是怎麼獲得這麼好的利率的？
(A) 我親自去銀行拜訪。
(B) 每個月 2%。
(C) 不，我沒有要買房子。

本題為以疑問詞 How 開頭的問句，詢問獲得較佳利率的「方法」，(A) 回答「親自到銀行一趟」，與問句構成完整對話，為最適當的答案。(C) 以疑問詞開頭的問句，不能以 Yes 或 No 開頭的答句回覆，因此可以直接刪除此選項；(B) 故意使用了與「利率」相關的數據 2%，引人混淆，作答時請特別小心。

- **interest rate** 利率　**in person** 親自、親身

15

How is he going to finish his project on time?
(A) Has he fixed the projector?
(B) He needs to stay late.*
(C) It's six o'clock now.

他要如何及時完成他的計畫？
(A) 他修好投影機了嗎？
(B) 他必須留到很晚。
(C) 現在是六點。

本題為以疑問詞 How 開頭的問句，詢問「如何準時完成」，(B) 回覆「方法」為「加班完成」，與問句構成完整對話，為正確答案。(A) 使用了 projector，與題目中的單字（project）發音相似，這類選項多半不會是答案。

- **fix** 修理 **stay** 留下

16

Does this school offer any classes on finance?
(A) Have a look at one of the brochures.*
(B) The financial analysis was wrong.
(C) Classes start in September.

這間學校有提供任何金融課程嗎？
(A) 看一下那些冊子。
(B) 那份財務分析是錯的。
(C) 九月開學。

本題詢問「是否有特定的課程」，(A) 提到有可以作為參考的資料（brochures），為最適當的回覆。其他選項，故意使用了與題目當中字根相同（finance, financial）或是相同的單字（classes），皆不是答案。

- **offer** 給予、提供 **finance** 金融、財政 **have a look at** 看一看 **financial** 金融的、財務的 **analysis** 分析

17

When did they build a fountain in front of the hospital?
(A) A large amount of water.
(B) Three or four months ago.*
(C) The architects.

他們何時在醫院前面蓋了噴水池？
(A) 大量的水。
(B) 三、四個月前。
(C) 幾位建築師。

疑問詞 When，用來詢問「時間」，本題詢問「何時蓋了」噴水池。(B) 回答了確切的時間資訊，為正確答案。

- **fountain** 噴泉、噴水池 **in front of** 在某人／某物前面 **amount** 總數、數量 **architect** 建築師

18

Is Mr. Sampson going to arrive today or tomorrow?
(A) It's okay. He doesn't want to.
(B) A flight schedule.
(C) He arrived late last night.*

山普森先生今天還是明天抵達？
(A) 沒關係，他不想要。
(B) 航班時刻表。
(C) 他昨天很晚才抵達。

題目為選擇疑問句，因此答案應為問句中所包含的兩種選項（①今天、②明天）之一，或是以其他的內容回覆。(C) 未選擇兩選項其中一個，而是回答「他已經抵達」，為正確答案。

- **flight** （飛機的）班次

19

You can change the meeting time, can't you?
(A) Remember to change your clothes.
(B) The directors are already on their way.*
(C) He was not present.

你可以更改會議的時間，不是嗎？
(A) 記得換衣服。
(B) 幾位總監已經在路上了。
(C) 他不在場。

自己已知的事實（更改會議時間），再次向對方確認或是取得同意時，會使用附加問句。(B) 回答「總監已經在路上」，表示無法更改，與問句構成完整對話，為正確答案。

• **be on one's way** 在去……的途中　**present** 出席的、在場的

20

Do you need help cleaning up this mess?
(A) The cleaners are new.
(B) The containers were empty.
(C) I can just use the vacuum.*

你需要人幫忙清理這團混亂嗎？
(A) 清潔人員是新來的。
(B) 容器是空的。
(C) 我只用吸塵器就可以了。

本題重點在詢問「是否要幫你打掃」，(C) 的回答中，省略了「沒關係（No）」，說道「我可以使用吸塵器」，為最適當的答覆；(A) 故意使用了字根相同的單字（cleaning, cleaner），並非答案。

• **mess** 髒亂的東西、混亂　**empty** 空的　**vacuum** 真空吸塵器

21

Why don't you ask the sales department for some advice?
(A) I hadn't thought of that.*
(B) The figures from last month.
(C) I won't leave my job.

你何不要求業務部提一些建議？
(A) 我沒有想到。
(B) 上個月的數據。
(C) 我不會辭職。

「Why don't you . . . ?」用來詢問對方的想法「何不……？」，針對題目句的建議，(A) 表示同意，說道：「我沒想到」，與題目句構成完整對話，為正確答案。

• **department** 部門　**advice** 建議、忠告　**figure** 數字　**leave** 辭去（工作等）

22

How do I get downtown from here?
(A) It's expensive to live there.
(B) Yes, she works at a shop.
(C) There's a subway map on the wall.*

我如何從這裡去市中心？
(A) 住那裡，花費很高。
(B) 是的，她在一間商店工作。
(C) 牆上有張地鐵的路線圖。

本題為以 How 開頭的問句，詢問到市區的「方法」，(C) 並未親切地直接予以回覆，而是以事不關己的口吻要對方自己看「地鐵路線圖」，為最適當的答案。在此補充，本題為以疑問詞開頭的問句，不可用 Yes 或 No 開頭的答句回覆，聽到的當下即可刪除 (B) 選項。

• **downtown** 市中心、鬧區　**expensive** 昂貴的

23

Which client signed our contract?
(A) At the conference.
(B) The increase in rent.
(C) The one from New York City.*

哪一位客戶簽了合約？
(A) 在研討會上。
(B) 租金上漲。
(C) 來自紐約市的那位。

本題使用疑問形容詞 Which，詢問「哪一位客戶簽約了？」，(C) 的回覆為「來自紐約的那位」，為正確答案。選項將題目中的名詞 client 換成指示代名詞 one，當選項中出現 one 時，多半為正確答案。

• contract 合約 increase 增加 rent 租金

24

Aren't you retiring at the end of the year?
(A) No, early next year.*
(B) A retirement party.
(C) Three full-time employees.

你不是年底要退休嗎？
(A) 不是，是明年初。
(B) 退休派對。
(C) 三名全職員工。

本題為否定問句，詢問「是否會在年底退休」，(A) 以 Yes 或 No 的答句回覆，並在後方補充說明，為最適當的回答；(B) 僅使用了 retirement，與題目句中的單字（retire）字根相同，並非答案。

• retire (v.) 退休 retirement (n.) 退休

25

Didn't you say the renovation would be done by today?
(A) I did, but we ran into a problem.*
(B) The workers are over there.
(C) No, we didn't order the appliances.

你不是說，整修工作今天會完成？
(A) 我是說過，但我們遇到了問題。
(B) 工人在那裡。
(C) 不，我們沒有訂家電產品。

雖然本題為否定問句，但請先將 not 拿掉，視為一般問句「你是說今天之內會完成嗎？」，就能掌握題目重點。(A) 回覆「發生了一些問題」，表示可能沒辦法，為最適當的回應，與問句構成完整對話。

• renovation 翻新、翻新工作 run into 陷入（困境、債務等） appliance 家電產品

26

Have they announced the nominees for the award yet?
(A) The picks are as expected.*
(B) To honor the company president.
(C) The first award ceremony.

他們宣布獎項的入圍者了嗎？
(A) 挑出的人選一如預期。
(B) 為了向公司總裁致敬。
(C) 第一屆頒獎典禮。

本題為一般問句，詢問「已經公布候選人了嗎？」，(A) 針對重點回覆「如同預料」，為最適當的答案。其他兩個選項的內容雖然也與 award 有關，卻不符合文意，解題時，請務必格外留意。

• nominee 被提名者 award 獎、獎品 pick 挑選、選擇 expect 預期、認為 honor 給……以榮譽 ceremony 典禮

27

Do you want me to pick you up at the station?
(A) It's almost 5 o'clock.
(B) A discounted ticket.
(C) I'm not coming today.*

你要我去車站接你嗎？
(A) 快要五點了。
(B) 打折的車票。
(C) 我今天不去。

本題詢問「需要我去車站接你嗎？」，(C) 回覆「我今天不去」，表示不需要接送，為最適當的答案。在 PART 2 中，經常出現這類題型，答案不再是一般預料之內的回覆，因此難度提升不少。

- discounted 折扣的

28

I think this seat is already taken.
(A) Sit down, please.
(B) Where do the chairs go?
(C) Sorry. I'll move in a second.*

我想這個位子有人坐了。
(A) 請坐。
(B) 椅子到哪裡去了？
(C) 對不起，我馬上換位子。

本題的情境為在活動會場之類的場所，向對方表示他坐到了自己的位置。(C) 針對「這個座位有人了」，給予最適當的回覆，為正確答案。其他選項故意使用了 sit 和 chair 兩個與 seat 有關的單字，文意並不相符，答題時請特別留意。

- be taken 就座　in a second 馬上

29

Have you seen my bag around here?
(A) We need to buy shopping bags.
(B) Yes, it's a textbook.
(C) Didn't you leave it in your car?*

你有沒有在這附近看到我的包？
(A) 我們需要買購物袋。
(B) 是的，是一本教科書。
(C) 你不是留在你的車上了嗎？

本題重點在詢問「是否看到包包」，(C) 將 bag 替換成代名詞 it 回覆：「不是放在車上嗎」，為最適當的答案。在 PART 2 中，以反問方式回覆的選項，極有可能為正確答案。在此補充，一般問句通常會以 Yes 或 No 答句回覆，(B) 故意利用這點使人混淆，內容上並不符合文意。

- textbook 教科書、課本　leave 遺留

30

We need to find a faster way to get to the airport.
(A) Some delicious pastries.
(B) He'll be traveling all week.
(C) Sorry, but this is the best route.*

我們必須找到較快能抵達機場的路線。
(A) 一些美味的糕點。
(B) 他整個星期都在旅行。
(C) 抱歉，但這是最便捷的路線了。

本題的重點為「提議找一條更快抵達的路」。(C) 回覆：「這條是最佳路線」，為最適當的答覆。在此補充，(A) 使用了 pastries，僅與題目句中單字 faster way 的發音相似；(B) 故意使用與 airport 有關的單字 travel，來讓人混淆，因此 (A) 和 (B) 皆非答案。

- route 路線、路途

31

What time does the conference start tomorrow?
(A) Oh, I thought you weren't going.*
(B) A very good business deal.
(C) In the convention center.

明天的研討會何時開始？
(A) 噢，我以為你不會去。
(B) 一次很成功的交易。
(C) 在會議中心。

本題詢問「會議幾點開始」，(A) 並未回覆確切的時間，而是以驚訝的口吻說道「我以為你沒有要參加」，和題目句構成完整對話，為最適當的選項。本題的答案亦屬於預料之外的回答，為難度較高的題目。

- **deal** 協議、交易

PART 3 19

Questions 32–34 refer to the following conversation.

W Hello. This is Margaret Brown calling. [32] I recently mailed the paperwork to update my car insurance policy, but I never received a call from your company.

M Sorry to hear that, Ms. Brown. I'll have a look at our records. Can you remember the date you sent the forms?

W Ummm . . . Actually, I don't know the date, but I think it was a month ago.

M Well, [33] unfortunately, it seems that your forms never arrived here. However, [34] I can give you our website and you can complete the paperwork online. It's a brand new system, but it's much easier than sending in mail.

女 哈囉，我是瑪格麗特・布朗。[32] 我最近寄了文件，要更新我的汽車保險，但一直沒接到你們公司的電話。

男 很抱歉發生這種事，布朗女士。我會查看一下我們的紀錄。您還記得寄出表格的日期嗎？

女 嗯，其實，我不知道日期，但我想是一個月前的事。

男 呃，[33] 很遺憾，您的文件似乎沒有寄到這裡。不過，[34] 我可以給您我們的網站，您可以上網完成文書處理。這是全新的系統，但是比寄送郵件要簡單多了。

• **recently** 最近、新近 **mail** 郵寄 **paperwork** 資料、文書工作 **insurance** 保險 **policy** 保單 **unfortunately** 遺憾地、可惜 **arrive** （郵件、物品等）被送來 **complete** 完成 **brand new** 全新的

32

What is the woman trying to do?
(A) Lease a new car
(B) Purchase an appliance
(C) Renew an insurance policy*
(D) Apply for a credit card

女子試圖做何事？
(A) 租一輛新車。
(B) 購買一件家電。
(C) 更新保單。
(D) 申請信用卡。

對話第一段，女子提到更新汽車保險的相關內容：「I recently mailed the paperwork to update my car insurance policy」，由此確認答案為 (C)。

答案改寫 update → renew

• **lease** 租借、租用 **purchase** 購買 **appliance** 家用電器、裝置 **renew** 更新、更換 **apply for** 申請

33

What has caused a problem?
(A) An application was rejected.
(B) Some mail did not arrive.*
(C) A payment method failed.
(D) Some information was wrong.

何事導致問題？
(A) 申請被拒。
(B) 有個郵件沒有送到。
(C) 付款方式無效。
(D) 有些資料是錯的。

當題目詢問 problem 時，在聆聽對話前，請先標示出各選項中的重點單字（rejected, arrive, payment, information）。對話最後一段，男子提及尚未收到申請書（unfortunately, it seems that your forms never arrived here），由此得知答案為 (B)。

答案改寫 form → mail

• **cause** 造成、導致 **application** 申請 **reject** 拒絕 **payment** 支付、付款 **method** 方法、方式

34

What does the man offer to do?
(A) Complete a profile
(B) Send a new contract
(C) Cancel a policy
(D) Provide a web address*

男子提議為何？
(A) 讓檔案完整。
(B) 寄送新的合約。
(C) 取消一分保單。
(D) 提供網址。

請格外仔細聆聽男子所說的話。對話最後一段，男子說道：「I can give you our website」，表示願意提供網址，因此答案為 (D)。

答案改寫 give → provide
website → web address

• contract 合約　cancel 取消　provide 提供

Questions 35–37 refer to the following conversation.

W Hi, Ben. Did you have a nice holiday?	女 嗨，班，你的假期過得好嗎？
M It was excellent. [35] I spent a lot of time in the brand new stores uptown.	男 棒極了。[35] 我在城北新開的店逛了好久。
W Oh, really? Did you buy anything nice?	女 噢，真的嗎？你有買什麼好東西嗎？
M A few things, but a lot of the best stuff was sold out. [36] There were so many sales at the time.	男 有一些，但很多最好的東西都賣光了。[36] 那段時間有好多拍賣。
W That's too bad. At least you got to browse the new stores.	女 太糟了。至少你逛了那些新開的店。
M Yeah, but I'm glad to be back. What did I miss while I was away?	男 是啊，不過我很高興回來。我不在時，錯過什麼了嗎？
W Well, [37] we just got a new client who wants us to install new telephone systems for her company. I'd better fill you in on the details of her company.	女 嗯，[37] 我們剛接到一個新客戶，她要我們幫她的公司安裝新的電話系統。我最好告訴你她公司的詳細資料。

• stuff 物品、東西　browse 隨意觀看（商品等）　miss 錯過　be away 不在、外出　client 客戶
install 安裝、設置　details 詳細資料

35

What did the man do on his holiday?
(A) He threw parties.
(B) He visited a farm.
(C) He camped.
(D) He shopped.*

男子休假時做了何事？
(A) 他舉行派對。
(B) 他去農場。
(C) 他去露營。
(D) 他去逛街。

本題的重點為「男子的近況」。對話第一段，女子問男子假期過得如何，男子回覆「在商圈內逛了很久（I spent a lot of time in the brand new stores uptown.）」，因此 (D) 為最適當的答案。

• throw 舉行（宴會等）　farm 農場、農家

36

What does the man say about the places he visited?
(A) They served free food.
(B) They had many discounts.*
(C) They were hard to find.
(D) They were next to a park.

關於造訪的地方，男子說了什麼？
(A) 它們供應免費食物。
(B) 它們有許多折扣。
(C) 它們很難找。
(D) 它們在公園旁邊。

請特別仔細聆聽男子所說的話。對話中間說道：「There were so many sales at the time.」，表示當時有許多優惠活動，因此答案為 (B)。

答案改寫 sale → discount

37

According to the woman, what did the company do recently?
(A) They gained a client.*
(B) They held a sale.
(C) They took a vacation.
(D) They changed management.

根據女子所述，公司最近做了何事？
(A) 他們得到一個客戶。
(B) 他們舉行了拍賣。
(C) 他們去度假。
(D) 他們改變了管理方式。

聆聽時，請特別留意「公司的近況」。對話最後一段，女子說道：「we just got a new client who wants us to install new telephone systems for her company」，由此確認答案為 (A)。

答案改寫 get → gain

• **gain** 得到、獲得 **management** 管理、經營手段

Questions 38–40 refer to the following conversation.

M Jane, I just got an e-mail from our clients in Taiwan. [38] They're visiting at the end of the month to inspect some of their factories. They asked if they could stop by our office since we're in the area.

W Oh, that's great. [39] This could be a good time to pitch them the new European advertisement campaign we've been working on. Do you think the designers can finish the samples in time?

M I believe so. However, [40] I should let them know right away that their deadline is moving up by a few weeks. They thought there was more time to finish up.

男 珍，我剛收到台灣客戶的電子郵件。[38] 他們月底要來拜訪，視察一些他們的工廠。他們問到，因為我們也在這一區，是否可以順道來我們公司一趟。

女 喔，那太好了。[39] 這會是一個好時機，向他們大力推銷我們持續在進行的歐洲新廣告。你覺得設計師能及時完成樣本嗎？

男 我相信可以。不過 [40] 我得立刻知會他們，截稿日期提前了幾個星期。他們原本以為還有很多時間可以完成工作。

• **inspect** 檢查、進行視察 **pitch** 極力推銷 **work on** 從事 **right away** 立刻、馬上 **deadline** 截止期限

38

What are the speakers mainly discussing?
(A) An office inspection
(B) A factory opening
(C) A client visit*
(D) An advertising launch

說話者的討論主題為何？
(A) 視察辦公室。
(B) 工廠開幕。
(C) 客戶來訪。
(D) 展開廣告活動。

在對話前半部，通常可以聽到對話主旨的相關線索。對話第一段，男子表示自己收到了顧客的郵件，並補充說明對方預計在這個月底前來拜訪（They're visiting at the end of the month to inspect some of their factories.），因此 (C) 為最適當的答案。

• **inspection** 檢查、視察　**launch** 發起

39

What does the woman suggest doing?
(A) Presenting a new campaign*
(B) Signing a contract
(C) Organizing an inspection
(D) Having some equipment repaired

女子提議做何事？
(A) 展現新的活動。
(B) 簽署合約。
(C) 安排視察。
(D) 修理一些設備。

請仔細聆聽女子所說的話。女子說道：「This could be a good time to pitch them the new European advertisement campaign we've been working on.」，表示這是展現歐洲廣告案的絕佳機會，因此 (A) 為最適當的答案。

答案改寫 pitch → present

• **organize** 安排、籌畫　**equipment** 設備　**repair** 修理

40

What does the man say he will do?
(A) Pass on some information*
(B) E-mail some samples
(C) Update a website
(D) Prepare an itinerary

男子說他將做何事？
(A) 傳達一些訊息。
(B) 以電子郵件傳送一些樣本。
(C) 更新網站。
(D) 規劃行程。

關於對話結束之後要做的事情，可以在對話後半部聽到相關線索。對話最後一段，男子表示現在得告訴對方截止日將提前幾週一事（I should let them know right away that their deadline is moving up by a few weeks.），因此答案為 (A)。

• **pass on** 傳遞　**prepare** 籌備　**itinerary** 旅程、行程、路線

Questions 41–43 refer to the following conversation with three speakers.

M1 Thank you both for coming in today. I think we've covered just about everything regarding the International Cultural Expo.

W Yes, [41] I'm really looking forward to taking over. I think James has done a great job organizing the event so far.

M1 James, can you think of anything else Trisha might need to know?

M2 Ah, yes. One more thing; [42] the vendors will need receipts for their participation fees for tax purposes. It's okay to send them by e-mail.

W I understand. So James, I heard you're going to be working on the east coast.

M2 Yes, [43] I'm moving to Florida, so I'll be working at the Orlando Expo Center. I'm excited about the change.

男 1 謝謝你們倆今天來。我想我們已經處理了所有關於國際文化展的事情。

女 是的，[41] 我真的很期待接手。我認為，詹姆士把到目前為止的活動籌劃工作做得非常好。

男 1 詹姆士，你還能想到任何崔夏可能需要知道的事情嗎？

男 2 啊，有的，還有一件事，[42] 攤販會需要報名費的收據以便報稅。可以用電子郵件寄給他們。

女 了解了。那麼，詹姆士，我聽說你要去東岸工作。

男 2 是的，[43] 我要搬到佛羅里達，所以我會到奧蘭多展覽中心工作。我對這個改變感到很興奮。

- **cover** 處理、涉及 **regarding** 關於 **take over** 接手 **vendor** 小販、攤主 **receipt** 收據 **participation** 參加、參與 **fee** 費用 **tax** 稅、稅金 **coast** 海岸、沿海地區 **change** 改變

41

What are the speakers discussing?

(A) Moving a business
(B) Negotiating a contract
(C) Traveling for business
(D) Changing event management*

說話者在討論何事？

(A) 搬遷一家公司。
(B) 協商一份合約。
(C) 出差。
(D) 更換活動管理人。

對話第一段，男子提到已經處理好展覽相關的所有事務，女子表示非常期待「交接」(I'm really looking forward to taking over.)，因此 (D) 為最適當的答案。

- **negotiate** 談判、協商 **management** 管理、管理部門

42

What does James advise the woman to do?

(A) Schedule another meeting
(B) Make a list of vendors
(C) Hire an assistant
(D) Send receipts by e-mail*

詹姆士建議女子做何事？

(A) 安排另一次會議。
(B) 列出攤販的名單。
(C) 僱用一位助理。
(D) 用電子郵件寄送收據。

請掌握本題的重點為「給女子的建議」。在聆聽對話時，請特別留意關鍵人名 James。對話中段，另一名男子向詹姆士詢問是否還有其他的話要向女子交代，James 回覆說要提供參加者收據，同時建議以郵件寄送 (It's okay to send them by e-mail.)，因此答案為 (D)。

- **hire** 僱用 **assistant** 助理

43

What does James say he is excited about?
(A) Moving to a new city*
(B) Managing more projects
(C) Earning more money
(D) Learning a new sport

詹姆士說，他對何事感到很興奮？
(A) 搬到新的城市。
(B) 管理更多專案。
(C) 賺更多錢。
(D) 學習新的運動。

聆聽時，請特別留意關鍵字 excited（感到興奮的）。對話最後一段，男子說道：「I'm excited about the change.」，表示自己很期待新的變化，並說道：「會搬到佛羅里達」，因此 (A) 為最適當的答案。

• **manage** 管理、處理事務 **earn** 賺得、贏得

Questions 44–46 refer to the following conversation.

W	Hi, Mitchell. This is Reba from the sales department. [44] I'm not sure if you know this, but the air conditioning in conference room B isn't working. Do you think you'd be able to fix it at some point today?	女	嗨，米契爾，我是業務部的芮芭。[44] 我不確定你是否知道這件事，但會議室 B 的空調故障了。你覺得你今天能找個時間來修嗎？
M	Oh, sorry to hear that. This happened with conference room A, too, but it was easy to fix. I can come take a look at it.	男	喔，很遺憾聽到這事。會議室 A 也是如此，不過很容易就能修好。我可以過來看看。
W	Right now? [45] Well, umm, I'm actually meeting a client here in a few minutes. We don't really need the air conditioning today.	女	現在嗎？[45] 嗯，其實我馬上要和一位客戶在這裡開會。我們今天不是非開空調不可。
M	Yes, [46] it is oddly cool for this time of the year. How about I come up and take a look at it when you're finished?	男	是啊，[46] 一年的這個時候，天氣異常涼爽。等你們結束後，我再過來看看，如何？
W	Sure. That would be great. Thanks!	女	當然，那太好了，謝謝！

• **work**（機器等）運轉 **fix** 修理 **take a look at** 看一看 **oddly** 怪異地、奇特地

44

Why is the woman calling the man?
(A) To provide directions to an office
(B) To request a room change
(C) To report a malfunction in equipment*
(D) To inquire about a missing file

女子為何打電話給男子？
(A) 提供到某個辦公室的方向指引。
(B) 要求換房間。
(C) 報告設備故障。
(D) 詢問一個遺失的檔案。

對話第一段，女子說道：「I'm not sure if you know this, but the air conditioning in conference room B isn't working.」，表示冷氣無法使用，因此答案為 (C)。

答案改寫 air conditioning → equipment
not working → malfunction

• **malfunction** 故障 **equipment** 設備、裝備

45

What does the woman mean when she says, "Right now"?
當女子說「現在嗎」，意指什麼？

(A) She feels sorry about bothering the man.
(B) She will cancel a meeting.
(C) She wants to delay a repair.*
(D) She is pleased with a plan.

(A) 她對於打擾男子感到抱歉。
(B) 她將取消會議。
(C) 她想要延後修理的時間。
(D) 她對計畫很滿意。

題目句後方提到，預計待會要進行會議（Well, umm, I'm actually meeting a client here in a few minutes.），因此 (C) 為最適當的答案。

- **bother** 煩擾、打擾　**delay** 使延期、延誤　**repair** 修理、修補

46

What does the man say is unusual?
男子說何事很不尋常？

(A) The weather is unseasonably cold.*
(B) The office is experiencing many problems.
(C) The meetings have been cancelled.
(D) The woman's schedule is busy.

(A) 天氣不合時宜地冷。
(B) 辦公室經歷許多問題。
(C) 會議取消了。
(D) 女子的時程表很忙碌。

請仔細聆聽男子所說的話。對話後半段，男子說道：「it is oddly cool for this time of the year.」，表示今年異常涼爽，因此答案為 (A)。

答案改寫 oddly cool → unseasonably cold

- **unseasonably** 不合時宜地、不合時令地

Questions 47–49 refer to the following conversation.

M Alice, I just called the box office and [47] apparently the last showing of the musical downtown has been canceled. Do you have any other ideas about where we can take our clients when they visit from Italy?	**男** 艾莉絲，我剛打電話給劇院售票處，[47] 看起來，市區音樂劇的最後一場表演取消了。對於客戶從義大利來訪時，可以帶他們去哪裡，妳有沒有其他點子？
W That's too bad about the musical. Hmm. Well, [48] I've heard the Harbor Ship Tour is really good. It takes place on a yacht and there's music and fine dining. Also, the night view of the coast must be spectacular.	**女** 關於音樂劇的事，真是太糟了。嗯，這樣的話，[48] 我聽說港口輪船之旅實在很棒。旅程是搭乘遊艇，遊艇上還有音樂和精緻的晚餐。此外，海岸的夜景一定很令人讚嘆。
M Oh, right! I've heard about those yachts. They serve fresh seafood, which is supposed to be really incredible. [49] Can you look up the number and call to find out how much tickets are?	**男** 喔，對！我聽說過那些遊艇。遊艇上供應新鮮的海鮮，應該真的非常美味。[49] 妳可以查一下電話號碼，然後打去問票價多少嗎？

- **apparently** 顯然、看起來　**cancel** 取消　**take place** 舉行、發生　**dining** 進餐　**spectacular** 壯觀的、令人驚嘆的　**seafood** 海鮮　**be supposed to** 應該、應當　**incredible** 極好的、難以置信的

47

What problem does the man mention? 男子提及什麼問題？

(A) A telephone number was lost. (A) 有串電話號碼遺失了。

(B) A ticket price was wrong. (B) 有個票價是錯的。

(C) A trip was postponed. (C) 有個旅程延後了。

(D) An event was canceled.* (D) 有個活動取消了。

聆聽時，請特別留意男子所說的話。對話第一段說道：「apparently the last showing of the musical downtown has been canceled」，由此確認答案為 (D)。

答案改寫 musical → event

- lose 遺失、丟失 postpone 延後、延期

48

What does the woman suggest? 女子有何建議？

(A) A visit to a museum (A) 參觀博物館。

(B) An evening on a boat* (B) 船上之夜。

(C) A vacation to Italy (C) 去義大利度假。

(D) A night at the opera (D) 歌劇之夜。

對話中，女子說道：「I've heard the Harbor Ship Tour is really good.」，聽說郵輪旅遊很不錯，因此 (B) 為最適當的答案。

49

What does the man ask the woman to do? 男子要求女子做何事？

(A) Inquire about a price* (A) 詢問價錢。

(B) Contact some clients (B) 聯絡一些客戶。

(C) Refund some tickets (C) 退還一些票券的錢。

(D) Make a reservation (D) 預訂。

對話最後一段，男子請對方打電話詢問票價多少錢（Can you look up the number and call to find out how much tickets are?），因此答案為 (A)。

- inquire 詢問、調查 refund 退還、退款 make a reservation 預訂

Questions 50–52 refer to the following conversation with three speakers.

M1 Please come in, Micha and Jennifer. Have a look around the rooms. As I mentioned, [50] the previous couple has recently vacated the space.	男 1 請進，米卡和珍妮佛，四處看看房間吧。正如我提過的，[50] 之前的那對夫妻最近搬離這個地方。
W I really like the size of the rooms and the windows, but there are a few things we're worried about.	女 我真的很喜歡這些房間的大小和窗戶，但我們有一些疑慮。
M2 Yes, [51] we're wondering about the cost of heating the place in the winter. Does this building have good insulation?	男 2 對，[51] 我們想知道這裡冬天的暖氣費用。這棟大樓的保暖效果好嗎？
M1 Yes, it was all replaced last year. Also, a new energy efficient furnace was installed, so it's actually quite cheap to heat the apartments.	男 1 是的，去年全都更換過了。除此之外，還安裝了新的節能暖爐，所以要讓公寓暖和起來，其實費用相當低廉。
M2 Wow, in that case, I'm surprised the previous couple decided to leave.	男 2 哇，那樣的話，我很驚訝，之前那對夫妻竟然決定搬走。
M1 Well, [52] they just retired and decided to move to a smaller place.	男 1 嗯，[52] 他們剛退休，決定搬到小一點的房子。

- **have a look around** 四處看看　**previous** 先前的　**vacate** 空出、搬出　**insulation** 隔離、絕緣　**replace** 更換、代替　**energy efficient** 節省能源　**furnace** 火爐、暖氣爐　**install** 安裝　**quite** 相當、非常　**retire** 退休

50

Who most likely are Micha and Jennifer?　米卡和珍妮佛最可能是誰？

(A) City inspectors　(A) 市府檢查員。
(B) Potential tenants*　(B) 可能的房客。
(C) Interior designers　(C) 室內設計師。
(D) Hotel receptionists　(D) 飯店接待人員。

對話第一段，男子叫了對方的名字後，請對方看一下房間，並提到之前住在這裡的人已經搬走了（the previous couple has already vacated the space），因此 (B) 為最適當的答案。

- **inspector** 檢查員、視察員　**potential** 可能的　**tenant** 房客、承租人

51

What are Micha and Jennifer concerned about?　米卡和珍妮佛擔心什麼？

(A) The location of the windows　(A) 窗戶的位置。
(B) The size of the rooms　(B) 房間的大小。
(C) The cost of heating*　(C) 暖氣的費用。
(D) The noise of the city　(D) 城市的噪音。

聆聽對話時，請特別留意「擔憂的事情」。對話中間，珍妮佛提到有幾件事情令他們擔憂，之後米卡說道：「we're wondering about the cost of heating the place in the winter」，想要知道冬天的暖氣費用，因此答案為 (C)。

- **noise** 噪音

52

What is mentioned about the previous couple?
(A) They are no longer working.*
(B) They own the whole building.
(C) They prefer warmer climates.
(D) They have not moved yet.

關於之前那對夫妻，文中提到什麼？
(A) 他們已經不再工作了。
(B) 他們擁有整棟大樓。
(C) 他們比較喜歡溫暖的氣候。
(D) 他們還沒搬走。

聆聽時，請特別留意關鍵字 the previous couple（之前那對夫妻）。對話後半段提到，（這裡的條件極佳）很驚訝之前那對夫妻會選擇搬走，對方則回覆是因為退休才決定搬家（they just retired and decided to move to a smaller place.），因此答案為 (A)。

答案改寫 retire → no longer work

• **no longer** 不再 **own** 擁有 **whole** 整個的、全體的 **prefer** 更喜歡 **climate** 氣候

Questions 53–55 refer to the following conversation.

M	Tammy, 53 is everything all set for our trade show next Monday?	男	譚美，53 我們下星期一的貿易展都準備好了嗎？
W	Yes, I've had all our products and banners packed into the van, and I've just finished printing out the new flyers.	女	是的，我已經把所有的產品和廣告布條都裝上卡車了，而且剛剛把新的傳單都印好了。
M	Did you ask some staff if they could come to the convention center on Monday to help us set up?	男	妳有沒有問過一些員工，他們能否星期一到會議中心來幫我們布置攤位？
W	Oh . . . 54 thanks for the reminder. I'm sure I can find some people who are willing to help out. But how will they get into the convention center? I only have one pass for myself.	女	噢……54 謝謝你提醒。我確定我可以找到一些願意來幫忙的人。但他們要如何進入會議中心？我只有一張自己的通行證。
M	55 We have bought extra passes just in case we wanted to invite our clients to the show. I'll go get a few for you now.	男	55 我們多買了一些通行證，以防萬一要邀請客戶進去會場。我現在去拿幾張給妳。

• **trade** 貿易 **banner** 橫幅廣告、旗幟 **flyer** （廣告）傳單 **reminder** 提醒（的話）、提示 **pass** 通行證、入場證 **extra** 額外的 **just in case** 以防萬一 **invite** 邀請

53

What will happen on Monday?
(A) A vehicle will be repaired.
(B) A training session will continue.
(C) A trade show will start.*
(D) A new product will launch.

星期一將發生何事？
(A) 有車要修理。
(B) 訓練課程會繼續。
(C) 貿易展將開始。
(D) 新產品要發表。

聆聽時，請特別留意關鍵時間點 Monday（星期一）。對話第一段，男子說道：「is everything all set for our trade show next Monday?」，因此答案為 (C)。

• **vehicle** 車輛、運載工具 **repair** 修理、修補

54

What did the woman forget to do? 女子忘記做何事？

(A) Find some volunteers* (A) 找一些義工。

(B) Contact a convention center (B) 聯絡會議中心。

(C) Set up some tables (C) 擺放桌子。

(D) Update an itinerary (D) 更新行程。

對話第二段，女子感謝對方的提醒，認為應該可以找到願意幫忙的人（I'm sure I can find some people who are willing to help out.），因此 (A) 為最適當的答案。

答案改寫 people who are willing to help out → volunteers

- **itinerary** 行程

55

What does the man say is available? 男子說有什麼可用？

(A) Extra passes into a show* (A) 額外的展場通行證。

(B) A company banner (B) 公司的廣告布條。

(C) Free refreshments (C) 免費茶點。

(D) Product samples (D) 產品的樣本。

請仔細聆聽男子所說的話。對話末段，男子說道：「We have bought extra passes in case we want to invite our clients to the show.」，表示可能會邀請客戶參觀博覽會，故已多準備一些通行證，現在就去拿，因此答案為 (A)。

- **refreshment** 茶點、飲料

Questions 56–58 refer to the following conversation.

W	This is Carole Strauss calling from Rubin Marketing. [56] I understand you left a message about contracting us to advertise your new store.	女	我是盧賓行銷公司的卡蘿・史特勞斯。[56] 我聽說您留了訊息，要和我們簽約宣傳新店面。
M	Yes, [56] thanks for getting back to me. [57] I opened a new hair salon, and I'd love to start advertising in local newspapers and maybe on a billboard downtown.	男	是的，[56] 謝謝妳回我電話。[57] 我新開了一家美髮沙龍，想要開始在地方報紙上，還有，也許在鬧區的廣告看板上刊登廣告。
W	Okay, great. I'd love to set up a meeting with you to get a sense about what you'd like to include in your ads and what price range you're comfortable with. [58] Are you available to come to our office tomorrow afternoon?	女	好的，很好。我想要安排和您開個會，了解您的廣告內容要包含什麼，還有哪個價位區間是您覺得可以輕鬆負擔的。[58] 您明天下午有空來我們辦公室嗎？
M	That would work great for me. I'll actually be in that area picking up supplies, so [58] I can stop by around 2:00 P.M.	男	那個時間很好。事實上，我正好要去那一帶補貨，所以 [58] 我可以大約下午兩點順路過去。

- **contract** 訂立合約 **billboard** （路旁的）大型廣告牌、告示牌 **set up** 設立 **sense** 了解、領會 **include** 包括、包含 **range** 範圍 **comfortable** 自在的 **supply** 補給品 **stop by** 順路拜訪

56

Why does the woman call the man?
(A) To ask for a payment
(B) To return a phone call*
(C) To cancel a meeting
(D) To make a hair appointment

女子為何打電話給男子？
(A) 要求付款。
(B) 回撥電話。
(C) 取消會議。
(D) 預約美髮。

對話第一段，女子說道：「I understand you left a message about contracting us to advertise your new store.」，表示有聽到對方的留言，因此 (B) 為最適當的答案。如果不小心漏聽了這段話，可以由後方男子所說的話：「thanks for getting back to me」，推測出正確答案。

- **payment** 支付、付款　**cancel** 取消　**make an appointment** 預約

57

What did the man recently do?
(A) Hired a graphic designer
(B) Cancelled a subscription
(C) Started a new business*
(D) Purchased a billboard

男子最近做了何事？
(A) 僱用一位平面設計師。
(B) 取消訂閱。
(C) 展開新事業。
(D) 購買廣告看板。

本題的重點為「男子的近況」。對話第一段，男子說道：「I opened a new hair salon」，表示自己開了一間新的髮廊，因此答案為 (C)。

答案改寫 hair salon → business

- **subscription** 訂閱　**purchase** 購買

58

What does the man say he will do tomorrow?
(A) Attend a lunch
(B) Get a haircut
(C) Sell some products
(D) Go to an office*

男子說，他明天有何事？
(A) 出席午餐餐會。
(B) 剪頭髮。
(C) 販售一些產品。
(D) 去一家公司。

聆聽時，請特別留意關鍵時間點 tomorrow（明天）。對話後半部，女子詢問對方明天下午是否可以來辦公室一趟（Are you available to come to our office tomorrow afternoon?），男子正面回覆說明天剛好要到附近辦事，會在下午兩點左右過去，因此答案為 (D)。

- **attend** 參加、出席　**haircut** 剪髮

Questions 59–61 refer to the following conversation.

W David, [59] how did your editorial meeting go this morning? You were planning to ask the senior editor to hire some more contract workers, correct?

M Yes. The senior editor agreed to allocate funds for three additional employees during our busy periods.

W Wow, isn't that too many? [60] Last year, we were only allowed to hire one.

M Well, actually, they've only agreed to hire part-time freelancers. Still, having a few extra writers will really help us tackle the workload. [61] The human resources department is planning to place some online ads next week, so we should have help soon.

女 大衛，[59] 今天早上的編輯會議結果如何？你打算要求資深編輯多找一些約聘人員，對嗎？

男 是的。資深編輯同意撥專款，在我們工作高峰期多請三個人。

女 哇，不會太多嗎？[60] 去年只准我們請一個人。

男 嗯，事實上，他們只同意僱用兼職的自由工作者。儘管如此，多幾個撰稿人員的確有助於我們應付工作量。[61] 人力資源部計劃下星期上網刊登廣告，所以我們應該很快就有幫手了。

• **allocate** 分配、分派 **fund** 資金、專款、基金 **additional** 額外的 **period** 時期、期間 **allow** 允許、准許 **tackle** 著手對付或處理 **workload** 工作量 **human resources** 人力資源

59

What department do the speakers work in?
(A) Finance
(B) Editorial*
(C) Advertising
(D) Design

說話者在哪個部門工作？
(A) 財務。
(B) 編輯。
(C) 廣告。
(D) 設計。

對話開頭說道：「how did your editorial meeting go this morning?」，提到了編輯會議，因此答案為 (B)。

60

Why does the woman say, "Wow, isn't that too many"?
(A) To express surprise about a decision*
(B) To suggest another option
(C) To correct a management mistake
(D) To request a change of policy

女子為何說「哇，不會太多嗎」？
(A) 為了對某個決定表達驚訝。
(B) 為了建議另一個選項。
(C) 為了改正一個管理上的錯誤。
(D) 為了要求政策上的改變。

題目句後方緊接著說道：「去年只僱用了一名新人（Last year, we were only allowed to hire one.）」，因此 (A) 為最適當的答案。

• **surprise** 驚奇、詫異 **option** 選擇、可選擇的東西 **correct** 改正、糾正

61

According to the man, what does the human resources department plan to do?
(A) Prepare a new manual
(B) Host a job fair at an office
(C) Hold a training workshop
(D) Run an advertisement online*

根據男子所述，人力資源部計畫做什麼？
(A) 準備新的手冊。
(B) 在辦公室主辦就業博覽會。
(C) 舉行訓練工作坊。
(D) 上網刊登廣告。

聆聽時，請特別留意關鍵字 the human resources department（人力資源部）。對話最後一段，男子說道：「The human resources department is planning to place some online ads next week.」，表示預定刊登網路廣告，因此答案為 (D)。

答案改寫 place → run

• manual 手冊、簡介 job fair 就業博覽會 run 刊登

Questions 62–64 refer to the following conversation and chart.

Package	Rate per Day
All Star Coverage	$35.00
64 Premium Coverage	$20.00
Advanced Coverage	$15.00
Basic Coverage	$10.00

套裝產品	每日費用
全星級保險	$35.00
64 優質保險	$20.00
高階保險	$15.00
基本保險	$10.00

W Hi, my name is Jane Simpson, and I'm calling from Redman Enterprises. One of our sales teams will be traveling abroad, and 62 I'd like to purchase travel insurance for them. I've heard that you have excellent rates.

M Yes, that's correct. We have a few main packages. Our All Star Coverage package is our most comprehensive. 63 Will your team be trying any extreme sports during their free time?

W No, I don't believe they'll have time for that during the trip.

M 64 Then, I recommend our Premium package. It includes health and accident insurance, but is much cheaper without the sports coverage.

W Okay. That sounds great. Can you e-mail me the paperwork I'll need to fill out?

女 嗨，我是瑞德曼企業的珍・辛普森。我們有個業務團隊要出國，62 我想幫他們保旅遊險。我聽說你們的費用非常超值。

男 是的，沒錯。我們有幾個主要的套裝產品。我們的全星級套裝保險是保障最全面的產品。63 您的團隊在空閒時間，會嘗試任何極限運動嗎？

女 不，我相信他們的旅程中沒有時間從事那個。

男 64 那麼我推薦我們的優質保險。它包含健康與意外險，但不包含運動保險項目，因此要便宜得多。

女 好，聽起來很棒。你可以把我需要填寫的文件，用電子郵件寄給我嗎？

• rate 費用、比率 coverage 保險項目（或範圍） advanced 高階的 insurance 保險 comprehensive 全面的、綜合的 extreme 極端的 recommend 推薦 paperwork 資料、文書工作 fill out 填寫（表格、申請書等）

62

What is the purpose of the phone call?
(A) To inquire about a discount
(B) To apply for a service*
(C) To make a reservation
(D) To schedule a meeting

這通電話的目的為何？
(A) 要求折扣。
(B) 申請某項服務。
(C) 預訂。
(D) 安排會議的時間。

在對話前半部，通常會出現打電話的目的。女子說道：「I'd like to purchase travel insurance for them.」，由此推測答案為 (B)。

答案改寫 purchase → apply for
travel insurance → service

• apply for 申請、請求 make a reservation 預訂

63

Why does the man ask if the employees will do any sports?

男子為何問，員工是否將會從事任何運動？

(A) To offer some free gifts
(B) To decide on the most suitable package*
(C) To recommend a travel destination
(D) To request some medical information

(A) 以提供免費禮物。
(B) 以選定最適合的套裝產品。
(C) 以推薦旅遊的目的地。
(D) 以詢問一些醫學資訊。

聆聽時，請特別留意「是否進行運動活動」。對話中間，男子針對套裝產品進行説明，並問道：「Will your team be trying any extreme sports during their free time?」，因此 (B) 為最適當的答案。

- **suitable** 適當的、合宜的 **destination** 目的地、終點 **medical** 醫學的、醫療的

64

Look at the graphic. How much will each employee likely pay per day?

請見圖表。每位員工每天可能要付多少錢？

(A) $35 (B) $20*
(C) $15 (D) $10

(A) $35。 (B) $20。
(C) $15。 (D) $10。

價格取決於所選擇的商品。男子建議選擇 Premium 套裝產品（Then, I recommend our Premium package.），女子表示同意，因此答案為 (B)。

Questions 65–67 refer to the following conversation and flight schedule.

Flight Number 班機編號	Departure City 出發地	On Time/Delayed 準時／誤點	Est. Arrival Time 預計抵達時間
BT091	Toronto 多倫多	Landed 已降落	11:00
AC550	Alberta 亞伯達	On Time 準時	11:35
HG330	Vancouver 溫哥華	On Time 準時	12:00
DT302	65 Montreal 65蒙特婁	Delayed 誤點	13:20

W I just had a look at the airport website. 65 It seems that Michael Park won't arrive on time.

M Yeah, I heard his city is experiencing a big storm, so 65 many flights had their takeoff times delayed.

W That's too bad. I suppose we should go pick him up later then.

M Actually, 66 traffic is supposed to be terrible today with all the construction around the airport. How about we just leave now?

W You're right. We don't want to be late. 67 If we get there too early, we can browse the gift shops.

女 我剛看了機場的網站。65 看來麥可・帕克無法準時抵達。

男 是啊，我聽說他的城市正遭受強勁暴風雨侵襲，因此 65 許多班機的起飛時間都延後了。

女 真是太糟了。那我猜想我們要晚一點去接他了。

男 事實上，66 機場周邊在施工，今天的交通狀況應該很糟。我們現在就出發怎麼樣？

女 你說得對。我們可不想遲到。67 如果太早到，我們可以逛逛禮品店。

- **flight** （飛機的）班次 **departure** 出發、離開 **delay** 使延期、延誤 **Est. (= estimated)** 估計 **arrival** 到達 **storm** 暴風雨 **takeoff** 起飛 **be supposed to** 認為應該 **terrible** 極差的 **construction** 建造、工程 **leave** 動身、出發 **browse** 瀏覽、隨意觀看

65

Look at the graphic. Which city is Michael Park traveling from?
請見圖表。麥可・帕克從哪個城市過來？

(A) Toronto　(A) 多倫多。
(B) Alberta　(B) 亞伯達。
(C) Vancouver　(C) 溫哥華。
(D) Montreal*　(D) 蒙特婁。

對話第一段，女子說道：「It seems that Michael Park won't arrive on time.」，提到麥可・帕克可能無法準時抵達，隨後男子回覆：「因為颶風導致很多班機延遲起飛（many flights had their takeoff times delayed）」。根據對話內容，對照表格後可以得知，延誤的為從蒙特婁起飛的班機，因此答案為 (D)。

66

According to the man, why should the speakers leave now?
根據男子所述，說話者為何應該現在動身？

(A) Traffic may cause delays.*　(A) 交通可能導致延誤。
(B) The airport is far away.　(B) 機場很遠。
(C) They need to take the bus.　(C) 他們必須搭公車。
(D) A flight was early.　(D) 有班機提早抵達。

請仔細聆聽男子所說的話。對話後半段提到，由於機場周邊的道路正在施工，可能導致交通壅塞（traffic is supposed to be terrible today with the construction around the airport），建議現在就出發。因此答案為 (A)。

- **cause** 造成、導致　**delay** 使延期、延誤

67

What does the woman suggest doing while they wait?
女子建議在等待時做什麼？

(A) Getting some food　(A) 吃點東西。
(B) Looking in some stores*　(B) 看看商店。
(C) Seeing a film　(C) 看場電影。
(D) Having coffee　(D) 喝咖啡。

對話最後一段，女子說道：「If we get there too early, we can browse the gift shops.」，建議若太早抵達（如果要花時間等待），可以去禮品店逛逛。因此 (B) 為最適當的答案。

答案改寫 browse → look in
gift shop → store

- **have** 吃、喝

Questions 68–70 refer to the following conversation and chart.

Plan	Contract Length	Monthly Payment
Bronze	6 months	$140.00
Silver	70 12 months	$100.00
Gold	24 months	$60.00
Platinum	36 months	$30.00

方案	合約期間	月費
銅	6 個月	$140.00
銀	70 12 個月	$100.00
金	24 個月	$60.00
白金	36 個月	$30.00

M Hello, I'm looking to purchase a new service plan for my cell phone, so I thought I'd drop in and ask about your plans.

W Of course. Well, we offer several different plans. Have a look at this chart. Obviously, you will pay the lowest monthly fee for the longest contract but [68] we charge a cancelation fee if a contract is cancelled before it ends.

M Umm . . . Okay, [69] I'm planning to do an exchange program abroad next year, so I don't think a two-year or three-year plan is right for me.

W All right, [70] I think the one-year plan would be best for your needs. Are you interested in signing a contract today?

M Yes, sure. I have some time now.

男 哈囉，我想購買新的手機方案，所以，我想就順路過來，詢問你們的方案。

女 當然。嗯，我們提供好幾種不同的方案。請看一下這張表。顯然合約期間最長，您付的月費也就最低，但是，[68] 如果合約還沒到期便要取消，我們會收取違約金。

男 嗯……是這樣的，[69] 我計畫明年出國當交換生，所以我覺得兩年或三年的方案不適合我。

女 好的，[70] 我認為一年的方案最符合您的需求。您想今天簽約嗎？

男 好，當然。我現在有時間。

• **length** (時間的)長短、期間 **drop in** 順便拜訪 **offer** 提供 **several** 數個的、幾個的 **obviously** 顯然地 **cancelation (n.)** 取消 **cancel (v.)** 取消 **end** 結束、終止 **exchange** 交換 **abroad** 到國外

68

According to the woman, when is an extra fee charged?

(A) When a product is delivered
(B) When a device gets broken
(C) When a client doesn't pay a bill
(D) When a service is canceled early*

根據女子所述，何時會收取額外的費用？

(A) 當產品交貨時。
(B) 當設備損壞時。
(C) 當客戶未付賬單時。
(D) 當服務提早取消時。

對話第一段，女子說道：「we charge a cancelation fee if a contract is cacelled before it ends」，表示如果在合約到期前提前解約，會索取違約金，因此 (D) 為最適當的答案。

• **device** 設備、裝置

69

What does the man say he might do next year?
(A) Purchase a new phone
(B) Go overseas*
(C) Sign a new contract
(D) Lease a device

男子說他明年可能會做何事？
(A) 買新的手機。
(B) 出國。
(C) 簽一份新合約。
(D) 租一個設備。

副詞片語 next year 用來表示「時間」，聆聽時，請先設想 next year 可能會出現在對話中。對話第二段，男子說道：「I'm planning to do an exchanged program abroad next year」，由此確認答案為 (B)。

答案改寫 abroad → overseas

- overseas 在國外、在海外　lease 租用

Look at the graphic. How much has the man agreed to pay per month?
(A) $140.00
(B) $100.00*
(C) $60.00
(D) $30.00

請見圖表。男子同意每月付多少錢？
(A) $140.00。
(B) $100.00。
(C) $60.00。
(D) $30.00。

對話後半段，女子建議選擇簽一年約（I think the one-year plan would be the best for your needs.），詢問男子是否現在簽約，對方表示同意，因此答案為 (B) 12 個月對應的簽約金額。

Questions 71–73 refer to the following talk.

M [71] Welcome to the Ancient Civilizations Museum. We're so pleased you could attend the opening of our new Cultures of Egypt exhibit and see some of the rarest and oldest artifacts discovered along the Nile River. [71] Before we start, [72] I'd like to offer you each a headset. This will allow you to hear me over the hum of the conversation in the museum. Additionally, [73] if you're interested in ancient pottery making techniques, there is a presentation at 3:30 in the auditorium. Follow me, so we can begin.

男 [71] 歡迎來到古文明博物館。很高興你們能參加埃及文明新展覽的開幕，看到一些在尼羅河沿岸發掘的最罕見且最古老的工藝品。[71] 在開始之前，[72] 我要發給你們每人一副耳機。這會讓你們在博物館的嘈雜交談聲中聽到我說的話。此外，[73] 如果你們對古代的陶器製作技術有興趣，三點半在禮堂有演講介紹。跟我來，我們可以開始了。

• civilization 文明 rare 稀有的、罕見的 artifact 手工藝品 hum 嗡嗡聲、嘈雜聲 additionally 此外、附加地 pottery 陶器 auditorium 禮堂、觀眾席 follow 跟隨

71

What is the purpose of the talk?
(A) To explain the rules
(B) To name some key features
(C) To ask for payment
(D) To begin a tour*

這段話的目的為何？
(A) 解釋規則。
(B) 列舉一些重要的特徵。
(C) 要求付款。
(D) 開始一趟導覽。

從獨白的開頭，可以推測說話地點可能在博物館內（Welcome to the Ancient Civilizations Museum.）。中間提到，在開始之前（Before we start），先將耳機發給大家，因此 (D) 為最適當的答案。

• name 列舉、陳述

72

What will the speaker distribute?
(A) Some headphones*
(B) A museum program
(C) Tickets to a performance
(D) A map of nearby galleries

說話者會分發何物？
(A) 一些耳機。
(B) 博物館的節目單。
(C) 表演的門票。
(D) 附近藝廊的地圖。

聆聽時，請特別留意要「分發的物品」。獨白中間說道：「I'd like to offer you each a headset.」，由此確認答案為 (A)。

答案改寫 offer → distribute
headset → headphone

• distribute 分發、分配

73

According to the speaker, what will begin at 3:30?
(A) A question and answer session
(B) A classical music concert
(C) An antiques auction
(D) An educational presentation*

根據說話者所述，什麼會在 3 點半開始？
(A) 問答時間。
(B) 古典音樂會。
(C) 古董拍賣。
(D) 教育主題演講。

聆聽時，請特別留意關鍵時間點「三點半」。獨白後段提到，三點半有一場與古代陶器的製作技法相關的講座（if you're interested in ancient pottery making techniques, there is a presentation at 3:30 in the auditorium.），因此答案為 (D)。

• **auction** 拍賣 **educational** 有關教育的

Questions 74–76 refer to the following talk.

M [74] I'd like to take this opportunity to talk about our company's expense policies. I know that many of you in the sales department frequently need to take clients out to lunch. However, some of you have not been submitting your expense reports on time. It's very important to submit your reports and receipts within one month of the expenses. It is also important to make sure the forms are filled out properly. [75] Veronica, our expense manager, will contact you if you've filled out a form incorrectly. [76] From next month, the company will be implementing a new policy. Expense reports that are submitted late will no longer be reimbursed.

男 [74] 我想利用這個機會談談我們公司的費用規定。我知道，有很多業務部的人經常需要帶客戶出去吃午餐。不過，你們有些人並未準時交出你們的費用報告。要在支出後的一個月內，交出你們的報告和收據，這很重要。確定表格都填寫正確也很重要。[75] 如果你們的表格未填寫正確，我們的財務經理，薇若妮卡會和你們聯絡。[76] 從下個月開始，公司將實施新的政策。遲交的費用報告將不再核銷。

• **opportunity** 機會 **expense** 費用、支出 **policy** 政策、方針 **department** 部門 **frequently** 經常地 **submit** 交出、呈遞 **on time** 準時 **receipt** 收據 **make sure** 確定 **fill out** 填寫 **properly** 正確地、恰當地 **incorrectly** 錯誤地、不正確地 **implement** 實施、執行 **reimburse** 報銷

74

What is being discussed?
(A) Company expense regulations*
(B) Training new sales employees
(C) Hiring an office manager
(D) Filling out insurance forms

獨白在討論何事？
(A) 公司的費用規定。
(B) 訓練新的業務人員。
(C) 僱用辦公室經理。
(D) 填寫保險表格。

獨白第一句說道：「I'd like to take this opportunity to talk about our company's expense policies.」，由此確認答案為 (A)。在獨白前段，通常可以聽到與主旨相關的重要線索。

答案改寫 policies → regulations

• **regulation** 規則、規定 **insurance** 保險

75

Why will Veronica contact listeners?
(A) To provide payment
(B) To request receipts
(C) To review a policy
(D) To resolve an error*

薇若妮卡為何聯絡聽者？
(A) 為了付款。
(B) 為了要求收據。
(C) 為了審核一項政策。
(D) 為了解決錯誤。

聆聽時，請特別留意關鍵人名 Veronica。獨白後段說道：「Veronica, our expense manager, will contact you if you've filled out a form incorrectly.」，表示如果表格填寫錯誤，將會直接聯絡本人。因此答案為 (D)。

- resolve 解決

76

What will the company do next month?
(A) Stop using a form system
(B) Begin using a new policy*
(C) Lengthen a project deadline
(D) Deposit payments electronically

公司下個月會做何事？
(A) 不再使用表格系統。
(B) 開始採用新政策。
(C) 延長一個計畫的最後期限。
(D) 以電子方式存款。

請仔細聆聽關鍵時間點 next month（下個月）。獨白後段說道：「From next month, the company will be implementing a new policy.」，由此得知答案為 (B)。

答案改寫 implement → use

- lengthen 使延長、使加長 deadline 截止期限、最後期限 deposit 存款 electronically 用電子方式

Questions 77–79 refer to the following announcement.

W [77] May I have your attention, Smithside Mall shoppers. Thank you for visiting our brand new location. Today, we have a special promotion happening for customers who fill out a customer satisfaction survey. We have two stations set up – [78] one at the north entrance and one at the east entrance. Please stop by and let us know how your shopping experience was today. Your participation is greatly appreciated. [79] All participants will have their name entered into a draw for a $100 gift card that can be used at any Smithside Mall stores. Thank you and enjoy your day!

女 [77] 史密斯塞德商場的各位顧客，請注意。謝謝你們光臨我們新開的分店。今天，我們為填寫滿意度調查的顧客推出特別促銷。我們設了兩個調查站，[78] 一個在北側入口，一個在東側入口。請順路前往，讓我們知道您今天的購物經驗。非常感謝您的參與。[79] 所有參加者都可以參加一百元禮物卡的抽獎，禮物卡可在任何一家史密斯塞德商場使用。謝謝各位，並祝您今天愉快！

- attention 注意 location 地點、位置 promotion 促銷 fill out 填寫（表格、申請書等） satisfaction 滿意 survey 調查 entrance 入口 stop by 順路拜訪 participation 參與 appreciate 感謝 participant 參加者 draw 抽（籤）

77

Where is the announcement taking place?
這項通知在何處發布？

(A) At an outdoor market　(A) 露天市場。
(B) At a shopping center*　(B) 購物中心。
(C) At a bus station　(C) 公車站。
(D) At an art gallery　(D) 藝廊。

獨白第一句說道：「May I have your attention, Smithside Mall shoppers.」，請商場顧客留意廣播內容，由此確認答案為 (B)。

• **take place** 發生、舉行

78

Why does the speaker say, "We have two stations set up"?
說話者為何說，「我們設了兩個調查站」？

(A) To correct a mistake　(A) 為了改正錯誤。
(B) To explain some locations*　(B) 為了解釋地點。
(C) To apologize for a delay　(C) 為延誤道歉。
(D) To express disappointment　(D) 為了表達失望。

請務必掌握題目句前後方句子的文意。題目句之後說道：「一個在北側入口，一個在東側入口（one at the north entrance and one at the east entrance）」，因此答案為 (B)。

• **correct** 改正、糾正　**apologize for** 道歉、認錯　**delay** 延緩、延誤　**disappointment** 失望

79

What does the speaker offer?
說話者提供何物？

(A) Entrance into a contest*　(A) 進入比賽場地的權利。
(B) A book of discount coupons　(B) 一本折扣券。
(C) Free beverages at a café　(C) 咖啡館的免費飲料。
(D) A discount on a purchase　(D) 購物折扣。

在獨白後半部，通常可以聽到說話者的建議或要求事項。最後提到：「All participants will have their name entered into a draw for a $100 gift card that can be used at any Smithside Mall stores.」，表示登錄名字參加抽獎活動，因此答案為 (A)。

答案改寫 draw → contest

• **beverage** 飲料

Questions 80–82 refer to the following broadcast.

M Good afternoon, Edge Radio listeners. Thank you for tuning into Business Talk with Tom Wiser. Today, I'll be talking to [80] professional employment counselor Michelle Bernstein. Over next half hour, Ms. Bernstein will be talking about strategies for landing a job that suits your education, interests, and lifestyle. During the last ten minutes of the show, we'll be taking questions from listeners, so [81] visit our website at www.edgeradio.com/businesstalk and leave a comment with your question. Let me kick off the show by welcoming our guest! Ms. Bernstein, [82] I heard you released a series of digital books last month.	男 優勢電台的聽眾午安，感謝您收聽湯姆‧魏瑟主持的商業講座。今天，我會和 [80] 專業求職顧問蜜雪兒‧伯恩斯坦對談。接下來半小時，伯恩斯坦女士會談論一些策略，教你如何找到一份符合你的學歷、興趣和生活方式的工作。在節目的最後 10 分鐘，我們會回答聽眾的問題，所以，[81] 請上我們的網站，www.edgeradio.com/businesstalk，在留言處寫下你的問題。節目一開始，讓我先歡迎我們的來賓！伯恩斯坦女士，[82] 我聽說妳上個月推出了一系列電子書。

- **tune into** 收聽或收看某個節目 **employment** 就業 **strategy** 策略 **land** 獲得 **suit** 適合 **leave** 留下 **kick off** 開始 **release** 發行、發表

80

What is Ms. Bernstein's area of expertise?
(A) Web development
(B) Entertainment
(C) Career guidance*
(D) Finance

伯恩斯坦女士的專業領域是什麼？
(A) 網頁開發。
(B) 娛樂業。
(C) 生涯輔導。
(D) 金融業。

獨白前段提到專業求職顧問（professional employment counselor Michelle Bernstein），因此 (C) 為最適當的答案。

答案改寫 employment → career

- **expertise** 專長

81

What are the listeners encouraged to do?
(A) Send in résumés
(B) Call Ms. Bernstein
(C) Purchase an e-book
(D) Leave a comment online*

說話者鼓勵聽眾做何事？
(A) 寄送履歷表。
(B) 打電話給伯恩斯坦女士。
(C) 購買電子書。
(D) 上網留下意見。

在獨白後半部，通常可以聽到說話者的建議或要求事項。後面提到：「visit our website at www.edgeradio.com/businesstalk and leave a comment with your question」，建議可以到網站上留下評論，因此答案為 (D)。

答案改寫 website → online

- **résumé** 履歷表

82

What does the speaker say happened last month? 說話者說上個月發生何事？

(A) A group interview was conducted. (A) 進行團體面試。

(B) A radio schedule changed. (B) 電台的節目表更改。

(C) A free seminar took place. (C) 舉辦免費研討會。

(D) A line of books was released.* (D) 發行一系列書籍。

聆聽時，請特別留意關鍵時間點 last month（上個月）。獨白最後一句說道：「I heard you released a series of digital books last month」，表示聽說上個月出版了電子書，由此可以確認答案為 (D)。

• **conduct** 進行

Questions 83–85 refer to the following excerpt from a meeting.

W We're just about finished for today, but I have one final thought to add. [83] I want to remind all the cashiers present that we've added another feature to our customer transactions here at Park Road Café and Bakery. As you know, many stores are now allowing customers to pay with the cell phone app, Pay Smart. [84] Our systems have just been upgraded to include this payment method, and [85] we've put signs at all our cash registers announcing the new feature. We will have a general training session about how to use the new system. Can everyone meet tomorrow afternoon for that?	**女** 我們即將結束今天的營業，但我還有最後一點意見要補充。[83] 我要提醒在場的所有收銀員，我們已經在「帕克路咖啡烘焙坊」的顧客交易流程中，增加了另一個功能。你們知道，現在有許多商店都允許顧客用手機 app「智慧付」來付款。[84] 我們的系統剛剛升級來含括這種付款方式，而且 [85] 我們在所有的收銀機上都貼了告示，宣布這項新功能。我們會有一個關於如何使用新系統的一般訓練課程。大家明天下午可以集合上課嗎？

• **final** 最後的 **thought** 意見、看法 **add** 增加、補充說 **remind** 提醒 **present** 在場的、出席的 **feature** 功能 **transaction** 交易 **allow** 允許 **pay** 付、支付 **payment** 支付、付款 **method** 方式 **sign** 公告、招牌 **cash register** 收銀機 **announce** 宣布

83

Who most likely are the listeners? 聽眾最可能是誰？

(A) Restaurant chefs (B) Café workers* (A) 餐廳主廚。 (B) 咖啡館員工。

(C) Software designers (D) Employee trainers (C) 軟體設計師。 (D) 員工訓練講師。

請透過獨白內容推測聽者是誰。獨白前段說道：「I want to remind all the cashiers present that we've added another feature to our customer transactions here at Park Road Café and Bakery.」，當中提到了公司名稱（Park Road Café and Bakery），由此可以推測答案應為 (B)。

84

What is the purpose of the talk? 這段談話的目的為何？

(A) To explain a customer complaint (A) 解釋顧客的抱怨。

(B) To announce a new sales procedure* (B) 宣布新的銷售步驟。

(C) To begin a training session (C) 開始一項訓練課程。

(D) To demonstrate some new equipment (D) 展示一項新設備。

獨白前段提到針對顧客交易，新增了一項功能，後方接著説明具體的結帳方式（Our systems have just been upgraded to include this payment method），因此 (B) 為最適當的答案。

• **complaint** 抱怨、抗議　**procedure** 步驟、程序　**demonstrate** 示範操作、展示　**equipment** 設備

85

What can be found at each cash register?
(A) Announcement signs*
(B) Membership cards
(C) Promotional coupons
(D) Updated menus

在每一台收銀機上可以發現什麼？
(A) 通知的告示。
(B) 會員卡。
(C) 促銷優惠券。
(D) 更新的菜單。

聆聽時，請特別留意關鍵字 cash register。獨白後段説道：「we've put signs at all our cash registers announcing the new feature」，由此確認答案為 (A)。

• **announcement** 布告、通知　**promotional** 促銷的

Questions 86–88 refer to the following telephone message.

M Hello, Ms. Wilford. This is Mike Drew calling. I just received your e-mail about the package that was delivered to you yesterday. [86] I'm sorry to hear that [87] the box was water damaged. I agree with you that you should not try to use the products in the box, as they are electrical and water damage could be dangerous. To remedy this problem, [88] I am going to send a brand new order at no charge to you. Please repackage the original order and give it to the deliveryman when he brings your new order. Again, I'm very sorry for the inconvenience.

男 哈囉，魏爾福女士，我是麥克德魯。我剛剛收到您關於昨天遞送包裹的電子郵件。[86] 很抱歉聽聞 [87] 盒子浸水損壞。我同意您所說的，您不應該嘗試使用盒內的產品，因為它們是電器用品，而泡水損傷可能很危險。為了補救這個問題，[88] 我打算免費送一個全新的貨品過去。請將原來的貨品重新包裝好，當送貨員把新的貨品送過去時，把舊的交給他。再次為造成您的不便致上歉意。

• **deliver** 投遞、送貨　**damaged** 損壞的　**agree** 同意　**electrical** 電的、與電有關的　**damage** 損害、毀壞　**remedy** 補救　**brand new** 全新的　**order** 所訂的貨　**at no charge** 無償、免費　**inconvenience** 不便

86

What is the purpose of the telephone message?
(A) To order some electronics
(B) To purchase insurance
(C) To apologize for a problem*
(D) To ask for a shipping address

這段電話留言的目的為何？
(A) 訂購一些電器。
(B) 購買保險。
(C) 為問題致歉。
(D) 詢問送貨地址。

在獨白前半部，通常可以聽到與目的相關的重要線索。當中提到：「I'm sorry to hear」，表示感到抱歉，因此 (C) 為最適當的答案。

答案改寫 sorry → apologize

• **purchase** 購買　**insurance** 保險　**apologize for** 因為……道歉

87

What problem does the speaker mention?
(A) Some electronics are broken.
(B) Some packaging is damaged.*
(C) A payment has been delayed.
(D) A new item is sold out.

說話者提及什麼問題？
(A) 有些電器用品故障。
(B) 有個外盒破損。
(C) 有筆款項延後。
(D) 有個新產品售完。

聆聽時，請特別留意「問題」所在。獨白前段說道：「the box was water damaged」，由此確認答案為 (B)。因為本題和上一題的解題線索在同一句獨白上，很容易就會漏聽，請特別留意。

答案改寫 box → packaging

• **payment** 支付、付款 **delay** 使延期、使延後 **item** 物品 **sold out** 售完的、售罄

88

What does the speaker say he will do?
(A) Pick up an item
(B) Contact a manager
(C) Provide a refund
(D) Send another package*

說話者說他會做何事？
(A) 拾起一件物品。
(B) 聯絡經理。
(C) 提供退款。
(D) 寄送另一個包裹。

獨白後段說道：「I am going to send a brand new order at no charge to you.」，表示會免費寄送全新商品，因此答案為 (D)。

答案改寫 order → package

• **refund** 退還、退款

Questions 89–91 refer to the following telephone message.

M Hi, Divia. This is Jeff calling. [89] I've just had a chance to look at your design for Sampson Real Estate's online advertisement, and I wanted to give you some feedback. Actually, the design has a few issues. Sampson Real Estate is one of the oldest companies in the area and they focus mostly on high-end properties. I'm sorry I didn't explain this better to you, but Sampson usually prefers more traditional graphics. [90] The ones you've used are a bit too young and casual. [91] How about I send you some of Sampson's previous advertisements so you can review them and get an idea about what they want? Call me back when you get a chance.

男 嗨，蒂薇亞，我是傑夫。[89] 我剛剛才有時間看妳為山普生不動產設計的線上廣告，我想給妳些意見。實際上，這個設計有幾個問題。山普生不動產是業界最老的公司之一，他們主要聚焦在高檔的房地產上。抱歉沒有把這一點跟妳解釋得更清楚些，但山普生通常偏愛較傳統的圖樣。[90] 妳所使用的圖，有點太過於年輕且不夠正式。[91] 我寄一些山普生之前的廣告給妳如何？這樣妳可以仔細看看，對他們想要什麼有個概念。等妳有空時，回我電話。

• **real estate** 房地產、不動產 **actually** 實際上 **issue** 問題、爭議 **focus on** 集中於 **mostly** 大部分地、主要地 **high-end** 高檔的 **property** 財產、資產、房地產 **explain** 解釋 **traditional** 傳統的 **casual** 非正式、隨意的 **previous** 先前的

89

What industry does the speaker work in?
(A) Internet sales
(B) Fashion retail
(C) Advertising*
(D) Publishing

說話者在哪個行業工作？
(A) 網路銷售。
(B) 服飾零售。
(C) 廣告業。
(D) 出版業。

獨白前段說道：「I've just had a chance to look at your design for Sampson Real Estate's online advertisement, and I wanted to give you some feedback.」，提到「針對網路廣告案的回覆」，因此 (C) 為最適當的答案。

• **retail** 零售

90

Why does the speaker say, "Actually, the design has a few issues"?
(A) To outline the survey results about a design
(B) To suggest that their budget is limited
(C) To indicate a problem with some finished work*
(D) To express some safety concerns

說話者為何說「實際上這個設計有幾個問題」？
(A) 為了概述一個設計的調查結果。
(B) 為了暗示他們的預算有限。
(C) 為了指出某項已完成作品的問題。
(D) 為了表達一些安全疑慮。

聆聽時，請特別留意題目句。題目句後方說明廣告客戶的特性，表示目前的設計有點過於年輕（The ones you've used are a bit too young and casual.），因此答案為 (C)。

• **outline** 概述、略述　**survey** 調查　**result** 結果　**budget** 預算　**limited** 有限的　**indicate** 指示、指出　**express** 表達　**safety** 安全　**concern** 關心的事、擔心

91

What does the speaker suggest the listener do?
(A) Study some prior designs*
(B) Work on another project
(C) Contact a client directly
(D) Consult a coworker

說話者建議聽者何事？
(A) 研究一些之前的設計。
(B) 進行另一項專案。
(C) 直接與客戶聯絡。
(D) 請教同事。

在獨白後半部，會提到說話者的建議或是要求。說話者表示可以將之前的廣告傳給對方，請對方參考看看（How about I send you some of Sampson's previous advertisements so you can review them and get an idea about what they want?），因此答案為 (A)。

答案改寫 previous → prior
advertisement → design
review → study

• **prior** 在前的　**directly** 直接地　**consult** 與……商量、請教　**coworker** 同事

Questions 92–94 refer to the following excerpt from a meeting.

W Hello, everyone. Thanks for attending this editorial meeting on such short notice. Some of our new publications were set to be released early next year. Unfortunately, the release dates have been pushed back again. This means those who have preordered books will now have to wait even longer to receive their copies. Who knows how many will cancel their orders? [92] I suggest we run another preorder promotion to ensure we don't lose sales. [93] I'd like everyone to come up with some promotional ideas. [94] I am available throughout this morning to discuss any concerns you might have about what kind of promotions are appropriate.

女 大家好，謝謝各位一接到通知就趕來參加編輯會議。我們有些新書本來預定明年初要發行，遺憾的是，發行日期已再度延後。這意謂著那些已經預訂新書的人，現在必須等更久才能收到他們的書。誰知道會有多少人取消訂單？ [92] 我建議，我們進行另一波預購促銷，以確保我們不會損失銷量。[93] 我想要每個人想出一些促銷的點子。[94] 我今天整個上午都有空，任何有關何種促銷可能適合的疑慮，都可以找我討論。

• editorial 編輯的　notice 通知　publication 出版物　release 發行　mean 意指、意謂　preorder 預購　ensure 確保　lose 損失（金錢）　come up with （針對問題等）想出　appropriate 適當的、恰當的

92

What does the woman imply when she says, "Who knows how many will cancel their orders"?

(A) She wants someone to report an exact figure.
(B) She is worried about a loss of business.*
(C) She would prefer to receive online orders.
(D) She was not expecting any problems to occur.

當女子說「誰知道會有多少人取消訂單」，意指什麼？

(A) 她想要有人報告確實的數字。
(B) 她擔心生意損失。
(C) 她比較喜歡接到線上訂單。
(D) 她不希望發生任何問題。

題目句後方說道：「I suggest we run another preorder promotion to ensure we don't lose sales.」，為確保銷售量不會下滑，提議舉辦預購促銷活動，因此答案為 (B)。

• exact 確切的、精確的　figure 數字　lose 損失　occur 發生

93

What is the topic of the meeting?

(A) Redesigning a book cover
(B) Reducing production costs
(C) Developing a marketing strategy*
(D) Attracting new authors

會議的主題為何？

(A) 重新設計一本書的封面。
(B) 降低生產成本。
(C) 發展行銷策略。
(D) 吸引新的作者。

獨白後段要求提出促銷相關的計畫（I'd like everyone to come up with some promotional ideas.），因此 (C) 為最適當的答案。

• reduce 減少、降低　strategy 策略　attract 吸引

94

What will the speaker probably do this morning?
(A) Attend a weekly meeting
(B) Conduct a telephone consultation
(C) Visit a broadcasting station
(D) Address employee questions*

說話者今天早上可能會做何事？
(A) 參加週會。
(B) 進行電話諮詢會議。
(C) 拜訪廣播電台。
(D) 處理下屬的問題。

聆聽時，請特別留意時間副詞片語 this morning（今天上午）。獨白最後一句說道：「I am available throughout this morning to discuss any concerns you might have about what kind of promotions are appropriate.」，由此確認答案為 (D)。

答案改寫 discuss → address
concern → question

• conduct 進行、實施　consultation 諮詢（會）　address 處理、應付

Questions 95–97 refer to the following instructions and seating chart.

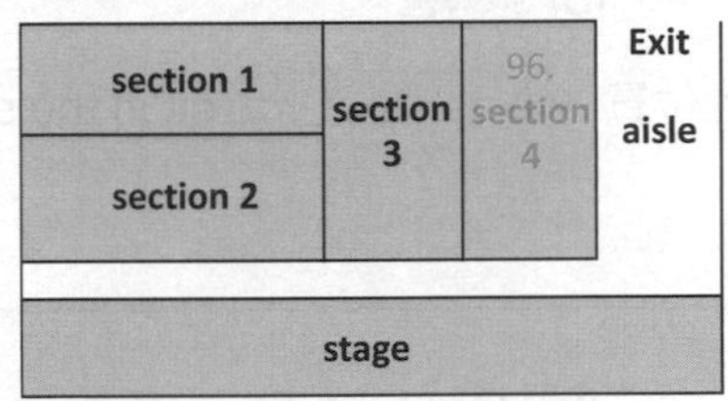

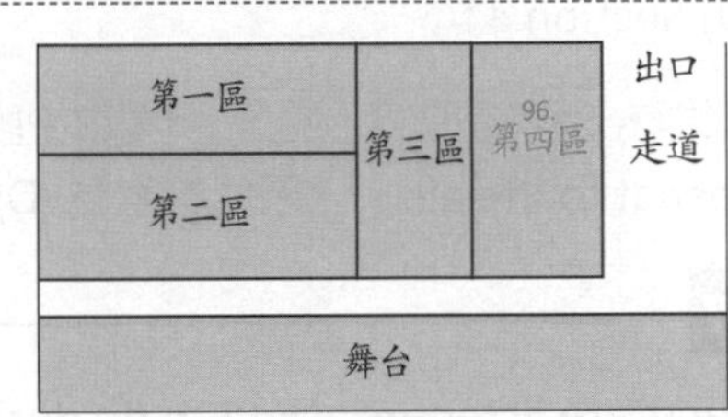

W Hello, everyone. I'm so excited [95] you were all able to attend our audition for a part in the International Ballet. Before we start the auditions, I'd like to let everyone know how things are going to happen today. Everyone has been given a number. When your number is close to being called, please make your way backstage. Everyone is free to watch the auditions. However, since many families are also here to watch, [96] we ask that you sit in the section closest to the aisle, so you do not disturb anyone when you are moving to and from your audition. [97] We also ask that you be quiet and courteous during performances. Following the auditions, our lead choreographers will make decisions and invite selected dancers to a second audition next week.

女 大家好。很高興 [95] 你們都能來參加我們國際芭蕾舞團的甄選。在開始之前，我想告訴各位今天的流程。每個人都拿到了一個號碼。快要叫到你的號碼時，請前往後台。各位都可以隨意觀賞甄選過程。不過，由於有許多人的家人也來這裡觀賞，因此，[96] 要請你們坐在最靠近走道的區域，這樣的話，你們要上下台時，才不會干擾到其他人。[97] 同時要求你們，演出進行時請保持安靜且遵守禮節。甄選之後，我們的首席舞蹈指導會作出決定，並邀請獲選的舞者參加下星期的第二輪甄選。

• aisle 走道、通道　attend 參加、出席　audition 甄選、試演／試唱／試奏　disturb 妨礙、打擾
courteous 有禮貌的、謙恭的　performance 表演　following 在……以後
choreographer 編舞者、舞蹈指導　make a decision 決定

95

Who most likely are the listeners?
(A) Directors
(B) Writers
(C) Performers*
(D) Reporters

聽眾最可能是誰？
(A) 導演。
(B) 作家。
(C) 表演者。
(D) 記者。

獨白前段説道：「you were all able to attend our audition for a part in the International Ballet」，針對「參加芭蕾舞團徵選的人」作説明，因此答案為 (C)。

96

Look at the graphic. What section does the speaker want the listeners to sit in?
(A) Section 1
(B) Section 2
(C) Section 3
(D) Section 4*

請見圖表。說話者要聽眾坐在哪個區域？
(A) 第一區。
(B) 第二區。
(C) 第三區。
(D) 第四區。

聆聽時，請特別留意「位置」。獨白中段建議選擇走道旁的位置（we ask that you sit in the section closest to the aisle），因此答案為 (D)。

97

What are listeners asked to do during the audition?
(A) Remain quiet*
(B) Take photographs
(C) Avoid cellphone use
(D) Speak to choreographers

在甄選時，要求聽眾做何事？
(A) 保持安靜。
(B) 拍照。
(C) 不要使用手機。
(D) 和舞蹈指導談話。

本題重點為 during the audition（甄選期間）的注意事項。獨白後段説道：「We also ask that you be quiet and courteous during performances.」，叮嚀在表演期間，請各位保持肅靜且遵守禮儀，因此答案為 (A)。

- **remain** 保持　**take a photograph** 拍照　**avoid** 避免

Questions 98–100 refer to the following instructions and flowchart.

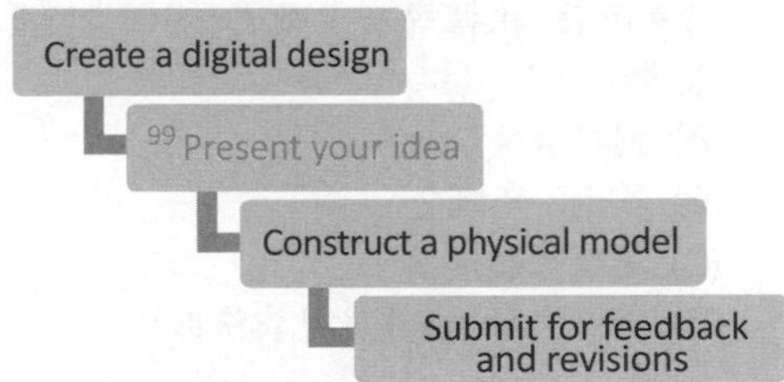

創建數位設計
99 展示你的概念
建造實體模型
交出作品以接受意見與修正

M Let's start with some great news. [98] Thanks to our recent merger, Frontier Architecture managed to pick up numerous contracts with private and city developers. As a result, we're going to have a lot of building designs to work on in the coming year. Now, I'd like to talk about our design development process. Take a look at this flowchart. [99] Notice that we've added a step between create a digital design and construct a physical model. This new step means you will need to get approval from a senior designer before constructing a model. Because we have so many projects to work on, we need to make sure we're not wasting our time building models that won't be approved. [100] This new process will help you focus your time and should ensure that we are able to meet our deadlines.

男 我們用一些很棒的消息來開始會議吧。[98] 由於我們最近的合併，「新領域建築」設法簽下了許多私人及市府開發單位的合約。因此，接下來一年，我們會有很多建物的設計要忙。現在，我想談談我們的設計發展步驟。請看這張流程圖。[99] 請注意，我們在創建數位設計與建造實體模型之間增加了一個步驟。這個新步驟，代表你在建造模型之前，必須得到資深設計師的認可。因為有那麼多專案要進行，我們必須確定沒有把時間浪費在建造不會得到認可的模型上。[100] 這個新的程序有助於你們集中時間，而且應該能確保我們在截止日前完成。

• **construct** 建造　**revision** 修正、修訂　**thanks to** 由於、幸虧　**merger** 合併　**numerous** 許多的　**contract** 合約　**as a result** 因此、結果　**notice** 注意　**approval** 認可、贊成　**senior** 資深的、年長的　**waste** 浪費　**approve** 贊成、同意　**meet** 達到、完成

98

What does the speaker say about Frontier Architecture?

(A) They lost several important clients.
(B) They recently merged with another company.*
(C) They hired a new design team.
(D) They won an international award.

關於新領域建築，說話者說了什麼？

(A) 他們失去好幾個重要的客戶。
(B) 他們最近和另一家公司合併。
(C) 他們僱用了新的設計團隊。
(D) 他們贏得一項國際大獎。

聆聽時，請特別留意關鍵字 Frontier Architecture。獨白前段說道：「Thanks to our recent merger, Frontier Architecture managed to pick up numerous contracts with private and city developers.」，由此確認答案為 (B)。

• **several** 好幾個　**merge** 合併

99

Look at the graphic. According to the speaker, which step was recently added?

(A) Create a digital design

(B) Present your idea*

(C) Construct a physical model

(D) Submit for feedback and revisions

請見圖表。根據說話者所述，哪個步驟是最近增加的？

(A) 創建數位設計。

(B) 展示你的概念。

(C) 建造實體模型。

(D) 交出作品以接受意見與修正。

本題重點在「新的步驟」。獨白中段說道：「Notice that we've added a step between create a digital design and construct a physical model.」，表示在數位設計製作和實體模型建造之間新增一個步驟，因此答案為 (B)。

100

What problem will the speaker's plan prevent?

(A) Losing digital files

(B) Paying overtime wages

(C) Working in a crowded office

(D) Not finishing work on time*

說話者的計畫能預防什麼問題？

(A) 遺失電子檔案。

(B) 付加班費。

(C) 在擁擠的辦公室工作。

(D) 未準時完成工作。

聆聽時，請特別留意新步驟的「目的或效用」。獨白最後一句提到，新程序不僅可以減少時間的浪費，還能確保在時間內完成（This new process will help you focus your time and should ensure that we are able to meet our deadlines.），因此 (D) 為最適當的答案。

- **wage** 薪水、報酬　**crowded** 擁擠的

ACTUAL TEST

中譯+解析

PART 1 ∩21

1

(A) They are putting on their helmets.
(B) They are passing by a bike.
(C) They are gathering on a bridge.
(D) They are riding next to the water.*

(A) 他們正在戴頭盔。
(B) 他們經過一輛腳踏車。
(C) 他們在橋上集合。
(D) 他們在水邊騎車。

(D) 針對人們沿著水岸邊(next to the water)騎(riding)腳踏車的狀況描述，為正確答案。當選項中出現 water 時，通常為正確答案。(A) 雖然不是答案，但在 PART 1 中，選項中常同時出現 put on 和 wear，請特別留意。另外，雖然兩者的意思皆為穿戴，但 putting on 用來表示動作；wearing 用來形容狀態，因此為了符合照片情境，應使用 wearing 較為適當。

• put on 穿上、戴上　pass 經過　gather 使聚集、集合　bridge 橋、橋樑　ride 騎、乘

2

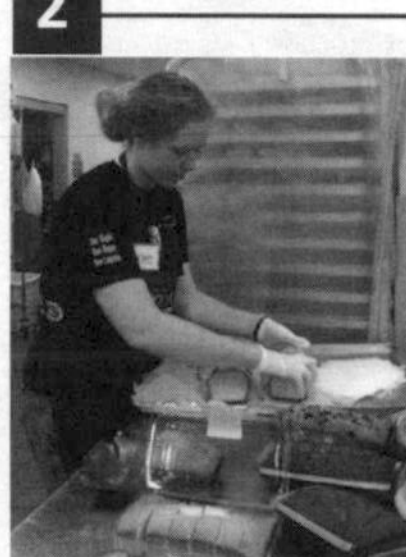

(A) A woman is buying some bread.
(B) A woman is wearing a pair of gloves.*
(C) A woman is carrying a tray.
(D) A woman is opening a container.

(A) 女子正在買麵包。
(B) 女子戴著手套。
(C) 女子端著托盤。
(D) 女子打開容器。

(B) 針對戴著手套的狀態(wearing a pair of gloves)說明，為正確答案。(A) 和 (C) 皆使用了出現在照片內的東西(bread, tray)，讓人混淆，並不符合照片情境；(D) 的內容與照片無關。

• bread 麵包　carry 攜帶、運送　tray 托盤　container 容器、貨櫃

3

(A) Some people are operating a machine.
(B) Some people are standing in rows.
(C) A man is speaking to a group of people.*
(D) A woman is examining her tools.

(A) 有些人在操作機器。
(B) 有些人成排站著。
(C) 一名男子對著一群人講話。
(D) 女子在檢查她的工具。

(A) 的內容無法從照片判斷；(B) in rows 並不符合照片情境；(D) 僅使用了照片內的人和物(a woman, tools)，並不符合照片情境。在此補充，單字 examine 主要用來形容「仔細觀看」某樣東西的動作。(A)、(B) 和 (D) 皆不符合照片情境，因此答案為 (C)。

• operate 操作、開動　stand 站立、站著　in a row 成一排　examine 檢查　tool 工具

4

(A) A musician is performing on a stage. (A) 音樂家正在舞台上表演。

(B) Some musical instruments are on display.* (B) 陳列著一些樂器。

(C) Some music stands have been set up. (C) 架好一些譜架。

(D) A guitar is being tuned. (D) 正在為一把吉他調音。

照片中並未出現任何人物，而 (A) 以 musician 當作主詞，可以直接刪除。另外，請先預想到這類題型的選項中，可能會出現現在進行被動式（be being p.p.），且以照片中的事物作為主詞，亦為錯誤選項。(D) 請先換成主動語態，當成是某人正在調音（Someone is tuning a guitar.），亦非答案；(C) 的說明雖然與照片中的樂器有關，但並不符合照片情境；因此答案為 (B)。這類照片，選項中若出現 be on display，通常會是答案。

• **perform** 表演　**stage** 舞台　**instrument** 樂器、儀器　**tune** 為……調音

5

(A) A plant is blocking the doorway. (A) 有棵植物擋在門口。

(B) A ladder is propped against the shelves.* (B) 一把梯子靠著架子。

(C) Books have been piled on the floor. (C) 書堆放在地上。

(D) A framed photograph is being hung up. (D) 正掛起一張裝在相框裡的照片。

照片中並未出現人物，因此須優先刪除現在進行被動式，也就是選項 (D)； (A) 的內容從照片中難以確認；(C) 僅使用了照片中的東西（books），使人混淆，內容並不符合情境。(B) 針對梯子倚靠著書架的狀態進行描述，為正確答案。本句亦可寫成「A ladder is leaning against the shelves.」。

• **plant** 植物　**block** 阻塞、堵住　**doorway** 門口、出入口　**ladder** 梯子　**prop** 支撐、支持　**shelf** 架子　**pile** 堆積　**hang up** 懸掛

6

(A) The workstations are illuminated by some lamps.* (A) 工作站靠一些燈照亮。

(B) The desks are positioned in a circle. (B) 書桌排成一個圓。

(C) A computer has been taken apart. (C) 電腦被拆開。

(D) Some cables are coiled around a pole. (D) 有些電纜捲在一根柱子上。

(A) 針對工作台上擺著燈客觀描寫，為正確答案；(B) 後方的 in a circle，為錯誤的說明；(C) 和 (D) 僅使用了照片中的東西（computer, pole），使人混淆，內容與照片情境不符。

• **workstation**（電腦）工作站　**illuminate** 照亮、照射　**position** 擺放　**take (something) apart** 拆開　**pole** 柱、竿

PART 2 22

7

Where is the bus station located?
(A) It departs at six o'clock.
(B) Downtown across from the arena.*
(C) We bought tickets today.

公車站位在哪裡？
(A) 它六點出發。
(B) 市區的體育場對面。
(C) 我們今天買了票。

疑問詞 Where 用來詢問「地點」，本題詢問「公車站的位置」，(B) 回答了確切的位置，和題目句構成完整對話，為正確答案。

- **depart** 出發、離開 **arena** （體育比賽或表演用的）場地、競技場

8

I think the new manager is very nice, don't you?
(A) I can't meet him this afternoon.
(B) No, they hired him last month.
(C) Yes, he tells great jokes.*

我覺得新來的經理很親切，你不覺得嗎？
(A) 我今天下午見不到他。
(B) 不，他們上個月僱用了他。
(C) 是啊，他很會講笑話。

本題和以往 PART 2 中常見的附加問句題型不太一樣。題目句中 don't you 的後方省略了 think so，因此本句詢問的重點為「是否覺得經理人還不錯」，(C) 表示同意（Yes），並補充說明原因，為最適當的回覆。

- **hire** 僱用

9

Didn't we receive the new shipment on June 1?
(A) No, there's been a delay.*
(B) To inspect the new merchandise.
(C) You should have canceled it by now.

我們不是 6 月 1 日收到新來的貨了嗎？
(A) 不，延後了。
(B) 為了檢查新商品。
(C) 你在這之前就該取消了。

碰到否定問句時，只要先將 not 拿掉，視為一般問句，就能更容易掌握住題目的重點。本題要詢問的是「是否有在 6 月 1 日收到」，(A) 回覆「延誤了」，表示並未準時收到，與題目句構成完整對話。

- **shipment** 運輸的貨物、運送 **delay** 延誤、延期 **inspect** 檢查 **merchandise** 商品、貨物

10

Where can I post this notice about the lecture?
(A) No, I didn't notice the change.
(B) Give it to the receptionist.*
(C) The lecturer has not replied yet.

我可以把這張演講的告示貼在哪裡？
(A) 不，我沒有注意到改變。
(B) 把它交給櫃檯人員。
(C) 演講者還沒有回覆。

本題為以 Where 開頭的問句，詢問可以貼公告的地方，(B) 以指示代名詞 it 代替「公告」，回答「請交給接待員」，為最適當的答案。在此補充，(A) 以疑問詞開頭的問句，不能以 Yes 或 No 開頭的答句回答，聽到的當下即可刪除此選項。另外，像 (C) 一樣，在選項中使用了與題目句（lecture）相同或相似的單字（lecturer）時，通常不太可能是答案。

- **notice** 公告、通知 **receptionist** 接待人員 **lecturer** 演講者、講師 **reply** 答覆、回答

11

Why is the office so cold this morning?
(A) Have you seen the movie yet?
(B) They're repairing the furnace.*
(C) Another room, please.

辦公室今天早上為什麼這麼冷？
(A) 你看過電影了嗎？
(B) 他們正在修暖氣。
(C) 另一個房間，謝謝。

本題為以 Why 開頭的問句，詢問冷的「原因」，(B) 回答了原因為「暖器正在修理」，為正確答案。這類題型的答案通常會省略掉連接詞 because，直接表明原因。

• **repair** 修理、修補　**furnace** 暖氣、暖爐

12

The CEO will arrive on September 10, right?
(A) Yes, that's the deadline.
(B) No, she rescheduled her trip.*
(C) I went there two days ago.

執行長會在 9 月 10 日抵達，對吧？
(A) 是的，那是截止日期。
(B) 不，她更改了旅程的時間。
(C) 我兩天前去過那裡。

本題使用「. . . right?」詢問「執行長是否會在 9 月 10 日抵達」。針對再次向對方確認的問題，(B) 為最適當的答覆。其他選項的內容也與「期限」和「時間」有關，答題時請特別小心。

• **arrive** 到達、到來　**deadline** 截止日期、最後期限　**reschedule** 將……改期、重新安排……的時間

13

The window in the conference room is broken.
(A) I'll notify maintenance.*
(B) An international conference.
(C) I will open the door for you.

會議室的窗戶破了。
(A) 我會通知維修人員。
(B) 一場國際會議。
(C) 我會幫你開門。

當題目為直述句時，請務必聽清楚每個選項的內容。由於必須先掌握每個選項的重點，再找出最適當的答案，因此此類題型的難度偏高。題目句表示「窗戶被打破了」，根據文意判斷應為「通報維修人員」，因此答案為 (A)。

• **notify** 通知、報告　**maintenance** 維修

14

When does the modern art exhibit begin?
(A) Over twenty famous artists.
(B) No, I don't enjoy galleries.
(C) The show kicks off this weekend.*

當代藝術展何時開始？
(A) 超過 20 位知名藝術家。
(B) 不，我不喜歡藝廊。
(C) 展覽本週末開始。

本題為以 When 開頭的問句，詢問「何時開始」，(C) 回答了確切的時間資訊（this weekend），與題目句構成完整對話。在此補充，(B) 以疑問詞開頭的問句，不能以 Yes 或 No 開頭的答句回答，聽到的當下即可刪除此選項。

• **exhibit** 展覽　**kick off** 開始

15

Can you tell me who the project leader will be?
(A) Barry MacDonald.*
(B) Beside Jacob's office.
(C) He suggested it in the meeting.

你可以告訴我，專案主持人是誰嗎？
(A) 貝瑞·麥唐諾德。
(B) 在雅各的辦公室旁邊。
(C) 他在會議上提出的。

題目為間接問句時，解題關鍵為句中的疑問詞。本題等同於以 Who 開頭的問句，詢問「是誰」負責，(A) 回覆了人名，為最適當的答覆。當題目為 Who 開頭的問句時，答案除了人名，還有可能是職稱、部門名稱或公司名稱。

16

Can you bring the report to the budget meeting tomorrow morning?
(A) It starts at ten o'clock every day.
(B) I'm off all day tomorrow.*
(C) We just finished the presentation.

明天早上的預算會議，你可以把報告帶來嗎？
(A) 每天十點開始。
(B) 我明天休假。
(C) 我們剛結束演講。

本題使用「Can you . . . ?」，「能帶報告來嗎？」，詢問對方的意願，(B) 解釋「因為明天休假」，表示可能沒有辦法，為正確答案。像這類明確回絕的答覆，通常會是正確答案。

- **budget** 預算

17

Which company takes care of the shipping?
(A) Within two to five days.
(B) The one located in Chicago.*
(C) No, they won't sail today.

哪一家公司負責運送？
(A) 二到五天之內。
(B) 位在芝加哥的公司。
(C) 不，他們今天不開船。

本題使用疑問形容詞 which，詢問「由哪一間公司負責」，(B) 以代名詞 one 代替公司（company），為最適當的答案，與題目句構成完整對話。在此補充，當題目改成詢問「配送時間」時，答案才可以選 (A)。which 開頭的問句，當選項中有 one 時，通常會是答案。

- **take care of** 處理、負責　**shipping** 運送、運輸　**sail** 開船、航行

18

Doesn't the manager usually arrive by nine o'clock?
(A) It usually finishes quickly.
(B) Unfortunately, he doesn't have any.
(C) Yes, but he's meeting with clients.*

經理不是通常九點會到嗎？
(A) 通常很快就完成。
(B) 不巧，他一個都沒有。
(C) 是的，但他正在見客戶。

請將本句視為一般問句，重點在詢問「是否會在九點前抵達」。(C) 回答「是，但是（Yes, but）」目前正在開會，所以現在不在，與題目句構成完整對話，為最適當的選項。

19

Should we drive to the restaurant or take the subway?
(A) A new train schedule.
(B) It's just across the street.*
(C) I'll give you a new invoice.

我們應該開車去餐廳還是搭地鐵去？
(A) 一張新的火車時刻表。
(B) 餐廳就在街道對面。
(C) 我會開張新的發票給你。

當題目為選擇疑問句時，可以預想到答案應為問句中所包含的兩種選項（①開車、②搭乘地鐵）之一，或是以其他內容回覆。(B) 以其他內容回覆「就在街的對面」，表示走過去即可，為正確答案。

- **invoice** 發票、發貨單

20

Do you know what Dr. Pike said about the research results?
(A) He hasn't reviewed them yet.*
(B) At least three more tests.
(C) During the medical conference.

你知不知道，關於研究結果，派克博士怎麼說？
(A) 他還沒看過。
(B) 至少還要檢驗三次。
(C) 在醫學研討會時。

當題目為間接問句時，解題關鍵為句中的疑問詞，請千萬不要漏聽重點。本句要詢問的重點是「他說了什麼」，(A) 為最適當的回答。在此補充，當 PART 2 中，出現「還不知道」或是「我不太清楚」這類意思的選項時，通常就是正確答案。

- **research**（學術）研究　**result** 結果　**at least** 至少　**medical** 醫學的

21

How frequently do you take a vacation?
(A) First Class seats, please.
(B) Once or twice a year.*
(C) Yes, she's already left.

你多久會度假一次？
(A) 頭等艙，謝謝。
(B) 一年一到兩次。
(C) 是的，她已經離開了。

本題詢問「有多常去」，重點為詢問「頻率」，(B) 回答「一年一到兩次」，與題目句構成完整對話。請特別留意，解題重點即為疑問詞 How 後方的單字。

- **frequently** 頻繁地、經常地　**leave** 離開（某處）

22

Will you apply for a new job or take some more classes? 你會應徵新工作還是再多修一些課？

(A) He will graduate in the fall. (A) 他今年秋天畢業。

(B) My updated résumé. (B) 我更新過的履歷表。

(C) I have an interview next week.* (C) 我下星期有個面試。

本題為選擇疑問句，兩個選項分別為①找新工作、②繼續上課。(C) 回答「之後要去面試」委婉表示選擇了①，為正確答案。

• **apply for** 應徵、申請 **graduate** 畢業 **resume** 履歷表

23

Why did the packages arrive so damaged? 包裹送來時，為何受損這麼嚴重？

(A) He will reimburse the costs. (A) 他會退還費用。

(B) There was heavy rain.* (B) 之前下大雨。

(C) A new delivery company. (C) 一家新的貨運公司。

疑問詞 Why 用來詢問「原因」，本題詢問「包裹破損的原因」。(B) 簡短回覆說：「因為下大雨」，為正確答案。

• **damaged** 受損的 **reimburse** 退還 **cost** 費用 **delivery** 運送、遞送

24

Maybe you could print the graphs in color this time. 也許這一次，你可以把圖表印成彩色的。

(A) That would be better.* (A) 那會好多了。

(B) The computer is new. (B) 電腦是新的。

(C) It's too big for the copy room. (C) 太大，放不進影印室。

助動詞 could 可以用來表示「建議」，題目句建議「彩色印刷」。(A) 回答：「效果會更好」表示同意，與題目句構成完整對話，為最適當的回應。其他選項中使用了與 print、 color 有關的內容，但與文意不符。

25

Where should we hold the awards dinner? 我們應該在哪裡舉行頒獎晚宴？

(A) Beef and vegetables. (A) 牛肉與蔬菜。

(B) He is the HR manager. (B) 他是人資部經理。

(C) We should check the budget first.* (C) 我們應該先核對預算。

本題為以 Where 開頭的問句，雖為詢問地點，但 (C) 回答在決定地點之前「應該先確認一下預算」，為最適當的回覆。最近在 PART 2 中，經常出現這類題型。針對題目句，並未給予正面回覆，因此難以從選項中直接找出答案，需仔細思考並剔除不適當的選項，來找出正確解答。

• **hold** 舉行 **award** 獎、獎品 **beef** 牛肉 **vegetable** 蔬菜 **budget** 預算

26

Would you mind sending me a copy of your report?
(A) How much paper is left over?
(B) Oh, I just turned off my computer.*
(C) They sent the receipt to my office.

寄一份你的報告給我，好嗎？
(A) 還剩多少紙？
(B) 噢，我剛剛關了電腦。
(C) 他們把收據寄到我的辦公室。

「Would you mind + V-ing . . . ?」意思為「你介意⋯⋯嗎？」。本題以此句型請求對方「傳送複本」，(B) 回答「我剛關掉電腦」，表示可能沒辦法傳，委婉拒絕了對方，為最適當的答覆。其他選項僅使用了與題目句中單字（send, copy）相關的詞彙（paper, sent），故意讓人混淆，答題時請特別留意。

• **mind**（用於否定句和疑問句）介意、反對　**turn off** 關掉

27

Was the client pleased with the photos we took?
(A) On the company website.
(B) I haven't spoken to her.*
(C) A new set of cameras.

客戶對我們拍的照片滿意嗎？
(A) 在公司的網站上。
(B) 我還沒機會和她說話。
(C) 一組新相機。

本題為一般問句，詢問「客戶是否滿意」，(B) 回答「尚未和她說到話」表示不太清楚，與題目句構成完整對話。(C) 使用了 cameras，使人容易與題目句中的 photos 聯想在一起，造成混淆，並非正解。

28

Who is checking the financial figures?
(A) Early next Monday morning.
(B) At least three charts, I'm sure.
(C) All of the team members, actually.*

誰在核對財務數字？
(A) 下星期一一大早。
(B) 我確定，至少有三張圖表。
(C) 實際上是整個團隊。

本題使用以 Who 開頭的問句，詢問「要由誰來確認」，(C) 回覆「全體團隊成員」，為正確答案。在 PART 3 或 PART 4 中，當選項中出現 actually 時，通常會是答案；在 PART 2 中，亦是如此。

29

Did you attend the ice sculpture show downtown?
(A) They're still in the museum.
(B) I don't really enjoy the cold.*
(C) What time will you go?

你參觀過市區的冰雕展了嗎？
(A) 他們還在博物館裡。
(B) 我不是很喜歡寒冷。
(C) 你何時要去？

本題詢問「是否參加過活動」，(B) 回覆「不太喜歡」，表示不太想去，與題目句構成完整對話。最近在 PART 2 中，答案常是拒絕或是表示不太願意的回覆。

• **attend** 參加、出席　**sculpture** 雕像

30

Can you help me with this new software?
(A) How long have we been waiting for it?
(B) The program is called "Easy Accounting."
(C) Bill was the one who installed it.*

你可以幫我看這個新軟體嗎？
(A) 我們已經等多久了？
(B) 這個軟體叫「輕鬆搞定會計」。
(C) 那是比爾安裝的。

「Can you . . . ?」用來請求對方「可以……嗎？」。本題以此詢問對方「可以教我怎麼使用新軟體嗎」。(C) 態度有點冷淡地表示「可以請負責安裝的 Bill 協助」，為最適當的答覆。

- **accounting** 會計　**install** 安裝

31

Do you think these sausages have gone bad?
(A) Check the date on the package.*
(B) From the butcher next door.
(C) I prefer bacon and eggs.

你覺得，這些香腸已經壞了嗎？
(A) 查看包裝上的日期。
(B) 向隔壁的肉販買的。
(C) 我比較喜歡培根和蛋。

本題詢問的是「香腸是否壞掉了」，(A) 請對方「確認一下日期吧」，與題目句構成完整對話。最新的考題中，答案大多為「我不知道、請問問看其他人、你自己確認一下」等較為事不關己的回覆。其他的選項中，僅使用了與 sausages 相關的單字（butcher, bacon, eggs），使人混淆，內容皆不符合文意。

- **butcher** 肉店老板、屠夫　**prefer** 更喜歡

PART 3 23

Questions 32–34 refer to the following conversation.

M	Hi, [32] I got an e-mail about a big sale happening at this outlet this week. The sale starts today, right? Does it apply to the leather winter jackets?	男	嗨，[32] 我收到一封電子郵件，說這家暢貨中心本週有大拍賣。拍賣是從今天開始，對嗎？包含冬季的皮外套嗎？
W	Yes, of course. Everything in the store is 50% off the tag price. [33] Did you bring the coupon included in the e-mail for an additional 10% off for members?	女	是的，當然。店裡所有商品，都照標價打對折。[33] 您帶了電子郵件所附的優惠券嗎？會員憑券可以再打九折。
M	No, my home printer ran out of ink. [34] I'll print it at the office and then come back in the evening. I'm hoping to get all my winter clothes shopping done today.	男	沒有，我家裡的印表機沒有墨水了。[34] 我會到辦公室列印，傍晚再帶過來。我希望今天可以把冬裝買齊。

• outlet 暢貨中心　apply to 適用於　leather 皮革　tag 標籤　additional 額外的　run out of 用完、耗盡

32

Why did the man choose to shop at the store?

(A) The store is next to his home.
(B) He received an e-mail notification.*
(C) His friend recommended the store.
(D) The store's selection is very large.

男子為何選擇到這家店購物？

(A) 這家店在他家隔壁。
(B) 他收到電子郵件發送的通知。
(C) 他的朋友推薦這家店。
(D) 這家店的選擇非常多元。

對話第一段，男子說道：「I got an email about a big sale happening at this outlet this week.」，表示收到了通知優惠活動的電子郵件，因此答案為 (B)。

• notification 通知　recommend 推薦　selection 選擇

33

What does the woman ask for?

(A) A credit card number　(B) A purchase receipt
(C) A membership card　(D) A discount voucher*

女子要求何物？

(A) 信用卡卡號。　(B) 購物收據。
(C) 會員卡。　(D) 折扣優惠券。

請仔細聆聽女子所說的話。女子詢問男子是否把電子郵件中所附的優惠券帶來（Did you bring the coupon included in the e-mail for an additional 10% off for members?），因此 (D) 為最適當的答案。

答案改寫 coupon → voucher

• purchase 購買　receipt 收據　voucher 票券

34

Why does the man say he will return at a later time?

(A) He left his wallet at the office.
(B) He wants to bring his wife.
(C) He needs to print something.*
(D) He has an urgent meeting.

男子為何說他稍晚再來？

(A) 他把皮夾留在辦公室沒帶。
(B) 他想帶他太太來。
(C) 他需要列印東西。
(D) 他有緊急會議要開。

針對女子詢問是否有帶優惠券，男子表示要先回辦公室印出優惠券後，晚上再來一趟（I'll print it at the office and then come back in the evening.），因此答案為 (C)。

• leave 留下、遺忘　wallet 皮夾、錢包　urgent 緊急的、急迫的

Questions 35–37 refer to the following conversation.

W	Hi, Mr. Witz. [35] I'm wondering if these blankets can be dry-cleaned. I spilled grape juice on them and I'm afraid I won't be able to remove the stains myself.	女	嗨，魏茲先生。[35] 我不知道這些毯子能不能乾洗。我把葡萄汁灑在上面了，我擔心光靠自己沒辦法把汙漬去掉。
M	It shouldn't be too hard to get them out. They'll be ready for pick up on Friday. Oh, and the dress you dropped off yesterday will be done that day as well.	男	要去除汙漬應該不會太難。毯子星期五就可以來拿。喔，還有，您昨天送來的洋裝，那天也會洗好。
W	I see. Actually, [36] I was planning on wearing that dress to a work dinner on Wednesday. Is it possible you could have it cleaned by then?	女	了解。其實 [36] 我原本打算星期三要穿那件洋裝去應酬晚餐。你有可能在那之前把它洗好嗎？
M	That's perfectly fine. [37] I'll have the staff get to work on it today, so you can pick it up Wednesday morning.	男	完全沒問題。[37] 我會請員工今天就做，這樣您星期三早上就可以來拿。

• **blanket** 毛毯、毯子 **spill** （使）灑出、（使）濺出 **remove** 去掉、脫掉 **stain** 汙點、缺跡 **hard** 困難的、費力的 **drop off** 遞送、留下 **actually** 實際上 **possible** 可能的 **perfectly** 完全地、絕對地

35

Where is this conversation most likely taking place?
(A) At a fabric store
(B) At a supermarket
(C) At a restaurant
(D) At a dry cleaner*

這段對話最可能發生在哪裡？
(A) 布料行。
(B) 超級市場。
(C) 餐廳。
(D) 乾洗店。

本題詢問對話所在的地點，屬於難度較高的題目。對話第一段，女子説道：「I'm wondering if these blankets can be dry-cleaned.」，由此推測答案應為 (D)。

• **fabric** 布料、織品

36

What is the woman doing on Wednesday?
(A) Traveling out of town
(B) Attending a company event*
(C) Making a presentation
(D) Going to a conference

女子星期三有何事？
(A) 出城去外地。
(B) 參加公司的活動。
(C) 做簡報。
(D) 去研討會。

在對話中，可以聽到題目當中的時間副詞。請仔細聆聽女子所説的話，並特別留意 Wednesday（星期三）。對話第二段，女子説道：「I was planning on wearing that dress to a work dinner on Wednesday.」，表示打算在應酬餐會時穿，因此答案為 (B)。

答案改寫 work dinner → company event

• **attend** 出席、參加

37

What does the man offer to do?
(A) Refund a service
(B) Replace an item
(C) Rush an order*
(D) Rent out a garment

男子提議何事？
(A) 退還某項服務的費用。
(B) 更換一項物品。
(C) 趕一個訂單。
(D) 出租一件衣服。

原本男子請女子週五來領取衣物，但在對話最後一段，出於女子的要求，男子表示會請員工盡快完成，以便她可以在週三上午領取（I'll have the staff get to work on it today, so you can pick it up Wednesday morning.）。因此 (C) 為最適當的答案。

- **refund** 退款、退還 **replace** 更換、代替 **item** 一件物品 **rush** 匆忙地做 **rent out** 出租 **garment** （一件）衣服

Questions 38–40 refer to the following conversation.

M	Hello, this is Mark calling from Direct Car Rentals. [38] My coworker and I are scheduled to come to your workplace to pick up the car you rented. However, we're running late, because traffic is really bad. We won't get there until after 7 P.M.	男	哈囉，我是汽車直租公司的馬克。[38] 我和同事排定要到貴公司取回您租的車。不過，因為交通狀況實在很糟，我們會晚一點到。晚上七點以後才會到。
W	Okay, thanks for notifying me. I usually leave at 6:30, but [39] I can leave the keys with the security guard.	女	好，謝謝你通知我。我通常六點半下班，不過，[39] 我可以把鑰匙留給警衛。
M	That sounds great. [40] I also have your updated membership forms I was going to give you. Should I give them to the security guard?	男	聽起來很不錯。[40] 我還帶了您最新的會員表要給您。我該交給警衛嗎？
W	You can just slip them into my mailbox next to the entrance. It's box number 101A.	女	你可以直接把它投進我的信箱，就在入口旁邊，號碼是 101A。

- **rental** 租賃、出租 **coworker** 同事 **be scheduled to** 安排、排定 **workplace** 工作場所 **rent** 租用 **notify** 通知、告知 **leave** 離開（某處） **security** 安全 **form** 表格 **slip** 塞入 **entrance** 入口

38

Why will the man visit the woman's office?
(A) To deliver an invoice
(B) To apply for a job
(C) To install some equipment
(D) To pick up a vehicle*

男子為何造訪女子的辦公室？
(A) 為了送一張發票。
(B) 為了應徵工作。
(C) 為了安裝某個設備。
(D) 為了取一輛車。

請仔細聆聽男子所說的話，並特別留意「拜訪的目的」。對話第一段，男子說道：「My coworker and I are scheduled to come to your workplace to pick up the car you rented.」，表示已經排定要去取回對方所租用的車，因此答案為 (D)。

答案改寫 car → vehicle

- **deliver** 投遞、運送 **invoice** 發票、發貨單 **apply for** 申請、應徵 **install** 安裝 **equipment** 設備 **vehicle** 車輛

39

What does the woman say she will do?
(A) Wait for a worker to arrive
(B) Give a key to an employee*
(C) Pay for a service online
(D) Use a discount coupon

女子說她會做何事？
(A) 等一位同事到來。
(B) 把鑰匙交給一位員工。
(C) 在線上支付服務費用。
(D) 使用折扣優惠券。

本題詢問女子所說的話，因此請務必仔細聆聽女子說話的內容，並在當中找尋答案。對話第一段，女子說道：「I can leave the keys with the security guard.」，表示會把鑰匙留給警衛，由此確認答案為 (B)。

答案改寫 leave → give
security guard → employee

• **arrive** 到達、到來　**pay for** 支付……的費用

40

What does the woman ask the man to put in her mailbox?
(A) Some client paperwork*
(B) A tax receipt
(C) A user's manual
(D) Some promotional vouchers

女子要求男子把什麼放進她的信箱？
(A) 一些客戶文件。
(B) 稅賦憑證。
(C) 使用手冊。
(D) 一些優惠券。

對話後半部，男子提到要順便將會員資料轉交給女子（I also have your updated membership forms），女子請男子將資料放在信箱內，因此 (A) 為最適當的答案。本題需要綜合兩人所說的內容，才能順利解題。考題裡，有時會出現這類較為棘手的題型。

答案改寫 form → paperwork

• **paperwork** 資料　**manual** 使用手冊　**promotional** 促銷的

Questions 41–43 refer to the following conversation with three speakers.

M1 Hello, welcome to Paper and Things. What can I do for you today?

W Hi, [41] I can't seem to find any folders. I'm looking for some plastic A4 size folders that will hold a few sheets of paper. I'm preparing some training materials for my new interns.

M1 Well, I'm sure we sell those, but they might be out of stock. I'll ask my coworker. Hey, Tim! [42] Do we have clear A4 size folders in stock?

M2 Yeah, but [42] they're in boxes in the stock room. I can go get you some. How many do you need?

W Fifteen. Also, do you know if there's a print shop nearby? I'd like to get these training booklets printed today.

M2 [43] We run a print shop here as well. Just head to the back of the store after I give you your folders and place your order at the counter.

W How convenient. Thank you.

男 1 哈囉，歡迎光臨「紙與用品」。您今天需要什麼服務？

女 嗨，[41] 我似乎找不到任何資料夾。我在找 A4 大小的塑膠資料夾，可以裝好幾張紙的那種。我在準備訓練教材給新來的實習生。

男 1 嗯，我確定我們有賣，但可能缺貨。我問一下同事。嘿，提姆！[42] 我們的透明 A4 大小資料夾還有嗎？

男 2 有，但是 [42] 在倉庫的箱子裡。我可以去幫你拿一些。你需要多少？

女 15 個。還有，你知道附近有沒有影印店嗎？我想要今天就把這些訓練手冊印出來。

男 2 [43] 我們這裡也有影印服務。等我把資料夾給您後，您只要走到店後方，把訂單放在櫃台上就可以。

女 真方便，謝謝你。

- **prepare** 準備 **training** 訓練 **material** 材料、資料 **out of stock** 無庫存、售完 **in stock** 有存貨 **stock** 存貨、庫存品 **head** （向特定方向）出發 **place an order** 下訂單 **convenient** 方便的、便利的

41

What is the woman shopping for?
(A) Books
(B) Printer ink
(C) Paper
(D) Folders*

女子要買什麼？
(A) 書。
(B) 印表機墨水。
(C) 紙。
(D) 資料夾。

對話第一段，女子說道：「I can't seem to find any folders.」，表示找不到資料夾，由此確認答案為 (D)。

42

What does Tim say about some items?
(A) They are still in storage.*
(B) They are out of stock.
(C) They are available at another store.
(D) They are currently on sale.

關於某些物品，提姆說了什麼？
(A) 它們仍有存貨。
(B) 它們缺貨。
(C) 另一家店還有。
(D) 它們目前在促銷。

聆聽時，請特別留意關鍵人名 Tim。對話中間，男子請提姆確認資料夾的庫存量（Do we have clear A4 size folders in stock?）。提姆表示保管在倉庫的箱子裡（they're in boxes in the stock room），因此答案為 (A)。

答案改寫 stock room → storage

- **available** 可買到的

43

What additional service does Tim mention?
(A) Free shipping
(B) In-store printing*
(C) Discounted membership
(D) Free book binding

提姆提到什麼額外的服務？
(A) 免費運送。
(B) 店內列印。
(C) 會費打折。
(D) 書籍免費裝訂。

聆聽時，請特別留意「額外提供的服務」。對話後半部，尋找資料夾的女子詢問附近是否有影印店。男子回覆可以在他們店內影印（We run a print shop here as well.），因此答案為 (B)。

- **free** 免費的 **shipping** 運輸、貨運 **binding** （書籍的）裝訂

Questions 44–46 refer to the following conversation.

W I just got a call from the Birch Hotel. [44] We booked their banquet room for our upcoming fundraiser, but [45] it seems the room has some electrical problems that cannot be fixed in time. Unfortunately, we won't be able to hold the event there.

M Really? That's too bad. Well, we should try to find an alternate location as soon as possible. The invitations are going to be printed early next week.

W Can you research some possible locations and call them about prices and availability?

M Actually, I think I have the perfect place—the new Fort Albert Hotel downtown. It's a brand new hotel and the architecture is stunning. Plus, it has multiple banquet rooms, so there will probably be something available when we need it. [46] I'll look up the number now.

女 我剛接到樺木飯店打來的電話。[44] 我們訂了他們的宴會廳來舉辦即將到來的募款活動，但 [45] 宴會廳的電路似乎出了問題，無法及時修好。很不幸，我們無法在那裡舉行活動。

男 真的嗎？真是太糟糕了。這樣的話，我們應該盡快找到替換的地點。邀請函下星期初就會印好。

女 你可不可以研究一下可能的地點，然後打電話問價格和是否接受預訂？

男 其實，我想，有個理想的地點——市區新開的艾伯特堡飯店。那是間全新的飯店，建築樣式迷人至極。不只如此，它有好幾間宴會廳，因此，在我們需要的時段，可能還有空房間。[46] 我現在查電話號碼。

- **book** 預訂 **banquet** 宴會 **upcoming** 即將來臨的 **fundraiser** 募款活動 **electrical** 電的、與電有關的 **fix** 修理 **alternate** 替代的 **location** 位置、場所 **invitation** 邀請、請帖 **availability** 有空與否 **architecture** 建築式樣、建築風格 **stunning** 極漂亮的、極迷人的 **multiple** 多個的 **probably** 很可能

44

What are the speakers organizing?
(A) A company trip
(B) A holiday event
(C) An awards dinner
(D) A fundraiser*

說話者在籌備何事？
(A) 公司旅遊。
(B) 假期的活動。
(C) 頒獎晚宴。
(D) 募款活動。

對話第一段，女子說道：「We booked their banquet room for our upcoming fundraiser」，由此確認答案為 (D)。

- **organize** 安排、籌畫

45

What problem does the woman mention?
(A) A hotel is in need of repair.*
(B) A reservation was lost.
(C) Some invitations were misplaced.
(D) Some customers complained.

女子提及什麼問題？
(A) 飯店需要整修。
(B) 預訂資料遺失。
(C) 有些邀請函放錯地方。
(D) 有些顧客抱怨。

當題目詢問 problem 時，請先標示出各選項的重點單字（例如：repair, reservation, invitations, complained），再來聆聽對話內容。對話第一段，女子提到電力問題發生後，似乎未能及時處理完畢 (it seems the room has some electrical problems that cannot be fixed in time)。在聽到 fix 後，即可找到 repair 所在的選項，因此答案為 (A)。

答案改寫 fix → repair

• **in need of** 需要、急需 **repair** 修理 **reservation** 預訂 **lose** 遺失、失去 **complain** 抱怨

46

What most likely will the man do next?
(A) Cancel an event
(B) Visit a hotel
(C) Find a contact number*
(D) Make a reservation

男子接下來最可能做何事？
(A) 取消一個活動。
(B) 造訪一家飯店。
(C) 找到聯絡電話號碼。
(D) 預訂。

當題目詢問「. . . do next?」時，在對話後半部，會出現解題的關鍵線索。對話最後一段，男子說道：「I'll look up the number now.」，表示要找一下電話號碼，因此 (C) 為最適當的答案。

答案改寫 look up → find

• **cancel** 取消 **contact** 聯絡、接觸

Questions 47–49 refer to the following conversation.

W Hi, Pierre. Have you checked out the new timetable for next month? [47] I put you on the schedule to teach two sculpture classes in the afternoon.	女 嗨，畢耶。你看過下個月的新課表了嗎？[47] 我幫你排了兩堂下午的雕塑課。
M Oh, hmmm. Do these classes need to be back-to-back?	男 噢，嗯……這些課必須連著上嗎？
W Why? Will that be a problem?	女 怎麼了？會有問題嗎？
M Well, sculpture classes can be quite messy. It takes about 15 to 20 minutes to clean up after, but with only a five-minute break, it would probably be impossible.	男 嗯，雕塑教室可能會弄得很亂。下課後，要花將近 15 到 20 分鐘清理，但下課時間只有五分鐘，很可能無法清理完畢。
W Ah. [48] I see your point. [49] What if we hold the next class in another room? We have two more classrooms available at that time.	女 啊，[48] 我懂你的意思。[49] 如果我們把第二堂課換到另一間教室呢？那個時段，我們還有兩間教室空著。

• **timetable** 時刻表、課程表 **sculpture** 雕塑術、雕塑品 **back-to-back** 緊接著 **quite** 相當 **messy** 混亂的、雜亂 **probably** 很可能 **impossible** 不可能 **available** 可用的

47

Where most likely do the speakers work? 說話者最可能在哪裡工作？

(A) A dance academy (A) 舞團。
(B) An art school* (B) 藝術學校。
(C) A paint supply shop (C) 美術用品店。
(D) A restaurant (D) 餐廳。

對話開頭為與「雕刻」課程時間表相關的內容（I put you on the schedule to teach two sculpture classes in the afternoon.），因此答案為 (B)。

• **supply** 供給、補給品

48

What does the woman imply when she says, "Will that be a problem"? 當女子說「會有問題嗎」，意指什麼？

(A) She disagrees with the man's statement. (A) 她不同意男子的說法。
(B) She does not want to edit a schedule. (B) 她不想修訂課表。
(C) She wants to know what she has overlooked.* (C) 她想知道哪裡疏忽了。
(D) She is eager to take the man's class. (D) 她渴望接男子的課。

本題為掌握意圖的題型，必須先理解題目句前後文意，才能順利解題。題目句後方，男子進一步說明，之後女子才回覆「我明白你的意思了（I see your point.）」，因此 (C) 為最適當的答案。

• **disagree** 不同意、不符 **statement** 陳述 **edit** 修訂、編輯 **overlook** 忽略、沒注意到 **eager** 渴望的、急切的

49

What does the woman offer to do? 女子提議為何？

(A) Change a classroom* (A) 換教室。
(B) Hire a cleaner (B) 僱一個清潔工。
(C) Recruit some students (C) 招收一些學生。
(D) Pay for art supplies (D) 付錢買美術用品。

對話最後一段，女子說道：「What if we hold the next class in another room?」，詢問下一堂課是否要換到其他教室，因此答案為 (A)。

• **change** 改變、更改 **hire** 僱用 **recruit** 吸收（新成員）

Questions 50–52 refer to the following conversation.

W	Maxwell, [50] I need the results of the e-survey we conducted for the marketing presentation next Monday. Have you downloaded all the results yet?	女	麥斯威爾，[50] 我需要我們線上調查的結果，下星期一的簡報要用。你下載所有結果了嗎？
M	I'm having trouble getting them. [51] The survey company website is down. I'm waiting for a call back from them. When do you need the results by?	男	我下載時遇到困難。[51] 民調公司的網站掛點。我在等他們回我電話。你什麼時間以前需要這些結果？
W	By tomorrow morning at the latest. [52] I have to print a report of the figures on Friday, so I'd like to get all the design work done by Thursday night.	女	最晚明天早上。[52] 我必須在星期五印出一份這些數字的報告，所以，我希望所有的版面設計在星期四晚上之前完成。

• **result** 結果、成果 **survey** 調查 **conduct** 實施 **have trouble (+V–ing)** 做某事有困難 **figure** 數字

50

What are the speakers discussing?
(A) Preparing for a presentation*
(B) Building a new website
(C) Submitting a budget review
(D) Hiring a new advertiser

說話者在討論何事？
(A) 準備簡報。
(B) 建立新的網站。
(C) 提出預算審核。
(D) 僱請新的廣告公司。

在對話前半部，通常可以找到與對話主旨相關的線索。對話第一段，女子說道：「I need the results of the e-survey we conducted for the marketing presentation next Monday.」，提到「下週有行銷簡報」，因此 (A) 為最適當的答案。

• **submit** 提出、呈遞　**budget** 預算

51

Why was the man unable to complete a task?
(A) A meeting lasted all day.
(B) A website was not working.*
(C) Some files went missing.
(D) Some fees were not paid.

男子為何無法完成任務？
(A) 會議開了一整天。
(B) 網站無法運作。
(C) 有些檔案遺失了。
(D) 有些費用未付。

對話第一段，男子表示網站有點問題，無法下載結果（The survey company website is down.），因此答案為 (B)。

答案改寫 down → not working

• **last** 持續　**missing** 遺失的、缺少的　**fee** 費用

52

What does the woman say she will do on Friday?
(A) Meet with a client
(B) Give a presentation
(C) Design a brochure
(D) Print a document*

女子說，她星期五要做何事？
(A) 和客戶見面。
(B) 發表簡報。
(C) 設計宣傳手冊。
(D) 列印文件。

對話中會提到 Friday（星期五），請仔細聆聽女子所說的話。對話最後一段，女子說道：「I have to print a report of the figures on Friday.」，由此確認答案為 (D)。

答案改寫 report → document

Questions 53–55 refer to the following conversation with three speakers.

M1	Hello, I'm Mitch Holland. I called yesterday about a repair quote for the damage done to my vehicle. [53] I need it to file my insurance claim.	男 1	哈囉，我是米契·霍蘭德。我昨天打過電話來要我車子受損修理費的報價。[53] 我需要報價單申請保險理賠。
W	Okay, sure. Who did you speak with yesterday?	女	好的，當然。您昨天和誰通電話？
M1	The mechanic's name was Kevin Rogers.	男 1	技工的名字是凱文·羅傑斯。
W	Okay, yes, [54] I think Kevin completed the quote yesterday. Just a moment. Kevin?	女	好，有的，[54] 我想凱文昨天就完成報價了。請稍等一下。凱文？
M2	Yes, what is it?	男 2	是，有什麼事？
W	Did you finish the quote for Mr. Holland? I can't seem to find it.	女	你完成霍蘭德先生的報價單了嗎？我似乎找不到。
M2	Yes, it's on your computer. [55] I just need you to print it out.	男 2	有，在妳的電腦裡。[55] 只是需要妳把它印出來。
W	No problem.	女	沒問題。

• **repair** 修理、修補 **quote** 報價 **damage** 損害、毀壞 **vehicle** 車輛 **insurance** 保險 **claim** （對保險公司的）索賠 **mechanic** 技工 **complete** 完成

53

What is Mr. Holland planning to do?
霍蘭德先生計劃做何事？

(A) Purchase a new car　(A) 買一輛新車。
(B) Make an insurance claim*　(B) 申請保險理賠。
(C) Apply for a license　(C) 申請執照。
(D) Rent a vehicle　(D) 租一輛車。

聆聽時，請特別留意關鍵人名。對話第一段，男子在介紹完自己的姓名後，向對方要求報價單，並補充說明為申請保險理賠所需（I need it to file my insurance claim.），因此答案為 (B)。

答案改寫 file a claim → make a claim

• **purchase** 購買 **apply for** 申請 **rent** 租用

54

According to the conversation, what did Kevin do yesterday?
根據這段對話，凱文昨天做了何事？

(A) He had a car towed.　(A) 他叫人來把車拖走。
(B) He ordered some new parts.　(B) 他訂購了一些新零件。
(C) He prepared a price quote.*　(C) 他做了一份報價單。
(D) He witnessed a car accident.　(D) 他目擊一場車輛。

聆聽時，請特別留意關鍵時間點 yesterday（昨天）。對話中間，女子說道：「I think Kevin completed the quote yesterday.」，表示已經完成報價單，因此 (C) 為最適當的答案。

• **tow** 拖、拉 **order** 訂購 **part** 零件 **prepare** 製作、準備 **witness** 目擊 **accident** 意外事故

55

What does Kevin ask the woman to do?
(A) Process a payment
(B) Call an insurance company
(C) Fill out a form
(D) Print a document*

凱文要求女子何事？
(A) 處理一筆款項。
(B) 打電話給保險公司。
(C) 填寫一份表格。
(D) 列印一份文件。

聆聽對話時，請務必掌握解題關鍵為「女子將要做的事情」。對話後半段，男子表示女子要印出報價單（I just need you to print it out.），因此答案為 (D)。

- **process** 處理　**payment** 支付的款項　**fill out** 填寫　**form** 表格

Questions 56–58 refer to the following conversation.

M Hi, I purchased some new boots from your online store on December 2 during your half-price event. [56] I just got them now, but the invoice says I was charged full price.	男 嗨，我在12月2日半價活動期間，在你們的網路商店買了幾雙新靴子。[56] 我現在剛收到貨，但發票上說，要收我全額。
W I'm sorry to hear that. [57] It seems there was an error on our website that day. Several customers reported the same problem.	女 很遺憾聽到這事。[57] 看來好像那天我們的網站出了錯。好幾位顧客都遇到同樣的問題。
M Oh, that's too bad.	男 喔，那太糟了。
W Yes, we're planning to refund the extra cost, but since I have you on the line, I can do that directly right now.	女 是啊，我們打算退回多收的費用，但既然您在線上，我可以現在直接幫您處理。
M I'd appreciate that. Thank you.	男 太感謝了。
W You're welcome. [58] I also noticed your membership is about to expire. Would you like to renew it now?	女 不客氣。[58] 我還注意到，您的會員資格快到期了。您要現在更新嗎？
M Sure. That's a good idea.	男 當然，真是個好主意。

- **invoice** 發票、發貨單　**charge** 收費、索價　**several** 一些、幾個　**refund** 退還　**extra** 額外的　**cost** 費用　**directly** 直接地　**appreciate** 感謝、感激　**notice** 注意、察覺　**expire** 屆期、終止　**renew** 使更新

56

Why is the man calling?
(A) He received the wrong order.
(B) He wants to return an item.
(C) He would like to visit the store.
(D) He was charged too much for an item.*

男子為何打電話？
(A) 他收到的貨品是錯的。
(B) 他想退一件貨品。
(C) 他想造訪這家店。
(D) 他有件貨品被收了太多費用。

在對話前半部，通常可以確認與打電話目的相關的關鍵線索。對話第一段，男子說道：「I just got them now, but the invoice says that I was charged full price.」，表示購買了半價的特價商品，卻被要求支付全額，因此 (D) 為最適當的答案。

答案改寫 full price → too much

- **order** 所訂的貨　**item** 物品

57

What does the woman explain?

(A) A technical malfunction*　(B) A discount policy
(C) A delivery failure　(D) A change in supplier

女子作何解釋？

(A) 技術性故障。　(B) 折扣政策。
(C) 運送失敗。　(D) 更換供應商。

請仔細聆聽女子所說的話。對話第一段，女子說道：「It seems there was an error on our website that day.」，解釋說明當天網站出了點問題，由此確認答案為 (A)。

答案改寫 error → malfunction

- **technical** 技術的　**malfunction** 發生故障　**policy** 政策　**delivery** 運送、投遞　**failure** 失敗　**supplier** 供應商

58

What does the woman ask the man to do?

(A) Send an order back　(B) Locate an invoice
(C) Renew a membership*　(D) Describe an item

女子要求男子何事？

(A) 把訂的貨送回去。　(B) 找出發票。
(C) 更新會員資格。　(D) 描述一項物品。

對話後半部，女子提到男子的會員資格即將到期（I also noticed your membership is about to expire），詢問男子是否需要更新（Would you like to renew it now?）。因此答案為 (C)。在此補充，對話中大多會以恭敬口吻的祈使句，或是表示建議的句型，來表達「要求」，請務必熟記。

- **locate** 找出、確定……的地點　**describe** 描述

Questions 59–61 refer to the following conversation.

W Hi, Max. This is Tracy. [59] I'm downstairs trying to park in the parking garage, but I forgot my pass in my office last night, so I can't open the gates to get in.	**女** 嗨，麥克斯，我是崔西。[59] 我在樓下，想把車停進停車場，但我昨天晚上把停車證忘在辦公室沒帶，所以，我沒辦法開啟柵欄進去。
M Oh, sorry to hear that. Can you ask the parking attendant to let you in?	**男** 喔，很遺憾聽到這事。妳可以請停車場管理員放妳進去嗎？
W He's not at his desk right now. I've been waiting for ten minutes but he hasn't come back. [60] Would you be able to bring my pass down to me? It's on my desk next to my computer.	**女** 他現在不在位子上。我已經等了十分鐘，但他還沒回來。[60] 你可以把我的停車證拿下來給我嗎？在我桌上，電腦的旁邊。
M I'm just heading into a meeting. [61] I'll send Patty down with your pass in just a moment.	**男** 我正要去開會。[61] 我馬上派佩蒂拿妳的停車證下去。
W Okay, thanks for your help!	**女** 好的，謝謝你的幫忙！

- **parking garage** 停車場　**attendant** 服務員　**head** 朝特定方向前進

59

Where most likely is the woman?

(A) At a parking entrance*　(B) On a bus
(C) In an office　(D) In a stairwell

女子最可能在哪裡？

(A) 在停車場入口。　(B) 在公車上。
(C) 在辦公室裡。　(D) 在樓梯間。

對話第一段，女子說道：「I'm downstairs trying to park in the parking garage, but I forgot my pass in my office last night, so I can't open the gates to get in.」，由此推測答案應為 (A)。

- **stairwell** 樓梯間

60

What does the woman ask the man to do?
(A) Call the parking attendant
(B) Deliver a parking pass*
(C) Cancel a meeting
(D) Recommend a venue

女子要求男子何事？
(A) 打電話給停車場管理員。
(B) 送停車證來。
(C) 取消會議。
(D) 推薦一個場地。

請仔細聆聽女子所說的話。對話第二段，女子表示已經等了好一陣子，但管理員還沒回來，詢問對方是否可以幫忙把通行證拿下樓（Would you be able to bring my pass down to me?），因此答案為 (B)。「Would you . . . ?」意思為「可以請你……嗎？」，用來表示請求。

• **deliver** 投遞、運送 **cancel** 取消 **recommend** 推薦 **venue** 舉行地點、會場

61

Why does the man say, "I'm just heading into a meeting"?
(A) To acknowledge a problem
(B) To ask for permission
(C) To suggest an option
(D) To decline a request*

男子為何說「我正要去開會」？
(A) 為了承認有問題。
(B) 為了請求許可。
(C) 為了建議一個選項。
(D) 為了拒絕一個請求。

本題詢問男子的意圖，請仔細聆聽對話，並掌握前後文意。題目句後方接著說道：「I'll send Patty down with your pass in just a moment.」，可以得知男子無法直接答應女子的請求，因此 (D) 為最適當的答案。

• **acknowledge** 承認 **permission** 允許、許可 **suggest** 建議 **option** 選擇、可選擇的東西
decline 婉拒、謝絕 **request** 要求、請求

Questions 62–64 refer to the following conversation and seat map.

=========== Front ===========

Aisle	63 seat 25C	seat 25D	Window
	seat 26C	seat 26D	

=========== 前面 ===========

走道	63 座位 25C	座位 25D	窗戶
	座位 26C	座位 26D	

W Excuse me. 62 Sorry, but I think you might be in my seat. 63 The flight attendant said I'm in seat C next to the aisle.
M Oh, really? I was pretty sure this was my seat. 62 Let's compare our boarding passes. Oh . . . I see the mistake. 63 I should be in seat 26C. Sorry about that. I'll move to the back now.
W Oh, that's okay. If you'd like to sit here, I could take your seat. Actually, my friend will be sitting in that row, so it would be better for us to sit together during the flight.
M Okay, that sounds good.
W Great, thanks. 64 I'll go let the flight attendant know about the change now.

女 不好意思，62 抱歉打擾了，但我想你可能坐到我的位子了。63 空服員說，我的位子是靠走道的 C。
男 噢，真的嗎？我很確定，這是我的位子。62 那我們來比對一下各自的登機證。噢，我發現問題出在哪了。63 我應該坐 26C。抱歉，我現在就移到後面那排。
女 噢，沒關係。如果你想坐這裡，我可以坐你的位子。其實，我朋友會坐在那一排，所以，飛航途中，我們坐在一起會更好。
男 好的，聽起來不錯。
女 太好了，謝謝。64 我去告訴空服員換位子的事。

• seat 座位　aisle 走道、通道　flight 飛行、搭機旅行　flight attendant 空服員　pretty 相當、非常　compare 比較、對照　boarding 登機、登船　row （一排）座位

62

What is the purpose of the conversation?
(A) To determine a cost
(B) To request a service
(C) To correct a mistake*
(D) To explain a process

這段對話的目的為何？
(A) 決定費用。
(B) 要求服務。
(C) 改正錯誤。
(D) 解釋流程。

對話第一段，女子向男子表示對方好像坐錯了位置（Sorry, but I think you might be in my seat.）。男子表示不太可能，建議雙方都出示自己的登機證（Let's compare our boarding passes.）。因此 (C) 為最適當的答案。

• correct 改正、糾正　determine 決定、確定

63

Look at the graphic. Which seat was the woman originally assigned to?
(A) 25C*
(B) 25D
(C) 26C
(D) 26D

請見圖表。女子原先分配到的是哪個位子？
(A) 25C。
(B) 25D。
(C) 26C。
(D) 26D。

首先請先在對話中找出有關「女子的座位資訊」。對話第一段，女子表示自己的座位在 C 靠走道（The flight attendant said I'm in seat C next to the aisle.）。在後面對話中，男子解釋自己的座位應該在 26C（I should be in seat 26C.）。根據兩人提供的資訊，對照座位表內容後，可以得知女子的座位靠走道在 25C，因此答案為 (A)。

• assign 分配、分派

64

What will the woman most likely do next?
(A) File a complaint with the airline
(B) Report a change to the flight staff*
(C) Get off the plane
(D) Request a vegetarian meal

女子接下來最可能做何事？
(A) 向航空公司申訴。
(B) 向機組人員報告換位子一事。
(C) 下飛機。
(D) 要求素食餐。

當題目以「. . . do next?」結尾時，用來詢問對話結束後的狀況，通常在對話後半部，會出現解題的關鍵線索。對話最後一段，女子說道：「I'll go let the flight attendant know about the change now.」，表示會告知空服員更換座位一事，因此答案為 (B)。

答案改寫　attendant → staff
let . . . know → report

• file a complaint 提出申訴　airline 航空公司　vegetarian 素食的　meal 一餐

Questions 65–67 refer to the following conversation and schedule.

Stage	Project Type
1	In-ground swimming pool installation
2	[66] Backyard landscaping and gardens
3	Veranda reconstruction (front and back)
4	Final roof repairs

階段	工程類型
1	地面泳池裝設
2	[66] 後院造景與園藝
3	陽臺重建(前、後)
4	最後的屋頂修補

W Hello, Andrew. [65] How is the construction on the Park Road house coming along?

M Very well. The house interior is in great condition, so we've been able to start on the exterior improvements right away.

W That's good to hear. I'm thinking of listing it for sale at the end of May. A lot of people will be looking for new homes at that time. Do you think your team can finish up by then?

M Let's have a look at the schedule. Well, we've managed to complete the in-ground pool and [66] we're going to start the backyard landscaping in a couple days. I think we'll be able to put the finishing touches on everything else by mid-May.

W That's great. [67] Just make sure to record all your labor hours for our cost analysis. That way, we can determine the price of the home in May.

女 哈囉,安德魯。[65] 公園路的房屋工程進展如何?

男 很順利。屋內的裝潢還很好,所以,我們可以立刻進行外部改善工程。

女 很高興聽到這個消息。我正考慮在五月底把它列入出售名單。到時候會有很多人在找房子。你覺得你的團隊可以在那之前完成嗎?

男 來看一下進度表。嗯,我們已設法完成地面泳池,[66] 過幾天要開始後院造景工程。我想我們可以在五月中以前,完成其他部分的收尾工作。

女 太好了。[67] 你要確定記錄下你們所有的工時,以便我們進行成本分析。那樣的話,我們五月可以決定房價。

- **in-ground** 地面 **installation** 安裝、設置 **backyard** 後院 **landscaping** 造景、景觀美化 **reconstruction** 重建 **construction** 建造、建設 **condition** 情況、狀態 **improvement** 改善 **manage** 設法做到 **labor** 工作、勞動 **cost** 成本 **analysis** 分析 **determine** 決定

65

What most likely is the man's profession?

(A) Interior decorator
(B) Delivery man
(C) Real estate agent
(D) Contractor*

男子的職業最可能為何?

(A) 室內裝潢人員。
(B) 送貨員。
(C) 不動產經紀人。
(D) 承包商。

對話第一段,女子向男子詢問目前的施工狀況如何(How is the construction on the Park Road house coming along?),因此 (D) 為最適當的答案。請特別留意,雖然本題為與男子有關的提問,但解題線索卻在女子所說的話當中。

- **real estate** 不動產、房地產 **contractor** 承包商

66

Look at the graphic. What stage of the improvements will begin in a couple days?

(A) Stage 1
(B) Stage 2*
(C) Stage 3
(D) Stage 4

請見圖表。幾天內會開始哪個階段的改善工程？

(A) 階段 1。
(B) 階段 2。
(C) 階段 3。
(D) 階段 4。

聆聽對話時，請先掌握本題重點為「施工進度」，並特別留意 in a couple days。對話第二段，男子說道：「we're going to start the backyard landscaping in a couple days」，由此得知為「後院造景」。對照表格內容可知，答案為 (B)。

67

What does the woman ask the man to keep?

(A) Receipts of all costs
(B) A list of available homes
(C) A record of time worked*
(D) Photos of his progress

女子要求男子要保留什麼？

(A) 所有費用的收據。
(B) 可買到的房子清單。
(C) 工時紀錄。
(D) 工程進度的照片。

對話最後一段，女子表示務必要好好記錄施工時間，以便進行成本分析（just make sure to record all your labor hours for our cost analysis），因此答案為 (C)。

答案改寫 labor hours → time worked

- receipt 收據　available 可買到的

Questions 68–70 refer to the following conversation and pie chart.

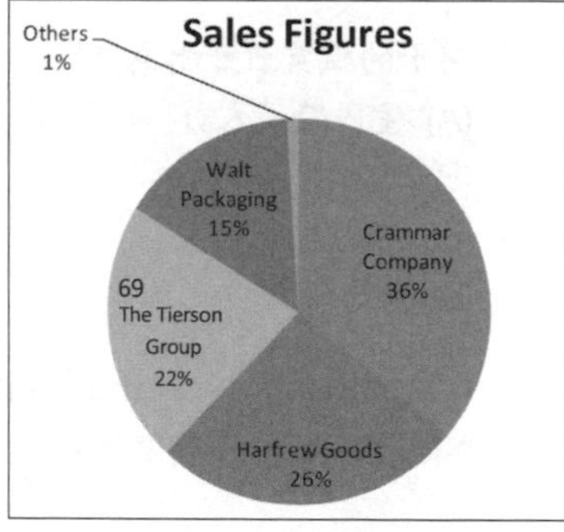

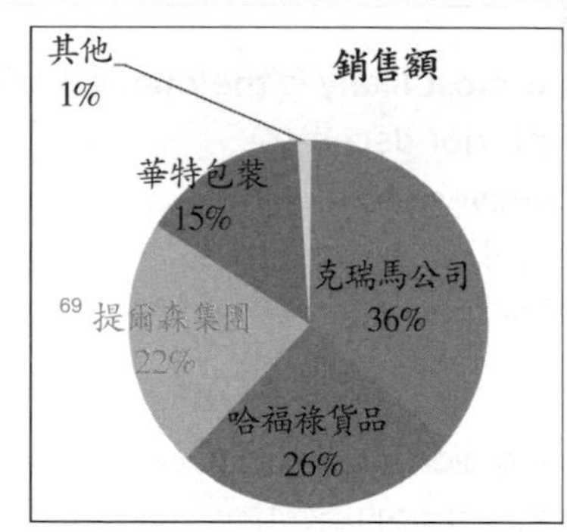

M Hi, Jane. 68 Did you hear the board is thinking of merging with Walt Packaging? I just got the e-mail report. Have you had a chance to look at it?

W No, I've been too busy with conference calls. What did the report say?

M Here, I printed it off. 69 We're already the third largest packaging company in the country, but if we merge with Walt Packaging, that should move us up to first place.

男 嗨，珍。68 妳有沒有聽說，董事會正考慮併購「華特包裝」？我剛收到電子郵件寄來的報告。妳看過了嗎？

女 沒有，我忙著開電話會議。報告上說了什麼？

男 這裡，我印出來了。69 我們已經是國內第三大包裝公司，但如果我們併購「華特包裝」，會讓我們升到第一名。

W Hmm. I'm not sure it would be a smart move, though. [70] Walt Packaging's sales figures for last year look pretty low. They could be even lower this year.

M Yes, but with our company's policies, I think we could increase their sales and maybe even surpass Crammar Company's figures by next year.

女 嗯。不過，我不確定這是不是聰明的一步棋。[70] 華特包裝去年的銷售額看起來相當低。今年甚至可能更低。

男 是的，但有了我們公司的策略，我認為我們可以提升他們的業績，明年甚至有可能超越克瑞馬公司的銷售額。

• goods 商品、貨物 board 董事會 merge 合併 figure 數字、金額、價格 pretty 相當 low 低 increase 增加、增大 surpass 超越、勝過

68

What are the speakers mainly discussing?

(A) A company merger*
(B) A budget report
(C) Department productivity
(D) Hiring a financial analyst

說話者討論的主題為何？

(A) 公司的併購。
(B) 預算報告。
(C) 部門的產能。
(D) 僱用財務分析師。

對話開頭第一句，男子說道：「Did you hear the board is thinking of merging with Walt Packaging?」，提到董事會正在考慮併購「華特包裝」，由此推測答案應為 (A)。在對話前半部，大多會出現與對話主旨有關的關鍵線索。

• budget 預算 department 部門 productivity 生產力 merger （公司等的）合併 hire 僱用 analyst 分析師

69

Look at the graphic. Where do the speakers work?

(A) Walt Packaging
(B) Harfrew Goods
(C) The Tierson Group*
(D) Crammar Company

請見圖表。說話者在哪裡工作？

(A) 華特包裝。
(B) 哈福祿貨品。
(C) 提爾森集團。
(D) 克瑞馬公司。

本題要找出對話者「所屬的公司」。對話第二段，男子提到自己的公司為國內第三大（We're already the third largest packaging company in the country），由此線索可得知答案為 (C)。

70

Why does the woman say she has doubts?

(A) The man did not understand some figures.
(B) A company was excluded from a report.
(C) Her company is located in another state.
(D) A company has not made many sales.*

女子為何說她有疑慮？

(A) 男子不了解一些數字。
(B) 報告不包括某家公司。
(C) 她的公司位在另一個州。
(D) 有家公司的銷售額並不高。

請特別留意女子所說的話，並找出她「感到不安」的原因。對話後半段，女子說道：「Walt Packaging's sales figures for last year look pretty low.」，表示銷售額十分低靡。因此 (D) 為最適當的答案。

• exclude 不包括、把……排除在外

PART 4 24

Questions 71–73 refer to the following advertisement.

W Do you have an old leather jacket or coat you don't wear anymore? Why not call New Again Leather? [71] We'll arrange to pick up your used leather clothes and recycle them. When you call, inquire about our Trade-In Program. [72] By signing up for a membership, you can get a discount on the purchase of recycled clothing items of your choice. [73] For more details or to schedule a pick-up, call 800-555-2222.	女 您有再也不穿的皮夾克或皮外套嗎？何不打電話給「重新皮件」？[71] 我們會安排人手去取您的舊皮衣，回收再利用。當您打電話來，請詢問我們的舊衣換現金活動。[72] 註冊加入會員後，您可以在購買所選的二手衣物時，享有折扣優惠。[73] 更多詳情或安排取件，請電洽 800-555-2222。

• leather 皮革、皮革製品　arrange 安排　inquire 詢問　trade-in 以舊折價換新　sign up for 註冊參加　purchase 購買

71

What service is being advertised? 廣告中是何種服務？

(A) Dry cleaning　(A) 乾洗。
(B) Furniture delivery　(B) 家具運送。
(C) A clothing recycling program*　(C) 衣物回收活動。
(D) A cooking course　(D) 烹飪課程。

本題詢問的是廣告的主題，請透過幾個單字找出答案。「如果有以後不會再穿的舊皮衣，我們將取來重新再利用（We'll arrange to pick up your used leather clothes and recycle them.）」。在本句話中聽到了 clothes 和 recycle，可以找出答案為 (C)。

• delivery 運送

72

How can listeners receive a discount? 聽眾如何獲得折扣優惠？

(A) By becoming a member*　(A) 成為會員。
(B) By ordering two items　(B) 訂購兩件物品。
(C) By registering online　(C) 在線上註冊。
(D) By entering a contest　(D) 參加比賽。

聆聽獨白時，請務必掌握解題關鍵為「獲得折扣的方法」。獨白後段說道：「By signing up for a membership, you can get a discount」，因此答案為 (A)。

答案改寫 sign up a membership → become a member

• order 訂購　register 註冊、登記

73

What does the speaker say is available over the phone? 說話者說，透過電話可以取得什麼？

(A) A customer survey　(A) 顧客意見調查。
(B) A list of stores　(B) 商店名單。
(C) The best discount　(C) 最好的折扣。
(D) An appointment*　(D) 預約。

獨白最後一段說道：「For more details or to schedule a pick-up, call 800-555-2222.」，表示如要獲得更多資訊或是預約服務，請以電話聯繫，因此答案為 (D)。

• **available** 可得到的 **survey** 調查 **appointment** 預約、約會

Questions 74–76 refers to the following announcement.

M [74] Attention all travelers. The 4 P.M. bus to St. Ellen has been canceled due to heavy snow fall. We apologize for this inconvenience and urge you to go to ticket booth 2 to get a refund for your ticket. [75] Those who are traveling to St. Ellen are encouraged to purchase a ticket for the 6 P.M. train instead. While you're waiting for the train, [76] please visit Coffee Madness for a free beverage and Wi-Fi access. Again, we're very sorry for the delays and thank you for visiting [74] Central Bus and Train Station.

男 [74] 各位旅客請注意。由於下大雪，下午四點開往聖艾倫的巴士已取消。造成您的不便，敬請見諒，並請您盡速前往 2 號票口辦理退票。[75] 欲前往聖艾倫的旅客，建議您改買六點的火車票。在您等候火車時，[76] 請到瘋咖啡享用免費飲料及 Wi-Fi 上網。我們再次為造成延誤致上歉意，並感謝您造訪 [74] 中央巴士暨火車站。

• **cancel** 取消 **due to** 由於、因為 **apologize** 道歉、認錯 **inconvenience** 不便、麻煩 **urge** 催促、力勸 **refund** 退還、退款 **encourage** 鼓勵 **purchase** 購買 **instead** 作為替代 **beverage** 飲料 **delay** 延誤、延緩

74

Where is the announcement being made?

(A) At a city hall
(B) At a shopping mall
(C) At a transit station*
(D) At a concert venue

這個廣播在哪裡發布？

(A) 市政府。
(B) 購物商場。
(C) 轉運站。
(D) 音樂會會場。

獨白第一句為：「Attention all travelers.」，當中可以聽到關鍵線索 travelers，因此 (C) 為最適當的地點。如果不小心漏聽了這句話，可以由獨白後方所使用的單字（bus, traveling, train），以及獨白最後一句：「Central Bus and Train Station」，再度確認。

答案改寫 bus and train → transit

• **transit** 中轉、運送 **venue** 舉行場所、會場

75

What does the speaker ask listeners to do?

(A) Proceed to a boarding gate
(B) Keep an original receipt
(C) Use a bank machine
(D) Purchase another ticket*

說話者要求聽眾何事？

(A) 前往登機門。
(B) 保留原始收據。
(C) 使用自動提款機。
(D) 購買另一張車票。

聆聽時，請特別留意「要求事項」。獨白中段說道：「Those who are traveling to St. Ellen are encouraged to purchase a ticket for the 6 P.M. train instead.」，表示（不必購買巴士票），請大家改買傍晚六點的火車票，因此答案為 (D)。

• **proceed** （朝特定方向）前進 **boarding** 上船（或火車、飛機等） **receipt** 收據

76

According to the speaker, what can customers get at Coffee Madness?

(A) A train ticket
(B) A complimentary drink*
(C) A loaned computer
(D) An updated bus schedule

根據說話者所述，顧客可以在瘋咖啡得到什麼？

(A) 一張火車票。
(B) 一杯免費飲料。
(C) 一台出租的電腦。
(D) 一張更新的巴士時刻表。

聆聽時，請注意關鍵字 Coffee Madness。獨白後段說道：「please visit Coffee Madness for a fee beverage and Wi-Fi access」，由此確認答案為 (B)。

答案改寫 free → complimentary　beverage → drink

• loan 借出　complimentary 贈送的

Questions 77–79 refer to the following telephone message.

W　Hi, Anna. It's Bethany calling. [77] Are you able to come to the store this afternoon? [78] I think we need to get some of the decorating decisions finalized. The boss is getting impatient. There are a lot of paint and flooring samples to look through, so [79] I'm going to choose the best ones now and bring them to the store. When we meet, we should see how the samples look in the actual store space. Please call me back. Thank you.

女　嗨，安娜，我是伯達妮。[77] 妳今天下午能來店裡嗎？[78] 我想我們必須對一些裝潢作出最後決定。老闆不耐煩了。有好多油漆和地板的樣本要看，所以 [79] 我現在會選出些最好的，帶到店裡。等我們碰面，我們可以看看這些樣本在實際店面空間裡看起來如何。請回我電話，謝謝妳。

• decorate 粉刷裝潢、裝飾　decision 決定　finalize 最後確定　impatient 不耐煩的　look through 瀏覽　choose 選擇　actual 實際的

77

What is the purpose of the message?

(A) To locate some materials
(B) To request a meeting*
(C) To hire a designer
(D) To ask about a product

這段留言的目的為何？

(A) 找出一些材料。
(B) 要求碰面。
(C) 僱用一位設計師。
(D) 詢問一個產品。

獨白前段詢問是否可以到辦公室一趟（Are you able to come to the store this afternoon?），表示有事需要一起作決定。因此 (B) 為最適當的答案。

• locate 找出　material 材料、原料　request 要求　hire 僱用

78

What does the speaker imply when she says, "The boss is getting impatient"?

(A) Her boss needs to reschedule a project.
(B) She needs to change some paint colors.
(C) The designers will start working soon.
(D) Some selections must be confirmed quickly.*

當說話者說「老闆不耐煩了」，意指什麼？

(A) 她的老闆需要重新編排一個專案的時間表。
(B) 她需要更換一些油漆的顏色。
(C) 設計師會很快開始工作。
(D) 有些選擇必須趕快確定。

當題目詢問說話者的意圖時，請務必特別注意聆聽前後句的文意。前句表示必須快點決定某些事情（I think we need to get some of the decorating decisions finalized.），根據文意，(D) 為最適當的答案。

• **selection** 選擇被挑選的人或物 **confirm** 確定

79

What most likely will the speaker do next?
(A) Decide on design samples*
(B) Contact a manager
(C) Visit a manufacturing site
(D) Go to a paint supply store

說話者接下來最可能做何事？
(A) 選定設計的樣本。
(B) 聯絡一位經理。
(C) 拜訪工廠。
(D) 去油漆行。

獨白後段表示將從眾多樣品中，挑選出最好的樣品帶去賣場（I'm going to choose the best ones now and bring them to the store.），因此答案為 (A)。在此補充，當題目問句以「. . . do next?」結尾，詢問獨白結束後，說話者將做什麼時，在對話後半部，通常會出現解題的關鍵線索，請特別熟記。

• **decide** 決定 **contact** 聯絡 **manufacture** （大量）製造 **supply** 供應

Questions 80–82 refer to the following talk.

M Good afternoon, interns. Thanks for coming to this meeting on such short notice. [80] I hope everyone is enjoying their interning experience at Parson Real Estate. [81] Tomorrow is the launch of our new branch office downtown, and I'd like you all to help out with the event. As you know, we'll be setting up tables outside with brochures about our services. [81] I'd like you to stay at the tables all morning and hand out brochures to people on the street. [82] I've had T-shirts made for you to wear so don't worry about dressing up. I'll be distributing them at the end of the meeting.

男 午安，各位實習生。謝謝大家一接到通知就趕來參加會議。[80] 希望大家在帕爾森不動產的實習都很愉快。[81] 我們在市區的分公司明天開幕，希望大家都來幫忙這次活動。你們都知道，我們要在外面擺桌子，放上關於公司業務的小冊子。[81] 我希望你們整個早上都留守桌邊，並向路人發放廣告小冊。[82] 我幫你們訂做了T恤穿，所以不用擔心要穿著正式服裝。會議結束時，我會分發T恤。

• **on short notice** 一接到通知 **real estate** 不動產、房地產 **launch** 啟動
branch 分公司、分店 **event** 活動 **set up** 擺放或豎起某物 **hand out** 分發 **dress up** 裝扮、盛裝
distribute 分發、分配

80

Where do the listeners work?
(A) At a bank
(B) At a fashion house
(C) At a university
(D) At a real estate agency*

聽者在哪裡工作？
(A) 銀行。
(B) 服裝設計公司。
(C) 大學。
(D) 不動產仲介公司。

獨白前段說道：「I hope everyone is enjoying their interning experience at Parson Real Estate.」，提到了公司名稱（Parson Real Estate），由此確認答案為 (D)。

81

What will the listeners be doing tomorrow? 聽者明天有何事要做？

(A) Conducting surveys (A) 進行調查。

(B) Interviewing interns (B) 面試實習生。

(C) Distributing pamphlets* (C) 分發傳單。

(D) Cleaning up an office (D) 打掃辦公室。

聆聽時，請特別留意關鍵時間點 tomorrow（明天）。獨白前段說道：「Tomorrow is the launch of our new branch office downtown, and I'd like you all to help out with the event.」，可以推測出分店開幕當天將舉行活動，後句則提到了更具體的內容：「I'd like you to stay at the tables all morning and hand out our brochures to people on the street.」，因此答案為 (C)。

答案改寫 hand out → distribute
brochure → pamphlet

• conduct 實施、進行

82

What has the speaker done for the listeners? 說話者為聽者做了何事？

(A) Prepared uniforms* (A) 準備制服。

(B) Bought some chairs (B) 買了些椅子。

(C) Shortened a schedule (C) 縮短時程表。

(D) Paid for a trip (D) 支付旅費。

獨白後段說道：「I've had T-shirts made for you to wear so don't worry about dressing up.」，表示已做好衣服，請對方不用擔心服裝問題，因此答案為 (A)。

答案改寫 T-shirt → uniform

• prepare 準備 shorten 縮短 pay for 支付……的費用

Questions 83–85 refer to the following excerpt from a meeting.

W [83] I'm very pleased to announce that Sampson National Bank will be awarded the Outstanding Community Outreach Award this year. This is truly a reflection of how much work we've done to improve our local community. I especially want to recognize the work of Mona Ruiz. [84] She arranged the fundraiser we sponsored to rebuild our city's youth club in June and was responsible for the success of our mentorship program. [85] Because of her work, our bank has doubled its charitable outreach. I'd like to ask Ms. Ruiz to say a few words now about what she foresees us doing next year.

女 [83] 很高興宣布，山普生國家銀行榮獲今年的傑出社會服務獎。這真實反映出我們為改善本地社區盡了多少心力。我尤其要表彰蒙娜·露薏絲的工作。[84] 為了我們重建本市青年俱樂部的贊助計畫，她於六月安排了募款活動，而我們的導師計畫之所以成功也要歸功於她。[85] 因為她的工作成果，我們銀行的慈善服務範圍得以加倍擴展。現在，我想邀請露薏絲女士來談談，她預測我們明年要做什麼。

• announce 宣布 outstanding 傑出的 outreach 擴大服務範圍 reflection 反映 improve 改善 recognize 表彰、賞識 sponsor 主辦、贊助 be responsible for 是……的原因 double 加倍 charitable 慈善的 foresee 預知、預見

83

What is the speaker announcing?
(A) Hiring a new employee
(B) A company fundraiser
(C) An upcoming mentorship program
(D) The winning of an award*

說話者宣布何事？
(A) 僱用一位新員工。
(B) 公司的募款活動。
(C) 即將來臨的導師計畫。
(D) 獲得獎項。

獨白第一句說道：「I'm very pleased to announce that Sampson National Bank will be awarded the Outstanding Community Outreach Award this year.」，宣布山普生國家銀行得獎，由此確認答案為 (D)。

84

What did the company sponsor in June?
(A) A sports club
(B) A fundraising event*
(C) A financial convention
(D) A university scholarship

公司在六月贊助主辦了什麼？
(A) 運動俱樂部。
(B) 募款活動。
(C) 金融研討會。
(D) 大學獎學金。

聆聽時，請特別留意關鍵時間點 June（六月）。獨白中段，「六月」出現的地方同時提到，為了重新組織青年俱樂部，進行了募款活動（She arranged the fundraiser we sponsored to rebuild our city's youth club in June），因此答案為 (B)。

答案改寫 fundraiser → fundraising event

• **fundraising** 募款 **financial** 金融的、財政的 **scholarship** 獎學金

85

What does the speaker say about Mona Ruiz's work?
(A) It improved the company image.
(B) It is outlined on the company's website.
(C) It increased the company's charity work.*
(D) It doubled the number of clients.

關於蒙娜・露薏絲的工作，說話者說了什麼？
(A) 它改善了公司形象。
(B) 公司的網站概述了內容。
(C) 它增加了公司的慈善工作。
(D) 它讓客戶人數加倍。

在獨白中段，出現與關鍵人名 Mona Ruiz 有關的內容，說明女子業績，使得慈善活動成長了兩倍（Because of her work, our bank has doubled its charitable outreach.），因此答案為 (C)。請特別留意，(D) 僅重複使用了 double，內容不符合文意，此選項並非正解。

• **outline** 概述、略述 **increase** 增加

Questions 86–88 refer to the following talk.

M [86] Let's start off the meeting by looking at an analysis of the online reviews for our new outdoor barbeque, the Grill Master 2000. As I'm sure you know, this barbeque has numerous features, and it seems our customers really love it. Based on the reviews, the aesthetic appeal appears to be the most popular feature. [87] The customers love that they have five colors to choose from, meaning they can match their barbeque to their

男 [86] 會議一開始，先來看看我們新戶外烤肉爐，「烤肉大師 2000」的線上調查分析。相信你們都知道，這個烤肉爐有許多特色，而且看起來，我們的顧客真的很喜歡它。根據評論，美學的吸引力似乎是最受歡迎的特色。[87] 顧客喜歡有五個顏色可選，表示他們可以讓烤肉爐和草地上的家具互

lawn furniture. However, our website does not display images of each color. [88] The web designers are going to work on updating the website with that information.

相搭配。不過，我們的網站並未列出每種顏色的圖片。[88] 網頁設計師將會更新網頁，加入這個資訊。

• **analysis** 分析　**outdoor** 戶外的　**numerous** 許多的、很多的　**feature** 特徵、特色　**based on** 以……為根據　**aesthetic** 美學的、藝術的　**appeal** 吸引力　**appear** 似乎、看來好像　**choose** 選擇　**match** 和……相配　**lawn** 草坪、草地

86

What is the main topic of the meeting?
會議的主題為何？

(A) Restructuring plans
(B) A new delivery method
(C) A product prototype
(D) Customer feedback*

(A) 重建計畫。
(B) 新的運送方式。
(C) 某個產品的原型。
(D) 顧客的意見回饋。

在獨白前半部，通常可以聽到與獨白主旨有關的關鍵線索。獨白第一句說道：「Let's start off the meeting by looking at an analysis of the online reviews for our new outdoor barbeque」，表示要開始針對新產品的網路評價進行分析，因此 (D) 為最適當的答案。

答案改寫 review → feedback

• **restructuring** 重建、改組　**delivery** 運送、投遞　**method** 方法

87

What feature of the product does the speaker mention?
說話者提到產品的何項特色？

(A) Removable grills　(B) Portability
(C) Color options*　(D) Energy efficiency

(A) 可拆卸烤肉架。　(B) 可攜帶。
(C) 顏色的選擇。　(D) 節能。

聆聽時，請特別留意 feature（特點）。獨白中段提及商品最具人氣的特色，後方補充說明「可以選擇顏色（The customers love that they have five colors to choose from）」，因此答案為 (C)。

• **removable** 可拆裝的　**portability** 可攜帶性、輕便　**option** 選擇、選擇權　**efficiency** 效率、效能

88

What does the speaker imply when he says, "Our website does not display images of each color"?
當說話者說「我們的網站並未列出每種顏色的圖片」，意指什麼？

(A) A website should be edited.*
(B) Images have been removed from a website.
(C) A photographer needs to be hired.
(D) Customers mostly chose one color.

(A) 網站應該修改。
(B) 圖片已從網站移除。
(C) 需要僱用攝影師。
(D) 顧客大部分選某種顏色。

請特別留意題目句前後的文意。題目句後方說道：「The web designers are going to work on updating the website with that information.」，表示將更新（顏色的）資訊，因此 (A) 為最適當的答案。

答案改寫 update → edit

• **edit** 修訂　**remove** 消除、移動　**hire** 僱用

Questions 89–91 refer to the following excerpt from a meeting.

W Hello, and welcome to our monthly Hamilton Township meeting. [89] I'm sure most of you are aware that we've been trying to persuade state officials to build a new community center downtown. [90] However, we're still short on signatures from local residents, and we'd like to plan a few events this summer to raise awareness. The Hamilton Restaurant Alliance has already agreed to host a street party near the waterfront to help us spread the word about the event. I think this will generate a lot of publicity and we'll reach our goal of 50,000 signatures. [91] I'd like everyone to schedule to work a shift and distribute flyers at the party.

女 哈囉，歡迎參加漢彌爾頓鎮的月會。[89] 相信你們大部分人都知道，我們持續致力於說服州政府官員在市區蓋一座新的社區中心。[90] 不過，本地居民的簽署人數還不夠，我們想在今年夏天規劃一些活動，喚起大家的注意。漢彌爾頓餐廳聯盟已經同意在靠近碼頭區的地方舉行一場街頭派對，協助我們把關於這個活動的訊息傳播出去。我認為，這會產生很大的宣傳效果，我們會達成五萬個簽名連署的目標。[91] 希望大家可以安排輪班並在派對上發傳單。

- **aware** 知道的、察覺的 **persuade** 說服 **state** 州的 **official** 官員、公務員 **short on** 缺乏 **resident** 居民 **raise** 喚起、引起 **awareness** 察覺、意識 **alliance** 聯盟 **agree** 同意、贊同 **host** 主辦、主持 **waterfront** 濱水區、碼頭區 **spread** 傳播、散布 **generate** 產生、引起 **publicity** 宣傳、(公眾的)注意 **reach** 達到 **shift** 輪班、輪班工作時間 **distribute** 分發、分配 **flyer** (廣告)傳單

89

What is the talk mainly about?
(A) Electing a new town mayor
(B) Planning a city anniversary
(C) Convincing state officials*
(D) Forming a charity group

這段談話的主題是什麼？
(A) 選出新的鎮長。
(B) 籌劃市府週年紀念日。
(C) 說服州政府官員。
(D) 組織慈善團體。

獨白前段說道：「I'm sure most of you are aware that we've been trying to persuade state officials to build a new community center downtown.」，由此可以找出答案為(C)。

答案改寫 persuade → convince

- **elect** 選舉、推選 **mayor** 市長、鎮長 **convince** 使信服、說服 **form** 組織、成立 **charity** 慈善

90

What problem does the speaker mention?
(A) Lack of public support*
(B) A delay in the release of funds
(C) Damaged facilities
(D) Lost signatures

說話者提及什麼問題？
(A) 缺乏公眾支持。
(B) 延後發放專款。
(C) 設備受損。
(D) 簽名遺失。

當題目詢問 problem 時，答案經常使用「換句話說」，聆聽時請務必留意。獨白中段說道：「However, we're still short on signatures from local residents」，表示居民署名的數量仍然不足，由此確認答案為(A)。答案通常會出現在 however 的後方。

答案改寫 short on → lack of

- **lack** 缺少、沒有 **delay** 延緩、使延期 **release** 發放 **fund** 資金、專款 **damaged** 損壞的

91

What are listeners asked to do?
(A) E-mail state officials
(B) Volunteer at an event*
(C) Sample some food
(D) Contact local media

聽眾被要求做什麼？
(A) 寫電子郵件給州政府官員。
(B) 當活動的義工。
(C) 試吃一些食物。
(D) 聯絡本地媒體。

在獨白後半段，會出現說話者的提議或是要求事項。獨白最後一句說道：「I'd like everyone to schedule to work a shift and distribute flyers at the party.」，要求大家調配工作時間，以發放宣傳單，因此 (B) 為最適當的答案。

• **sample** 品嚐、嘗試 **volunteer** 志工、義工 **contact** 聯絡

Questions 92–94 refer to the following announcement.

M Good morning, everyone. Thanks for attending [92] Parker Hospital's administrative new-hire training. We hope you'll have a long career in Parker Hospital's many award-winning medical departments. Today, we'll go over hospital policies and then you'll meet with your department heads for more specific training. We're sure you'll gain a lot of useful information today, but don't worry if you forget something. We'll be handing out employee conduct manuals for you to review when you go home today. Not all seats are full right now, so [93] we'll wait a few more minutes for the rest of the group to arrive. [94] In the meantime, I'll pass out the handbooks. Please read through the introduction page.

男 大家早。感謝大家參加 [92] 帕克醫院的行政新人訓練。我們希望你們在帕克醫院的許多得獎醫學部門都能有長久的職業生涯。我們今天要細看醫院的政策，接著，你們會和所屬部門主管見面，接受更精確的訓練。我們確信，你們今天會獲得許多實用的資訊，如果你忘記了某些內容，也別擔心。在你們今天回家前，我們會分發員工指導手冊讓你們複習。現在，還有座位是空的，所以，[93] 我們再多等幾分鐘，等其他人到來。[94] 在這期間，我會分發手冊。請讀完引言。

• **attend** 參加、出席 **administrative** 行政的、管理的 **award-winning** 獲獎的 **medical** 醫學的、醫療的 **policy** 政策 **specific** 詳細精確的、特定的 **gain** 獲得、得益 **useful** 有用的、有助益的 **hand out** 分發、免費給予 **conduct** 指導、引導 **manual** 手冊 **review** 複習 **the rest of** 其餘的 **in the meantime** 在⋯⋯期間之內、同時 **introduction** 引言、序言

92

What type of business does the speaker work for?
(A) A transit company
(B) A medical facility*
(C) An advertising firm
(D) A pharmacy

說話者在何種行業工作？
(A) 運輸公司。
(B) 醫療機構。
(C) 廣告公司。
(D) 藥局。

關於說話者工作的地方或是職業，常常會以專有名詞表示。獨白開頭提到 Parker Hospital（帕克醫院），由此專有名詞可以找出答案為 (B)。

• **facility**（有特定用途的）場所 **firm** 公司、商號 **pharmacy** 藥局、（醫院的）藥房

93

What does the speaker imply when he says, "Not all seats are full right now"?
(A) Some participants have not arrived.*
(B) The chairs can be rearranged.
(C) The venue will be changed.
(D) The event is not successful.

當說話者說「現在，還有座位是空的」，意指什麼？
(A) 有些參加者還沒到。
(B) 椅子可以重排。
(C) 場地要換。
(D) 活動不成功。

當題目詢問說話者的意圖時，請先理解題目句前後句的文意後，再進行解題。題目句後方提到要繼續等（尚未抵達的）人（we'll wait a few minutes for the rest of the group to arrive.），因此答案為 (A)。

• **participant** 參加者 **rearrange** 重新排列、重新布置 **venue** 舉行地點、會場

94

What does the speaker ask the listeners to do?
(A) Write down their medical history
(B) Go to their assigned departments
(C) Fill out contact information
(D) Review some materials*

說話者要求聽眾何事？
(A) 寫下他們的病史。
(B) 前往指定部門。
(C) 填寫聯絡資料。
(D) 仔細看一些資料。

在獨白後半段，可以找到與要求事項有關的線索。「I'll pass out the handbooks. Please read through the information page.」，要求讀一下 handbook，因此答案為 (D)。

答案改寫 handbooks → materials read through → review

• **assigned** 指定的 **material** 資料、原料

Questions 95–97 refer to the following recorded message and order form.

Quantity	Item Description
10	Ballpoint Pens (10 per package)
20	Black toner cartridge
35	Clear plastic A4 file
[95] 60	Glossy copy paper (1000 sheets per box)

W Hi, I'm calling to leave a message for Mike Wentz. I've just reviewed your monthly order, and I wanted to confirm something with you. [95] It seems you've listed ten times the amount of paper you usually order. I think it may be a mistake. I'd be happy to correct it for you. [96] Just call me back and give me the okay, and I'll process your order. Also, I wanted to let you know that [97] we're using a new courier starting next week, but your order should arrive within the same timeframe. [97] If you have any problems, though, feel free to call Tina in customer service.

數量	品名
10	原子筆（一盒十隻）
20	黑色碳粉
35	A4 透明塑膠資料夾
[95]60	光面影印紙（一箱一千張）

女 嗨，我打來留言給麥克·溫茲。我剛看過您的每月訂單，想和您確認一件事。[95] 您似乎列了平常訂購量十倍的紙張。我想也許是寫錯了。我很樂意為您更正。[96] 只要回電給我，表示同意，我就會處理您的訂單。此外，我想告訴您，我們從下星期開始換成新的快遞公司，但您訂的貨應該會在同樣的時間送達。[97] 不過，若您有任何問題，請隨時打給客服部的緹娜。

• **quantity** 數量 **clear** 透明的 **glossy** 光滑的、用亮光紙印的 **review** 檢閱 **monthly** 每月的、每月一次的 **order** 訂單、所訂的貨 **confirm** 證實、確定 **correct** 改正 **process** 處理 **courier** 快遞公司、快遞員 **timeframe** 時間範圍、一段時間

95

Look at the graphic. Which quantity on the order form will probably be changed?
(A) 10
(B) 20
(C) 35
(D) 60*

請見圖表。訂單上的哪個數量最可能會修改？
(A) 10。
(B) 20。
(C) 35。
(D) 60。

有時候第一題就是與圖表相關的題目。解題線索大多會依照題目順序逐一提及，因此請從獨白前段找出本題答案。從「It seems you've listed ten times the amount of paper you usually order.」，可以推測出問題在於紙張的訂購上，因此答案為 (D)，與紙張有關的數量。

96

What will the speaker do before processing the order?
(A) Wait for a confirmation*
(B) Give a phone number
(C) Inspect a package
(D) Review a product manual

說話者在處理訂單之前會做何事？
(A) 等候確認。
(B) 給一個電話號碼。
(C) 檢查一個包裹。
(D) 檢閱產品使用手冊。

聆聽獨白時，請先預想到當中將會出現與題目 processing the order（處理訂單）相關的內容。在「Just call me back and give me the okay, and I'll process your order.」當中，可以將「call me back and give me the okay（請回電表示同意）」理解成 (A) 等待對方確認那件事。

- confirmation 確定、確認　inspect 檢查

97

What does the speaker say about Tina?
(A) She will not be in the office.
(B) She will deliver some items herself.
(C) She will take care of shipping problems.*
(D) She will refund some purchases.

關於緹娜，說話者說了什麼？
(A) 她不會在辦公室。
(B) 她會親自送一些物品。
(C) 她會處理貨運的問題。
(D) 有些購買的東西，她會退款。

在提及關鍵字 Tina 的地方，將可以找到答案。獨白最後一句說道：「If you have any problems, though, feel free to call Tina in customer service.」，當中便提到了 Tina。因為句中出現了 problem，所以可以直接選擇 (C)。如果希望更加確定答案，可以透過前句：「we're using a new courier」，理解前後文意後，再行解題。

- refund 退還、退款　purchase 所購之物　take care of 處理　shipping 貨運

Questions 98–100 refer to the following announcement and graph.

Employee Feedback

100
80
60
40
20
0

Employee Breakrooms | [99] Food Court Discounts | Better Parking Spaces | Free Transit Passes

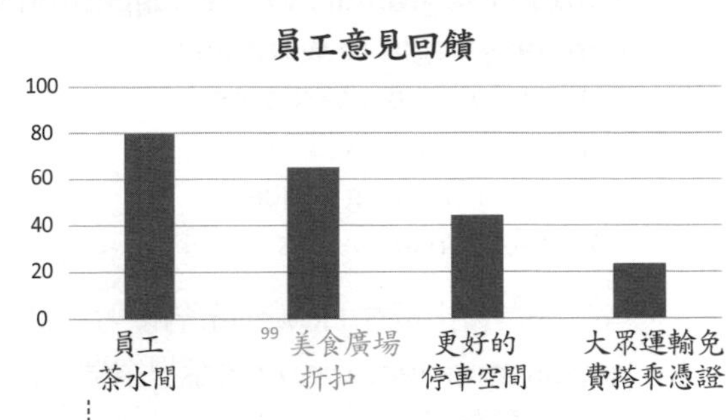

M Thank you so much for filling out our employee feedback comment cards. [98] At Rodsmart Shopping Center, we value your opinions and will try to make changes to ensure a happy and productive work environment. Many of you offered suggestions about employee breakrooms. I'm sure everyone would love a quiet place to spend their breaks, but unfortunately, we just don't have rooms available for this. [99] However, the second most popular suggestion seems more feasible. I will be speaking with upper management in the next few days to see if we can get working on that. [100] For participating in this feedback session, you can all collect a mall gift card on your way out.

男 非常感謝你們填寫員工意見卡。[98] 羅德史邁特購物商場重視你們的意見，並會努力改變以確保有個愉快且具生產力的工作環境。你們許多人都建議設置員工茶水間。我確信每個人都愛安靜的地方休息，但是，很不湊巧，我們沒有空間可用。[99] 不過，第二多人提的建議似乎比較可行。這幾天，我會和管理高層談，看看我們是否能開始進行。[100] 因為參與了這次意見反應，你們離開時都可以拿到一張商場的禮物卡。

- **breakroom** 茶水間、休息室 **transit** 公共交通運輸系統、運輸 **fill out** 填寫 **value** 重視、珍視 **opinion** 意見 **ensure** 確保 **productive** 有生產力的 **environment** 環境 **quiet** 安靜的 **unfortunately** 不湊巧、遺憾的 **available** 有空的、可利用的 **feasible** 可行的 **upper** 上層的、較高的 **participate in** 參加 **collect** 領取 **on the way out** 離開時

98

Where does the talk take place?
(A) At a museum
(B) At a restaurant
(C) At a shopping mall*
(D) At an office

這段談話發生在哪裡？
(A) 在博物館。
(B) 在餐廳。
(C) 在購物商場。
(D) 在辦公室。

關於說話者所在的地點或是職業，常會以專有名詞表示。獨白前段說道：「At Rodsmart Shopping Center, we value your opinions」，指出確切的地點「shopping Center（購物商場）」，由此可以找出答案為 (C)。

答案改寫 shopping center → shopping mall

99

Look at the graphic. Which suggestion will the company begin to work on?

(A) Employee breakrooms
(B) Food court discounts*
(C) Better parking spaces
(D) Free transit passes

請見圖表。公司會開始進行哪一項建議？

(A) 員工茶水間。
(B) 美食廣場折扣。
(C) 更好的停車空間。
(D) 大眾運輸免費搭乘憑證。

答案通常會出現在 However 的後方。獨白中段說道：「However, the second most popular suggestion seems more feasible.」，表示提案第二多的內容有機會實行（之後將對此進行討論）。對照圖表後，可以得知答案為 (B)。

100

What will employees receive for completing comment cards?

(A) A gift card for the mall*
(B) Entrance into a contest
(C) A voucher for a free drink
(D) A new work uniform

員工完成意見表會收到什麼？

(A) 商場的禮物卡。
(B) 參加比賽的資格。
(C) 免費飲料券。
(D) 新的員工制服。

聆聽獨白後段時，請特別留意題目當中的 receive（獲得）。在「For participating in this feedback session, you can all collect a mall gift card on your way out.」當中，可以聽到 gift card，由此找出答案為 (A)。

答案改寫 collect → receive

- **entrance into** 進入　**voucher** 票券

答案紙

ACTUAL TEST 01

LISTENING SECTION																				
	1	Ⓐ Ⓑ Ⓒ Ⓓ	11	Ⓐ Ⓑ Ⓒ Ⓓ	21	Ⓐ Ⓑ Ⓒ Ⓓ	31	Ⓐ Ⓑ Ⓒ Ⓓ	41	Ⓐ Ⓑ Ⓒ Ⓓ	51	Ⓐ Ⓑ Ⓒ Ⓓ	61	Ⓐ Ⓑ Ⓒ Ⓓ	71	Ⓐ Ⓑ Ⓒ Ⓓ	81	Ⓐ Ⓑ Ⓒ Ⓓ	91	Ⓐ Ⓑ Ⓒ Ⓓ
	2	Ⓐ Ⓑ Ⓒ Ⓓ	12	Ⓐ Ⓑ Ⓒ Ⓓ	22	Ⓐ Ⓑ Ⓒ Ⓓ	32	Ⓐ Ⓑ Ⓒ Ⓓ	42	Ⓐ Ⓑ Ⓒ Ⓓ	52	Ⓐ Ⓑ Ⓒ Ⓓ	62	Ⓐ Ⓑ Ⓒ Ⓓ	72	Ⓐ Ⓑ Ⓒ Ⓓ	82	Ⓐ Ⓑ Ⓒ Ⓓ	92	Ⓐ Ⓑ Ⓒ Ⓓ
	3	Ⓐ Ⓑ Ⓒ Ⓓ	13	Ⓐ Ⓑ Ⓒ Ⓓ	23	Ⓐ Ⓑ Ⓒ Ⓓ	33	Ⓐ Ⓑ Ⓒ Ⓓ	43	Ⓐ Ⓑ Ⓒ Ⓓ	53	Ⓐ Ⓑ Ⓒ Ⓓ	63	Ⓐ Ⓑ Ⓒ Ⓓ	73	Ⓐ Ⓑ Ⓒ Ⓓ	83	Ⓐ Ⓑ Ⓒ Ⓓ	93	Ⓐ Ⓑ Ⓒ Ⓓ
	4	Ⓐ Ⓑ Ⓒ Ⓓ	14	Ⓐ Ⓑ Ⓒ Ⓓ	24	Ⓐ Ⓑ Ⓒ Ⓓ	34	Ⓐ Ⓑ Ⓒ Ⓓ	44	Ⓐ Ⓑ Ⓒ Ⓓ	54	Ⓐ Ⓑ Ⓒ Ⓓ	64	Ⓐ Ⓑ Ⓒ Ⓓ	74	Ⓐ Ⓑ Ⓒ Ⓓ	84	Ⓐ Ⓑ Ⓒ Ⓓ	94	Ⓐ Ⓑ Ⓒ Ⓓ
	5	Ⓐ Ⓑ Ⓒ Ⓓ	15	Ⓐ Ⓑ Ⓒ Ⓓ	25	Ⓐ Ⓑ Ⓒ Ⓓ	35	Ⓐ Ⓑ Ⓒ Ⓓ	45	Ⓐ Ⓑ Ⓒ Ⓓ	55	Ⓐ Ⓑ Ⓒ Ⓓ	65	Ⓐ Ⓑ Ⓒ Ⓓ	75	Ⓐ Ⓑ Ⓒ Ⓓ	85	Ⓐ Ⓑ Ⓒ Ⓓ	95	Ⓐ Ⓑ Ⓒ Ⓓ
	6	Ⓐ Ⓑ Ⓒ Ⓓ	16	Ⓐ Ⓑ Ⓒ Ⓓ	26	Ⓐ Ⓑ Ⓒ Ⓓ	36	Ⓐ Ⓑ Ⓒ Ⓓ	46	Ⓐ Ⓑ Ⓒ Ⓓ	56	Ⓐ Ⓑ Ⓒ Ⓓ	66	Ⓐ Ⓑ Ⓒ Ⓓ	76	Ⓐ Ⓑ Ⓒ Ⓓ	86	Ⓐ Ⓑ Ⓒ Ⓓ	96	Ⓐ Ⓑ Ⓒ Ⓓ
	7	Ⓐ Ⓑ Ⓒ Ⓓ	17	Ⓐ Ⓑ Ⓒ Ⓓ	27	Ⓐ Ⓑ Ⓒ Ⓓ	37	Ⓐ Ⓑ Ⓒ Ⓓ	47	Ⓐ Ⓑ Ⓒ Ⓓ	57	Ⓐ Ⓑ Ⓒ Ⓓ	67	Ⓐ Ⓑ Ⓒ Ⓓ	77	Ⓐ Ⓑ Ⓒ Ⓓ	87	Ⓐ Ⓑ Ⓒ Ⓓ	97	Ⓐ Ⓑ Ⓒ Ⓓ
	8	Ⓐ Ⓑ Ⓒ Ⓓ	18	Ⓐ Ⓑ Ⓒ Ⓓ	28	Ⓐ Ⓑ Ⓒ Ⓓ	38	Ⓐ Ⓑ Ⓒ Ⓓ	48	Ⓐ Ⓑ Ⓒ Ⓓ	58	Ⓐ Ⓑ Ⓒ Ⓓ	68	Ⓐ Ⓑ Ⓒ Ⓓ	78	Ⓐ Ⓑ Ⓒ Ⓓ	88	Ⓐ Ⓑ Ⓒ Ⓓ	98	Ⓐ Ⓑ Ⓒ Ⓓ
	9	Ⓐ Ⓑ Ⓒ Ⓓ	19	Ⓐ Ⓑ Ⓒ Ⓓ	29	Ⓐ Ⓑ Ⓒ Ⓓ	39	Ⓐ Ⓑ Ⓒ Ⓓ	49	Ⓐ Ⓑ Ⓒ Ⓓ	59	Ⓐ Ⓑ Ⓒ Ⓓ	69	Ⓐ Ⓑ Ⓒ Ⓓ	79	Ⓐ Ⓑ Ⓒ Ⓓ	89	Ⓐ Ⓑ Ⓒ Ⓓ	99	Ⓐ Ⓑ Ⓒ Ⓓ
	10	Ⓐ Ⓑ Ⓒ Ⓓ	20	Ⓐ Ⓑ Ⓒ Ⓓ	30	Ⓐ Ⓑ Ⓒ Ⓓ	40	Ⓐ Ⓑ Ⓒ Ⓓ	50	Ⓐ Ⓑ Ⓒ Ⓓ	60	Ⓐ Ⓑ Ⓒ Ⓓ	70	Ⓐ Ⓑ Ⓒ Ⓓ	80	Ⓐ Ⓑ Ⓒ Ⓓ	90	Ⓐ Ⓑ Ⓒ Ⓓ	100	Ⓐ Ⓑ Ⓒ Ⓓ

ACTUAL TEST 02

LISTENING SECTION																				
	1	Ⓐ Ⓑ Ⓒ Ⓓ	11	Ⓐ Ⓑ Ⓒ Ⓓ	21	Ⓐ Ⓑ Ⓒ Ⓓ	31	Ⓐ Ⓑ Ⓒ Ⓓ	41	Ⓐ Ⓑ Ⓒ Ⓓ	51	Ⓐ Ⓑ Ⓒ Ⓓ	61	Ⓐ Ⓑ Ⓒ Ⓓ	71	Ⓐ Ⓑ Ⓒ Ⓓ	81	Ⓐ Ⓑ Ⓒ Ⓓ	91	Ⓐ Ⓑ Ⓒ Ⓓ
	2	Ⓐ Ⓑ Ⓒ Ⓓ	12	Ⓐ Ⓑ Ⓒ Ⓓ	22	Ⓐ Ⓑ Ⓒ Ⓓ	32	Ⓐ Ⓑ Ⓒ Ⓓ	42	Ⓐ Ⓑ Ⓒ Ⓓ	52	Ⓐ Ⓑ Ⓒ Ⓓ	62	Ⓐ Ⓑ Ⓒ Ⓓ	72	Ⓐ Ⓑ Ⓒ Ⓓ	82	Ⓐ Ⓑ Ⓒ Ⓓ	92	Ⓐ Ⓑ Ⓒ Ⓓ
	3	Ⓐ Ⓑ Ⓒ Ⓓ	13	Ⓐ Ⓑ Ⓒ Ⓓ	23	Ⓐ Ⓑ Ⓒ Ⓓ	33	Ⓐ Ⓑ Ⓒ Ⓓ	43	Ⓐ Ⓑ Ⓒ Ⓓ	53	Ⓐ Ⓑ Ⓒ Ⓓ	63	Ⓐ Ⓑ Ⓒ Ⓓ	73	Ⓐ Ⓑ Ⓒ Ⓓ	83	Ⓐ Ⓑ Ⓒ Ⓓ	93	Ⓐ Ⓑ Ⓒ Ⓓ
	4	Ⓐ Ⓑ Ⓒ Ⓓ	14	Ⓐ Ⓑ Ⓒ Ⓓ	24	Ⓐ Ⓑ Ⓒ Ⓓ	34	Ⓐ Ⓑ Ⓒ Ⓓ	44	Ⓐ Ⓑ Ⓒ Ⓓ	54	Ⓐ Ⓑ Ⓒ Ⓓ	64	Ⓐ Ⓑ Ⓒ Ⓓ	74	Ⓐ Ⓑ Ⓒ Ⓓ	84	Ⓐ Ⓑ Ⓒ Ⓓ	94	Ⓐ Ⓑ Ⓒ Ⓓ
	5	Ⓐ Ⓑ Ⓒ Ⓓ	15	Ⓐ Ⓑ Ⓒ Ⓓ	25	Ⓐ Ⓑ Ⓒ Ⓓ	35	Ⓐ Ⓑ Ⓒ Ⓓ	45	Ⓐ Ⓑ Ⓒ Ⓓ	55	Ⓐ Ⓑ Ⓒ Ⓓ	65	Ⓐ Ⓑ Ⓒ Ⓓ	75	Ⓐ Ⓑ Ⓒ Ⓓ	85	Ⓐ Ⓑ Ⓒ Ⓓ	95	Ⓐ Ⓑ Ⓒ Ⓓ
	6	Ⓐ Ⓑ Ⓒ Ⓓ	16	Ⓐ Ⓑ Ⓒ Ⓓ	26	Ⓐ Ⓑ Ⓒ Ⓓ	36	Ⓐ Ⓑ Ⓒ Ⓓ	46	Ⓐ Ⓑ Ⓒ Ⓓ	56	Ⓐ Ⓑ Ⓒ Ⓓ	66	Ⓐ Ⓑ Ⓒ Ⓓ	76	Ⓐ Ⓑ Ⓒ Ⓓ	86	Ⓐ Ⓑ Ⓒ Ⓓ	96	Ⓐ Ⓑ Ⓒ Ⓓ
	7	Ⓐ Ⓑ Ⓒ Ⓓ	17	Ⓐ Ⓑ Ⓒ Ⓓ	27	Ⓐ Ⓑ Ⓒ Ⓓ	37	Ⓐ Ⓑ Ⓒ Ⓓ	47	Ⓐ Ⓑ Ⓒ Ⓓ	57	Ⓐ Ⓑ Ⓒ Ⓓ	67	Ⓐ Ⓑ Ⓒ Ⓓ	77	Ⓐ Ⓑ Ⓒ Ⓓ	87	Ⓐ Ⓑ Ⓒ Ⓓ	97	Ⓐ Ⓑ Ⓒ Ⓓ
	8	Ⓐ Ⓑ Ⓒ Ⓓ	18	Ⓐ Ⓑ Ⓒ Ⓓ	28	Ⓐ Ⓑ Ⓒ Ⓓ	38	Ⓐ Ⓑ Ⓒ Ⓓ	48	Ⓐ Ⓑ Ⓒ Ⓓ	58	Ⓐ Ⓑ Ⓒ Ⓓ	68	Ⓐ Ⓑ Ⓒ Ⓓ	78	Ⓐ Ⓑ Ⓒ Ⓓ	88	Ⓐ Ⓑ Ⓒ Ⓓ	98	Ⓐ Ⓑ Ⓒ Ⓓ
	9	Ⓐ Ⓑ Ⓒ Ⓓ	19	Ⓐ Ⓑ Ⓒ Ⓓ	29	Ⓐ Ⓑ Ⓒ Ⓓ	39	Ⓐ Ⓑ Ⓒ Ⓓ	49	Ⓐ Ⓑ Ⓒ Ⓓ	59	Ⓐ Ⓑ Ⓒ Ⓓ	69	Ⓐ Ⓑ Ⓒ Ⓓ	79	Ⓐ Ⓑ Ⓒ Ⓓ	89	Ⓐ Ⓑ Ⓒ Ⓓ	99	Ⓐ Ⓑ Ⓒ Ⓓ
	10	Ⓐ Ⓑ Ⓒ Ⓓ	20	Ⓐ Ⓑ Ⓒ Ⓓ	30	Ⓐ Ⓑ Ⓒ Ⓓ	40	Ⓐ Ⓑ Ⓒ Ⓓ	50	Ⓐ Ⓑ Ⓒ Ⓓ	60	Ⓐ Ⓑ Ⓒ Ⓓ	70	Ⓐ Ⓑ Ⓒ Ⓓ	80	Ⓐ Ⓑ Ⓒ Ⓓ	90	Ⓐ Ⓑ Ⓒ Ⓓ	100	Ⓐ Ⓑ Ⓒ Ⓓ

ACTUAL TEST 03

LISTENING SECTION																				
	1	Ⓐ Ⓑ Ⓒ Ⓓ	11	Ⓐ Ⓑ Ⓒ Ⓓ	21	Ⓐ Ⓑ Ⓒ Ⓓ	31	Ⓐ Ⓑ Ⓒ Ⓓ	41	Ⓐ Ⓑ Ⓒ Ⓓ	51	Ⓐ Ⓑ Ⓒ Ⓓ	61	Ⓐ Ⓑ Ⓒ Ⓓ	71	Ⓐ Ⓑ Ⓒ Ⓓ	81	Ⓐ Ⓑ Ⓒ Ⓓ	91	Ⓐ Ⓑ Ⓒ Ⓓ
	2	Ⓐ Ⓑ Ⓒ Ⓓ	12	Ⓐ Ⓑ Ⓒ Ⓓ	22	Ⓐ Ⓑ Ⓒ Ⓓ	32	Ⓐ Ⓑ Ⓒ Ⓓ	42	Ⓐ Ⓑ Ⓒ Ⓓ	52	Ⓐ Ⓑ Ⓒ Ⓓ	62	Ⓐ Ⓑ Ⓒ Ⓓ	72	Ⓐ Ⓑ Ⓒ Ⓓ	82	Ⓐ Ⓑ Ⓒ Ⓓ	92	Ⓐ Ⓑ Ⓒ Ⓓ
	3	Ⓐ Ⓑ Ⓒ Ⓓ	13	Ⓐ Ⓑ Ⓒ Ⓓ	23	Ⓐ Ⓑ Ⓒ Ⓓ	33	Ⓐ Ⓑ Ⓒ Ⓓ	43	Ⓐ Ⓑ Ⓒ Ⓓ	53	Ⓐ Ⓑ Ⓒ Ⓓ	63	Ⓐ Ⓑ Ⓒ Ⓓ	73	Ⓐ Ⓑ Ⓒ Ⓓ	83	Ⓐ Ⓑ Ⓒ Ⓓ	93	Ⓐ Ⓑ Ⓒ Ⓓ
	4	Ⓐ Ⓑ Ⓒ Ⓓ	14	Ⓐ Ⓑ Ⓒ Ⓓ	24	Ⓐ Ⓑ Ⓒ Ⓓ	34	Ⓐ Ⓑ Ⓒ Ⓓ	44	Ⓐ Ⓑ Ⓒ Ⓓ	54	Ⓐ Ⓑ Ⓒ Ⓓ	64	Ⓐ Ⓑ Ⓒ Ⓓ	74	Ⓐ Ⓑ Ⓒ Ⓓ	84	Ⓐ Ⓑ Ⓒ Ⓓ	94	Ⓐ Ⓑ Ⓒ Ⓓ
	5	Ⓐ Ⓑ Ⓒ Ⓓ	15	Ⓐ Ⓑ Ⓒ Ⓓ	25	Ⓐ Ⓑ Ⓒ Ⓓ	35	Ⓐ Ⓑ Ⓒ Ⓓ	45	Ⓐ Ⓑ Ⓒ Ⓓ	55	Ⓐ Ⓑ Ⓒ Ⓓ	65	Ⓐ Ⓑ Ⓒ Ⓓ	75	Ⓐ Ⓑ Ⓒ Ⓓ	85	Ⓐ Ⓑ Ⓒ Ⓓ	95	Ⓐ Ⓑ Ⓒ Ⓓ
	6	Ⓐ Ⓑ Ⓒ Ⓓ	16	Ⓐ Ⓑ Ⓒ Ⓓ	26	Ⓐ Ⓑ Ⓒ Ⓓ	36	Ⓐ Ⓑ Ⓒ Ⓓ	46	Ⓐ Ⓑ Ⓒ Ⓓ	56	Ⓐ Ⓑ Ⓒ Ⓓ	66	Ⓐ Ⓑ Ⓒ Ⓓ	76	Ⓐ Ⓑ Ⓒ Ⓓ	86	Ⓐ Ⓑ Ⓒ Ⓓ	96	Ⓐ Ⓑ Ⓒ Ⓓ
	7	Ⓐ Ⓑ Ⓒ Ⓓ	17	Ⓐ Ⓑ Ⓒ Ⓓ	27	Ⓐ Ⓑ Ⓒ Ⓓ	37	Ⓐ Ⓑ Ⓒ Ⓓ	47	Ⓐ Ⓑ Ⓒ Ⓓ	57	Ⓐ Ⓑ Ⓒ Ⓓ	67	Ⓐ Ⓑ Ⓒ Ⓓ	77	Ⓐ Ⓑ Ⓒ Ⓓ	87	Ⓐ Ⓑ Ⓒ Ⓓ	97	Ⓐ Ⓑ Ⓒ Ⓓ
	8	Ⓐ Ⓑ Ⓒ Ⓓ	18	Ⓐ Ⓑ Ⓒ Ⓓ	28	Ⓐ Ⓑ Ⓒ Ⓓ	38	Ⓐ Ⓑ Ⓒ Ⓓ	48	Ⓐ Ⓑ Ⓒ Ⓓ	58	Ⓐ Ⓑ Ⓒ Ⓓ	68	Ⓐ Ⓑ Ⓒ Ⓓ	78	Ⓐ Ⓑ Ⓒ Ⓓ	88	Ⓐ Ⓑ Ⓒ Ⓓ	98	Ⓐ Ⓑ Ⓒ Ⓓ
	9	Ⓐ Ⓑ Ⓒ Ⓓ	19	Ⓐ Ⓑ Ⓒ Ⓓ	29	Ⓐ Ⓑ Ⓒ Ⓓ	39	Ⓐ Ⓑ Ⓒ Ⓓ	49	Ⓐ Ⓑ Ⓒ Ⓓ	59	Ⓐ Ⓑ Ⓒ Ⓓ	69	Ⓐ Ⓑ Ⓒ Ⓓ	79	Ⓐ Ⓑ Ⓒ Ⓓ	89	Ⓐ Ⓑ Ⓒ Ⓓ	99	Ⓐ Ⓑ Ⓒ Ⓓ
	10	Ⓐ Ⓑ Ⓒ Ⓓ	20	Ⓐ Ⓑ Ⓒ Ⓓ	30	Ⓐ Ⓑ Ⓒ Ⓓ	40	Ⓐ Ⓑ Ⓒ Ⓓ	50	Ⓐ Ⓑ Ⓒ Ⓓ	60	Ⓐ Ⓑ Ⓒ Ⓓ	70	Ⓐ Ⓑ Ⓒ Ⓓ	80	Ⓐ Ⓑ Ⓒ Ⓓ	90	Ⓐ Ⓑ Ⓒ Ⓓ	100	Ⓐ Ⓑ Ⓒ Ⓓ

ACTUAL TEST 04

LISTENING SECTION																				
	1	Ⓐ Ⓑ Ⓒ Ⓓ	11	Ⓐ Ⓑ Ⓒ Ⓓ	21	Ⓐ Ⓑ Ⓒ Ⓓ	31	Ⓐ Ⓑ Ⓒ Ⓓ	41	Ⓐ Ⓑ Ⓒ Ⓓ	51	Ⓐ Ⓑ Ⓒ Ⓓ	61	Ⓐ Ⓑ Ⓒ Ⓓ	71	Ⓐ Ⓑ Ⓒ Ⓓ	81	Ⓐ Ⓑ Ⓒ Ⓓ	91	Ⓐ Ⓑ Ⓒ Ⓓ
	2	Ⓐ Ⓑ Ⓒ Ⓓ	12	Ⓐ Ⓑ Ⓒ Ⓓ	22	Ⓐ Ⓑ Ⓒ Ⓓ	32	Ⓐ Ⓑ Ⓒ Ⓓ	42	Ⓐ Ⓑ Ⓒ Ⓓ	52	Ⓐ Ⓑ Ⓒ Ⓓ	62	Ⓐ Ⓑ Ⓒ Ⓓ	72	Ⓐ Ⓑ Ⓒ Ⓓ	82	Ⓐ Ⓑ Ⓒ Ⓓ	92	Ⓐ Ⓑ Ⓒ Ⓓ
	3	Ⓐ Ⓑ Ⓒ Ⓓ	13	Ⓐ Ⓑ Ⓒ Ⓓ	23	Ⓐ Ⓑ Ⓒ Ⓓ	33	Ⓐ Ⓑ Ⓒ Ⓓ	43	Ⓐ Ⓑ Ⓒ Ⓓ	53	Ⓐ Ⓑ Ⓒ Ⓓ	63	Ⓐ Ⓑ Ⓒ Ⓓ	73	Ⓐ Ⓑ Ⓒ Ⓓ	83	Ⓐ Ⓑ Ⓒ Ⓓ	93	Ⓐ Ⓑ Ⓒ Ⓓ
	4	Ⓐ Ⓑ Ⓒ Ⓓ	14	Ⓐ Ⓑ Ⓒ Ⓓ	24	Ⓐ Ⓑ Ⓒ Ⓓ	34	Ⓐ Ⓑ Ⓒ Ⓓ	44	Ⓐ Ⓑ Ⓒ Ⓓ	54	Ⓐ Ⓑ Ⓒ Ⓓ	64	Ⓐ Ⓑ Ⓒ Ⓓ	74	Ⓐ Ⓑ Ⓒ Ⓓ	84	Ⓐ Ⓑ Ⓒ Ⓓ	94	Ⓐ Ⓑ Ⓒ Ⓓ
	5	Ⓐ Ⓑ Ⓒ Ⓓ	15	Ⓐ Ⓑ Ⓒ Ⓓ	25	Ⓐ Ⓑ Ⓒ Ⓓ	35	Ⓐ Ⓑ Ⓒ Ⓓ	45	Ⓐ Ⓑ Ⓒ Ⓓ	55	Ⓐ Ⓑ Ⓒ Ⓓ	65	Ⓐ Ⓑ Ⓒ Ⓓ	75	Ⓐ Ⓑ Ⓒ Ⓓ	85	Ⓐ Ⓑ Ⓒ Ⓓ	95	Ⓐ Ⓑ Ⓒ Ⓓ
	6	Ⓐ Ⓑ Ⓒ Ⓓ	16	Ⓐ Ⓑ Ⓒ Ⓓ	26	Ⓐ Ⓑ Ⓒ Ⓓ	36	Ⓐ Ⓑ Ⓒ Ⓓ	46	Ⓐ Ⓑ Ⓒ Ⓓ	56	Ⓐ Ⓑ Ⓒ Ⓓ	66	Ⓐ Ⓑ Ⓒ Ⓓ	76	Ⓐ Ⓑ Ⓒ Ⓓ	86	Ⓐ Ⓑ Ⓒ Ⓓ	96	Ⓐ Ⓑ Ⓒ Ⓓ
	7	Ⓐ Ⓑ Ⓒ Ⓓ	17	Ⓐ Ⓑ Ⓒ Ⓓ	27	Ⓐ Ⓑ Ⓒ Ⓓ	37	Ⓐ Ⓑ Ⓒ Ⓓ	47	Ⓐ Ⓑ Ⓒ Ⓓ	57	Ⓐ Ⓑ Ⓒ Ⓓ	67	Ⓐ Ⓑ Ⓒ Ⓓ	77	Ⓐ Ⓑ Ⓒ Ⓓ	87	Ⓐ Ⓑ Ⓒ Ⓓ	97	Ⓐ Ⓑ Ⓒ Ⓓ
	8	Ⓐ Ⓑ Ⓒ Ⓓ	18	Ⓐ Ⓑ Ⓒ Ⓓ	28	Ⓐ Ⓑ Ⓒ Ⓓ	38	Ⓐ Ⓑ Ⓒ Ⓓ	48	Ⓐ Ⓑ Ⓒ Ⓓ	58	Ⓐ Ⓑ Ⓒ Ⓓ	68	Ⓐ Ⓑ Ⓒ Ⓓ	78	Ⓐ Ⓑ Ⓒ Ⓓ	88	Ⓐ Ⓑ Ⓒ Ⓓ	98	Ⓐ Ⓑ Ⓒ Ⓓ
	9	Ⓐ Ⓑ Ⓒ Ⓓ	19	Ⓐ Ⓑ Ⓒ Ⓓ	29	Ⓐ Ⓑ Ⓒ Ⓓ	39	Ⓐ Ⓑ Ⓒ Ⓓ	49	Ⓐ Ⓑ Ⓒ Ⓓ	59	Ⓐ Ⓑ Ⓒ Ⓓ	69	Ⓐ Ⓑ Ⓒ Ⓓ	79	Ⓐ Ⓑ Ⓒ Ⓓ	89	Ⓐ Ⓑ Ⓒ Ⓓ	99	Ⓐ Ⓑ Ⓒ Ⓓ
	10	Ⓐ Ⓑ Ⓒ Ⓓ	20	Ⓐ Ⓑ Ⓒ Ⓓ	30	Ⓐ Ⓑ Ⓒ Ⓓ	40	Ⓐ Ⓑ Ⓒ Ⓓ	50	Ⓐ Ⓑ Ⓒ Ⓓ	60	Ⓐ Ⓑ Ⓒ Ⓓ	70	Ⓐ Ⓑ Ⓒ Ⓓ	80	Ⓐ Ⓑ Ⓒ Ⓓ	90	Ⓐ Ⓑ Ⓒ Ⓓ	100	Ⓐ Ⓑ Ⓒ Ⓓ

ACTUAL TEST 05

LISTENING SECTION

No.	Answer	No.	Answer	No.	Answer	No.	Answer	No.	Answer	No.	Answer	No.	Answer	No.	Answer	No.	Answer	No.	Answer
1	Ⓐ Ⓑ Ⓒ Ⓓ	11	Ⓐ Ⓑ Ⓒ Ⓓ	21	Ⓐ Ⓑ Ⓒ Ⓓ	31	Ⓐ Ⓑ Ⓒ Ⓓ	41	Ⓐ Ⓑ Ⓒ Ⓓ	51	Ⓐ Ⓑ Ⓒ Ⓓ	61	Ⓐ Ⓑ Ⓒ Ⓓ	71	Ⓐ Ⓑ Ⓒ Ⓓ	81	Ⓐ Ⓑ Ⓒ Ⓓ	91	Ⓐ Ⓑ Ⓒ Ⓓ
2	Ⓐ Ⓑ Ⓒ Ⓓ	12	Ⓐ Ⓑ Ⓒ Ⓓ	22	Ⓐ Ⓑ Ⓒ Ⓓ	32	Ⓐ Ⓑ Ⓒ Ⓓ	42	Ⓐ Ⓑ Ⓒ Ⓓ	52	Ⓐ Ⓑ Ⓒ Ⓓ	62	Ⓐ Ⓑ Ⓒ Ⓓ	72	Ⓐ Ⓑ Ⓒ Ⓓ	82	Ⓐ Ⓑ Ⓒ Ⓓ	92	Ⓐ Ⓑ Ⓒ Ⓓ
3	Ⓐ Ⓑ Ⓒ Ⓓ	13	Ⓐ Ⓑ Ⓒ Ⓓ	23	Ⓐ Ⓑ Ⓒ Ⓓ	33	Ⓐ Ⓑ Ⓒ Ⓓ	43	Ⓐ Ⓑ Ⓒ Ⓓ	53	Ⓐ Ⓑ Ⓒ Ⓓ	63	Ⓐ Ⓑ Ⓒ Ⓓ	73	Ⓐ Ⓑ Ⓒ Ⓓ	83	Ⓐ Ⓑ Ⓒ Ⓓ	93	Ⓐ Ⓑ Ⓒ Ⓓ
4	Ⓐ Ⓑ Ⓒ Ⓓ	14	Ⓐ Ⓑ Ⓒ Ⓓ	24	Ⓐ Ⓑ Ⓒ Ⓓ	34	Ⓐ Ⓑ Ⓒ Ⓓ	44	Ⓐ Ⓑ Ⓒ Ⓓ	54	Ⓐ Ⓑ Ⓒ Ⓓ	64	Ⓐ Ⓑ Ⓒ Ⓓ	74	Ⓐ Ⓑ Ⓒ Ⓓ	84	Ⓐ Ⓑ Ⓒ Ⓓ	94	Ⓐ Ⓑ Ⓒ Ⓓ
5	Ⓐ Ⓑ Ⓒ Ⓓ	15	Ⓐ Ⓑ Ⓒ Ⓓ	25	Ⓐ Ⓑ Ⓒ Ⓓ	35	Ⓐ Ⓑ Ⓒ Ⓓ	45	Ⓐ Ⓑ Ⓒ Ⓓ	55	Ⓐ Ⓑ Ⓒ Ⓓ	65	Ⓐ Ⓑ Ⓒ Ⓓ	75	Ⓐ Ⓑ Ⓒ Ⓓ	85	Ⓐ Ⓑ Ⓒ Ⓓ	95	Ⓐ Ⓑ Ⓒ Ⓓ
6	Ⓐ Ⓑ Ⓒ Ⓓ	16	Ⓐ Ⓑ Ⓒ Ⓓ	26	Ⓐ Ⓑ Ⓒ Ⓓ	36	Ⓐ Ⓑ Ⓒ Ⓓ	46	Ⓐ Ⓑ Ⓒ Ⓓ	56	Ⓐ Ⓑ Ⓒ Ⓓ	66	Ⓐ Ⓑ Ⓒ Ⓓ	76	Ⓐ Ⓑ Ⓒ Ⓓ	86	Ⓐ Ⓑ Ⓒ Ⓓ	96	Ⓐ Ⓑ Ⓒ Ⓓ
7	Ⓐ Ⓑ Ⓒ Ⓓ	17	Ⓐ Ⓑ Ⓒ Ⓓ	27	Ⓐ Ⓑ Ⓒ Ⓓ	37	Ⓐ Ⓑ Ⓒ Ⓓ	47	Ⓐ Ⓑ Ⓒ Ⓓ	57	Ⓐ Ⓑ Ⓒ Ⓓ	67	Ⓐ Ⓑ Ⓒ Ⓓ	77	Ⓐ Ⓑ Ⓒ Ⓓ	87	Ⓐ Ⓑ Ⓒ Ⓓ	97	Ⓐ Ⓑ Ⓒ Ⓓ
8	Ⓐ Ⓑ Ⓒ Ⓓ	18	Ⓐ Ⓑ Ⓒ Ⓓ	28	Ⓐ Ⓑ Ⓒ Ⓓ	38	Ⓐ Ⓑ Ⓒ Ⓓ	48	Ⓐ Ⓑ Ⓒ Ⓓ	58	Ⓐ Ⓑ Ⓒ Ⓓ	68	Ⓐ Ⓑ Ⓒ Ⓓ	78	Ⓐ Ⓑ Ⓒ Ⓓ	88	Ⓐ Ⓑ Ⓒ Ⓓ	98	Ⓐ Ⓑ Ⓒ Ⓓ
9	Ⓐ Ⓑ Ⓒ Ⓓ	19	Ⓐ Ⓑ Ⓒ Ⓓ	29	Ⓐ Ⓑ Ⓒ Ⓓ	39	Ⓐ Ⓑ Ⓒ Ⓓ	49	Ⓐ Ⓑ Ⓒ Ⓓ	59	Ⓐ Ⓑ Ⓒ Ⓓ	69	Ⓐ Ⓑ Ⓒ Ⓓ	79	Ⓐ Ⓑ Ⓒ Ⓓ	89	Ⓐ Ⓑ Ⓒ Ⓓ	99	Ⓐ Ⓑ Ⓒ Ⓓ
10	Ⓐ Ⓑ Ⓒ Ⓓ	20	Ⓐ Ⓑ Ⓒ Ⓓ	30	Ⓐ Ⓑ Ⓒ Ⓓ	40	Ⓐ Ⓑ Ⓒ Ⓓ	50	Ⓐ Ⓑ Ⓒ Ⓓ	60	Ⓐ Ⓑ Ⓒ Ⓓ	70	Ⓐ Ⓑ Ⓒ Ⓓ	80	Ⓐ Ⓑ Ⓒ Ⓓ	90	Ⓐ Ⓑ Ⓒ Ⓓ	100	Ⓐ Ⓑ Ⓒ Ⓓ

ACTUAL TEST 06

LISTENING SECTION

No.	Answer	No.	Answer	No.	Answer	No.	Answer	No.	Answer	No.	Answer	No.	Answer	No.	Answer	No.	Answer	No.	Answer
1	Ⓐ Ⓑ Ⓒ Ⓓ	11	Ⓐ Ⓑ Ⓒ Ⓓ	21	Ⓐ Ⓑ Ⓒ Ⓓ	31	Ⓐ Ⓑ Ⓒ Ⓓ	41	Ⓐ Ⓑ Ⓒ Ⓓ	51	Ⓐ Ⓑ Ⓒ Ⓓ	61	Ⓐ Ⓑ Ⓒ Ⓓ	71	Ⓐ Ⓑ Ⓒ Ⓓ	81	Ⓐ Ⓑ Ⓒ Ⓓ	91	Ⓐ Ⓑ Ⓒ Ⓓ
2	Ⓐ Ⓑ Ⓒ Ⓓ	12	Ⓐ Ⓑ Ⓒ Ⓓ	22	Ⓐ Ⓑ Ⓒ Ⓓ	32	Ⓐ Ⓑ Ⓒ Ⓓ	42	Ⓐ Ⓑ Ⓒ Ⓓ	52	Ⓐ Ⓑ Ⓒ Ⓓ	62	Ⓐ Ⓑ Ⓒ Ⓓ	72	Ⓐ Ⓑ Ⓒ Ⓓ	82	Ⓐ Ⓑ Ⓒ Ⓓ	92	Ⓐ Ⓑ Ⓒ Ⓓ
3	Ⓐ Ⓑ Ⓒ Ⓓ	13	Ⓐ Ⓑ Ⓒ Ⓓ	23	Ⓐ Ⓑ Ⓒ Ⓓ	33	Ⓐ Ⓑ Ⓒ Ⓓ	43	Ⓐ Ⓑ Ⓒ Ⓓ	53	Ⓐ Ⓑ Ⓒ Ⓓ	63	Ⓐ Ⓑ Ⓒ Ⓓ	73	Ⓐ Ⓑ Ⓒ Ⓓ	83	Ⓐ Ⓑ Ⓒ Ⓓ	93	Ⓐ Ⓑ Ⓒ Ⓓ
4	Ⓐ Ⓑ Ⓒ Ⓓ	14	Ⓐ Ⓑ Ⓒ Ⓓ	24	Ⓐ Ⓑ Ⓒ Ⓓ	34	Ⓐ Ⓑ Ⓒ Ⓓ	44	Ⓐ Ⓑ Ⓒ Ⓓ	54	Ⓐ Ⓑ Ⓒ Ⓓ	64	Ⓐ Ⓑ Ⓒ Ⓓ	74	Ⓐ Ⓑ Ⓒ Ⓓ	84	Ⓐ Ⓑ Ⓒ Ⓓ	94	Ⓐ Ⓑ Ⓒ Ⓓ
5	Ⓐ Ⓑ Ⓒ Ⓓ	15	Ⓐ Ⓑ Ⓒ Ⓓ	25	Ⓐ Ⓑ Ⓒ Ⓓ	35	Ⓐ Ⓑ Ⓒ Ⓓ	45	Ⓐ Ⓑ Ⓒ Ⓓ	55	Ⓐ Ⓑ Ⓒ Ⓓ	65	Ⓐ Ⓑ Ⓒ Ⓓ	75	Ⓐ Ⓑ Ⓒ Ⓓ	85	Ⓐ Ⓑ Ⓒ Ⓓ	95	Ⓐ Ⓑ Ⓒ Ⓓ
6	Ⓐ Ⓑ Ⓒ Ⓓ	16	Ⓐ Ⓑ Ⓒ Ⓓ	26	Ⓐ Ⓑ Ⓒ Ⓓ	36	Ⓐ Ⓑ Ⓒ Ⓓ	46	Ⓐ Ⓑ Ⓒ Ⓓ	56	Ⓐ Ⓑ Ⓒ Ⓓ	66	Ⓐ Ⓑ Ⓒ Ⓓ	76	Ⓐ Ⓑ Ⓒ Ⓓ	86	Ⓐ Ⓑ Ⓒ Ⓓ	96	Ⓐ Ⓑ Ⓒ Ⓓ
7	Ⓐ Ⓑ Ⓒ Ⓓ	17	Ⓐ Ⓑ Ⓒ Ⓓ	27	Ⓐ Ⓑ Ⓒ Ⓓ	37	Ⓐ Ⓑ Ⓒ Ⓓ	47	Ⓐ Ⓑ Ⓒ Ⓓ	57	Ⓐ Ⓑ Ⓒ Ⓓ	67	Ⓐ Ⓑ Ⓒ Ⓓ	77	Ⓐ Ⓑ Ⓒ Ⓓ	87	Ⓐ Ⓑ Ⓒ Ⓓ	97	Ⓐ Ⓑ Ⓒ Ⓓ
8	Ⓐ Ⓑ Ⓒ Ⓓ	18	Ⓐ Ⓑ Ⓒ Ⓓ	28	Ⓐ Ⓑ Ⓒ Ⓓ	38	Ⓐ Ⓑ Ⓒ Ⓓ	48	Ⓐ Ⓑ Ⓒ Ⓓ	58	Ⓐ Ⓑ Ⓒ Ⓓ	68	Ⓐ Ⓑ Ⓒ Ⓓ	78	Ⓐ Ⓑ Ⓒ Ⓓ	88	Ⓐ Ⓑ Ⓒ Ⓓ	98	Ⓐ Ⓑ Ⓒ Ⓓ
9	Ⓐ Ⓑ Ⓒ Ⓓ	19	Ⓐ Ⓑ Ⓒ Ⓓ	29	Ⓐ Ⓑ Ⓒ Ⓓ	39	Ⓐ Ⓑ Ⓒ Ⓓ	49	Ⓐ Ⓑ Ⓒ Ⓓ	59	Ⓐ Ⓑ Ⓒ Ⓓ	69	Ⓐ Ⓑ Ⓒ Ⓓ	79	Ⓐ Ⓑ Ⓒ Ⓓ	89	Ⓐ Ⓑ Ⓒ Ⓓ	99	Ⓐ Ⓑ Ⓒ Ⓓ
10	Ⓐ Ⓑ Ⓒ Ⓓ	20	Ⓐ Ⓑ Ⓒ Ⓓ	30	Ⓐ Ⓑ Ⓒ Ⓓ	40	Ⓐ Ⓑ Ⓒ Ⓓ	50	Ⓐ Ⓑ Ⓒ Ⓓ	60	Ⓐ Ⓑ Ⓒ Ⓓ	70	Ⓐ Ⓑ Ⓒ Ⓓ	80	Ⓐ Ⓑ Ⓒ Ⓓ	90	Ⓐ Ⓑ Ⓒ Ⓓ	100	Ⓐ Ⓑ Ⓒ Ⓓ